FALLING FOR HER WOUNDED HERO

BY

MARION LENNOX

THE SURGEON'S BABY SURPRISE

BY

CHARLOTTE HAWKES

D1352836

MILLS & BOON

Marion Lennox has written over a hundred romance novels, and is published in over a hundred countries and thirty languages. Her international awards include the prestigious RITA® award (twice) and the *RT Book Reviews* Career Achievement award for 'a body of work which makes us laugh and teaches us about love'. Marion adores her family, her kayak, her dog, and lying on the beach with a book someone else has written. Heaven!

Born and raised on the Wirral Peninsula, England, **Charlotte Hawkes** is mum to two intrepid boys who love her to play building block games with them and who object loudly to the amount of time she spends on the computer. When she isn't writing—or building with blocks—she is company director for a small Anglo/French construction company. Charlotte loves to hear from readers, and you can contact her at her website: charlottehawkes.com.

FALLING FOR HER WOUNDED HERO

BY
MARION LENNOX

MILLS & BOON

Published in Great Britain 2016
By Mills & Boon, an imprint of HarperCollins*Publishers*
1 London Bridge Street, London, SE1 9GF

© 2016 Marion Lennox

ISBN: 978-0-263-92624-8

Printed and bound in Spain
by CPI, Barcelona

Dear Reader,

I've recently moved to a small coastal village where the sand squishes between my toes, where the waves are a gentle background murmur, and where I lie in bed at night and listen to the foghorns of ships as they head off into the unknown. And as I get to know my new home I'm realising that many of its residents are here for a reason. This place can be wild, windswept and awe-inspiring…or it can be calm and breathtakingly beautiful. Either way, it seems a place for healing.

The thought of such healing is what's inspired *Falling for Her Wounded Hero*. My heroine has lost her baby, and my hero has suffered life-changing injuries in a surfing accident. They're both doctors, but they can't heal themselves. Not alone.

But for the last few months my dog and I have walked my beach, over and over, until I've worked out how their strength, their hope, their love and their laughter, combined with the support of their wonderful seaside community, can finally let them find their future.

Enjoy,

Marion Lennox

CHAPTER ONE

THE SURF OUTSIDE his surgery window was calling like a siren's song. Sunlit waves were rolling in with perfect symmetry. Dr Tom Blake had been watching them between patients, crossing his fingers that his list for the afternoon stayed short.

It did. Cray Point was a small town tucked away on a peninsula on Australia's south-east coast, and almost without exception its residents loved the ocean. On a day like this, only the most urgent medical problems replaced the call of the surf.

Which meant Tom could surf, too.

'That's it,' he called to his receptionist as he closed his last patient file. 'We're out of here.'

'One more,' Rhonda called back. 'A last-minute booking. Mrs Tasha Raymond's here to see you.'

Tasha Raymond.

A tourist? Something easy, he hoped, and headed out to usher her in.

And stopped.

The woman was sitting at the far side of his waiting room. She was close to thirty, he thought, and very pregnant. She had the exhausted and shadowed look he sometimes saw when pregnant women had too much to cope with—toddlers at home, too many work commitments, or a deep unhappiness at the pregnancy itself.

She was small, five four or five, and fair skinned, with brown curls caught into an unruly knot. She was wearing maternity jeans and an enormous windcheater. The shadows under her eyes suggested she hadn't slept for days.

And he knew her. Tasha Raymond? He'd met her as Tasha Blake.

'Tasha,' he said, and she managed a smile and struggled to rise.

'Tom. I didn't think you'd recognise me.'

Fair point. Tasha was his half-brother's widow but he'd only met her once, at Paul's funeral four years ago.

He'd attended because he'd thought he should, not because he'd thought he was wanted. His stepmother had made it clear she'd prefer it if he stayed away. He'd gone, though, and had stayed in the background, and then one of Paul's climbing mates who knew the family background had decided to intervene and introduce him.

'Tom, I doubt if you've met Tasha. Did you know Tasha and Paul were married?'

The news that Paul had died trying to scale Everest had come as no huge surprise. Paul had spent his life moving from one adventure to another, taking bigger and bigger risks along the way. The knowledge that he'd found time to marry had been a bigger shock.

But the slight figure surrounded by Paul's climbing friends had seemed almost a ghost. He'd told her how sorry he was, but he'd only had time for few perfunctory words.

For of course his stepmother had moved in. Afterwards he'd never been able to figure if her contempt was only for him, or if it had included Tasha. Tasha had been a pale figure huddled into someone else's greatcoat to protect her from the icy winds at the graveside—and maybe also from her mother-in-law?

There'd seemed little point in pursuing the acquaintance, though. And after giving his condolences he'd left.

Four years ago.

Why was her face etched on his memory? Why was recognition so instant?

The notes in his hand said she was Tasha Raymond. She was obviously pregnant. Had she remarried? Four years was time to have moved on.

Rhonda was looking from Tom to Tasha with bright interest. Rhonda was the world's worst gossip—well, maybe apart from her twin sister. Tom employed them both. Rhonda was his receptionist and Hilda was his house-keeper. The widowed, middle-aged sisters were excellent at their jobs but to say they were nosy was an understatement.

'I can manage from here, Rhonda,' he told her, smiling at Tasha with what he hoped was a brisk, professional nod. 'You can go.'

'Oh, but Mrs Raymond—'

'Mrs Raymond is my late half-brother's widow,' he told her. He might as well. Rhonda would have asked Tasha to fill in a patient form and she'd have probably figured her history before he had. 'I imagine she's here on family business. There's no need for you to stay.'

Rhonda reluctantly gathered her belongings and departed.

Tasha was left with Tom. She felt ill.

What was she doing here?

She knew what she was doing here. She was here because she was desperate. She had to have help.

I can manage alone. It had been her mantra when her parents had been killed by a roadside bomb in Afghanistan when she'd been in her teens. It had held her up when Paul had died on Everest.

Two days ago it had crumbled.

Paul had been big-boned and muscular, his tall frame made larger by pushing himself to the limits of endurance in every possible physical endeavour.

This man was his half-brother and she hardly knew him.

Tom's hair was a deep brown, like Paul's, but sun-bleached at the tips as if he spent time in the surf she could see outside his surgery window. He was taller than Paul, six feet two or three. His blue eyes were creased at the edges and his skin was tanned. He was lean, muscled, taut. Another who pushed his physical limits? Who thought risks were fun?

She couldn't help it. She shuddered.

She was here because she needed him. Needing another Blake? The thought made her feel ill.

'Tasha,' he said softly, and his attention was all on her. 'How can I help?'

It would have been a shock to see her, she thought. It had been a surprise to meet him at Paul's funeral. This man and Paul had never been permitted to be brothers.

'My mother would disown me if she ever caught me talking to that side of the family,' Paul had told her. 'Which always seemed a shame. When I was a kid my father took me on a holiday, supposedly just father and son. Unbeknown to my mother, he invited my half-brother, too. Tom's four years older than me and I thought he was cool. Kind, too, to a kid who trailed after him. But of course Mum found out and hit the roof and as a kid I never saw him again. We met a couple of times later on with Dad, but then we lost touch. In an odd way, though, it's always seemed like I have a brother. If anything happened to me, Tasha, I reckon you could go to him.'

If anything happened to him. Like being crushed by tons of ice on Everest.

She hadn't needed Tom then, though, and she'd made a vow. She'd never *need* anyone again. Not like she'd needed her parents or thought she'd needed Paul. Paul had made her world crumble even before he'd been killed.

So what was she doing now, asking for help from another

Blake? Paul and his father had both been charming, undependable womanisers. Why should this man be different?

Because she needed him? Because she'd taken yet another risk and failed.

Her last risk.

'Tasha?' Tom's voice was still gentle, that of a concerned family doctor. Maybe that was the way to go, she thought. She could talk to him as one medic to another.

Only she didn't feel like a medic. She felt like a terrified single mum who'd just heard the worst of news.

'Tea,' Tom was saying, suddenly brisk, and his hands were on her shoulders and he was propelling her back into her seat. 'You look exhausted. I'm thinking tea with lots of sugar and then take your time and tell me all.'

'I should have booked for a long consultation,' she managed, trying to joke. 'I only booked for standard. You'll be out of pocket.'

'Do you think I'd charge?' His voice was suddenly strained but he had his back to her, putting on the kettle at the little sink behind Rhonda's desk. 'You're family.'

Family. She stared blankly at his broad back, at the tanned and muscled arms emerging from his crisp, white short-sleeved shirt, at the stethoscope dangling casually from his back pocket.

He oozed competence. He oozed caring.

He was a family doctor. This was what he did. There was no reason for her to want to well up and demand a hug and turn his shoulder into a sodden mess just because he'd said the word 'family'.

She wouldn't.

But she needed him and the very thought had her terrified.

So she sat on, silent, trying to keep her thoughts in check.

Tom spent time making tea, checking how she had it,

measuring sugar, stirring for maybe longer than it needed, as if he sensed she needed time to get herself together. By the time he set the mug into her cupped hands and tugged a chair up before her so he could sit down and face her, she had the stupid tears at bay again. She was under control—or as under control as she could be after the appalling news of two days ago.

'Now.' Tom was smiling at her, his very best patient-reassuring smile, a smile she recognised as one she'd practised as a new doctor. Family or not, she was clearly in the category of new client who may or may not have something diabolical going on.

There was a box of tissues on the side bench. He swiped it surreptitiously forward—or not so surreptitiously as she noticed and she even managed a smile.

'I won't cry on you.'

'You're very welcome to cry if you want. I wouldn't have minded it you'd cried on me four years ago. That one meeting and then you were gone...'

'To England,' she told him. 'I couldn't stay here. Paul's mother blamed—'

'Paul's mother is a vituperative cow,' he said solidly, and Tasha thought of Deidre and thought she couldn't have put it better herself.

'She thought I should have stopped Paul trying to climb.'

'No one could ever stop Paul doing what he wanted to do.'

'You knew him?'

'Not much. My mum was happy for me to meet Paul but Paul's mother...not. When Dad moved on from Deidre as well, it made things even more complicated. Dad was a serial womaniser. My mum coped okay—she got on with her life—but Deidre stayed bitter. She fought Dad's access to Paul every inch of the way. Dad cared about both Paul and me, but with Paul he ended up sidelined. As we got older

Paul and I used to meet a bit. We'd have a drink with Dad occasionally, but after Dad's death we lost touch. Tasha, you need to drink.'

'What…?'

He took her cupped hands in his and propelled the mug to her lips. 'Tea. Drink.'

She drank and was vaguely surprised by how good it tasted. When had she last had tea?

Come to think if it, when had she last eaten?

Great. Collapsing would help no one.

Neither would coming here. She should face this herself.

She couldn't. She needed… Tom.

'So tell me why you're here?' he asked.

She'd come this far but she didn't want to tell him. She didn't want to tell anyone.

Telling people made it real. It couldn't be real. It had to be a nightmare.

'Tasha, spill,' Tom said, in that gentle voice that did something to her insides. It made things settle. It made the battering ram in her heart cease for a moment.

Though of course it started up again. Some things were inescapable.

'My baby…' she started, and Tom sat back a little and eyed her bulge.

'Close to term?'

'I'm due to deliver next week.'

He nodded, as if it was entirely sensible that a close-to-term pregnant woman had decided to drive to Cray Point just to see him.

She should keep talking.

She couldn't.

'Do you have a partner?' he asked tentatively when she couldn't figure what to say next. 'Is the baby's dad around?'

And finally she found the strength to make her voice work. 'The baby's father is Paul.'

'Paul…'

'He left sperm,' she managed. She'd started. She had to find the strength to continue. 'That last climb… I was so angry with him for going. There'd been two landslides on Everest, major ones. The Sherpas were pulling out for the season, as were most of the climbers, but he still insisted on going. Then he came home that last night before he left, laughing. "I've got it sorted, babe," he told me. "I've been to the IVF place and left sperm. It's all paid for, stored for years. If worst comes to worst you can have a little me to take my place."'

She paused, searching for the words to go on. 'I think it was a joke,' she said. 'Maybe he thought it'd make me laugh. Or maybe he was serious—I have no way of telling. But I knew… I waved goodbye to him and somehow I knew that I'd never see him again.'

She tilted her chin, meeting his look head on. 'I was almost too angry to go to his funeral,' she told him. 'It was such a stupid, stupid waste. And then Deidre was in my face, blaming me, making nasty phone calls, even turning up at work to yell at me. So I left for England. You know I'm a doctor, too? I took a job in the emergency department in a good London hospital and I decided I'd put Paul behind me. Only then…then I sort of fell in a heap.'

Tasha shrugged. How to explain the wall of despair that had hit her? The knowledge that her marriage to Paul had been a farce. That her judgement was so far off…

She remembered waking one morning and thinking she was never going to trust again, and the thought had been followed by emptiness. If she couldn't trust again, that excluded her from having a family. A baby. The thought had been almost overwhelming.

'So you decided to use the sperm,' Tom said, as if he was following her thoughts, and she felt a surge of anger that was pretty much directed at her naïve self.

'Why not?' she flashed. 'Paul left it to me in his will. I could bring our baby up knowing the good things about Paul, feeling like it knew its dad. It seemed better—safer— than using an unknown donor, so I decided I'd be brave enough to try.'

And then she hugged her swollen belly, and the tears at last welled over.

'I wanted this baby,' she whispered. 'I wanted her so much...'

Wanted. Past tense. The word was like a knife to her heart. She heard it and tried to change it.

'I want her,' she said, and her voice broke on a sob, but there was no changing what the scans had shown.

And Tom leaned forward and put his hands over hers, so there were four hands cupped over her belly.

'Has your baby died, Tasha?'

And there it was, out there in all its horror. But it couldn't be real. Please...

'Not yet,' she managed, and his grip on her hands tightened. I wonder if this is the way he treats all his patients, she thought, in some weird abstracted part of her brain that had space for those things. He was good. He was intuitive, empathic, caring. He'd be a good family doctor.

A good friend?

'If anything happened to me, Tasha, I reckon you could go to him.'

Paul had been right, she thought. For just about the only time in his life, Paul had been right.

Oh, but laying this on him...

And he was a Blake. He even looked like his brother.

'Tell me,' he said, and it was an order, calm and sure, a direction she had to follow no matter how she was feeling. And she took a deep breath because this was what she'd come for. She had no choice but to continue.

'My baby's a girl,' she whispered. 'Emily. I've named her

Emily after my grandma. I had to come back to Australia to access Paul's sperm. I'm Australian and I have Aussie health insurance so I stayed here during my pregnancy. I've been doing locums. Everything was fine until the last ultrasound. And they picked it up. She has hypoplastic left heart syndrome. The left side of her heart hasn't developed. That…that's bad enough but I thought…well, the literature says there's hope and there are good people in Melbourne. With the Norwood procedure there's a good chance of long-term survival. I hoped. But two days ago I went for my last visit to the cardiologist before delivery and the ultrasound's showing an atrial septal defect as well. And more. Nothing's right. Everything's wrong. While she's in utero, she doesn't need her heart to pump her lungs, so she's okay, but as soon as she's born…'

She took a deep breath. 'As soon as she's born the problems will start. The cardiologist says I need to wait as long as possible before delivery so she's strong enough to face the faint possibility of surgery, but I'm not to hope for miracles. He says she'll live for a little while but it'll be days. Or less. The defect is so great…'

Strangely her voice was working okay. Strangely the words didn't cut out. It was like the medical side of her was kicking in, giving her some kind of armour against the pain. Or maybe it was simply that the pain was so unbearable that her body had thrown up armour of its own.

Tom's face had stilled. He'd be taking it in, she thought, like a good doctor, taking his time to assess, to figure what to say, to think of what might be the most helpful thing to say.

There wasn't anything to say. There just…wasn't.

Hypoplastic left heart syndrome…

He'd never seen a case but he'd read of it. He'd read of the Norwood procedure, a radical surgical technique giving hope to such babies, but with an atrial septal defect as well…

His hands were still gripping Tasha's. They were resting against the bulge that was her baby, and he felt a faint movement. A kick…

In cases like this there usually weren't any outward signs during pregnancy. A foetus only needed one ventricle. It didn't use its lungs to get oxygen to the body, so while it was in utero there was nothing wrong.

If the experts were right, Tasha was carrying a seemingly healthy baby, a little girl who'd only survive for days after she was born.

This woman was a doctor. She'd have gone down every path. Her face said she had, and she'd been hit by a wall at every turn.

'Transplant?' he said, still holding her hands, and he thought maybe it was for him as well as for her. He had a sudden vision of his half-brother as a child, a tousled-haired wild child, rebellious even as a kid. A bright kid who'd tumbled from scrape to scrape. Paul had done medicine, too. Their father had been a doctor so maybe that's why it had appealed to both of them, but the moment Paul had graduated he'd been off overseas. He'd helped out in some of the wildest places. He'd been a risk taker.

And now he was dead and his baby was facing the biggest risk of all. Being born.

A transplant? Without research it sounded the only hope.

'You must know the odds,' Tasha said flatly, echoing his thoughts.

He did. To find a suitable donor in time… To keep this little one alive until they found one, and then to have her fight the odds and survive…

He glanced up at Tasha's ravaged face and he thought, *Where are your friends? Where are your family? Why are you here alone?*

And something inside him twisted.

He'd been a family doctor for ten years now. He loved the work. He loved this little community and when his patients were ill he couldn't help but be personally involved.

But this woman was different.

She was his half-brother's widow and as such there was a family connection. Her story was heartbreaking.

And yet there was something more. Something that made him want to loosen the grip on her hands and gather her into him and hold.

It was almost a primeval urge. The urge to protect.

The urge to take away her pain any way he knew how.

Which was all getting in the way of what she needed from him, which was to be useful. She was here for a reason. She didn't need him to be messed up with some emotional reaction he didn't understand.

'So what can I do for you, Tasha?' he asked, in a voice he had to force himself to keep steady. 'I'll help in any way I can. Tell me what you need me to do.'

She steadied. He could see her fighting back emotion, turning into the practical woman he sensed she was.

She let go his hands and sat back, and he pushed back too, so the personal link was broken.

'I need an advocate,' she told him. 'No. Emily needs an advocate.'

'Explain.'

She had herself under control again now—sort of.

'I'm only part Australian,' she told him. 'My dad was British but Mum was Australian. I was born here but my parents were in the army. We never had a permanent home. Mum and Dad died when I was fifteen and I went to live with my aunt in the UK. That's where I did medicine. Afterwards I took a job with Médecins Sans Frontières, moving all around the world at need, which is when I met Paul. Paul owned an apartment here so Australia was our base but we still travelled. I've never stayed still long enough to get roots, to make long-term friends. So now I'm in a city I don't know very well. I'm about to deliver Emily by Caesarean section and straight after her birth I'll be expected to make some momentous decisions.'

She faltered then, but forced herself to go on. 'Like… like turning off life support,' she whispered. 'Like accepting what is or isn't possible and not attempting useless heroics. Tom, I don't trust myself but Paul said I could trust you. He spoke of you with affection. You're the only one I could think of.'

And what was he to say to that?

There was only one answer he could give.

'Of course I'll be your advocate,' he told her. 'Or your support person. Tasha, whatever you need, I'll be there for you. You have my word.'

'But you hardly knew Paul.'

'Paul's family and so are you,' he said, and he reached out and took her hands again. 'That's all that matters.'

'Hilda?'

Hilda Brakenworth, Tom's housekeeper, twin of Rhonda, answered the phone with some trepidation. She'd just finished making beef stroganoff and was contemplating the ingredients for a lemon soufflé. 'Make it lovely,' Tom had told her before he'd left for work. 'Alice will be here at eight, just in time for sunset. Can you set the table on the veranda? Candles. Flowers. You know the drill.'

She did, Hilda thought dourly. Tom's idea of a romantic evening never changed. But she was used to his priorities. Medicine came first, surfing second. His love life came a poor third, and the phone call she was receiving now would be like so many she'd received in the past. 'Change of plan,' he'd say and her dinners would go into the freezer or the trash.

'Yes?' she said, mentally consigning her lemon soufflé to oblivion.

'Change of plan. I've invited a guest to stay.'

This was different. 'You want a romantic dinner for
three?'

He chuckled but Hilda had known him for a long time.
She could hear strain in his voice—strain usually reserved
for times when the medical needs of the community were
overwhelming.

But did a guest staying warrant stress? She needed to
phone Rhonda and find out what was going on.

'I'll put Alice off,' he said. 'She'll understand.'

No, she won't, Hilda decided, thinking of the beautifully
groomed, high-maintenance Alice, but she didn't comment.

'Do you want me to make up the front room?'

'I… Yes. And could you put flowers in there?'

'It's a woman?'

'It's a woman called Tasha.' He hesitated and then he
told it like it was. 'She's my half-brother's widow and she's
in trouble. I'm hoping she'll stay as long as she needs us.'

Cray Point was a tiny, seemingly forgotten backwater, a village on a neck of land stretching out from Port Philip Bay.

'It's one high tide away from being an island, but the
medical emergency chopper can get here from Melbourne
within half an hour,' Tom told her. 'Your Caesarean's
booked in a week and you're not due for two weeks. We're
both doctors. We can surely detect early signs of labour
and get you to the city fast.'

So a couple of hours after she'd arrived she was on the
veranda, trying to eat the beautiful dinner Tom's house-
keeper had prepared.

Somewhat to her surprise she did eat. She'd looked at
the meal and felt slightly nauseous, which was pretty much
how she'd felt since that appalling last consultation with

the cardiologist, but Tom had plonked himself down beside her, scooped stroganoff onto both their plates and directed her attention to the surf.

'It's too flat tonight,' he told her. 'It's been great all day but the wind's died and the waves have died with it. That's the story of my life. I sweat all day trying to finish but the moment my patients stop appearing, so do the good waves. Dawn's better but once I hit the water I forget what I'm booked for. So I have a great time and come in to find Rhonda ready to have my head on a platter and the waiting room bursting at the seams.'

'Rhonda...'

'Rhonda's my receptionist. She and Hilda—she's the housekeeper you just met leaving—are sisters. They rule my life.'

'So no family? No wife and kids?'

'With my family history?' He grinned, a gorgeous, engaging grin that reminded her a little of Paul. 'Paul must have told you about my dad. He did the right thing twice in that he married my mum and then Paul's mother when they were pregnant, but he never stayed around long enough to be a father. He fancied the idea of his sons as his mates but the hard yards were done by our mums, and while they were raising us he went from woman to woman.'

'You think that's genetic?'

He grinned again. 'I reckon it must be. Dating's fun but I'm thirty-four years old and I've never met a woman I'd trust myself to commit to spending the rest of my life with.' His smile faded. 'But, unlike Dad, I won't make promises I can't keep. This life suits me. Mum was born and raised in Cray Point and this community nurtured both of us when Dad walked out on her. I left to do medicine but it's always called me home. The surf's great and the wind here in winter is enough to turn me into a salted kipper. I have a theory that the locals here don't age, they just get more and more preserved. If you dig up the graveyard you'll find old leather.'

'That sounds like you have nothing to do as a doctor.'

'Preserved leather still falls off surfboards,' he said, and the smile came back again. 'And tourists do dumb tourist things. I had a lady yesterday who rented a two-bedroom house for an extended family celebration and wanted it beautifully set up before they arrived. So she blew up eight air beds. On the seventh she started feeling odd but she kept on going. Luckily her landlady dropped in as she keeled over on the eighth. Full infarct. We air ambulanced her to Melbourne and she should make a good recovery but it could have been death by airbed. What a way to go.'

And for the first time in days—weeks?—months?— Tasha found herself chuckling and scooping up the tasty stroganoff. This man may well be a charming womaniser like his father and brother, but at least he was honest about it, she thought. And that side of him didn't affect her. Just for the moment she could put tragedy aside.

As she ate he kept up a stream of small talk, the drama of being a small-town doctor in a town where access could be cut in a moment. As a doctor she found her interest snagged.

'We can't rely on the road,' Tom told her as he attacked some lemon soufflé. 'It floods. It also takes one minor traffic accident or one broken-down car to prevent access for hours or even days. As a village we're pretty self-reliant and the medical helicopter evac team is brilliant. You sure you don't want more of this?'

'I… No.' She'd surprised herself by eating any at all.

'We'll feed you up for the next week,' Tom said calmly. 'You and Emily. Did you know there are studies that say taste comes through? This is a truly excellent lemon soufflé. Who's to say that Emily isn't enjoying it, too?'

It was an odd thought. Unconsciously her hands went to her belly, and Tom's voice softened.

'Cuddling's good,' he told her. 'I bet she can feel that as well, and I know she can hear us talking.'

'She might…' Her voice cracked. 'But the doctor said…'

'I know what's been said,' Tom told her, and his hand reached over and held hers, strong and firm—a wash of stability in a world that had tilted so far she'd felt she must surely fall. 'But, Tasha, your baby's alive now. She's being cuddled. She's sharing your lemon soufflé and she's listening to the surf. That's not such a bad life for a baby.'

It was a weird concept. That Emily could feel her now…

And suddenly Emily kicked, a good solid kick that even Tom could see under her bulky windcheater. They both looked at the bulge as Emily changed position, and something inside her settled. The appalling maelstrom of emotions took a back seat.

She was here overlooking the sea, feeding her baby lemon soufflé. It was true, Emily could hear the surf—every book said that babies could hear.

'Maybe you could take her for a swim tomorrow,' Tom suggested. 'Lie in the shallows and let the water wash over you—and her. She'll feel your body rocking and she'll hear the water whooshing around. How cool would that be, young Emily?'

And he got it.

She looked up at him in stupefaction but Tom was gazing out to sea again, as if he'd said nothing of importance.

But he'd said it.

How cool would that be, young Emily?

No matter how short Emily's life would be, for now, for this moment, Emily was real. She was her own little person, and with that simple statement Tom was acknowledging it.

The tangle of grief and fear and anger fell away. It was there for the future—she knew that—but for now she was eating lemon soufflé and tomorrow was for tomorrow. For now Emily was alive and kicking. She had no need for her faulty heart. She was safe.

And for the moment Tasha felt safe, too. When Tom had suggested staying she'd thought she'd agree to one night, when she could get to know him so she could figure whether she really could trust him to be her advocate. She knew if the birth was difficult and there were hard decisions to be made then she'd need a friend.

And suddenly she had one.

Thank you, Paul, she thought silently, and it was one of the very few times when she'd thought of Paul with gratitude. He had pretty much been the kid who never grew up, a Peter Pan, a guy who looked on the world as an amazing adventure. His love of life had drawn her in but she hadn't been married for long before she'd realised that life for Paul was one amazing adventure after another. Putting his life at risk—and hers too if the need arose—was his drug of choice.

And as for Tom saying his father's womanising was a genetic fault…yeah, Paul had pretty much proved that.

But now… He'd died but he'd left his sperm and it seemed he'd also left her a link to a man who could help her. Tom might be a womaniser like his brother. He might be any number of things, but right now he was saying exactly what she needed to hear. And then he was falling silent, letting the night, the warmth, the gentle murmur of the sea do his talking for him.

She could trust him for now, she thought, and once more her hands tightened on her belly.

She could trust this man to be her baby's advocate.

And her friend?

By the time dinner ended Tasha looked almost asleep. Tom had shown her to his best spare room and she hit the pillow as if she hadn't slept for a month. As maybe she hadn't.

Tom checked on her fifteen minutes after he'd shown her to her bedroom. He knocked lightly and then opened the door a sliver. He'd thought if she was lying awake, staring at the ceiling, he could organise music or maybe a talking book.

She was deeply asleep. Her soft brown curls were splayed out over the pillows and one of her hands was out from under the sheets, stretched as if in supplication.

She hadn't closed the curtains. In the moonlight her look of appalling fatigue had faded.

She looked at peace.

He stood and looked at her for a long moment, fighting a stupid but almost irresistible urge to stoop over the bed and hold her. Protect her.

It was because she was family, he told himself, but he knew it wasn't.

Impending tragedy? Not that either, he thought. In his years as a country doctor he'd pretty much seen it all. Experience didn't make him immune. When this community hurt, he hurt, but he could handle it.

He wasn't sure he could handle this woman's hurt.

And it wasn't being helpful, staring down at her in the moonlight. It might even be construed as creepy. Like father, like son? He gave himself a fast mental shake, backed out and closed the door.

He headed to his study. Tasha had handed her medical file to him diffidently back at the surgery. 'If you're going to be our advocate you need to know the facts.'

So he hit the internet, searching firstly for the combination of the problems in Emily's heart and then on the background of the paediatric cardiologist who had her in his charge.

The information made him feel ill. He was trawling the internet for hope, and he couldn't find it.

He rang a friend of a friend, a cardiologist in the States. He rang another in London.

There was no joy from either.

In the end he headed back out to the veranda. This was a great old house, slightly ramshackle, built of ancient timber with a corrugated-iron roof and a veranda that ran all the way around. It was settled back from the dunes, overlooking the sea. The house had belonged to his grandparents and then his mother. It was a place of peace but it wasn't giving him peace now.

This child was what…his half-niece? He'd scarcely known Paul and he'd only just met Tasha. Why should this prognosis be so gut-wrenching?

He couldn't afford to get emotional, he told himself. Tasha needed him to be clear-headed, an advocate, someone who could stand back and see the situation dispassionately.

Maybe she should find someone else.

There wasn't anyone else—or maybe there was, but suddenly he knew that even if there was he wouldn't relinquish the role.

He wanted to be by her side.

Her image flooded back, the pale face on the pillow, the hand stretched out…

It was doing his head in.

It was three in the morning and he had house calls scheduled before morning's clinic.

'That's the first thing to organise,' he said out loud, trying to find peace in practicality. At least that was easy. Mary and Chris were a husband-and-wife team, two elderly doctors who'd moved to Cray Point in semi-retirement. They'd helped out in an emergency before and he knew they would now.

'Because this is family,' he said out loud, and the thought was strange.

The woman sleeping in his guest room, the woman who looked past the point of exhaustion, the woman who was twisting his heart in a way he didn't understand…was family?

CHAPTER TWO

Eighteen months later...

THE SURF WAS EXTRAORDINARY. It was also dangerous. The wind had changed ten minutes ago, making the sea choppy and unpredictable.

The morning's swells had enticed every surfer in the district to brave the winter's chill, but a sudden wind change had caught them by surprise. The wind was now catching the waves as the swell rolled out again, with force that had wave smashing against wave.

Most surfers had opted for safety and headed for shore, but not Tom. There were three teenagers who hadn't given up yet, three kids he knew well. Alex, James and Rowan were always egging themselves on, pushing past the limits of sensible.

As the wind had changed he'd headed over to them. 'Time to get out, boys,' he'd told them. 'This surf's pushing into the reef.'

'This is just getting exciting,' Alex had jeered. 'You go home, old man. Leave the good stuff for us.'

They were idiots, but they were kids and he was worried. He'd backed off, staying behind the breakers while he waited for them to see sense.

Maybe he was getting old.

He was thirty-six, which wasn't so old in the scheme of

things. Susie was coming to dinner tonight and Susie was gorgeous. She was thirty-seven, a divorcee with a couple of kids, but she looked and acted a whole lot younger.

If she was here she'd be pushing him to ride the waves, he thought, instead of sitting out here like a wuss.

He glanced at the kids, who were still hoping for a clean wave. Idiots.

Was it safe to leave them? He still had to walk up to the headland before dinner, to take this week's photograph for Tasha.

And that set him thinking. He'd promised the photographs but were they still needed? Was anything still needed? She didn't say. He tried to write emails that would connect as a friend, but her responses were curt to the point of non-existent.

Maybe he reminded her of a pain that was almost overwhelming.

Maybe he was doing it for himself.

For Tom had stayed at Tasha's side for all of Emily's short life and it still seemed natural to keep tending her grave. In the few short days he'd helped care for the baby girl, she'd twisted her way around his heart.

But if Emily's death still hurt him, how was Tasha doing? She never said.

Suddenly, lying out behind the breakers, overseeing idiots taking risks, he had a ridiculous urge to take the next plane and find out.

Which was crazy. He was Tasha's link to her baby, nothing more, and she probably no longer wanted that.

But then he needed to stop thinking of Tasha.

A massive swell was building behind him, and the wind was swirling. He glanced towards the shore and saw the wave that had just broken was surging back from the beach. It was almost at a right angle to the wave coming in.

But the teenagers weren't looking at the beach. They

were staring over their shoulders, waiting for the incoming wave.

'No!' He yelled with all the power he could muster. 'It'll take you onto the reef. No!'

The two boys nearest heard. Alex and James. They faltered and let the wave power under them.

But Rowan either hadn't heard or hadn't wanted to hear. He caught the wave with ease and let its power sweep him forward.

It was too late to yell again, for the outgoing wave was heading inexorably for them all. For Tom and Alex and James it was simply a matter of head down, hold fast, ride through it. For Rowan, though... He was upright on the board when the walls of water smashed together.

The reef was too close. Rowan was under water, caught by his ankle rope, dragged by the sheer force of the waves.

He was on the reef.

Tom put his head down and headed straight for him.

There was no email.

Every Sunday since she'd returned to England Tom had sent an email, and there wasn't one now.

At first she wasn't bothered. Tom was a lone medical practitioner. Things happened. He'd send it later.

He didn't...and so she went to bed feeling empty.

Which was stupid.

It had been eighteen months since Emily's death. She'd left Australia as soon as the formalities were over, desperate to put the pain behind her. She hadn't had the energy to head back to her work with Médicins Sans Frontières. Instead she'd taken a job in an emergency department in London and tried to drown herself in her job.

Mostly it was okay. Mostly she got to the end of the day thinking she could face the next.

And Tom's emails helped. He sent one every Sunday,

short messages with a little local gossip, snippets of his life, his latest love interest, any interesting cases he'd treated. And at the end he always attached a photograph of Emily's grave.

Sometimes the grave was rain-washed, sometimes it was bathed in sunshine, but it was always covered in wildflowers and backed by the sea. He'd promised this on the day of the funeral and he'd kept his word. 'I'll look after this for you, Tasha. I'll look after it for Emily and I'll always make sure you can see it.'

It hurt but still she wanted it. She usually sent a curt thank you back and felt guilty that she couldn't do better.

For Tom had been wonderful, she conceded. He'd been with her every step of the way during that appalling time.

It had been Tom who'd intervened when various specialists had decreed Emily needed to be in ICU, saying that spending time with her mother would decrease her tiny life span. Tom had simply looked at them and they'd backed off.

It had been Tom who'd organised discreet, empathic photographers, who'd put together her most treasured possession—an album of a perfect, beautiful baby being held with love.

It had been Tom who'd taken her back to Cray Point, who'd stood beside her during a heartbreaking burial and then let her be, to sit on the veranda and stare out at the horizon for as long as she'd needed. He'd been there when she'd felt like talking and had left her alone when she'd needed to be alone.

And when, three weeks after Emily's death, she'd woken one morning and said she needed to go back to London, she needed to go back to work, he'd driven her to the airport and he'd hugged her goodbye.

She'd felt as if leaving him had been ripping yet another part of her life away.

But his emails had come every Sunday, and he was seemingly not bothered that she could hardly respond.

'So what?' she demanded of herself when there was still no email the next morning. 'Tom was there when you needed him but it's been eighteen months. You can't expect him to photograph a grave for the rest of his life.'

Could she move on, too?

And with that came another thought. The idea had seeped into her consciousness a couple of months ago. It was stupid. She surely wasn't brave enough to do it, but once it had seeded in her brain the longing it brought with it wouldn't let her alone.

Could she try for another baby?

What would Tom think? she wondered, and her instinctive question was enough to make her stop walking and blink.

'Tom's not in the equation,' she said out loud, and the people around her cast her curious glances.

She shook her head and kept going. Of course Tom wasn't in the equation.

'It's good that the contact's finally over,' she told herself, but then she thought of Emily's grave at Cray Point and knew that part of her heart would always be there.

With or without Tom Blake.

CHAPTER THREE

Six weeks later...

TODAY HAD BEEN an exhausting shift in the emergency department of her London hospital. The hospital was on the fringe of a poor socio-economic district, where unemployment was rife and where the young didn't have enough to do. The combination was a recipe for disaster and the disasters often ended up in Tasha's care.

She'd had two stabbings this shift. She was emotionally wiped—but, then, she thought as she changed to go home, she wanted to be emotionally wiped. She wanted to go home exhausted enough to sleep.

She'd hardly slept for weeks. Why?

Was it because the emails had stopped?

It was her own fault, she thought. She hadn't made it clear she was grateful, because a part of her wasn't. Tom's emails were a jagged reminder of past pain. She didn't want to remember—but neither did she want to forget.

And now Tom had obviously decided it was time to move on. She should be over it.

Could she ever be *over it*? She stared at her reflection in the change-room mirror and let her thoughts take her where they willed. How to move on?

Part of her ached for another baby, but did she have the courage?

'Tasha? You have visitors.' Ellen, the nurse administrator, put her nose around the door. 'Two ladies are here to see you. They arrived two hours ago. They wouldn't let me disturb you but said as soon as you finished your shift could I let you know. I've popped them into the counselling room with tea and biccies. They seem nice.'

'Nice?'

Emergency departments saw many tragedies. Often family members came in, days, weeks, sometimes months after the event to talk through what had happened. Ellen usually pre-empted contact by finding the patient file and giving her time to read it. It helped. For doctors like Tasha, after weeks or months individual deaths could become blurred.

But Ellen wasn't carrying a file and she'd described them as nice, nothing more.

'It's personal,' Ellen said, seeing her confusion. 'They say it's nothing to do with a patient. They're Australian. Hilda and Rhonda. Middle-aged. One's knitting, the other's doing crochet.'

Hilda and Rhonda.

She stilled, thinking of the only two Australians she knew who were called Hilda and Rhonda.

'Shall I tell them you can't see them?' Ellen asked, watching her face. 'I'm sure they'll understand. They seem almost nervous about disturbing you. One word from me and I suspect they'll scuttle.'

Did she want them to...scuttle?

No. Of course she didn't.

For some reason her heart was doing some sort of stupid lurch. Surely something wasn't wrong? With Tom?

It couldn't be, she thought. He'd be safe home in Cray Point with his latest lady. Who? He'd mentioned his women in his emails. Alice? No, Alice had been a good twelve months ago. There'd been Kylie and Samantha and Susie since then.

The Blake brothers were incorrigible, she thought, and she even managed a sort of smile as she headed off to see what Rhonda and Hilda had in store for her.

But they weren't here to tell her about Tom's latest lady.

'A subarachnoid haemorrhage?' She stared at the two women in front of her and she couldn't believe what she was hearing. 'Tom's had a subarachnoid haemorrhage?'

The women had greeted her with disbelief at first—'You look so different!' —

'I'm wearing scrubs,' she'd told them, but they'd shaken their heads in unison.

'You look prettier. Younger. Though that time would have made anyone look old.' They'd hugged her, but then they'd moved onto Tom.

These two women had formed a caring background during her time in Cray Point but now they seemed almost apologetic. Apologising for what they were telling her.

'It was the surf,' Rhonda said. 'A minor accident, he said, just a cut needing a few stitches, but then his neck was stiff and he got a blinding headache. He collapsed, scaring the life out of us. We had to get the air ambulance and the doctors say he only just made it.'

'But they say he's going to be okay,' Hilda broke in, speaking fast. Maybe she'd seen the colour drain from Tasha's face. 'Eventually. But it did some damage—the same as a minor stroke. Now he's trying to pretend it's business as normal but of course it's not.'

'What happened?' Tasha asked, stunned.

'It was the first of the winter storms,' Hilda told her, sniffing at the idiocy of surfers in general and one surfer in particular. 'The surf was huge and of course people were doing stupid things. They were surfing too close to the rocks for the conditions and he hit his head—a nasty, deep gash. Mary and Chris...did you meet them? They're the medical couple who help out sometimes. They stitched his head and tried to persuade him he needed a scan but would he listen? And that night… Well, it was lucky I decided to stay on, though cleaning the pantry was an excuse. He'd put off having his latest woman for dinner so I thought he must be feeling really ill. And he was toying with his meal when all of a sudden he said "Hilda, my neck… My head…" And then he sort of slumped.'

'There was no loss of consciousness but by the time the ambulance arrived he couldn't move his left arm or leg,' Rhonda told her. She took a deep breath and recited something she must have learned off by heart. 'His scans showed a skull fracture and infarct in the right lentiform nucleus corona radiata.'

'That's in the brain,' Hilda said helpfully, and Rhonda rolled her eyes. But then she got serious again.

'Anyway, the air ambulance was there fast and got him to Melbourne. They operated within the hour and they're saying long-term he should be fine. He spent two weeks in hospital, protesting every minute. Then they wanted him to go to rehab but he wouldn't. He says he can do the exercises himself. So now he's back in Cray Point, pretending it's business as usual.'

'But it's not,' Hilda told her. 'He has left-sided weakness. He's not allowed to drive. The doctors only let him come home on the condition he has physio every day but of course he says he's too busy to do it. He should concentrate on rehab for at least two months but will he?'

'He doesn't have time,' Hilda told her. 'And I was dusting in his study and he'd requested a copy of the specialist's letters and I just…happened to read them. Anyway the specialist's saying there's a risk of permanent residual damage if he doesn't follow orders. But Mary and Chris have a new grandbaby in Queensland, their daughter's ill and they had to go. There's no other doctor to help.'

'And of course it's winter in Australia.' Rhonda took over seamlessly. 'No doctor will take on a locum job in Cray Point in winter. We know he advertised—we weren't supposed to know that either but...'

'Hilda saw it on his study desk?' Tasha suggested, and Hilda flushed and then smiled.

'Well, I did, dear. But of course no one answered, and the oldies in Cray Point are still getting ill and he knows how much they need him. He cares too much to let us look after ourselves. So he's hobbling around, still working. The night before we left there was a car crash and out he went. It was filthy weather and he was crawling into the wreckage to stop bleeding...'

'And then we had to leave.' Up until now Rhonda had sounded resigned, full of the foolishness of men, but suddenly her voice wobbled. 'You know we're both English? We married brothers and moved to Cray Point thirty years ago but our parents stayed here. Last week our mam died and our dad's in a mess so we had to drop everything and come. Including abandoning Tom. We'll take our dad home with us but first there's his house to be sorted, immigration, so much to do...'

'But we're worrying about Tom all the time,' Hilda told her. 'We know he's not coping. It'll be weeks before we can get back, and who's to boss him around? He'll push himself and push himself. We have one district nurse and no one else. Cray Point's in real trouble. And then in the middle of last night Rhonda sat up in bed and said, "What about Tasha? She's family."'

The word seemed to echo around the counselling room. Family.

'I knew nothing about this,' she said faintly, and Rhonda nodded.

'Well, of course you wouldn't. He doesn't talk to anyone about it, and of course he worries about you. We all do.

He'd never bother you. Tasha…dear, it seems really unfair to ask, but Hilda knew your address…'

'From Tom's desk?' She couldn't help herself but she won a couple of half-hearted smiles.

'Well, yes, dear,' Hilda agreed. 'Though of course I didn't go looking. I just happened to have seen it on a certificate he left out for me to post to you. So we knew you were living in a hospital apartment and I remembered which hospital. So we thought we'd just come and let you know…'

'Because he needs someone,' Rhonda told her. And then she paused and told it like it was. 'He needs you.'

To say Tasha's mind was in overdrive was an understatement. She'd just finished a frantic shift. Normally it took hours to debrief herself, to rid herself of the images of the various crises bursting through the ambulance doors, but suddenly all she could think of was Tom.

The sudden end to contact hadn't been because he thought she should move on. It had been because he was in trouble himself.

'W-what about Susie?' she stammered. The thought of Tom needing her was such a switch that it had her unbalanced. 'Can't she help?'

And the two women snorted in unison.

'One thing Dr Tom Blake can't do and that's choose a woman who's any use,' Rhonda declared. 'She's hardly been near him since his accident. And she's not a doctor or even a nurse. How can she help? You're a doctor, dear. That's why we're here.'

'You want me to go?' Even saying it sounded wrong.

But both women were trying to smile. Their smiles were nervous. Their smiles said they didn't hold out much hope but they were like headlights, catching her and holding her. She couldn't move.

'Could you?' Hilda sounded breathless.

'Is it possible?' Rhonda whispered.

She stood and stared at the two rotund little ladies. They stared back, their eyes full of hope. And doubt. And just a touch of guilt as well.

Tom...

He needed her.

She didn't want to go.

Why not?

She could go. She knew she could. There'd been an intake of brand-new doctors only last week and there was crossover from the last lot. Her shift could be covered.

She could walk out of her barren little apartment within an hour.

But to go to Tom...

She didn't want to go back to Australia. Australia was full of memories of her little girl, her little fighter who'd lived just seven days. How could she go back to the place of all that pain?

But there was more to this than grief, she acknowledged. Her reaction wasn't all about not wanting to be where Emily had lived and died, and she had the courage to acknowledge it. She'd never avoided thinking about Emily and, to be fair, Tom had had a hand in that. He'd been with her all that time.

It was Tom who'd made sure she'd shared every precious moment of Emily's tiny life. It was Tom who'd sat by her, fielding well-meaning professionals, admitting those who could help, firmly turning away those who couldn't.

There had been so much support. There had been so much love.

For Tom had loved, too. 'She's my niece,' he'd told her when she'd been so exhausted she'd had to sleep but the thought of closing her eyes on her little girl had been unbearable. 'You sleep and I'll hold her every single moment. And I promise I won't sleep while you've entrusted her to me.'

He'd just…been there. She could hardly think of Emily without thinking of Tom.

And then, after Emily had died…

Being bundled back to Cray Point. A simple, beautiful ceremony on the headland because she couldn't think where else was right. Then sleeping and sleeping and sleeping, while Tom picked up the threads of…being Tom.

Which included his women. Alice was there, vaguely resentful of Tasha's presence. And then Alice was no longer around and Tasha knew it was partly because of her.

She'd said something to him—apologised—and Tom had grinned. 'Don't fuss yourself, lassie,' he'd told her. 'Alice knows I don't take my love life seriously. The whole town knows it.'

So he was like Paul. That was the thought that was holding her rigid now.

He was lovely, kind, gentle, caring.

He went from woman to woman.

He'd just suffered a cerebral bleed from a surfing accident. He was yet another man who took crazy risks…

The Blake brothers spelled trouble. She didn't want to go anywhere near him, but she owed him so much.

She thought of him now, the image that was burned into her mind. Waking up from sleep and finding him crooning down to her little daughter.

'Surfing's awesome,' he'd been telling her tiny baby. 'The feel of cool water on your toes, the strength of the wave lifting you, surging forward… Feel my fingers as I push under your toes. Imagine that's a wave, lifting you, surging… That's right, our Emily, curl your toes. You have such a tiny life, our Emily, but we need to fill it with so much. I wish I could take you surfing but feel the power under your toes and know that surfing's wonderful and you're wonderful and I hope you can take all this with you.'

And Tasha found herself blinking and Hilda gasped

and glared at Rhonda, who grabbed a handful of tissues from the counselling table. Tasha suddenly found she was being hugged. 'Dear, no,' Rhonda gasped. 'We shouldn't have come. We never should have asked. Tom will be okay. Cray Point will survive. Forget it, sweetheart, forget we ever came.'

Somehow she disengaged from their collective hug. Somewhere she'd read a research article that said hugging released oxytocin and oxytocin did all sorts of good things to the body. It made you more empathic. It made you want to connect more with your fellow humans.

With Tom? She'd be playing with fire.

Why? Because he was like Paul? He wasn't. Not really. She'd stayed with him for a month and there'd never been a hint that he was interested in her…that way.

Besides, she was older, wiser, and she knew how to protect herself.

And this time she didn't need Tom. Tom needed her, and Rhonda and Hilda were waiting for an answer.

And in the end there was only one answer she could give. No matter what Tom's personal life was like, what he'd done for her had been beyond price.

And then the idea that had been playing at the edges of her mind suddenly, unexpectedly surfaced. The idea had been growing, like an insistent ache, an emptiness demanding to be filled, a void it took courage to even think about.

She could still scarcely think about it but if she went to help Tom she'd be returning to Australia, where an IVF clinic still held Paul's gift.

She'd agonised over using Paul's sperm last time, but in the end it had come down to thinking her baby could know of its father. This time the tug to use the same sperm was stronger. Another baby would be Emily's brother or sister.

And suddenly that was in her heart, front and centre, and she knew what her answer would be.

'Of course I'll go,' she told them swiftly, before she had the time to change her mind. Before fear took over. 'It'll take me a couple of days to get there but I'll do it.'

'Oh, Tasha,' Hilda breathed.

'But don't tell him,' Rhonda urged. 'He won't let you come if you tell him. He'll say he's fine. He'll fire us for contacting you.'

'I'd like to see him try,' Hilda declared, but she sounded nervous and Tasha summoned a grin.

'Okay,' she told them. 'I won't warn him. But he'd better not be in bed with Susie when I get there.'

'I wouldn't think so,' Hilda declared, though she didn't sound absolutely certain.

'Sure,' Tasha said, but she didn't feel sure in the least.

CHAPTER FOUR

THERE WERE THINGS to do and he should be doing them. It was driving him nuts.

Old Mrs Carstairs hadn't had a house call for weeks. She'd been hospitalised with pneumonia in late autumn and it had left her weak. She should be staying with her daughter in Melbourne but she'd refused to stay away from her house a moment longer.

And who could blame her? Tom thought morosely. Margaret Carstairs owned a house high on the headland overlooking the sweeping vista of Bass Strait. She was content to lie on her day bed and watch the changing weather, the sea, and the whales making their great migration north. She was content to let the world come to her.

Except the world couldn't. Or Tom couldn't. And unlike Margaret Carstairs, he was far from happy to lie on a couch and watch the sea. Any reports about Margaret came from the district nurse and he knew Brenda was worried.

But he couldn't drive and he'd have trouble walking down Margaret's steep driveway when he got there. When he'd first woken after surgery he'd been almost completely paralysed down his left side. His recovery had been swift, but not swift enough. He still had a dragging weakness, and terror had been replaced by frustration.

He couldn't ignore his body's weakness. He couldn't drive. He used Karen, the local taxi driver, but since his leg had let him down while crawling into a crashed car, even Karen was imposing limits.

'He would have died if I hadn't done it,' he muttered to no one in particular. It was true. The driver had perforated a lung. It had been a complex procedure to get him out alive and if Tom had waited for paramedics it would have been too late. The fact that he'd become trapped himself when his leg hadn't had the strength to push himself out was surely minor. It was an excellent result.

But he still couldn't drive and he still had trouble walking in this hilly, clifftop town. So here he was, waiting for the next emergency that he couldn't go to.

His phone went and he lunged for it, willing it to be something he could handle.

It wasn't.

Old Bill Hadley lived down the steepest steps in Cray Point. He was lying at the bottom of them now, whimpering into his cellphone.

'Doc? I know you're crook, but I reckon I might have sprained me ankle. I'm stuck at the bottom of the steps. I've yelled but no one can hear me. Middle of the day, everyone must be out. Lucky I had me phone, don't you think? Do you reckon you could come?'

Bill Hadley was tough. If he was saying he might have sprained his ankle it was probably a fracture. Tom could hear the pain in the old man's voice, but he couldn't go. Not down those steps.

'I'll call the ambulance and get the district nurse to come and stay with you until it arrives,' he told Bill, and he heard silence and he knew there was pain involved. A lot of pain. 'Brenda can stabilise your ankle and keep you comfortable.'

'She…she can give me an injection, like?'

'She can.' Once again he felt that sweep of helplessness. He could authorise drugs over the phone but it was a risk. Bill had pre-existing conditions. Without being able to assess the whole situation...

He couldn't.

'Sorry, Bill, it's the best I can do,' he told him. 'Just keep that ankle still. There's no other way.'

And then he was interrupted. 'Yes, there is.'

He looked up from the settee and he almost dropped the phone.

Tasha was standing in the doorway.

Tasha...

This was a Tasha he'd never seen before. Tasha on the other side of tragedy?

When last he'd seen her she'd been post-pregnancy and ravaged by grief. Her hair had needed a cut. She'd abandoned wearing make-up and she'd worn nothing but baggy jogging pants and windcheaters. Even the day he'd put her on the plane to return to England he'd thought she'd looked like she'd just emerged from a war zone.

This woman, though, was wearing neat black pants and a crisp white shirt, tucked in to accentuate a slender waist. A pale blue sweater was looped around her shoulders. Her curls were shiny and bouncing, let loose to wisp around her shoulders.

She looked cool, elegant...beautiful.

She was carrying a suitcase. She set it down and smiled, and her smile was bright and professional.

'Hi,' she said, and beamed.

'H-hi.' Her smile almost knocked him into the middle of next week, but she was already switching to professional.

'Are you knocking back work? When I've come all this way to do as much work as possible? An injured ankle? Bill who?'

'Bill Hadley...'

'Ankle injury? House call? That's what I'm here for.'

'What the—?'

'Is it urgent? Is it okay if I use your car? Or I can ring the taxi again. I'll need his patient file if there is one, and an address. Can I use your medical kit?'

Tom couldn't answer. It felt like all the oxygen had been sucked out of the room. All the oxygen was in her smile.

She shook her head in mock exasperation and lifted the phone from his grasp.

'Bill? I've come in on the end of this conversation but this is Tasha Raymond. I'm Dr Blake's sister-in-law, a doctor, too, and I'm here to help until Tom's on his feet again. Could you tell me what the problem is?'

'You can drive?' Tom could hear Bill's quavering hope.

'I can,' Tasha assured him. 'You'll have heard that Dr Blake's had an accident, so we need to look after him. That means using me until he's recovered. What's happened?'

There was a moment's pause and then, 'I reckon I've sprained me ankle. If you could come, Doc, that'd be great.'

Doc. The transition was seamless, Tom thought, astounded. The community was desperate for a doctor and Tasha was here. Therefore Tasha was *Doc.*

'Five minutes tops,' Tasha said, as Bill explained the problem and outlined where he lived. 'I walked down those very steps when I was here eighteen months ago. Hang in there.'

And she disconnected and turned to Tom. 'Hey,' she said, and gave him her very warmest smile. 'It's good to see you. I'm so sorry about your accident but Rhonda and Hilda say you need me and it seems they're right. We can talk later but this sounds like I should go. Patient history? Anything else I should know?'

'You can't.' He was feeling like he'd been punched in the solar plexus. This was a whirlwind and it wasn't stopping. 'Tasha, I'm coping. I'll go.'

And her smile softened to one of understanding. And

sympathy. 'How weak is your leg, scale one to ten?' she said gently. 'Ten's strong. One's useless.'

'Eight,' he said, and she fixed him with a don't-mess-with-the-doctor look.

'Really?'

'Okay, six,' he conceded. 'But—'

'I didn't fly from London for buts. I flew from London because you've been injured, you need care and Cray Point needs me.' She stooped then and brushed her lips against his forehead, a faint touch. A sisterly gesture? 'I'm so sorry you've been hurt but for now it seems you need to rest. Can I take your car?'

He stared and she gazed calmly back. Waiting for him to accept the inevitable.

He had no choice. She'd flown all the way from England to help him. He should be grateful.

He was grateful but he was also…overwhelmed? That she come all this way…

Tasha was the one who needed help, not him, but for now…he had no choice.

'I'd appreciate your help,' he said stiffly. 'I… Thank you. But, Tasha, I'm coming with you.'

She drove. He sat in the passenger seat and tried to get his head around what had just happened.

A whirlwind had arrived. A woman he scarcely recognised.

The last time he'd seen Tasha she'd been limp with shock and grief. Now she was a woman in charge of her world. She was doctor reacting to a medical call with professional efficiency.

She was a woman who looked, quite simply, gorgeous.

His head wasn't coping.

He directed while she drove but she would have gotten there fine without him. In the weeks after Emily's death she'd walked Cray Point, over and over. He'd thought she'd hardly seen it. She obviously had.

'So…Rhonda and Hilda…' he said at last. It was almost the first question he'd been able to ask. She'd been all brisk efficiency, checking his medical supplies, watching him—as if she wasn't sure could manage—climb into the car, then turning towards Bill's like a homing pigeon. It was as if she'd been a doctor here for years.

'They came to see me in London,' she was saying. 'They told me you were in trouble.'

'They had no right.'

'They had every right.' Her voice softened. 'Eighteen months ago Cray Point was here when I needed it. So were you, but if we're taking the personal out of it then I'm paying back Cray Point.'

'So you just dropped everything…'

'As you dropped everything for me. I didn't leave anyone in the lurch, as you didn't. Next question?'

He sat back and tried to think of questions. He had a thousand.

He couldn't think of any.

And she had the temerity to grin. 'Very good, Dr Blake.'

'You want to say "Good boy" and pat my head?'

Her smile widened. 'Not yet. You have two months of behaving yourself before you get any elephant stamps.'

'Behaving myself?'

'Doing what the doctor says. Lots of rest. Lots of rehabilitation. Rhonda says you should be going to physio daily, but you won't leave Cray Point with no doctor. She also says you hurt more than you let on, and that you're not sleeping.'

'How does she know?'

She chuckled. 'Their intelligence system is awesome. I'm to report back.'

'Maybe you should stay somewhere else,' he said, but her smile didn't slip.

'Maybe I should, and I can, if you want privacy. All I care about is that you can get to rehab. What you do is your business as long as you're tucked up in bed when your doctor says you should be.' She considered for a moment and then added. 'Probably by yourself? I'm willing to bet that nights of endless passion aren't what your doctors are ordering.'

They weren't. He stared down at his weak leg with loathing.

'Nights of passion aren't exactly on the agenda,' he said through gritted teeth, and she chuckled again.

'I'll give you your elephant stamp for that one. It's this street, isn't it?'

Cray Point was an historic fishing village perched on a high headland. A few of the older houses were built at the foot of the cliffs, with narrow flights of steps twisting down to their entrances. They were a nightmare to access, increasingly owned and maintained by holidaymakers who didn't mind a few weeks of carting groceries down a hundred steps. Bill was one of the last fishermen living in one.

'History?' she demanded as they pulled to a halt, and somehow Tom pulled himself together and told her that Bill was an unstable diabetic.

'He's put on a power of weight since he stopped fishing, though heaven knows how he manages it when he has to come up and down these steps. He's had diabetes for years but he lives on fish and chips and beer, and takes his insulin when he feels like it. He's had more than one hypo. I suspect one might have contributed to this fall. He has peripheral nerve damage to his feet.'

'Yikes,' Tasha said. 'Okay, you stay up here and direct the ambulance.'

'Do I have a choice?'

She grinned again, an endearing grin that if he wasn't

so frustrated he might even enjoy. 'No,' she told him. 'But you may be useful. I'll ring for advice if I need it.'

'Why does that sound so patronising?'

'Because Rhonda and Hilda say you need patronising,' she told him, and before he could begin to realise what she intended she leaned across and kissed him. It was a feather kiss, the merest brush of lips against his nose. Why it had the power to pack a jolt as fierce as an electric charge...

But she was out of the car and in the back seat, fetching his doctor's bag, before he had a chance to analyse it.

'See you later,' she told him. 'Be good.'

He was left in the car to glower.

Bill had fractured his ankle. She suspected he also had fractured ribs. His blood sugar was so low it was a wonder he wasn't unconscious and it took skill to get him stabilised.

If she hadn't been here the outcome might have been fatal, she thought as she worked, and as Brenda, the district nurse, came bustling down the steps and immediately starting to berate Bill for living in such a dumb place, she was sure of it.

'Leave him be,' she said gently. She'd packed him with insulating sheets to keep him warm. She had a drip up and drugs on board and she'd given him enough glucose to get his sugars up but he was drifting in and out of consciousness regardless.

'And Doc shouldn't be out,' Brenda scolded. 'There he is, sitting at the top of the steps, and it's cold. You should make him stay home.'

That warranted an inward smile. She'd been in Cray Point for an hour and already she was being treated as part of the furniture. That's what it was like to be needed, she thought. There'd been a gap here and she'd slipped seamlessly into it.

'Tasha?' It was Tom.

She'd conceded his need to know and had left her phone on speaker. Tom might be up the top of the cliff, but in spirit—and in voice—he was right there.

'Yep?' She was adjusting the drip, wondering whether it was worth trying to move him inside.

'The ambulance is five minutes away,' Tom told her, and she relaxed a little. Bill's breathing was starting to get shallow. Shock, or something more sinister?

'Excellent.'

'You're worried.' He'd got it, she thought. Her one word must have contained a thread of concern.

'Nothing we can't handle,' she said brightly. Bill was looking up at her, dazed. The last thing she wanted was to frighten him.

'He looks like death, Dr Blake,' Brenda breathed. 'He looks awful.'

And Tasha gave her a glare that would have curdled milk.

'He does.' How to turn this around? 'He looks like he hasn't washed for days and he smells like dead fish,' she told Tom. 'Bill, I don't know what you've been doing but I suspect the first thing the nurses do in their nice clean hospital is give you a wash. Nurses are fussy about who they put between their sheets.'

Amazingly Bill managed a faint chuckle and Tasha chuckled, too, and then they settled back to wait for the ambulance.

She was stunning.

He sat in the car and directed the paramedics down the steps when they arrived and he felt the weight of the world lift from his shoulders.

She'd come from half a world away to help him.

He wanted to be down those steps instead of her, he

thought, and then he thought, no, he wanted to be down there *with* her.

Tasha.

He'd thought of her almost every day since she'd left. He'd thought of tapering off the dumb, newsy emails he'd sent her but sending a photograph of a grave without a note seemed wrong, and somehow the contact seemed important. He was family and he had to show he cared.

And here she was. Family. Caring.

The thought did his head in. He was the carer and yet she'd abandoned her life and come to help him.

The paramedics brought Bill up the steps strapped onto a stretcher and Tom eased himself out of the car to greet him. To his amazement, Bill was recovering his good humour.

'Practically don't hurt at all now, Doc,' he told him. 'Tasha fixed me right up. She's a good 'un and she says she's staying till you're better. Cray Point's lucky. You're lucky.'

Behind him, Brenda was talking to Tasha, and he realised his nurse was outlining home-care visits for the next day.

'Hey,' he said, interrupting Brenda's riveting account of Doris Mayberry's leg abscess. 'I haven't employed Tasha yet.'

And Brenda looked astonished. 'What do you mean, you haven't employed her? She's here to work and we need her. What possible quibble could you have?'

Quibble? He tried to think of any.

'Do you have registration to work in Australia?' he asked.

'Of course,' Tasha told him.

He couldn't think of anything more to say. It was starting to rain. He stood in the drizzle and watched as the paramedics loaded Bill into the ambulance and Brenda listed all the urgent things she had for Tasha to do.

He'd never felt more helpless in his life.

At last the ambulance drove away. Brenda gave a cheery wave—'See you tomorrow, Tasha!'—and he was left with Tasha.

She returned to his car—to the driving side—climbed in and looked out at him.

'Aren't you getting in?'

He did. He had to use his hands to heave his weak leg into the car and that made him more frustrated still.

'You will go surfing,' she said.

'What?'

'Rhonda and Hilda told me you hit your head on the rocks, surfing. Why don't the Blake boys choose nice safe hobbies?'

'Like macramé.'

'Macramé's good,' she said thoughtfully. 'Though needles can be sharp.'

'Tasha…'

'Yes?' She'd started the car and was heading for home. For his place.

'You shouldn't have come.' It came out as a snap and he winced, but she was smiling, amused rather than offended.

'Of course I should. You need me, but, then, you're a Blake boy so you think you don't need anyone.'

He wasn't sure how to answer that. 'I can't sit back and watch you work.'

'Of course you can't,' she said equitably. 'And you're not going to. Rhonda and Hilda gave me a list of the rehab routine you should be following. The most important thing to do after a head injury is to get your body back to what it was, fast, before the damage can't be reversed. So medical emergencies are for me to deal with, not you.'

He stared. 'You're not bossy!'

'What do you mean, I'm not bossy?'

'When you were here before. You were…'

'Traumatised?' she suggested for him when he didn't come up with a word. 'Of course. That's what I was when you knew me.' Once again her voice gentled. 'But I'm not traumatised now, Tom, and you are. That's what I'm here for. You were my support person. Now I'm yours.'

There seemed nothing left to say. He stared out at the rain-swept road and felt things shift inside him that he'd had no idea could shift.

This was Tasha, a widow, the mother of a baby who'd died. She was battered by life and she'd needed him in the most desperate of circumstances.

Now she was here to help him, but that wasn't what was throwing him. Or not so much. What was throwing him was that she looked…like Susie?

No. She looked nothing like Susie but there was a common thread. The women he dated were beautiful but, more important, they were self-reliant.

Tom Blake didn't need women. He'd trained himself not to need them. He'd seen the heartache his father had caused when he couldn't commit himself to a long-term relationship and Tom didn't trust himself not to do the same. He'd never understood how people committed themselves to a monogamous relationship. He liked people—he liked women—too much.

The women he dated knew it. He was always honest. Cray Point had a limited pool of single women but there were enough. Divorcees. Older women who loved the idea of dating but who'd been burned before. Of course there were women who thought they could change his mind but he was honest from the start.

His mind couldn't be changed and he knew it. He had no intention of hurting anyone as his mother had been hurt. So he stepped back and he never dated anyone he thought was the least bit vulnerable.

That didn't mean he wasn't attracted, though, and the woman beside him now…

Was his stepbrother's widow. Was out of bounds.

Why? She was beautiful. She was competent. She seemed like she was taking over his life as he knew it.

She seemed almost…fun.

That was a weird concept but it was the one that sprang into his mind and stayed. Since the accident his life had been grey, filled with pain and boredom. He hadn't had the energy to keep up with past relationships or start another. But now there was Tasha…

'The first thing we need to decide is where I live,' she told him.

'Where you live… You really intend staying?'

'I told Rhonda and Hilda I'll stay as long as you need me, and one look at you tells me you'll need me for a while.'

'Thanks.'

'Tom, you do need to admit you need help. Your left leg's dragging. There's a faint slur in your voice, and did you know your smile's lopsided?'

He wasn't smiling now. 'I'm fine.'

'You're not, and without rehab you risk not being fine permanently. You know that. Surely it's just commitment to the medical needs of this town that's stopped you focusing, so I'm not leaving. Rhonda and Hilda say I can use their cottage. They have cats, which their next-door neighbour is currently feeding, and cats make me sneeze, but I'd rather sneeze than interfere with your love life.'

'I don't have a love life.'

'And that was inappropriate. Sorry.' She was serious now. 'Tom, when I stayed with you last year I was shocked and numb and I was very, very grateful, which is why I'm here now. But I'm no longer shocked and numb and if Susie or anyone else is on the scene, or if you simply want privacy… Be honest, Tom. If you'd like me to stay at

Rhonda and Hilda's I'll make a deal with the cats. There are two bedrooms. They can have one, I can have the other.'

'Stay with me.' To say he was disconcerted was an understatement and his voice came out a growl, but she smiled.

'So you're happy for me to stay until that limp disappears?'

'I seem to be stuck with you.'

'That's gracious.'

It wasn't but she was looking amused, and that disconcerted him even more.

But he was behaving like a bore. She'd come a long way to help him. He needed to get his act together and be grateful.

'I'm sorry.' He closed his eyes. 'Tell me you haven't messed with your career path or given up your holidays for the next ten years to come here.'

'I haven't.' Her voice softened. 'Tom, I've just reached the end of my contract and to be honest I was thinking of changing workplaces anyway. This gives me time to consider where I'll go next.'

'Back to your work with Médicins Sans Frontières?'

'I'm not sure, but I need to think and Cray Point is as good a place to think as any. Your house, or Rhonda and Hilda's place with cats? It's up to you, Tom, but be honest, if you'd rather I'm out of your hair then Rhonda and Hilda's it is.'

'If you stay at my place you'll boss me,' he said, and that grin flashed out again, the grin he hadn't known she'd possessed until today.

'Of course I will. Exercise, exercise, exercise. I've made a commitment. I'm staying until you're recovered and I can't see myself spending the rest of my life in Cray Point.'

'There are worse places to stay.'

'There are,' she agreed. 'But the problem is that Cray Point comes with a Blake boy and this is messing with another vow. And that's to never have anything to do with anyone resembling a Blake boy ever again.'

'You're labelling me with my brother and father?'

'I surely am,' she said cordially. 'And I intend to keep doing so. Believe me, it's the only safe thing to do. So you can do what you like. Our lives shouldn't mesh—just as long as you do your rehab.'

He lay in bed that night and thought of the gift she'd given him. The freedom to get himself back to normal.

What was normal?

Nothing felt normal any more.

His body had once been what he was. When he'd wanted to move, his body had moved. When he'd wanted to surf, run, put himself in peril hauling people out of crashed cars, make love, his body had come along with him. It had done what he'd demanded of it, no questions asked.

But now it was like his body belonged to one of his patients—not him. Since that night when a blinding headache had suddenly seen him crash, limp, helpless, his body had seemed separate from what he was. The sensation had been terrifying.

What he should have done—and he knew this—was stay away from Cray Point and put his all into rehab. He should be working with his body until it felt like it belonged to him again. Only in some weird way that'd be acknowledging that his damaged body had control, not him. His body would be dictating that he leave Cray Point without a doctor. His body would be dictating what he could and couldn't do.

So he'd hunkered back down in Cray Point. Dating had stopped. Everything had stopped but work while he fought for control again.

And now here was Tasha, proposing a course of action

it was sensible to accept but which meant he was out of control again.

He was being dumb. Paranoid. Hers was a magnificent gesture and he should accept it with gratitude. But to calmly sit back and let her take over his life…

That was an overstatement.

He closed his eyes and fought for sleep but it wouldn't come. He felt like he was flailing, almost as helpless as that first day in Intensive Care, when he'd realised his arm and leg wouldn't respond to his commands.

How could Tasha make him feel like that?

Control…

It had been his mantra all his life. He'd seen the emotional mess his father had caused. He'd seen his mother's pain and he'd sworn he'd never cause it and never have it happen to him.

But during these last few weeks his body had shown him how little control he really had, and now Tasha was showing him the same.

'It's dumb to feel like this.'

He said it out loud and it echoed in the darkened room. His body was recovering and with Tasha's help then maybe…no, make that surely, it would recover completely.

All he had to do was let Tasha take control.

All he had to do was let go.

CHAPTER FIVE

SHE WOKE TO the sound of thumping. It wasn't steady, though. It was a decidedly wobbly thump.

Someone was thumping on the veranda outside her bedroom window.

She glanced at her bedside clock and practically yelped. It was after eight. She'd gone to bed over twelve hours ago. Despite the feigned chirpiness she'd put on for Tom, her body had demanded sleep.

Maybe that was a defence.

For now she was here, the place she'd left eighteen months ago, wondering if she could ever forget.

She didn't want to forget, but the pain of remembering was appalling. At least in London she could throw herself into her work, but here…

Up on the headland was a tiny grave. She'd thought she'd go there last night but in the end she just couldn't. She'd declined Tom's invitation to share dinner. She'd pleaded jet lag, eaten eggs on toast and hit the pillows.

But now… Thump…thump…thump…

Intrigued, she tossed back the covers and hauled up the window. Her bedroom looked straight over the veranda to the ocean beyond. The sea air felt blissful. She breathed in the salt and then she looked along the veranda and decided to stop breathing for a while.

The mixed emotions of moments ago came to a grinding halt.

For Tom was here, and Tom was gorgeous.

There was no other word for it. He was totally, absolutely gorgeous.

He was wearing boxers and nothing else. The weak winter sun was doing its best to make his bronzed body glisten. A sheen of sweat on his chest and brow made him look even more...

Gorgeous. She couldn't get past that word.

Tom had a skipping rope and was doing his best to skip, but his lazy leg was dragging. He was forcing himself on, but every second or third skip his leg didn't lift. He'd swear and keep going.

'Good morning.'

Tasha's greeting made him miss the rope again.

She was just along the veranda. She'd stuck her head out the window and she smiled as he turned to look at her.

'What's the sound of a centipede with a wooden leg?' she asked.

'I don't know—what?' he demanded, goaded, knowing something corny was coming.

'Ninety-nine thump,' she told him, and grinned as if it was an entirely original joke and she expected applause. 'That's you, only you don't get to ninety-nine.' She swung her legs over the window sill and perched. She was wearing a long white nightie with lace inserts. It reached her ankles and reminded him of something his grandma would have worn, but there the similarity ended.

Tasha didn't look like anyone's grandma, Tom thought. Her brown-gold curls were tousled from sleep, tumbling to her shoulders. She wore no make-up but she needed none. She looked pert and wide awake and beautiful.

And interested.

'What's causing the leg to drag?' she asked, as if it was any of her business.

'A subarachnoid haemorrhage,' he said carefully. 'Pressure in the brain.'

'I get that, you idiot,' she told him. 'In case you've forgotten, I have a medical degree, too. So, let me see... Balance problems can be due to muscle weakness and paralysis, damage to the cerebellum—that's the part of the brain that controls balance,' she added kindly. 'You could have loss of sensation in the leg itself, with high-tone or low-tone damage to the vestibular system, though I see no evidence of spasticity. You could have impaired vision, hypotension, ataxia, or poor awareness of body position. You have been assessed?'

'In hospital.' He hated talking of his medical problems—especially to a woman in a nightgown, a woman who until now he'd thought of as someone he could help.

Their roles were suddenly upside down and the sensation made him feel like snapping and retreating.

He couldn't. She'd come here to help. He owed it to her to be cordial, even grateful.

'But not since you came home, which was three weeks ago,' she was saying. 'You have foot-drop. You probably need a brace to support the ankle. Are you having pain?'

'No!'

'I'll bet you get tired. Fatigue is one of the most common after-effects of what's happened to you, especially if you entertain on the side.'

'I am not tired and I don't entertain!'

'And crabbiness, too,' she said equitably. 'Personality changes. You weren't crabby last time I was here.'

'Tasha...'

'So you need a thorough physiotherapy assessment.' She gave him an almost apologetic smile. 'You know, I'm not the only bossy woman in your life right now. Rhonda was in full organisation mode before I left England. She's determined you make the most of me being here, so she's booked an assessment for you this afternoon. The plan is for me to take your morning clinic and then to drive you to Summer Bay. They have a full physio clinic, with all the rehab equipment you need. They'll do a full assessment and start you this very afternoon. And every afternoon I'm here.'

'What…?'

'Rhonda's set it up and I agreed,' she told him calmly. 'I know you will, too. It's not worth me coming all this way for you to be put on a waiting list.'

'I don't need—'

'Of course you do and you know it.' She softened. 'Tom, you haven't had time to take care of yourself. I get that, but I'm here now. You know you need specialised physio, targeted specifically for your problems. Jumping rope's good but it has limitations. The Summer Bay clinic has a neurophysiotherapist on site and she sounds excellent. She'll coordinate the team.'

'Who told you…?'

'Rhonda explained the situation,' she said. 'You hired a bossy boots, not me, so you have only yourself to blame that she's getting us organised. But you know she's right. Muscle weakness, speech… Your recovery needs to be a multidisciplinary effort.'

'I don't need…' He was starting to sound like a parrot.

'You know you do need,' she said patiently. 'You're trying to be your own doctor and it doesn't work.' Her voice gentled again. 'Tom, when I hit the wall I knew to come to you for help. You took over and I let you. I needed to let you. So now it's you who's in trouble. We can't make you but why not relax and go with what Rhonda and Hilda and I have planned?'

'"Blast of the trumpet…"' he managed, and she grinned.

'"Against the monstrous regiment of women"?' She even

had the temerity to chuckle. 'John Knox knew what he was up against, although I think it was only two women he was complaining of—the women on the throne. You have three women to rail against—me, Rhonda and Hilda. Now... could you walk me through the clinic work after breakfast? Then you can take a nice nap while I do morning surgery.'

'A nice nap...' He was almost speechless.

'I might need to wake you if there's something I don't understand,' she told him. 'But I hope I won't.'

'Are you really registered to work in Australia?'

'Of course,' she said, sounding wounded. 'I hold an Australian passport and I organised Australian registration and worked here during IVF and the first part of my pregnancy. I know the system. Okay, I'm heading for the shower. Then breakfast. Let's get this show on the road.'

She stood under the shower and let the hot water wash away the cobwebs left from jet lag.

She tried not to shake.

She'd done well, she thought. She'd acted as if she knew what she was doing, as if she was on top of her world.

Except she wasn't. And she wasn't because when all was said and done, Tom Blake was just that. A Blake boy. The sight of his near naked body on the veranda had shaken her as she'd had no intention of being shaken.

Paul Blake had entered her life like a whirlwind, sweeping her off her feet with his love for adventure, his exuberance and his passion. She'd fallen hard and was married before she knew it. Then she'd spent years watching him take crazy risks. Being terrified for him. Not knowing that he was betraying her and he'd been betraying her almost from the start.

In the end she'd realised marriage vows meant nothing. Personal loyalty meant nothing.

Tom seemed kinder and gentler, but in essence he seemed the same. He admitted openly that he loved women—serial women—and he took the same crazy risks Paul had.

Was she being unfair? Was she judging Tom because of Paul?

No. She was judging Tom because of Alice and Susie, and all the Alices and Susies before, all the women he'd chatted about in his newsy emails. Plus the fact that he'd been injured because of a reckless surfing accident.

She was sensible to judge—so why was she shaking?

Because she was vulnerable? Because the sight of him on the veranda had made something twist inside her that frightened her?

Because she didn't trust herself.

'There's no reason to be scared,' she said out loud. 'I have no intention of going down that road again. Besides, he's not the slightest bit interested.'

'But if he was?' She was talking to herself.

'Then I'd run. I'd head to the cats. Much safer.'

'Even if they make you sneeze?'

'Sneezing's harmless,' she told herself. 'As opposed to the Blake boys, who aren't harmless at all.'

Stuck in the corner of the dressing table was the appointment card outlining the details of the booking she'd made the day before she'd left for Australia.

She'd thought—hoped?—she could be brave enough to try again for a baby.

Now she glanced out the window at Tom, who was still doggedly skipping. She remembered how much she'd needed him.

Fear flooded back.

She picked up the appointment card and thrust it back into the bottom recess of her suitcase.

Her reaction to Tom said that she wasn't very brave at all.

* * *

Any doubts as to Tasha's ability to take over were allayed the moment Tom took Tasha into the clinic.

Rhonda and Hilda's niece was currently filling in for Rhonda. To say Millie was less than satisfactory was an understatement. She was cute and blonde and dimwitted. She chewed gum and watched while Tom and Tasha sorted the morning files. There was half an hour before the first patient was due, and Tom had no intention of leaving unless Tasha seemed capable.

She proved it in moments.

He handed her the list of appointments and watched as she did a fast check of the associated files. As she reached the end of the list she turned to him, looking worried.

'Mrs Connor?' she said. 'Margie Connor? Millie's booked her in for last on the list but according to her file her last three appointments have been for serious cardio. events. The reason for today's visit is that her legs are swelling and she's feeling breathless. Should we—?'

And Tom swore and reached for the phone. Rhonda would have picked this up.

'Margie Connor never rings unless it's something major, and her heart failure's getting worse,' he told Tasha. 'Good call.'

Margie answered on the second ring, which was another confirmation that all was far from well. Normally Margie would be on the beach with her dogs at this time of the morning.

'Margie? You're coming in this morning? Millie says it's your legs and you're short of breath?' He listened and grimaced.

'If they're that swollen get Ron to bring you in straight away. Pack a nightie and toothbrush—you know the drill. We might get away with adjusting your medication but if the swelling's too much you could need a couple of days in hospital to get rid of the fluids. It's nothing to panic about but the sooner we see you, the less fluid we'll have to get rid of. I'll be waiting at the clinic. Straight away, Margie. Don't spend time making yourself beautiful for me. You're gorgeous as you are.'

He replaced the receiver and turned and Tasha was glaring at him. Strangely her glare made him want to chuckle. She was like a mother hen, defending her territory.

Only her territory was actually his.

'You aren't staying here,' she said severely. 'I can deal with this.'

'Margie's scared,' he said simply. 'She has grounds for being scared. I'm not having her face a strange doctor.'

'I'm not strange.'

'No,' he said, and he had to suppress a grin as her glare continued. 'You're not. Apologies. But you are different. I need to be here and you need to accept it. Tasha, what you're proposing will only work if you let me share when it's appropriate. It's appropriate now.'

Was it a glare or was it a glower? He couldn't decide, but either way it was cute.

Um…cute wasn't on the agenda. She was a colleague.

He held up his hands, as if in surrender. He wasn't in control. He knew it, he didn't like it but he had to accept it. 'Tasha, I know I've been pig-headed in keeping on working,' he told her. 'But until now I haven't had much choice. I accept I need help. Believe it or not, I'm deeply grateful that you're here and I will do the rehab. Of course I will. But this is my town and these are my people. You need to accept that I care.'

'You're supposed to rest.'

'Rest doesn't mean lying in bed for the next couple of months. We can share. I'll back off when I need to—and, yes, I'll concede you may be a better judge of that than I am—but we have two consulting rooms. I'll work mornings, but at half-pace. You'll work next door and if you need me, call.'

She stood back and considered, while on the sidelines Millie watched on with vague interest. It was like an intellectual decision was being made, he thought. A clinical assessment with a prognosis at the end.

She was very, very cute.

'Okay,' she said at last. 'That seems fair but there's a deal-breaker. In the mornings we share your work. In the afternoons you let me share your rehabilitation.'

That took him aback. 'What do you mean?'

'Just that. You let me come with you this afternoon and hear what the physios say. I have no intention of watching as you complete every exercise, but someone close to you should have an overview. You know patients often hear only what they want or think they need to hear. You don't have a mum and you don't have a partner—unless you're considering taking Millie or Susie. Are you?'

'No!' he said, as Millie recoiled in horror at the idea.

She grinned. 'Then let me in, Tom. You know rehab is gruelling. You'll need encouragement and sometimes you'll need pushing. You need to share.'

'I don't need...'

'You keep saying that, but is it true? You don't need my help? Like Bill didn't need a doctor at the foot of the steps yesterday? Tom, be honest.'

'I don't want to share.' How ungracious was that, but the words seemed to come from deep inside. Handing over to Tasha was losing even more of the control he valued so much.

She raised her brows and gave him a long, hard look. And then she seemed to come to a decision.

'Tom, the way I see it, we have three alternatives. One—you leave everything to me. Two—you share. Three—I leave.'

Things were suddenly serious. 'What the...?'

'I told Rhonda and Hilda I'd take over your workload, whether you want me or not. But of course I can't.'

'It's good of you to see it.'

That earned him a wry smile. 'I am being good,' she told him. 'I'm trying my hardest to see this from your point of view. I'm thinking of you as yet another gung-ho Blake boy, but what you just said has made me brave enough to push my luck. You said, "This is my town. You need to accept that I care." So I accept you care, but—accepting that—do you concede that the town needs me? You can't cope yourself. Do you need me to be here?'

There was a moment's silence. He met her gaze and she met his gaze right back. Her eyes flashed a challenge.

And amazingly he also saw the faintest hint of laughter, as if she knew the dilemma he was in and was faintly enjoying it. Whereas he wasn't.

'Yes,' he said at last, and then added a grudging 'Thank you.'

'And do you also concede that most people dealing with head injuries need a support person?'

'I don't—'

'Concede it,' she said. 'You said it yourself—for now, I may be a better judge than you are. I'm here not only for this town or for your patients. I'm here for your care as well.' The laughter faded. 'Tom, eighteen months ago I realised I needed a support person and I came to you. I followed your advice and you were with me every step of the way. If you were treating someone for a head injury now, would you say they needed to take someone with them for at least the initial assessment at rehab?'

'I don't need...' He stopped. The three words were like a repetitive mantra in his head but the worst thing about this mantra was he knew it wasn't true.

'The Blake boys don't need,' she said, and her voice was

suddenly grim. 'Not usually. But for now face the fact that you do. When people are listening to what medical practitioners are telling them their hearing's often limited. They hear the first thing but they're so busy taking it in that they miss the next.'

'I'm a doctor,' he snapped. 'I don't miss things.'

But at that Millie chimed in with something like glee. 'Like the top step yesterday? You missed that. You bruised yourself, too, though you wouldn't let anyone help. And your medical bag.' Millie was enjoying herself. 'On Tuesday you left your bag in the surgery and you had to get the taxi to turn around. You're missing things all the time.'

'I normally leave my bag in my car,' he said through gritted teeth. 'I'm not used—'

'Exactly,' Tasha told him. 'Thank you, Millie. That's just the point. You're not used to any of this. Give up, Tom,' she said, her voice gentling. 'For once, accept that you're human like the rest of us. And I will leave if you don't accept my help.'

'What, go back to England?'

'There are other reasons I need to be in Australia,' she said, diffidently. 'Right now the overriding one is you, but I don't need to be in Cray Point. It's co-operation or nothing.'

'Or you'll go where?'

'What I do from now on is none of your business. Do you want my help or not?'

'I… Yes.' There was nothing else to say.

And she smiled, a smile that held understanding as well as satisfaction. 'Excellent,' she said, and strangely he got the feeling that she understood where he was coming from. 'Is that a car? Could Margie be here already?'

She was, and she was in almost complete heart failure. Medical need took over.

A truce had been reached. Sort of. For a while Tom was

able to forget his doubts as he and Tasha fought to stabilise her.

Finally Margie was loaded onto the medevac chopper and evacuated to Melbourne, her prognosis a whole lot better than when she'd arrived. Tom took himself to his room. Tasha took the spare room and they started working through patients.

It was a normal day, Tom told himself. Except that Tasha was in the next room and Tasha was bossy and Tasha was...

Disturbing.

He'd been out of his comfort zone ever since the accident, floundering with loss of control.

Tasha's arrival should have helped, he told himself. So why did he feel even more out of control now than he had before she'd arrived?

Later that afternoon Tasha drove him across to Summer Bay, while he tried not to grit his teeth beside her.

Tasha didn't mind his silence. The sun had come out. Tom's car was a soft top and she'd asked that they take the roof down. Tom had consented with bad grace but the wind from the sea blew her curls out behind her and she felt like the fog of the last eighteen months was lifting a little.

This really was the most beautiful place. Every curve seemed to open a wilder view of the ocean and the air was so salty she could almost taste it.

The sea was winter wild. She felt clean and refreshed and ready for anything.

Another try at pregnancy?

She thought of the card at the bottom of her suitcase. How much courage would she need to be to go there?

Too much.

Focus on what comes next, she told herself, which was getting Tom through rehab. She glanced across at his grumpy face and smiled.

'You look like a kid heading for the dentist.'

'That's what I feel like,' he admitted. 'You know I can do this on my own.'

'I know you can't.'

'What made you so know-all?'

'A medical degree,' she said serenely. 'Same as you. If you were your patient you'd be saying exactly the same.'

'And my patient would have the right to refuse.'

'He would,' she said equitably. 'And you'd tell him exactly what he'd be losing in the future by doing so.' She considered for a little, and then glanced at him again. 'Tom... would I be right in thinking you're afraid you might fail? That you won't recover the power you once had?'

He didn't reply. The look on his face said she'd nailed it.

'You've come so far,' she said gently. 'Rhonda and Hilda told me how much damage there was, and you've fought back. You know it's still early days. You know...'

'I do know.'

'But the world was yours before and now... You're no longer invincible. But you must have felt like that before. You and Paul and your dad before you. Daring all, and never thinking of the cost.'

'Do you really think—?'

'I know,' she snapped, and then got herself under control again. 'Sorry. That's past anger from watching Paul go off to climb mountains. And knowing your dad was killed test-driving a car at...what speed? And looking at the damage you've done surfing in stupid conditions. But you will get better, Tom. Every prognosticator tells me you will, so you might as well just get on with it.' She steered the beautiful little car around the next curve and took in the stunning vista before her and then she grinned. 'How often have you been bossed by a woman?'

There was no answer. She tried to suppress her grin and she kept on driving.

* * *

How often had he been bossed by a woman?

Never?

He'd been raised by a woman who'd been so in love with his father that she'd never got over it. She'd adored her son but her ambitions for herself had disappeared the day her husband had walked out on her. The house had been a shrine to that short marriage. She'd been loving but weak and Tom had learned early that he could pretty much do what he liked.

He loved his mum. He loved Cray Point, but even as a child he'd learned to be deathly afraid of the love that consumed his mother. That kind of love meant misery and heartache and he had no intention of going down that road.

His mother had lost control of her life the moment she'd met his philandering father. To Tom, control was his mantra. He put up with Rhonda and Hilda's bossiness—he even enjoyed it—but theirs was bossiness at the edges. The big decisions in life were his.

He was still in control now, he told himself. He didn't need to accept Tasha's presence at his physiotherapy session. Would she leave if she didn't think he was putting a hundred and ten percent into these sessions?

She may well.

Right now she looked like she was enjoying the sun on her face, the wind in her hair, but underneath her smile was a determination he'd had no clue about.

Had losing Paul and then losing her baby caused that determination, or had it already been there?

'Where do you call home?' he asked, tangentially, and she glanced at him for a moment before turning her attention back to the road.

'Why do you ask?'

'It's just…you went back to England. Is home there?'

'No.' She hesitated. 'I've never really had a home.'

'Never?'

'My mum and dad were with the Australian army but they were based all over the world. They were Special Services, so for half of my childhood I was never allowed to know where they were. When they were killed I was in a boarding school in Sydney but I'd only been there for eighteen months. Before that I'd been in an international school in Egypt. Before that…a list of countries I can hardly remember. After they died I stayed with my aunt in London, but she doesn't like me. I remind her of my mother and it still makes her cry. You can't imagine how wearying that is. But I'm her duty so she's still constantly wondering why I'm not staying with her. I think that's one of the reasons I joined Médicins Sans Frontières where I met Paul. So, no, I don't have a home.'

'If Emily had lived?' It was a hard question but as a doctor he knew that hard questions were too often left unasked.

'I would have made a home,' she said without missing a beat. 'That was the plan. To settle and stay. To find a community. To give her a childhood where she could have best friends. And a puppy. She would have loved a puppy.'

Her voice faltered and then she steadied. He knew that about her too, by now. Whatever life threw at her, she steadied.

But he could tell the young Tasha had ached for a puppy.

'But that's the past,' she told him, moving on with a briskness he guessed she'd cultivated from years of deflecting sympathy. 'I need to figure a way forward and I will, but one thing at a time. Next step is to get you working at full capacity. Thus your physiotherapy, and here we are.'

She was his support person.

He'd never imagined he could need such a thing.

A cute, blonde dynamo came out to greet them. 'I'm Dr

Sally Myers, neuro-physiotherapist, but I'd prefer it if you called me Sally. Can I call you Tom and Tasha?'

'Of course,' Tasha said. They'd been sitting in the waiting room for ten minutes, with Tom growing more and more impatient while Tasha calmly photographed recipes from housekeeping magazines with her phone. She tucked her phone away as they both rose to greet Sally. 'Tom can see you on his own if he'd like,' she told Sally. 'But would it be more helpful if I came in, too?'

'It always is,' Sally said frankly. 'You'll be needing support, Tom, and if Tasha's happy to give it…'

'Fine,' Tom snapped, and both women looked at him, astonished.

'Sorry,' he muttered. 'It's just that I'm used to doing things alone.'

'Of course you are,' Sally said, sympathetic but firm. 'I'm sure Tasha understands and so do I. But if you don't mind me saying so, you should have been here weeks ago. We have a lot of catching up to do and if Tasha's prepared to help then your chances of a full recovery are greater. Do you want to look a gift horse in the mouth?'

And Tom looked at Tasha and she raised her brows in mock enquiry. She was smiling. Laughing?

Anything less like a horse he'd yet to see.

She was offering him a faster way to recovery. What was he doing, being a bore?

'Let's do it,' he growled.

'So you'd like Tasha to sit in and learn the exercises?' Sally was making him say it out loud.

'Yes.'

And then he glanced at Tasha and her eyes were still dancing. She understood, he thought, and then he thought that if he had to share there was no one he'd rather share with.

She was a loner. She wouldn't push past his boundaries—maybe she even understood them.

'Yes, please,' he said.

He was learning to stand.

It sounded simple. Tasha had been with Tom for almost twenty-four hours now and she'd seen him sit and stand scores of times.

She'd also seen the way he'd favoured his good leg every time.

Sally had assessed him, prepared his programme, told him bluntly what he risked by not doing it, told him the importance of attending clinic every day and then disappeared to deal with the next recalcitrant client. A more junior physiotherapist took over.

She proceeded to have Tom sit and stand and walk, sit and stand and walk, sit, stand and walk. Tom was forced to favour his bad leg every time.

Tasha saw that it hurt. She saw how much of an effort it cost him. She saw the beads of sweat on his forehead and something inside her clenched.

She hated this, and she was forcing him to do it.

No. Her presence let him do it. She knew Tom accepted the need for such hard work. His skipping this morning had shown her how hard he'd been trying himself, but he needed this professional approach.

She was right to have come, even if arriving at Cray Point, being with Tom, being so close to her daughter's grave, did stir up all sorts of emotions she'd rather not face.

Emily...

'Let's end with swimming,' the physio decreed at last. 'Did you bring your swimmers?'

'Yes,' Tasha told her, and Tom swivelled and stared.

'Pardon?'

'Sally told me swimming might be involved. Just lucky

I made myself useful with the laundry last time I was here. I knew they were in the laundry cupboard. I brought your boardies rather than the budgie smugglers you wear under your wetsuit.'

'Thanks,' he said through gritted teeth. And then… 'You know, if you were serious you'd swim with me.'

'I thought you'd never ask,' she told him, and grinned and pulled a pair of rainbow-coloured swimmers from her bag. 'I came here to be a hands-on support person, Tom Blake, and I'm with you all the way.'

Why not? she thought. She'd learned a whole lot about pain in the last eighteen months and one thing stood out. Sitting thinking about it didn't help. She needed to be distracted—and how much more could she be distracted than by jumping into the pool with Tom Blake?

And in the end it was fun. Ridiculously fun. The young physio—Liselle—ran him through some basic water exercises, leg, arm and neck, and then produced a stretchy band, which she used to rope his good arm to his body. Then she turned to Tasha.

'We can do this three ways,' she told them. They were standing chest deep in the warmed pool. 'I can toss a ball back and forth to Tom, making him use his weak arm, while Tasha watches. That's pretty boring. Or, Tasha, I can tape your favoured arm and have you and Tom have a competition as to who can catch the most. But what's most fun is if I play, too. See this neat little net? I get to play goalie. You two work together, both using only your weaker arms. You guys have to stand behind the three-metre line and stay at least two metres apart. The rule is that you need to toss the ball to each other before you aim for goal and it doesn't matter how many times you do it. You feint to try and get the ball past me. Every time you miss I get a point, but every time you work together and get a goal then it's a point to the Wobble Team.'

'The Wobble Team,' Tasha said blankly, and Liselle grinned.

'You're both wobblers, Tom because of your head injury and Tasha because I'm taping your right arm and you'll find even that sets you off balance. Game?'

And Tom and Tasha looked at each other.

'I'm in,' Tasha said. 'Wobblers, huh?'

'No one calls me a wobbler and lives to tell the tale,' Tom growled.

'Prove it, big boy.' Liselle laughed and tossed him the ball.

He caught it and grinned with his success. Too easy. But apparently it was.

'I threw it straight and slowly,' Liselle told him. 'But something tells me you don't like being treated with kid gloves, so sharpen up.'

'Right,' he said, and tossed the ball to Tasha. His arm felt stiff and strange but there was no way he was letting it stop him. 'Let's show this lady what wobblers are capable of.'

And for the first time for six long weeks he had...fun.

It was fun. Yes, his body still didn't feel as if it belonged to him. He had two disadvantages—one was that he was forced to use his weak arm and the other was that his movement was restricted because his leg didn't obey orders the moment he sent it. And Liselle was good. 'I play water polo,' she admitted. 'And, yes, state level.'

But he had Tasha, and Tasha was amazing.

She looked amazing. Her costume wasn't anything to write home about—a simple one-piece—but it was in a myriad of tropical colours. She was trim and lithe and agile, and she ducked and weaved in the water as if water was her second home. She hadn't tied her curls back. She was soaked the first time he threw an awkward ball to her and she dived for it. She surfaced laughing, her curls spiralling every which way, and she tossed the ball back to him and he was so distracted that he missed.

He didn't get that distracted again. Her look of disappointment at his easy miss had him focusing, and she was, too. She was laughing, diving, yelling to him, feigning tosses towards goal, pretending to toss towards the goal and then tossing to him, pretending to toss to him and then tossing straight at the goal.

For all her laughter she was taking this game very seriously. So did he and at the end of half an hour, when Liselle called time, the score was dead even and even Liselle was looking exhausted.

'I need to find you guys a greater handicap,' she told them. 'You work too well together as a team. Tasha, if you keep working Tom like this we'll have him a hundred percent in no time. Will you come to every session?'

'There may be medical imperatives that stop me coming,' Tasha told her. 'But I'll try. And I do the driving so unless Tom wants to catch a taxi I need to bring him.'

Did he want to catch a taxi?

He looked at Tasha, who was swinging herself out of the pool. Water was streaming from her curls, running in rivulets down the smooth surface of her throat and the curve of her breasts. Her legs were perfect—no, make that everything about her was perfect.

No, he didn't want a taxi.

'I think we could do this until we get to the stage where it's Liselle and me against you, and we play until we lose,' she told him. 'You reckon we could do that in two months?'

'There's a challenge,' Liselle said, grinning. 'I could bring in the rest of my polo team as reinforcements.'

And for the first time since the accident Tom suddenly felt normal. These women were smiling at him, daring him, challenging him. And they were expecting him to get back to normal or better.

'You think I can do it?' he demanded, facing his fears front on.

'I'm sure of it,' Liselle said. 'Look how far Tasha's driven you today.'

'It was you,' Tasha said.

'It was all of us,' Liselle admitted. 'But, Tom, with Tasha driving you, there are no limits to what you can do. I know it.'

'There are no limits to what you can do.'

The words kept playing in her head, a mockery.

It was almost dusk. The sun was sinking in the west. Tom was fast asleep in front of the fire. For all his protestation that he'd coped well, the rehab had knocked him around. While he slept Tasha finally found the time and the courage to walk up the headland to the Cray Point cemetery. To Emily's grave.

It was a place of tranquil beauty, overlooking the sea. Emily's grave was a simple headstone surrounded by carefully cultivated flowers.

Planted by Tom.

She had so many conflicted emotions they were playing havoc with her mind.

Tom. Being here. Grief.

Trying for another baby.

To have another baby feeling as she did wasn't fair, she thought. She was still gutted by Emily's death. The pain and humiliation she'd received from Paul was still with her, and yet she hadn't managed to build defences.

For that was what was bothering her most now. She knew she could fall for Tom. His very smile seemed dangerous.

'So how weak does that make me?' she asked Emily, as

she crouched by the little grave and ran her fingers through Tom's flowers.

She hadn't been strong enough for Emily. She'd needed Tom. 'And something keeps whispering that I still need him,' she said out loud, whispering to her little girl. 'How can I think of another baby without the strength to face whatever comes?'

'There are no limits to what you can do...'

'Maybe there are,' she told herself. 'And maybe I've reached them. I loved Mum and Dad. I thought I loved Paul, and, oh, I loved you, my Emily. But each time... How can I think of trying again?'

But it wasn't just the thought of another baby that had her asking the question.

Tom... How she felt, seeing him again...

It was weakness.

But for some reason the question kept hammering in her brain.

How could she think of trying again?

CHAPTER SIX

LIFE SETTLED INTO a routine—sort of—but a medical house was never normal. As soon as the locals realised Tasha was available, the phone went all the time.

'Do you spend all your time in the clinic?' Tasha demanded at the end of the second week. She'd just finished an extra clinic and Tom had come to find her.

'I can't,' Tom told her. 'We have a huge elderly population. I need to do house calls.'

But Tasha was doing the house calls now, and was astounded by how many were needed. 'You need two permanent doctors,' she told him.

'We do. Are you interested?'

He'd just returned from a long rehab session to which he'd had to go alone. Ray Desling had spilt his toe with an axe just as they'd been preparing to leave. It had nearly killed Tom to climb into a taxi and leave Tasha to clean and stitch, but her threat was still there.

'You stop doing rehab, I stop being here.'

What was he doing? Proposing she stay? For ever?

'What would I do in Cray Point?' she asked, sounding astounded.

'Live?' He limped behind the reception desk so he could see the files she was processing. It felt good to stand beside her at the end of the day, figuring how much they'd achieved. That included how much he'd achieved. The left-sided weakness was lessening by the day.

'Live?' she said now, sounding puzzled. 'Just live?'

'Like everyone else,' he told her. 'That's what we do in Cray Point. You could learn to surf and fill your spare time patching people up. That's the story of my life.'

'With ladies on the side,' she retorted. 'Which reminds me, I've been here for two weeks and nary a lady. Is there a problem?'

He managed a smile. Since his accident he hadn't felt the least bit like dating. In truth, ever since Emily's death his heart hadn't been in it, and maybe the women he'd spent time with sensed it. But he wasn't telling Tasha that.

'Susie's tossed me over for the guy who fixes her computer,' he told her, and tried to look glum.

'Really?'

'Really.'

'Are you heartbroken?'

He forgot the glum and grinned. 'How can I compete with someone who knows how to increase internet speed? In times gone by, legend says women found doctors sexy but I suspect they only found them useful. Geekiness now seems a strong draw card.'

'I'm sorry.'

'Don't be. I don't get involved. I never have.'

'Because?'

'Because I suspect I'm like my father and my brother,' he said honestly. 'I have no idea how to play happy families and I suspect it's too late to learn. Now, about you staying…'

'You're offering me a job?'

'If you're interested.'

'I'm not,' she said, too quickly.

'Then I guess it's my turn to ask: because?'

'Same reason. Because I suspect you're like your father and your brother.'

He frowned. 'Tasha, I'm offering you a job, not proposing marriage.'

'That's right,' she agreed. 'You are. But working together… It couldn't work long-term. I don't know if you're aware of the tensions…'

And of course he was. He'd have to be an insensitive idiot not to feel them, but to talk about them out loud…

They'd been in the same house for two weeks now and the tensions she'd talked of were building. There was nothing tangible, just an undercurrent of awareness that couldn't be avoided.

It was a big old house with a rabbit warren of rooms, yet somehow he always knew where Tasha was. When she walked into the room, tension escalated. When they cooked together, when their bodies brushed in passing, or sometimes at sunset when he sat on the veranda and she came out to join him, the tension was so great it felt almost a physical thing.

It wasn't helped by the physio sessions. The water play was something he looked forward to more and more. He'd felt almost gutted today when Tasha hadn't been able to come. He loved her skills and her excitement. He loved the way she beamed whenever he pushed himself to the limit and achieved more and more.

So what? She was a friend, not a lover. There was no reason for tension.

She was a woman without a home, without a base. She was a fully qualified medical practitioner. A colleague. It was entirely sensible to be offering her a job.

But she'd been feeling the tension, too, and the knowledge set him aback.

'It's hormonal,' he said, trying to sound knowledgeable, trying to set things on a medical footing. 'Two single adults, working closely together… But there's nothing between us…'

'There's a whole lot between us, but attraction isn't possible.'

'No?'

'No,' she said flatly. 'You need to find yourself another Susie.'

'That sounds insulting.' He thought about it for a little longer. 'It sounds like you're afraid.'

'I'm not afraid,' she told him. 'And I didn't mean to be insulting. But I'm aware, and I don't want to stay aware. I don't intend to feel that tension for the rest of my life.'

'Hey, we're adults,' he said, striving for lightness. 'Surely we can get over a bit of physical attraction.'

'Is that what it is?'

'You're hot,' he said honestly.

'Like Susie and Alice and the rest.'

'Tasha…'

'Too right, it's insulting,' she said flatly. 'Don't you ever call me hot again. This is an inappropriate conversation to be having with a colleague, which demonstrates my point. We can't be colleagues. I leave in six weeks. You'll be fit enough to drive again and take over here. I'll get on with my life.'

'What will you do?'

'I have plans.'

'Care to share?'

'No.' How could she talk to Tom about what she'd hardly faced herself? What she probably didn't have the courage to face.

'Because you don't know?'

'I'm a doctor. I can go anywhere I want in the world and get a job.'

'Drift, you mean.'

'It's better than staying here and being seduced by you.'

Silence.

The words hung. And hung and hung.

Tasha closed her eyes. *Beam me up, Scottie,* she thought. What had she just said?

'I wouldn't,' Tom said at last in a voice that didn't sound like his own. 'I have no intention—'

'I know. I'm sorry. I have no idea where that came from.'

Another silence. And then...

'Because we both want it?' Tom asked.

She covered her face with her hands. 'No.'

'Why not?'

'This is a reaction from not having a Susie or someone like her around,' she whispered into her hands. 'It reflects badly on both of us.'

'It has nothing to do with Susie. It's the way you make me feel.'

'Then don't feel. We both know it's impossible.'

'Why is it impossible?'

'Because I have no intention of being one of your brief flings and you don't know how to do anything else. You've said it yourself. And me... I have no intention of being involved with another Blake boy.'

'I'm not Paul.'

'You're not, but you're like him in so many ways. I have no idea why he married me. He managed to stay by my side for our honeymoon but that was the extent of it. Then he was off adventuring, challenging himself, pushing himself to the limit. Heaven knows if there were other women. I only found out about the last, but looking back, he made our lives so separate there may well have been others.'

'So why did you marry him?'

'Who knows?' She shrugged. 'Maybe he reminded me of my parents. Maybe I'm genetically drawn to risk-takers, or maybe I'm just stupid. Persuading me to marry him must have seemed a challenge to Paul, but once the challenge was met he moved on. For a time I tried to keep up. I learned to abseil and we climbed in places I still can't believe. I went caving and scuba diving, and we did it in some of the most dangerous countries in the world. I pushed myself to the limit but pretty soon I realised that no matter what I did I wasn't important to him. It was the thrill of conquering that was important. And finally I discovered that included women... Who needed a wife? There could always be another Susie or another Alice.'

'That's not fair.'

'To who?'

'To me. I'm not Paul.'

'Of course you're not,' she agreed. 'But you said yourself you don't know about being faithful. And then there's the fact that you threw yourself onto rocks in the surf on a day everyone knew it was stupid to be there.'

'I—'

'Please, Tom,' she said wearily. 'This is a dumb conversation. I never meant to say those things and I regret it already. I'm being rude and judgemental and I have no right to be either. I'm sorry. It's my problem, not yours, but it is a problem and it means I can't stay. So can we just go back to how we were fifteen minutes ago? I have Emma Ladley bringing her daughter in any minute. Megan has menstrual problems, which Emma thinks have been compounded by boyfriend woes. Women's business. You need to leave.'

'You don't need me?'

'Of course I don't need you,' she managed. 'I needed you once and I'm very grateful but I have no intention of needing you again.'

'Tasha, the job...we could help each other.'

'We could destroy each other,' she told him. 'Please... Leave me be.'

* * *

He left and she shook, which was an entirely inappropriate reaction. She'd overreacted to the point of ridiculous, she told herself. Tom had offered her a job and suddenly they'd been talking about lust. They'd even talked of the impossibility of a long-term relationship, which was something neither of them had even thought of.

Except she had considered it. Of course she had. She'd been living with Tom for two weeks now and she'd been aware of him every moment. She'd acknowledged the attraction and she hadn't been able to put it aside.

Tom was her friend. He'd helped her at a time when she had been most vulnerable. She even acknowledged that she loved him—as a friend.

Except it wasn't quite as a friend, for every time he was near her, her body reacted in a way that was entirely inappropriate. She loved being near him. Tension or not, she loved sitting out on the veranda late at night and having him sit beside her. She loved his body in the pool, the vulnerability he exposed during rehab, the way he pushed himself to the limit and the exultation when he achieved the next step in physical fitness.

She loved the way he locked his gaze with hers as they passed the ball in their weird version of water polo. They were getting harder and harder to beat.

They were becoming a team.

'But only for now,' she muttered. 'It's transient. Long-term? No and no and no.'

But living here…

The thought was suddenly like a siren song. Living in Cray Point? Buying her own little cottage? Maybe taking courage in both hands, taking up that appointment for another attempt at IVF, using here as a base…?

Tom was her friend and she knew by now that she could

depend on him. She could surely live here, work here, with Tom in the background.

She couldn't because she felt...

'Like I have no intention of feeling,' she muttered. 'Like I'd be nuts to feel. You don't need to take risks—you know where that gets you. Get on with your life, Tasha Raymond, and go and greet your next patient. She has women's troubles and boyfriend troubles. Who needs either? Not me, that's for sure.'

Tom went home and pulled a casserole out of the freezer. How many casseroles had Hilda left? He stared at it for a long moment and then replaced it.

He rang for the taxi.

Five minutes later the taxi pulled up. Karen, the local cab owner, greeted him with cheer.

'Hey, Doc. Got an emergency?' In truth, Karen had been enjoying being on call for him. Until Tasha had arrived she'd been making a fortune.

'I need to go to the supermarket.'

She raised her eyebrows. 'Really? I thought Hilda had organised you everything. Casseroles, pies, deliveries twice a week. When she left she told me you wouldn't need for anything.'

'I don't always need what Hilda thinks. I want a change for dinner tonight.'

'Something special? I heard Susie's going out with Donald. Hmm...' She grinned. 'I'm guessing...you and Tasha...'

'Karen!'

'Just saying.'

'I'm only buying steak!'

'Whatever you say, Doc,' she said expansively. 'Whatever you say.'

* * *

Tasha arrived back at the house half an hour later to find the house empty. Her footsteps echoed on the ancient floorboards.

It felt strange. Wrong.

'How fast have I got used to company?' she demanded of herself. Too fast. Apart from her brief, disastrous marriage she'd been a loner all her life, yet here she was reacting with a shiver of desolation because Tom wasn't home.

She walked out to the veranda and the table was set. Two places.

Candles. Flowers.

She'd seen this set-up before, on that appalling night she'd arrived, eighteen months ago.

She'd hardly registered then but she did now. He must have had a date.

Did he think he had a date now?

'You idiot,' she said out loud and, she wasn't sure whether she was talking to herself or to Tom. She'd have an egg on toast later, she told herself. By herself. And then she'd go to bed early.

She didn't need this tension between them and she had no intention of escalating it.

But she couldn't settle. She needed a walk and she knew where she wanted to go.

Five minutes later she was walking along the cliffs, up towards the headland.

Emily was waiting, and tonight of all nights it seemed imperative to talk to her.

His car was back. That meant Tasha was home—except she wasn't.

Her coat was missing from the back veranda, as were her walking boots.

She was upset and that upset him. He still didn't understand what had happened this afternoon. All he knew was that he'd messed with their relationship and it felt bad.

He took his gear into the kitchen and set it out. Salad, steak, fruit and cream. It wasn't nearly as professional as the meals Hilda had prepared, but for some reason tonight it felt important to cook himself.

In truth, he wasn't sure what he was doing. The ground under him felt shaky and it wasn't just his weak leg that was the cause.

He opened an excellent wine. He checked the dining table on the veranda and decided to ditch the candles and flowers. Then he put them back again.

Then he ditched them again, dumping them in the trash so he couldn't change his mind. He brought the place settings into the kitchen and set the table there.

Better.

She still wasn't home.

The night was mild and clear. The moon was just coming up, hanging low over the eastern sky. The sounds of the surf and the call of distant plovers were the only things that cut the silence.

He thought of putting on music and decided not to.

What was he doing? He should be getting things back to a normal setting, except he wasn't sure what a normal setting was any more.

Why had he asked her to continue to work here, and why had it escalated so fast?

He headed back out to the veranda. He knew where she'd be. He'd watched her walk up there many times since she'd arrived. There was a tiny grave...

He should let her be. Her time with Emily was not his to share.

But tonight he needed to share. He'd messed with something deeply important. Friendship?

Something more?

She'd made it quite clear she didn't want more and he didn't either.

Or did he?

How could he? The last thing he wanted was to hurt her. How could he promise not to?

He should leave her be. He should...

He didn't. He shrugged on his jacket and took the walking pole he kept beside the door. His leg wasn't up to climbing the headland without support and he had no intention of becoming Tasha's patient.

What did he want?

He didn't know. All he knew was that he was out the door, walking towards the headland with the intention of finding out.

'Should I run?'

She'd lost Emily eighteen months ago but she'd spoken to her every day since she'd lost her.

'You never completely lose a child.' A midwife had told her that, some time in the dark days as Emily had slipped away. 'A baby is part of you. You may lose her from your body but she's carved a space inside you and that space will always be hers.'

She hadn't believed it then. In those appalling first few months, all she'd felt had been an aching, searing loss that threatened to destroy her. But always at the back of the pain had been the slip of comfort, the remembrance of Emily in her arms, the sweet smell of her, the sensation of tiny fingers curving around hers.

And they'd stayed with her. Even back in England she'd felt them, and she'd known that Emily was still real, still a part of her life. So she'd talked to her, and now, high on the headland in Cray Point's tiny cemetery where Emily lay buried, her little girl seemed closer than she'd been since she'd lost her.

'I'm making a mess of things,' she told her. 'I came back because Tom needed me and I owed him.' She took a deep breath. 'The problem is, I'm scared of how I'm feeling.'

And there it was, out there, the thing she was most afraid of.

Surely she couldn't. She'd have something deeply wrong with her to fall for another Blake boy.

She made herself think back to those appalling last few weeks with Paul. They'd had plans to go on vacation to Sardinia. After a gruelling two years of dreadful marriage, she'd clung to it with a final despairing hope.

Not only would it be a fabulous vacation, she'd told herself. It would also be a chance to patch up a marriage that was in real trouble.

And start a baby?

But then Paul had burst back into their apartment, beaming with excitement. 'Change of plans, sweetheart. It's the chance of a lifetime. There's an Australian team heading for Everest next month and someone's dropped out. They've offered me the chance and I can't say no. I know we planned Sardinia but you could come to base camp, do a few easy walks while you wait for me. Tasha, this is amazing...'

'You're not experienced enough,' she'd managed, stunned, and he'd turned angry.

'I'm fit. I've done enough climbing to know the basics. I can do this. I'll need to head back to Australia to organise visas and the like. I still have the apartment in Melbourne and the team will be leaving from there. You can come with me if you want. Stay in Australia or come to base camp.' And then, as she'd said nothing, he'd turned away. 'It doesn't matter. Support me or not, babe, I don't care.'

And then had come the phone call late at night, the call where she'd unashamedly stood in the dark and listened as her husband had talked to his lover.

'She's not coming to base camp—I knew she wouldn't.

She'll stay in Melbourne. That means we can spend a few days in Nepal before we go. Yeah, it means we cut acclimatisation short, but you and me, babe… Everest together and the rest. You just need to peel off that husband and get your act together. Yeah, sweetie, love you, too.'

She hadn't confronted him. She'd been too empty, too sad and shocked. She'd gone to Melbourne with him and helped him pack, all the time thinking this needed to be the last goodbye.

And then the day before he'd left he'd come back to the apartment looking triumphant.

'It's all fixed. I've been to the IVF place and made a deposit. I know you want a baby, sweetie, so if anything happens to me you can still have your baby. You can go to Sardinia, lie on the beach and dream of me.'

She hadn't gone to Sardinia and when the call had come to say Paul and his other 'sweetie' had perished, the emptiness inside her had hardly grown deeper.

She'd thought she loved him.

'What do I know about love?' she asked Emily, and there was no answer.

There were seaside daisies growing around the edges of the cemetery. It was almost dark but the daisies were white and easy to see. She gathered handfuls and piled them around the edges of the little grave, and then sat there, soaking in the silence, trying to make her jumbled thoughts line up.

She was in so much trouble.

She should leave.

She couldn't leave. She'd promised.

'I'll move to Hilda and Rhonda's house,' she told Emily. 'It makes sense. Even if the cats make me sneeze, they can't be as dangerous as Tom.'

'I'm not dangerous.'

She jumped and when she came back to earth Tom was

right beside her. He'd emerged from the dusk like a shadow. He stood in his dark coat, leaning on his cane, surveying her with concern. 'Tasha, don't make this bigger than it is.'

'I... What?'

'Me,' he told her. 'You sound afraid and I can't bear it.'

'I'm not afraid of you.' Except she was.

'Should I go away again?' he asked. 'I don't want to disturb you.'

'You're not.' That was another lie. But he was here and he was Tom and there were things she needed to say.

'Thank you for doing this,' she whispered. Because there was no concrete slab over Emily's grave as there was over most other graves. Instead, there was a rim of sea-tough plants, carefully chosen to create a tiny island of protection from the blast of the sea winds. Within that island were flowers, hellebores at the moment, Christmas roses, flowers that would bloom in mid-winter. And when Tasha had dug down to pull a recalcitrant weed she'd found daffodils bulbs ready to spring to life in late winter, and what looked like tiny ranunculi and anemone bulbs for spring.

Tonight she'd set her daisies at the rim of the grave where there was a space, but she knew instinctively that when she hadn't been here, that space would have been filled by Tom. He'd been tending her baby's grave and the thought did something to her heart she couldn't understand.

Sense or not, she had no defence against Tom's caring.

And he was caring still. 'I'm sorry I upset you,' he said gently. 'It's the last thing I intended.'

'It was me,' she said. 'I had no business to turn a professional proposition into something more.'

'You don't want it to be more?'

'No.'

'I guess that's good,' he told her. 'Because, as you say, I'm a Blake and I didn't learn relationships.'

'You do a nice line in caring despite it,' she told him,

carefully focusing her attention on rearranging her daisies. 'I love you for what you've done for us. For what you've done for Emily. But what's between us… It must be because of Emily. We were thrown into a hothouse of emotions. It's hardly surprising we're in a place now we don't recognise.'

'I guess that's right.

He stood back a little, saying nothing more, while she knelt beside Emily's grave and tried to get her emotions under control.

Let him think it's all about Emily, she told herself, but she knew it wasn't.

Finally she stood, brushed herself down and turned to look out at the moonlit sea. There was a long silence, a silence, though, that didn't feel uncomfortable. It was more… peace.

'Thank you for sending me the photographs,' she said at last. 'I… I'm sorry I couldn't respond…the way you deserved for sending them but they were important to me. I loved your emails, too. It sort of meant, even though I'd left, I hadn't abandoned her. She was with a friend.'

'That's quite a compliment.'

'It's the way I feel. But I couldn't write back.'

'I understood.'

'I know you did,' she whispered, and then there was more silence.

And then: 'Would you ever think about another baby?' Tom asked.

The peace was shattered. It was as if the question had opened a locked door, and the space behind was so flooded with emotion that she almost staggered.

But Tom was beside her. He touched her arm, a simple gesture of friendship, and the chaos settled a little.

'Don't answer if you don't want to,' he said, but he was probably the one person in the world who deserved an answer.

'I don't think I'm brave enough.'

'But you want...'

'I don't think I can want.'

He didn't reply. His hand still rested on her arm, and the contact helped. They stood side by side, looking out over the sea while she tried to think of where to take this. While she tried to think of where to take her life?

'So you don't want to stay here,' Tom said at last. 'And you don't think you can try for another baby? What do you want, Tasha?'

Why did the question seem so huge? Why did it seem so impossible?

'Medicine's good,' she said at last, gripping to the one thing that had stayed constant. 'I'm needed.'

'Medicine can't fill your life.'

'Does it fill yours?'

'In a way, yes,' he said simply. 'But medicine for me is more than caring for the next person who comes in the door. My medicine's all about caring for this community. Cray Point took care of me as a kid. It fills something inside me that I can give something back.' He hesitated and then forged on and she sensed he was warring with himself as to whether to say it or not. But then he said it. He asked it.

'What fills that void inside you, Tasha Raymond?'

And it was all she could do not to sob. For there was such a gaping wound inside...

She should be used to it. For heaven's sake, it had been with her all her life. Her parents had practically abandoned her at birth, leaving her with one carer after another. Then—and psychoanalysts would have a field day with this, she thought grimly—she'd fallen for a guy who'd been just like her parents. A man who'd said he loved her and had then betrayed her.

And then there was Emily.

The hole inside her wasn't diminishing. She couldn't fill it with work and it seemed to be getting bigger every day.

But she couldn't fill it here, not with this man, not with this place. And not with another baby?

She'd run out of courage.

'You would find the courage,' Tom said gently, and astonishingly it was as if he'd followed her train of thought. 'Tasha, I've cared for mums who've lost babies. In ten years of general practice I've seen it enough to know how massive that loss is.'

'Tom…'

'I've also seen it enough to sense that moving on is the hardest thing in the world,' he kept on. 'Having another baby seems impossible. But it's the thought that hurts, not the baby that comes. You know you can't ever replace Emily—why would you want to?—but the heart expands. There'll always be a hole where Emily should be, but it can't stop you living. It can't stop you searching for joy and accepting joy when you find it.'

'Tom, I can't…'

'I know,' he said simply, and he touched her cheek, lightly, the faintest of brushes. 'But if you ever feel you can and you need help to find the courage…Tasha, I accept that you can't stay here. I accept we have a relationship that causes you pain. But I'll always be here for you, Tasha. In the background. Egging you on every way I know how.'

'Th-thank you.'

'Think nothing of it,' he said, striving for lightness. He managed a smile. 'I can't do families myself but, wow, I'm good at giving advice. But now… Time to go home?'

And there was nothing else to say. She nodded mutely and turned towards the path.

Tom fell in beside her. His words kept echoing in her head. She needed space to think about them. She needed space to think about what she was feeling.

About a baby?

About Tom.

They walked on in silence. She hardly needed to slow her steps to pace his now. With his cane he was almost as sure as she was on the rough path. He was improving so fast.

Maybe she wouldn't need to stay for six weeks.

The thought was suddenly a desolate one.

But even as she thought it, his weak leg struck a tree root and he stumbled. Not enough to fall but enough for her to instinctively reach out and catch his hand. And hold.

He swore. She knew he hated showing weakness, hated being dependent—but he didn't pull away. His fingers linked through hers with a strength and warmth that made her feel...like she had no business feeling.

Maybe he did need her.

But the Blake men didn't need, and he was a Blake.

Stop it, she told herself. Stop categorising him. He's just Tom.

Just Tom? That was a thought that almost made her laugh. He was so much more than just Tom.

His hand still linked to hers and it felt right. It felt good.

She found herself thinking of the pseudo water-polo games they played, where they teamed against Liselle. Where their gazes stayed almost constantly locked as they fought for a strategy to get the ball through. She loved those games. She'd hated missing this afternoon.

It was fun, but it was more than that. She and Tom were working as a team. They had no hope of scoring a goal by themselves.

Tom was better in the water than she was, stronger, more agile, a better swimmer when he wanted to move fast, but he was handicapped with a weak arm and leg.

He needed her.

On her own she had neither the ability nor the strength to get the ball through the goal net. She needed Tom.

Why did that mesh with the feeling of his hand holding hers?

Why was that thought such a tantalising siren song? To need. To be needed.

'Friends,' Tom said softly as they reached the final rise before the house.

And she thought, Yes. To lose his friendship would break her heart.

But then…friends?

She wanted more.

No. It was her body that wanted more. Her head said it was ridiculous, that she needed no one, that she'd been solitary forever and it was far, far safer that way.

She'd learned life's lessons the hard way, and she had no choice but to accept them.

CHAPTER SEVEN

By the time they reached the house she almost had herself under control again. Tom unlatched the gate and he had to release her hand while he did. It was the natural time to let go. Friends would have let go then. He no longer needed her support.

He hadn't been holding her hand for support, though, a little voice whispered. Men and women didn't hold hands unless...

Stop it, her head commanded. There's no point thinking like this.

'I have steak for dinner,' Tom said, sounding proud of the concept.

And she thought of the table set on the veranda with the candles and the flowers and she mentally closed down.

'Can you freeze one?' she asked. 'I'm not hungry.'

'You don't want my steak? I was hoping to show off my prowess?'

'You have prowess?' He'd sounded wounded. *Prowess?*

'Hilda's filled my freezer with enough casseroles to keep me going until Armageddon so it's really hard to show off my splinter skills.'

'Your splinter skills being steak.'

'And salad. Until you've seen me toss a salad you haven't lived.'

And despite herself she chuckled, but then she thought of the candles and the flowers and her laughter faded.

'Not a good idea, Tom.'

'Not?' They were taking off their jackets in the hallway. He flicked on the hall lights and they lit the veranda as well. She glanced at the table she'd seen earlier.

The candles were gone. So were the flowers. The beautiful table setting had disappeared.

He followed her gaze.

'I'm not trying to add you to my list of serial women,' he told her, and she choked.

'Honestly, Tom, to admit you have such a thing...'

'Well, I do,' he said honestly. 'There are some lovely women in this town. I enjoy their company and they seem to enjoy mine. Take Susie. She's just been through a messy divorce. She has two teenage children who run her ragged. She hardly has any time for Susie but for a while she came here, dressed to the nines, ready for a night out. I put an effort into making dinner great and we enjoyed our nights.'

'Your whole nights,' she said before she could stop herself, and he grinned.

'Tasha, I'm no virgin,' he told her. 'But I've always been honest. No strings. I'm good at figuring how far we can take things before anyone gets hurt.'

'You're sure of that? How do you know Susie isn't secretly nursing a broken heart?'

'Hey, Susie called it quits, I didn't. She's in love with her geek.'

'So no one's ever broken their heart over you?'

'That's how my life's designed,' he said. 'That's what happened to my mother. I won't be responsible...'

So that was that. Another irresponsible Blake.

But she stood in the hallway and the space was a bit too narrow. His body was brushing against hers, and at every touch her nerve endings were sending sparks from her toes to her head and back again.

Move on, she told herself harshly, and headed for the kitchen.

She swung open the door and stopped.

The kitchen table was covered with a simple gingham tablecloth. There was the plain cutlery Tom's grandmother must have used, ancient bone-handled knives and forks. Plain crockery, mismatched, some of it cracked and worn.

No flowers. No candles. A bowl of salad sat on the bench and it was a pretty ordinary bowl of salad. Lettuce, tomatoes, cucumbers.

The fire stove at the far end of the kitchen was sending out its gentle warmth. Apart from a gleaming microwave and modern toaster, this room looked like it hadn't changed in a hundred years.

She'd sat here in the days after Emily had died, with Hilda fussing around her and Tom checking in and out to make sure she was okay. She'd hardly noticed the kitchen then, but when she'd returned it had seemed…like coming home? Now it seemed to fold itself around her like a warm cloak. Tom was ushering her in, opening the refrigerator, producing two steaks in a bowl.

'I've made a red wine marinade with an excellent shiraz,' he told her. 'I used half a bottle, which means there's only two glasses left. One for me because that's all I'm permitted. One for you because the last thing I want you to think is that I'm setting the scene for seduction. So, Tasha, steak and salad with me, or are you really intending to go hungry while I hop into both steaks?' And then he grinned and raised an eyebrow in mock enquiry. 'Dare you,' he said. 'Live dangerously. Steak and a glass of wine. What can possibly go wrong?'

If only you knew, Tasha thought helplessly. Oh, Tom, if only you knew.

But she had no choice. She sat and Tom produced an apron with a picture of a monster steak on the front.

'It's my recipe,' he told her, tying his apron strings with a flourish, and she had to grin. The apron read:

Rare: One Beer
Medium: Two Beers
Well Done: Three Beers

It broke the ice and she found herself relaxing a little. The frying pan started to sizzle and Tom had a flash of gourmet inspiration and started frying onions. He added the steak and she was suddenly starving. The smell filled the room and she thought…

Home is where the heart is?

It was an insidious thought, a siren song. Tom had his back to her. He was wearing jeans and a T-shirt, and his T-shirt was a touch too tight. It stretched over his pecs, delineating a build that could send any woman's heart rate up. His neck was sexy, too, she thought idly. It was a good neck. Broad. Strong. He hadn't had a haircut for a while, so the line where his hair started wasn't clearly defined. She could run her fingers up and trace…

Um…not. She poured herself water and then headed for the refrigerator and found herself some ice. It'd be better to pour it over her head, she thought, but she was a sensible woman so she sat and drank it and then concentrated on marshalling her thoughts into some sort of disciplined order. By the time he put a plate of sizzling steak in front of her and sat before her with his, she almost had herself under control.

And then he smiled and her control was shot to pieces again. He poured her wine and she tasted it and it was gorgeous. The night was gorgeous, the steak was gorgeous and Tom was even more gorgeous, and she thought what had this guy been thinking when he'd decided he needed candles and flowers?

'How did you and Liselle go today?' she asked, feeling a bit desperate, hoping to get the conversation to a level where she could operate without her hormones charging in and taking over.

'We did fine motor skills with my left hand,' he told her. 'We put little pegs into little holes until I started going crazy. Then we moved onto the really exciting stuff—we played marbles. You wouldn't believe the adrenalin rush.'

She chuckled, but her heart twisted yet again. Since she'd arrived he hadn't complained—not once. She knew his clumsiness was driving him crazy. She knew there were so many small things that he couldn't do. Even now, cutting his steak was a challenge. His right hand was fine but his stiff left hand didn't hold the way he needed to hold. There was a reason Hilda had left him so many casseroles.

He wouldn't have tried eating steak in front of his myriad women friends, she thought with sudden intuition. But he was cutting his steak in front of her, and she knew by doing it he exposed a vulnerability he hated.

And suddenly she felt herself close to tears.

He was different, she thought. She'd categorised him as a Blake boy but maybe she was wrong. Maybe...

The phone rang.

'Steakus Interruptus,' Tom said, and groaned and headed out to answer it.

Two weeks ago Tasha would have cut him off but she was learning to back off. She'd learned not to rush to the phone to cut him off from trying to deal with everything himself. In turn, Tom accepted that most calls were Tasha's responsibility. He'd come a long way, she thought. He'd finally accepted that if his body was to heal he had to face its current limitations.

Now he turned to her, his face resigned.

'House call,' he told her. 'Gut pain. I don't know any more. Ron Wetherall. He's a local real estate guru, a big man about town. He's also a bombastic, loud-mouthed bully. He has a mouse of a wife—Iris. Rumour has it that she's his punching bag and I'm sure rumour's right, though I can never get her to admit it. Now he won't tell her exactly what's wrong. Seems he's curled up on the bed, clutching his gut, demanding she ring the doctor. She says he's demanding I be there in two minutes or less—he's in agony.'

Food poisoning? Bowel blockage? Renal colic? There was little to go on, Tasha thought. It could be anything.

'I know he'd rather have me,' Tom told her. 'Macho doesn't even begin to describe our Ron. A woman doctor will just about do his head in. Maybe you could drive me.'

'You're tired,' she said. 'Aren't you?'

And it was a measure of how far they'd come that he agreed. 'Maybe it's time for our macho Ron to accept that women are as skilled as men,' he conceded. 'Are you okay to go?'

'After only one glass of wine?' she said. 'I can do it with my hands behind my back.'

'Then call me if you need me,' he told her, and she smiled at him and he smiled back. She headed out to get her jacket but she had to brush past him as she went.

And she came so close…so incredibly close…to kissing him goodbye that when she reached the veranda it was all she could do not to run.

Iris Wetherall, as Tom had described, was a worried mouse of a woman. She opened the door with a hand to her face, but Tasha could see the beginnings of an ugly bruise under her eye. She ushered Tasha in with relief but Tasha hadn't got two steps inside the door before an agonised moan filled the house. Two small King Charles spaniels put their paws over their heads and moaned in sympathy.

'I don't know what's happening,' Iris whispered. 'I was mopping the kitchen floor. I... Something spilt.' Her hand went to her eye again. 'Ron went to bed and left me to clean but suddenly he started screaming. He's partly undressed, hunched up on the bed, but he won't let me near. He won't say what's wrong, just get the doc, get the doc. He's upstairs.'

Iris hardly had to lead her. All she had to do was follow the moans.

The bedroom was vast. Actually, the whole house was vast, an ode to real-estate luxury surely almost unheard of in modest Cray Point. As she entered the bedroom Tasha had to stop and blink. Acres of white carpet. Vast French windows opening to a massive balcony with spotlights illuminating the swimming pool below. A bed that looked big enough to house a couple of families at a time, and the families wouldn't need to be small. Plush, plush and more plush and in its midst was a florid, overweight man in his fifties, stripped to the waist, his bedcovers half pulled up to hide his nether regions. He was lying almost in a foetal position, moaning fit to die.

'The doctor's here,' Iris quavered, and Ron managed to writhe around so he could see.

'Thank God...'

And then he saw Tasha and his yell almost split the night.

'I said the doc, you stupid cow. I don't want some woman. Get me the doc, now!'

'I'm a doctor.' Tasha was trying to assess what was happening. He was certainly in pain but he was almost apoplectic with rage and his yell had contained strength as well as fury. 'You know Dr Blake's been ill,' Tasha told him. 'I've taken over his house calls. Can you tell me what's wrong?'

'No!' It was a vicious yell, and he turned to his wife

again. 'Get her out. I don't want any more stupid women. It's your fault in the first place. Did I ask for new…?' And then he caught himself. 'Get out,' he screamed. 'Now.'

And Tasha was starting to guess what was wrong. If she was right… Ouch.

He did need help. There was no doubting his pain was real, but if he wouldn't let her help…

'I could call an ambulance,' she said.

'I don't want an ambulance. They'll take ages and women work those things now. Get Doc Blake!'

'He isn't on call.'

'Get him,' Ron shouted again.

Tasha hesitated. What she'd like to do was walk away until he saw reason, but there was a chance this was a torsion, something that could mean long-term damage.

'You understand Dr Blake is unwell himself,' she said, playing for time.

'I don't care,' he snarled.

What had Tom's assessment been? *A bombastic, loud-mouthed bully.*

She could call Tom. If she was right in her guessed diagnosis, he might even enjoy it, she conceded, but there was no way she was simply caving to this man's demands. A woman had some pride.

'I could ask Tom to assist,' she said, making herself sound doubtful.

'Get him!'

'Only in an assistant capacity,' she said firmly. 'On that understanding only.'

'He'll do what I tell him.'

'Dear, don't upset the doctor,' Iris quavered, and Tasha gave her a pat on the shoulder.

'I'm not upset,' she told her. 'If Ron doesn't want me to help, then we'll leave him be while we call for back-up.'

* * *

'Tom?'

Tom answered on the first ring. He hated Tasha doing these calls without him but he had no choice. The deal was, though, that she call him the moment she was worried.

'Problem?'

'Who would know?' she said softly. 'It might be something serious or it may not. Mr Wetherall is currently clutching his privates, screaming in agony and telling every woman in sight—that's Iris and me—where to go. Iris has the beginnings of a black eye. She looks like she's just been struck. Ron won't say what's wrong but he's demanding that you come. I've finally agreed to call you—but only in an assistant capacity.'

'What do you think's happening?' Ron Wetherall was a beefy oaf, known for his unscrupulous business dealings as well as for his appalling treatment of his rather nice little wife. But if he was really ill…

'He was undressing when it came on,' Tasha said blandly. 'Iris says he had no symptoms until then. He took off his shirt, then his shoes and socks and then started to remove his brand-new pants. That's all the information I've been able to glean. He's told me where to go in no uncertain terms when I asked to examine him, but based on the information…'

And Tom was with her. 'The dreaded zipper stick?'

'That's what I'm assuming. But I'm a girl, what would I know? And it could be something more serious. He's being so obnoxious I could walk out but he could do some real damage.'

'There are those in this town who'd enjoy a bit of real damage,' Tom said thoughtfully. 'But you're right. It'd be negligent to leave him as he is.'

'So you'll come?'

'Of course.' He paused, thinking it through. 'Tasha, I've been worried about Iris for some time. I'm sure she's being assaulted but she won't say. Two months ago I treated her for a broken cheekbone but all she'd say was that she'd fallen. She's had broken bones before but he's always with her when she comes in.'

'She won't talk about her eye now.'

'So we have two patients.' He hesitated and then came to a decision. 'I'm thinking… If he's really incapacitated then maybe we can use this situation to treat the two of them. Will you follow my lead?'

'Of course.'

'Excellent,' Tom told her. 'I'll call the taxi and be right with you.'

Tasha and Iris followed orders and got out of Ron's sight. They drank tea in the kitchen and tried to settle the dogs, while overhead the air was filled with Ron's obscenity-laden moans.

Iris seemed more and more frightened. If this was zipper stick, Ron would need to take his fury out on someone at the end of this, Tasha thought, and she hoped Tom had a plan.

Then Tom arrived—with back-up.

He had a huge surgical case and he had company. Brenda bustled in behind him, carrying surgical scrubs encased in plastic wraps and her own nursing case. She was followed by Karen, the taxi driver, carrying an oxygen canister big enough to fuel an elephant. Tasha tried to take it from her—Tom, plus the district nurse, plus the local taxi driver were all heading for the sick room—but Karen shook her head.

'Doc wants me to carry it,' she said. 'I spend my life hauling luggage. No sweat.'

'Straight up to the bedroom,' Tom ordered. 'I'm not sure what we're facing but Dr Raymond suspects it's serious so we need to get things moving. Dr Raymond, could you come into the bedroom, please? And Iris, too? If this is a surgical procedure we need you to sign consent forms. Karen, could you stay? Karen was a nurse before she and her husband took over the taxi company,' he explained to Tasha. 'We've used her before when we've had to do emergency surgical procedures. She's great.'

And then he reached Ron's bedside and all at once he turned into the Tom Tasha knew. Gentleness itself. 'Hi, Ron. You have a problem? We're here to help and we'll get the pain under control as fast as we can. Let's see what's happening.'

Let's see. Let *us* see. Plural.

There were now five people and two dogs in Ron's bedroom, and Ron was staring wildly up at the assortment of people around his bed. His eyes were almost popping out of his head.

'Get these people out of here!'

'You know I can't do that,' Tom said soothingly. 'I have to assume it's not a minor problem or you would have let Dr Raymond deal with it. And with your request for no ambulance we've come prepared for anything.'

'No,' Ron screamed, and Tom sighed.

'We may need a sedative, Nurse,' he told Brenda. 'Could you administer five milligrams of diazepam, intramuscularly. Karen, would you mind helping? Tasha, I'll get you to hold his hips. Karen, if you could hold that arm? We'll twist him around so he's facing upwards and I can see what we're dealing with. Okay, on my count. Three, two…one…'

And before he knew it, Ron was on his back and Brenda was slipping in the intramuscular sedative.

And they could all see what the problem was.

One penis. One zipper. Inextricably entwined.

Tom grimaced. 'You know, you really should have let Dr Raymond deal with this,' he said gently. 'Swelling around the entrapped tissue makes this procedure more difficult. We need a penile block. Brenda, could you administer...?'

'Certainly, Doctor,' Brenda said.

'You do it,' Ron screamed and Tom shook his head.

'Maybe Dr Raymond could have managed by herself if you'd agreed to let her examine you,' he told him. 'But we've gone past that now. Iris, do you have cooking oil? Excellent. Brenda, can we have a plastic sheet from your bag? Let's move, people. Ron, the sedation will be taking hold any minute. Just try your best to relax until it does.'

Tasha could only watch in admiration. Tom had the situation under complete control.

Once the sedative took hold and they could get a clear idea of how bad the problem was, cooking oil might solve the problem without any other intervention, she thought. The pain was easing but Ron was still breathing fire. He was demanding—expecting—a quick surgical fix, but to his chagrin Tom simply poured cooking oil over everything in sight and told him to stay where he was while the oil had a chance to penetrate.

'It's important you stay still,' he told him. 'The oil may well take half an hour to soften everything around it. Would you like Iris to stay with you? Or Brenda? No? Then I suggest we all retire to the kitchen. Call us if there's any change.'

So, much to Ron's fury, they ended up around the kitchen table again. Iris tentatively produced a bottle of wine, which Tom and Tasha refused because they were on duty but which Karen had no qualms in accepting. And Brenda had one too because, as she said, she was only a little bit on duty. Iris watched them drink, and then suddenly poured one for herself.

She drank it too fast, and then Tom poured her another.

He was watching her with sympathy. He was waiting, Tasha thought. *What's he doing?*

There was a little small talk. The moans upstairs were decreasing as the drugs took hold.

Iris was relaxing.

And then, after the second glass of wine, Tom asked Iris about the bruise on her face. She shook her head.

'Tell us,' Tom said gently, and reached over and brushed her cheek, lightly, a gesture of caring that made something inside Tasha twist.

And it must have hit Iris exactly the same way. She gave a half-strangled sob, looked wildly round the table— and then tugged her blouse down to reveal bruises right to where they disappeared under her bra. 'R-Ron,' she said simply. 'All the time.'

'You've never admitted,' Tom said gently. 'Iris, I've asked…'

'He'd hit me harder if he knew I told you. But…but he'll hit me again tonight anyway. He was angry with me before…'

'Do you want to leave him?' Tom asked, and Iris took another gulp of wine and looked wildly about her. Four sympathetic faces looked back.

'Y-yes. But he'd never let me. I don't have any money and I have nowhere to go. He told me once if I ever left him he'd hide everything and he knows how. He says he'll come up on paper as bankrupt. And he'd come after me. No one defies Ron.'

'Iris, we can,' Karen said, in a voice that brooked no opposition. 'And we will. You have two dogs who'd get on fine with my two dogs, who just happen to be German Shepherds. Big ones. My boys are gentle as lambs but they don't look gentle. We have a granny flat at the back of our house and Brian and I and the dogs can see anyone off who needs to be seen off. Promise.'

'And if you don't like the granny flat there's a spare room at my place,' Brenda told her. 'If you let us…if you allow us to help you, you'll find you're surrounded. Iris, you have friends in this town. Ron's never let them close but we're here for you.'

And suddenly Tasha realised just why Tom had come armed with Karen and Brenda. They'd turned from two nurses into two fierce advocates for a downtrodden sister. Had he known they would? She glanced at him and saw the satisfaction. Of course he'd known.

He cared.

'But then there's money.' Karen sounded not only help- ful, she was also practical. 'Ron's loaded but Iris is right— he's smart enough to hide everything. The whole town knows he's a financial snake. I wouldn't mind betting ev- erything's in offshore accounts.'

'Iris, where does he keep his financial records?' Tom's question was gentle but firm. Iris had crossed a line and he didn't want her retreating.

She gazed at him as if he was crazy. As if they were all crazy. But suddenly a flare of hope lit her bruised face. The beginnings of revolt.

'In his study. I'm not allowed in except to dust and hoover.'

'Then let's dust,' Tom said cheerfully. 'And maybe we should dust the insides of his filing cabinet, too. What do you think?'

And, to Tasha's amazement, they were suddenly all in Ron's study. Five people sifting financial documents fast… Operating the copier. Being very, very quiet. At the end of half an hour Iris had a suitcase packed and the dogs and Iris were in Karen's taxi, Brenda following behind to give the impression of solidarity, and Tasha was almost breath- less with astonishment.

'We'll get these documents to the local solicitor before

his morning coffee,' Tom declared. 'There's no way Ron can hide what he owns now. Iris, you're safe.'

There was still the small matter of one entrapped penis. Ron was still lying rigid in his bed. Tom had warned him not to move and he hadn't.

He looked almost emasculated, Tasha thought, and she could have felt sorry for him if she hadn't seen those bruises. Their staging spoke of constant beatings, over and over.

Tom had taken photographs with his cellphone. 'If it's okay with you, Iris, I'll talk to the police,' he'd said.

And Brenda and Karen had both said, 'Do it.'

Iris had taken another gulp of wine and said yes.

Ron had quite a day in front of him tomorrow.

But for tonight his pain was almost over. Tasha was happy to stay in the background. Ron lay rigid while Tom examined him. The oil had softened the trapped foreskin. The zipper was oiled to the maximum.

Tom touched the head of the zipper with wire cutters, the teeth came apart and the skin flopped free.

There was a tiny bit of bleeding. Tom cleaned it with care, then he and Tasha removed his oiled clothing and the plastic sheeting, and helped Ron into clean pyjamas. Their care couldn't be faulted.

'We're leaving you another sedative and a couple of painkillers,' Tom told him. 'It's eleven now. You can take them any time after two. We'll leave you a glass of water.'

'Iris'll get it,' Ron growled. 'Where is she? I want a whisky.'

'No alcohol tonight,' Tom decreed. 'Not with the drugs you have on board.'

'Tell Iris to come up.' And they knew he had no intention of following orders.

'Iris can't come,' Tom said smoothly. 'We noticed bruising on her face and examination proves it's extensive. We've organised for her to stay somewhere where she can be fully examined. Many of those bruises are old. We need to find their cause.'

There was a moment's pause. It stretched.

'She falls,' Ron growled at last. 'Stupid cow. She's clumsy. Don't listen to a word she says. Tell her to come here now.'

'She's already gone,' Tom said gently. 'You get some sleep, Ron. You may need all your strength tomorrow.'

They left him not sleeping. They left him almost rigid with rage and frustration—and fear.

They left and Tom was grinning like the proverbial Cheshire cat.

'I've been waiting for years,' he said in satisfaction. 'I suspected but there was nothing I could do. I can't believe one zipper and it's sorted.'

'She might rescind,' Tasha reminded him. It was sadly normal for battered women to respond to threats and return.

'You think Karen and Brenda will let that happen? They're two of the toughest women I know. Iris has her dogs, a safe place to stay and a couple of German Shepherd watchdogs. She has Karen and Brenda at her back and a file on Ron's dealings that I bet will make our local solicitor's eyes water. Nailed by a zipper.'

'You really do care,' Tasha said slowly. They were back in the car, heading home.

'Do you doubt that? These are my people.'

'Paul never cared.' She hadn't meant to say it. It just... happened.

'I'm not Paul.'

'You surf to the point where you smash yourself on the rocks. You love women.'

'I do,' he said. 'Guilty as charged. So shoot me.'

She fell silent.

So did he.

Guilty as charged.

He accepted it. He knew it.

His care was extraordinary. What had just happened showed a depth of insight and tenderness that almost did her head in. He'd watched and worried about Iris for years, and tonight he'd found an opportunity to put things right.

His care made something inside her twist so hard it hurt. He loved this town. He loved its people.

So what? The voice inside her head was hammering the question. *It doesn't make any difference. He still loves women. He still loves risk.*

And then the thought of Iris was suddenly front and centre. Once upon a time Iris had loved Ron, she thought. Iris must have gone into marriage as a blissful bride, sure that her man loved her back.

How could you trust your judgement?

She couldn't. Her judgement was skewed by a lousy childhood, but maybe she'd been born with a lack of survival instinct in the first place. Like Iris.

Make decisions with your head, not your heart. She'd said that to herself after Paul's funeral. She'd put the rule aside when she'd tried to have Emily, and hadn't she paid the price?

The night suddenly seemed darker, bleaker, and the exultation from what had just taken place receded. She drove on in silence. Tom stretched his bad leg and winced and she didn't ask about it. She couldn't.

She didn't want to care.

Tom's phone rang and she was almost grateful. He had his phone on speaker and she listened. Croup. A young mum with an eighteen-month-old baby plus two other children. Her husband was away. She couldn't come to the surgery and Tasha could hear the fear in her voice.

She also heard the unmistakable sounds of croup in the background.

'We're already in the car,' Tom told the young mother. 'We'll be there in less than five minutes.'

'You should be home in bed,' Tasha told him. 'I can do this. Tom, you must be dead on your feet.'

'I have adrenalin bouncing off the walls,' he told her. 'If you think I can go home and sleep...'

'You should do something about your adrenalin. It gets you into all sorts of trouble.'

'Does it?' he asked, and his voice suddenly softened. 'Is that what you're afraid of?'

She didn't answer. She couldn't.

Meg Ainsling was eighteen months old and near to exhaustion. Hannah Ainsling opened the door holding Meg, and she practically fell into their arms with relief.

'I'm so frightened.'

Then she broke off as Meg started wheezing again. It was a fragile, weak cough, a child at the end of her strength.

'You should have rung earlier,' Tom said, swinging his bag onto the table and then taking Meg into his arms.

And here was yet another example of Tom's caring, Tasha thought as he carried the little girl through to the warm kitchen, holding her as if he'd been holding babies all his life. The firmness and his soft growl of reassurance seemed to relax the little one rather than frighten her.

'Let's get some steam into the room,' he ordered. 'Hannah, get every pot you can fit onto the stove, filled with hot water, and see how much we can bring to the boil. Boil the kettle, too. Let's get this room full of vapour.'

That was the old-fashioned way of treating croup, Tasha knew. It worked to an extent but Meg was beyond using that as a sole remedy. Tasha could hear the stridor, which marked the upper airway obstruction secondary to infection or swelling.

She unpacked the medical bag while Hannah started filling the kitchen with steam. Tom performed a swift examination, talking to the little girl as he did. Meg was limp in his arms, as if she sensed that finally here was someone who could help her.

They worked fast, not needing to speak to each other as they worked. There was no need. Tom spooned the little girl back into her mother's arms—after that swift examination there was no need to stress her more than necessary. Then they administered nebulised adrenalin. They used a nebuliser mask with oxygen, and it was a sign of how close Meg was to the edge that the little girl didn't fight it.

Her breathing was rapid. Her pulse was fast and there was a drawing in of the muscles between her ribs and in her neck. It hurt to listen, and Tasha glanced at Hannah's face and glanced away.

She knew this terror. Here it was again, the black wall. The impossibility of moving on.

How could she ever put herself near this dread again? How could she think of having another baby?

How could she let herself love again?

She couldn't.

Hannah had herself under control. 'The stridor will get worse if she cries,' Tom had told her, so every ounce of Hannah's concentration was in keeping her little girl calm.

If it had been Tasha's call she'd probably be sending her to hospital but Tom seemed content to wait.

Another ten minutes. Another dose.

Tasha accepted his cue. She made them all tea and they waited some more.

Another ten minutes. Another dose.

And finally the stridor faded. The little girl relaxed in her mother's arms, and ten minutes after that she was asleep.

Drama over.

'Keep the steam up tonight,' Tom told her. 'But I think she'll be fine.' They stood by the cot they'd pulled into the kitchen and watched the steady rise and fall of Meg's chest. 'But why did you leave it so long to call?'

'I didn't like to worry you,' Hannah told him. 'I know you need your rest.'

'I'm almost better.'

'But you're not fully better. The whole town knows it. And Tasha—'

'You know Tasha's here to help.'

'But Tasha's little girl would have been the same age as Meg,' Hannah whispered. 'We all know about your Emily, Tasha. We're all so sorry. I didn't want to hurt you.'

And Tasha's chest tightened.

It did hurt. Of course it hurt and it hurt the most because time stood still when it should move on.

Emily was still a part of her, a deep and abiding centre she could never lose. But Emily didn't grow. That was the heartbreak. In her mind Emily was still a beloved, beautiful newborn, not an eighteen-month-old. She should be coping with childhood illnesses, bumps, bruises, all the things that made a normal childhood.

'I don't think about it,' she whispered, and Hannah and Tom looked at her with identical expressions. Expressions that said they knew she was lying.

'I'm not avoiding children for the rest of my life because I've lost Emily,' she said, forcing herself to sound brisk, efficient, professional. 'Are you sure you don't want Meg to go to hospital?'

'She's better with me,' Hannah said, her eyes suddenly welling.

And Tasha thought, *I need to get out of here.*

'Can you take my case out to the car?' Tom asked. 'Sorry, but my leg…'

'Of course.' She knew it was a ruse, an escape Tom sensed she needed, but she was too grateful to protest. 'Goodnight, Hannah. Good luck with Meg.'

'I don't need luck when I have you two,' Hannah whispered. 'God bless both of you.'

Once more she drove. Tom gazed out into the darkness and said nothing. There were things unsaid all over the place.

Hannah's words hung between them.

She wasn't starting any conversation that could end up with her weeping, she decided. She'd spent eighteen months tamping down emotions and she wasn't about to let them flare now.

'How do you cope?' Tom asked, and the tamping got a whole lot harder.

She should say 'I'm fine.' She should say 'It doesn't bother me, seeing kids every day of my working life. Watching parents with kids in strollers, pushing swings in playgrounds, coping with howling kids in supermarkets.'

'I don't cope,' she said quietly. 'I just suck it up and keep it down there. Being a sodden mess for the rest of my life's not an option. Emily's with me as much as she can be. The rest… I think it's like amputation. You learn to get on with your life but nothing's going to put it back.'

He swore.

'And that doesn't help either,' she said. 'You can't imagine the new words I've attempted.' She tried a smile, which didn't come off. 'I know this is dumb,' she confessed. 'But I used to be afraid of flying. I didn't like thunder either. Now, though, I don't seem to be afraid of anything. It's like the worst has happened, so what can I possibly be afraid of?' She tried for the smile again and finally succeeded. 'So see me indomitable. See me fearless. Just like a Blake boy.'

He didn't smile back. 'I don't like the analogy,' he said softly. 'Because I can't imagine how empty that must feel. If there's anything I can do…' He paused. 'But of course there's not.'

'You did everything you could do.'

'Taking away hurt…'

'It's not possible. It's not worth trying.'

'Tasha, pull in here.' They were driving along the coast road, along the cliffs above the town. There was a track off to the east, innovatively named 'View Road'.

She shouldn't obey, Tasha thought. She was feeling numb, tired by the emotion of the night, exposed by the worry she sensed in Tom's voice. She should keep going, head to bed, hide her pain under her pillows as she fought for sleep.

But the car seemed to turn of its own accord, and a moment later they were parked under a sign that was even more innovative—'View Point'.

It was indeed View Point. The moon hung low over the water, sending silver shards from the horizon straight to Tom's little car. The night was still and calm. The ocean was a plane of moonlit shimmer.

While they watched, a pod of dolphins broke the surface just beneath the cliffs. They leaped in and out of the water as they made their way south, growing smaller and smaller until all that was left was a trail of moonlit phosphorescence.

'I ordered those guys,' Tom said smugly. 'Right on cue. They're good. They'll start demanding a pay rise soon if they do it any better.'

She'd been lost, caught by the emotion still welling inside her. Tom's words broke the moment and made her choke on a bubble of laughter.

This was okay. She was moving on.

'What you did tonight was brilliant,' she told him. 'I can't believe that Iris is safe. And Meg... How can you care so much?'

'When I'm really like Paul?'

'That's not what I meant.'

'I'm sure it is,' he told her. 'You think I can't care about anyone because I won't care about someone in particular. Because I know I'm a risk as husband material, I won't go there, but that doesn't mean I can't care in other ways.'

'I know. I'm sorry.'

'I'm sorry, too. I wish you hadn't had to help treat Meg tonight. I know how much it hurt.'

'I need to get over hurt.' She was trying her hardest to keep this conversation grounded. 'Like you. You're improving every day.'

'I'm not talking about physical hurt. It's the other hurt that stays with us. Watching my father break my mother's heart... Watching your husband betray you... Watching Emily die...' And then he stopped.

There was a long, long silence. She couldn't break it. She didn't know how.

And then...

'Tasha, I'd really like to kiss you.'

This was a bad idea. Her head knew it but somehow tonight she'd passed the point where her head was in control.

The night. The pain she'd just tried to express. His pain. Tom...

She'd never talked to anyone as she and Tom had just talked. She'd tried to hide her pain, not put it out there for anyone to see.

Only this wasn't *anyone*.

Tom was her friend. He was the man she'd gone to when she'd been in trouble. He was a colleague, someone who'd helped her, and she could help back. A man who'd suffered a cerebral bleed.

He was all of those things but above all he was Tom.

A man sitting beside her, reaching out to touch her face, swiping away an errant tear that had welled up despite her best efforts to hold it back.

She hadn't cried since she'd left Australia eighteen months before. She'd left her tears in a graveyard high on the headland of Cray Point and she'd shed no tears since.

But somehow Tom exposed her.

She'd just told him she could never feel fear again, and here it was, in the car with them. She was fearful.

Not of Tom. Never of Tom.

She was frightened of how he made her feel.

Turn on the ignition, she told herself. Head for home. Her head was screaming it, but Tom's touch on her face was light, wondering, gentle.

Her friend.

A Blake boy?

The analogy seemed to have gone out the window. She'd watched him comfort a tiny child, calm her, settle her.

She'd watched him care for Iris. Care *about* Iris.

And despite her fears, a flicker of hope lit within her and refused to be quelled.

Maybe she could try... Maybe they could try...

Move forward with your head, not your heart.

Her mantra was wavering. She was trying to clutch at it but it was vaporising at his touch.

'I won't hurt you.' He said it like it was the most sacred vow and somehow she managed to smile.

'By kissing me? You have five o'clock stubble. Of course you'll hurt me.'

'You want to risk it?' The fingers traced her cheekbones, then moved to cup her face, but as if he could sense her fear, his hands held her lightly so she could pull back at any moment.

But fear was receding. Those last tugs from that appalling mantra couldn't hold her. This was Tom.

She raised her face to his and let herself be pulled in to be kissed.

She hadn't expected it. She hadn't wanted it.

She wanted it now.

His mouth met hers, lightly, tentatively, ready to pull away if she made the least move of protest.

But how could she protest when it felt as if his mouth belonged to her? Was part of her. Was…hers?

For the feel of his mouth on hers wasn't complicated at all. The first touch had deepened in an instant as both their bodies recognised something bigger than each of them.

Heat. Passion. Desire.

For she wanted him. Her body was screaming its need and she had no defence. She wanted no defence. She sank into the kiss and melted into its heat. She felt his arms wrap around her as if she was the most precious thing in the world, and that's what she felt like. Cherished.

Helpless in the face of mutual desire.

Melting and wanting to melt.

But this wasn't exactly a private place. View Point was also known as Passion Point and for a reason. The local kids used it as a parking spot and why wouldn't they? The place breathed romance.

And now a car zoomed in behind them, all eight cylinders of heated-up metal. It cruised up beside them, the sound system sending out a booming bass that was pretty much guaranteed to break any romantic moment. The driver's window came down and a head poked out.

'Hey, Doc, not expecting to see you up here. You got a chick?'

'That's what I get for not buying a generic sedan,' Tom breathed, and tugged away.

'You too busy to talk?' the kid in the car called, and Tom sighed and wound down his window.

'Time you were home in bed, Benny Lannard,' he said sternly. 'Does your dad know you have his car?'

'Got my licence last week,' Benny said proudly. 'Me and Kylie's just trying things out.'

'Yeah, well don't go trying too much out,' Tom said bluntly. 'You guys know how babies are made and they mean the end of life as you know it. You make Kylie pregnant, mate, you'll be a grandpa at forty and you'll be paying child maintenance for the next twenty years.'

There was a moment's deathly silence.

'Child maintenance...'

'I know you'd do the right thing by Kylie,' Tom said inexorably. 'But if you don't support her the government garnishes your wages. They take half or sometimes more, until the kid's as old as you are. But of course you know that. And by the way, Kylie, if you end up pregnant you won't get into your nineteen-fifties dresses ever again, and who can go clubbing with a baby in tow? If you think your mum will take over, think again. I know your mum.'

'Uh, gross,' Kylie muttered. 'Benny, maybe...'

'Yeah, babe,' Benny said hurriedly, and Tasha had to choke back laughter at the sudden lack of enthusiasm in both their voices. And then Benny said... 'Who you got there, Doc?'

'A friend,' Tom said, winding his window up firmly. 'A friend who's mature enough to know it's time to go home. We'll leave you to it but if you're planning on starting a family tonight, drop in tomorrow and I'll give you both a brochure on the responsibilities of parenthood.'

They drove home. Tasha was torn between laughter and something else. Something she couldn't name.

The kiss had changed all sorts of things. So had Tom's lecture on responsibility. He cared so much, she thought. He loved this little community and the thought was suddenly, inexplicably sexy.

A doctor giving a lecture on teenage pregnancy? What was sexy about that?

But he'd made her laugh and he'd kissed her again lightly before they'd driven from View Point and every single sense was aware of him. Achingly aware. Nothing else seemed to matter.

Where was sense when she needed it? She couldn't grasp it and she didn't.

And when they reached home the sensation became almost unbearable.

'Cup of tea?' Tom said, and his voice was suddenly unsteady. His voice had been starting to lose the faint slur the stroke had caused and she missed it. Which was dumb. Inexplicable. And then she thought, was she missing it because it meant that soon he'd have no need of her?

Soon she could go home. Wherever home was.

'Or bed?' Tom asked before she could answer the tea question, and the world seemed to still.

Tea and bed. A normal question between friends.

Friends to lovers... It could happen.

It shouldn't happen, she told herself fiercely. It was dumb. She'd fallen for one Blake.

Tom wasn't Paul. He was just... Tom.

And there was no pressure. They ditched their jackets, stowing their medical gear in the hall cupboard. They were two professionals home from the job.

Home. There was that word again.

She was home with Tom.

Home was where the heart was and she knew where her heart lay. Up until now the sense of belonging had seemed everything to do with a tiny grave on a headland but suddenly she knew it wasn't true. Or it was partly true but there was more.

Where was her heart?

It was well and truly here. It was entwined with all the things Tom had done for her. It was entwined with Tom's caring, Tom's laughter, Tom's smile.

Surely not. That'd make a mockery of every vow she'd made after the disaster of her marriage to Paul, but right now her heart didn't seem to connect to her head.

He was so near. So close.

He should have a bigger hallway, she thought tangentially.

And then he said, 'Tasha…' in a voice she hadn't heard before.

A voice full of tenderness. A voice that was husky with a passion that matched what she was feeling.

A voice that said he wanted her as much as she wanted him.

A voice that said bed was inevitable.

'Tom,' she whispered, and the thing was decided. He had her in his arms and he was lifting her…

'Your leg,' she squeaked. 'Your arm…'

'It's therapy,' he told her, smiling. 'You don't think my rehab team would approve of me exercising any way I know how?'

'It's not on your list,' she managed.

'Then it's a dumb list. It needs all sorts of things added to it, starting now.'

CHAPTER EIGHT

SHE WOKE. THE sun was streaming into Tom's bedroom and when she opened her eyes she could see the light glinting on the sapphire surface of the sea. She was in Tom's arms and she'd never felt this way in her life.

She'd thought marriage to Paul had been good. For a short time, before Paul's love of adventure had eclipsed his desire for her, she'd loved their marriage. She'd believed she was loved.

But she'd never felt like this. She lay spooned in Tom's arms and she felt the world settle. This was her place. This was where she was meant to be. Bliss.

But…this was where she'd vowed never to be again.

And bliss or not, her stupid mantra surfaced, uncalled for, unwanted, but it was there all the same. Head, not heart. What had happened last night?

Bliss had happened and it had taken every single piece of sense from her head and dissolved it, until all she'd felt was joy.

And joy was a fleeting, cheating thing. Hadn't she learned that?

But joy was now. She closed her eyes again and pushed away the sense of panic. Surely all that mattered was that she was being held by Tom. This was the man who'd been there for her when she'd needed him most. He'd seen her at her most vulnerable. He'd held her while she'd sobbed and then, as she'd finally tugged herself out of despair, he'd made her laugh again.

He was her lover.

He shouldn't be her lover. That appalling little voice was breaking the moment, ruining the feeling of utter contentment. She lay spooned in Tom's arms, skin against skin, and it felt so right... It felt so wonderful...

Go away, she told her stupid beetle of a mantra, and the mantra backed off a little and tucked itself into a dark corner of her brain.

It was the best she could do. She couldn't wrench it out entirely.

But she wanted to give herself up entirely to this man. She wanted to think happy ever after. She wanted the whole fantasy.

But the beetle was still asking questions. How many women had he had in this bed? How many more would share it in the future?

She stirred and his hold on her tightened, strong, warm, possessive. 'Good morning, my love,' he whispered, his voice muffled by her hair, and she felt like screaming at her beetle. Go away, go away, go away.

She'd gone this far. Why not embrace this moment? She turned within his arms and felt herself melt again. She was where she wanted to be more than anything else in the world.

She was home.

I don't think so, the beetle told her, and she knew it spoke the truth. But for now... Please let me believe it as truth.

And she did. Sort of. Her body turned to his again and it felt right. It felt perfect.

She was so in love.

She was so in trouble.

* * *

Tasha was different.

He'd never felt this way with a woman before.

She was his friend. He felt as if he'd known her forever. He felt as if he knew her through and through, and making love with her had been inevitable.

He loved her.

Until last night he would have said he loved her as a friend, nothing more. Or maybe he was lying. Maybe he'd wanted her for a very long time but he hadn't acknowledged it until now.

But there was no choice but to acknowledge it now. The way he felt...

Was it possible that he could trust himself to commit?

Was it possible that Tasha was the one?

And there it was, a thunderbolt of knowledge so deep it almost knocked him sideways. He'd never thought he could be faithful to a woman, but he'd never met Tasha.

With Tasha all bets were off. Family history be damned. He could be faithful. He would be faithful and suddenly, fiercely, he knew it at a level so deep that the years of doubt fell away.

He'd teach her to trust, he thought. If he could learn the lesson then so could she.

But for now... Enough of the introspection, he told himself as he gathered her against him yet again. He had this woman in his arms and that was all that mattered.

He asked for nothing more in the world.

But then the world broke in.

Susie...

Theirs had been a fleeting relationship, not even consummated. She'd been fun. She'd now found a man she wanted a permanent relationship with, and that was fine by him. They were still friends.

But why was she on his veranda at this hour?

'Tom. Yoo-hoo… Tom, love, are you awake? It's Susie. Sorry, sweetheart, I understand you should be resting but you know I left my shawl here? Donald's taking me away for the weekend and I need it.'

If there was anything surer to bring Tasha's mantra beetle out of its dark corner, this was it.

Susie. A woman from Tom's past.

Only how did she know she was from his past?

Because he'd told her? Because she trusted Tom?

Maybe she did—but, oh, the level of faith she had to have…

She didn't have enough.

Tom hauled on a pair of pants while Tasha lay back and cringed and the gorgeous feeling of being cherished turned to smut.

He opened his wardrobe and grabbed a shawl, which made her feel even worse.

This was innocent, she told herself. This was Tom's past life and it had nothing to do with her, but head was suddenly ruling heart in no uncertain terms. It was fear. It wasn't logical but she was a coward, and she knew it.

Tom had walked out onto the veranda. He was speaking briefly to Susie, but she wasn't listening. Fear had her hauling on knickers, bra, jeans and windcheater, and by the time he came back to the bedroom she was dressed.

'Tasha…' He came straight to her. He must be able to see the fear on her face. She couldn't disguise it from herself, much less him. 'Love, it's not what it seems. Susie left her shawl here months ago, before the accident. Hilda must have packed it into the wardrobe. I saw it when I came home from hospital but I didn't have the energy to do anything about it. She asked me about it last week. I told her where it was but then I forgot again. Then…to be honest…Tasha, I haven't been thinking of Susie. You've been here…'

'Your latest conquest,' she muttered. 'How can I have been so dumb?'

'Tasha…'

'Leave it, Tom,' she said roughly. She felt sick. Betrayed.

Not betrayed by Tom, though. He'd broken no promises. She was even sure that he was speaking the truth.

The betrayal she felt was worse. She'd betrayed herself, her own beliefs, her own hard-earned self.

'I never slept with Susie,' he said flatly.

'Tom, I believe you. I'm sorry. The conquest jibe was unfair. I do know you better than that. But you're my friend, Tom, not my lover, and risking that by fancying myself in love with you is just plain dumb. It scares me. It makes me feel out of control and I've vowed never to go down that path again.'

And then she took a deep breath and said what had to be said. What her mantra dictated she had to say.

'Tom, I'll be grateful for you forever. Please, if possible I'll always be your friend, but because there's this attraction between us then the friendship has to be at a distance. We both know that. So I'll stay in Cray Point until you can drive again. I'll stay until you don't need to do rehab every day, but I won't stay here.'

'That's crazy.'

'Cats make me sneeze,' she said, striving desperately for lightness, and then she decided to say it like it was. 'But they don't break my heart, and if I stay here that's what I'm risking. I never meant you to be my lover and I don't want that.'

'I didn't think I wanted it either.' His voice was serious, troubled, and she saw real concern for her in his gaze. It was almost her undoing.

But the feeling she'd had as he'd tugged Susie's shawl from the wardrobe was one she'd never wanted to feel again. Okay, she believed him. Susie was simply an ex who'd left her shawl here, but it had opened a chasm in her heart that had been ripped open the moment she'd heard Paul on the phone to the other woman.

She hadn't wanted to believe it. She'd asked Paul calmly who he'd been on the phone to. Honesty in marriage, she'd thought, and she'd expected a confession.

And then he'd lied, and she'd known he'd lied. She knew Tom was speaking the truth now, but lies or truth, that chasm was still there. To trust herself…

No. She was self-contained. What had started with Paul had torn her heart. She'd got over his deceit and his death— sort of—and then she'd thrown her hat into the ring again in the loving business and she'd tried to have a baby. And that had ripped her heart almost out of her body.

What was she doing, thinking she could start again?

She couldn't.

She had an appointment with the IVF clinic in six weeks. The prospect had been so huge it had terrified her, but the seed of hope had flared and grown.

And now…one night of passion and one stupid shawl had shown her how stupid that hope was. She couldn't be brave. She'd had the brave crushed out of her.

She had no courage left.

'Tasha, you look terrified.' Tom was watching her, worried for her, reaching for her, but she backed away.

'I'm not. At least, I'm not as long as I can get away. Tom, you've been the best friend but now… I don't want this to go further and in your heart I don't think you do either. I'm sorry, Tom, but it's you or the cats, and it's time I was sensible. I choose cats.'

'I'm scared, too,' he said, almost as if he hadn't heard her, and she blinked.

'I said I wasn't.'

'I know you are. Like me. We're peas in a pod. Tasha, I've spent my life thinking guys who married and remained faithful for the rest of their lives had some sort of gene that was missing in my family.' He took a deep breath. 'It turns out I was wrong. It turns out it was just that I hadn't met the right woman.'

It should have made her melt, but how could she? She was holding herself rigidly under control, clinging to the knowledge of past hurt. 'I'm not that woman,' she managed.

'You've been burned. First by my idiot half-brother. Second by the loss of Emily, though the loss of your parents has to be in the mix there as well. You don't trust love, just as I didn't. But it's past tense, Tasha. I trust it now. You can choose to trust me or not...'

'How can I do that?'

Silence. The room was deathly still. It was as if the weight of the world was right above their heads, ready to descend.

Tasha was feeling ill.

Trust. Her heart was crying for it, longing for it, aching for it as if there was a void in there that only trust could fill.

She could take this one step...

And fall into the arms of Tom Blake. And try for another baby.

And let the whole disastrous cycle start again.

And her heart clenched. She could almost feel it shrivel at the thought of what could lie ahead if she fell into the arms of this man.

She'd hurt so much...

Cats.

'I'm... I'm leaving,' she whispered. 'Please, Tom, don't try and stop me. If you keep pressuring I won't be able to stay at Hilda and Rhonda's. I'll have to go away completely.'

'Are you so afraid?'

And finally she gave him the truth. 'Yes,' she said, openly and honestly. 'Yes, I am.'

'You can't take a chance on me?'

'I can't take any more chances. I'm being sensible.'

'So sensible means we stay alone for ever?'

'I know how much it hurts…'

'So you'll teach me?' Anger was obvious now, raw and exposed. 'I've finally met the woman I want to spend the rest of my life with, but she's scared I might betray her.'

'Tom…'

'I wouldn't,' he said fiercely. 'I won't. But of course you're right, I have no evidence to back that with. You've judged me on my father and on Paul…'

'I'm not…'

'There's no need to go on,' he snapped. 'You've said enough. I care about you, Tasha, but I have nothing more than my word to prove it. So I can't prove it. We'll leave it there, then. We'll work out the nuts and bolts of how we plan the workload later. You've made your choice. Go and live with cats.'

CHAPTER NINE

'I THINK WE can safely say you're all right to drive again.'

Of all the things he'd been hoping for, this should have been the biggest. Sally had just performed intensive neurological tests. She'd pushed him every way she could. His left leg was still weaker than the right. He still had a slight limp. His fingers didn't flex instantaneously but they were pretty fast. In these last four weeks he'd pushed himself to the physical edge and now he was reaping the rewards.

He was cured. Well, almost. Recovery from cerebral damage was slow. His brain was making new neural pathways. He still had a way to go before he could balance well on a surfboard again, but essentially his body could almost be classified as normal.

He should be over the moon.

He walked out of the physiotherapy clinic and missed Tasha.

She still came with him occasionally, but she'd ceased joining in. She sat on the sidelines, silently, reading a book, pretending she wasn't watching. Anger still vibrated between them. It felt as if they'd betrayed each other. A normal friendship was impossible.

She hadn't come today. Darryl and Louise Coad had turned up at the surgery to discuss their worries about their elderly mother. Tasha could have put them off until tomorrow, or she could have asked Tom to see them later—

they were, after all, his patients—but instead she'd welcomed them.

'Of course I can see you. Tom, can you ask Karen to drive you?'

She'd sounded almost relieved, which was the story of their lives right now. She didn't want anything more to do with him than she had to.

Her fear left him feeling angry. Why couldn't she trust when he'd made such a leap himself?

'Why the black face?' He'd been sitting in Karen's cab, silent, his thoughts grim as Cray Point's taxi driver took him home. 'I would have thought you'd be on top of the world,' she said. 'Great report from your physio. And, hey, did you know the solicitors have put a freeze on Ron's assets? Iris should be set for life. There's also a question about the legality of Ron's financial dealings. Some of those documents we copied are red hot. The local cop says we might end up with Ron facing charges other than assault and battery. How cool's that?'

'Really cool,' Tom said, and tried a smile, but Karen looked sideways at him and grimaced.

'You got it bad, huh?'

'What?'

'Don't *what* me. The whole town knows you're loopy over Tasha. We all know why she moved out and we're all really sorry. And now you've recovered, she can leave and we'll be stuck with your sorry face for the rest of our lives. Whatcha going to do about it, Doc?'

'There's nothing I can do,' he said explosively. 'She loved my half-brother and he was a toe rag. She lost her baby. How do I persuade her to trust again?'

And there it was, out in the open. He'd said it. He sat back, aghast, feeling more exposed than he'd ever felt in his life.

Karen didn't say anything. There was nothing to say, at

least for the moment. It took her a good two minutes before she opened her mouth again and even then it wasn't to impart wisdom.

'Guess flowers and candles and Hilda's casseroles won't work on this one, hey, Doc?'

He almost lost it. He gritted his teeth and they drove on in silence.

When finally they pulled up outside the surgery he had himself under control—almost. 'Thank you,' he said curtly. 'Put it on my account.'

'Sure thing, Doc.'

'And don't go saying—'

'I don't need to. The whole town knows. Tasha's looking as grim-faced as you. I don't know why we don't just knock your heads together and be done with it.'

'And put us both back into hospital with cerebral bleeds?'

'Not funny, Doc,' she said. She paused. 'You know Rhonda and Hilda and their dad will be back on Sunday. If you've got your driving licence back and they're wanting their house, what's to stop Tasha from leaving?'

'Nothing.' Except a small grave up on the hill, but that wouldn't hold her, he thought.

And he couldn't hold her.

'Think of something, Doc,' Karen said urgently. 'There must be some way...'

'Leave it, Karen,' he said heavily, and slammed the taxi door and headed up to the house.

He limped. When he concentrated he no longer limped but he wasn't concentrating on his leg now.

He was thinking of nothing but Tasha.

The post box was full. He grabbed it as he went past, and riffled through. He wanted something—anything—to distract him, but there seemed nothing out of the ordinary. They all looked like specialist letters sent after referrals, all like the dozen or more he sorted at the end of each day.

He poured himself a beer and settled down to read. Work... It was the only way he could think of to get his head away from where it most wanted to be.

Rhonda and Hilda shared a picturesque cottage in the centre of town. It was cute to the point of twee, filled with mementos of lives back in England, husbands now gone, shells collected over years, pieces of driftwood, china ornaments, cats past and present.

Tasha was currently sitting on the back step overlooking a hundred or so pot plants. Cats were twining through her legs and her eyes were watering.

She wasn't noticing. She was staring in horror at a small white stick.

A stick with two red lines in the centre.

How had this happened? *How?*

She'd been a bit queasy yesterday and the day before. And tired. Then she'd woken in the middle of the night thinking dates. Thinking horror.

This morning she'd lost her breakfast.

She tested herself at the surgery and told herself it must be a mistake. She'd pleaded that it was a mistake. Then she'd worked all day, thrusting it on the backburner.

She'd just tested herself again.

If she was asked to describe her feelings right now, she couldn't. Of all the dumb, terrifying, catasmotic—was that a word?—things to happen...

She was pregnant with Tom's child.

One night.

They'd used condoms. Of course they had—they weren't kids like Benny and Kylie. They'd stopped before things had got out of hand. They'd decided—like mature adults—to go ahead but to be careful.

She'd been sensible. Tom had been sensible.

Okay, they might have been in a hurry...

This was too big. Her head couldn't take it in. She was staring at the red lines until they blurred.

She was exposed again. She was totally, absolutely out of control, when she'd made a conscious, intelligent decision to stay in control. She'd moved out of Tom's house four weeks ago and she'd kept her distance. Even if her heart did give this crazy hammer every time she saw him, she had it under wraps. She was being sensible.

Rhonda was due home tomorrow and Hilda and their dad soon after. She'd intended to stay on in their guest room, work here for a couple more weeks until she was sure Tom could cope, and then go... Where?

It didn't matter. She'd intended to start looking at job offers soon. Somewhere busy, she'd thought. Somewhere demanding where her head didn't have to think.

Of Emily. Or Paul. Or her parents.

Or betrayal and loss.

Or Tom.

She'd written to the IVF clinic and asked them to destroy the last vials of Paul's sperm. She had no use for it. She knew she didn't have the courage to start again.

The plastic stick in her hand with its red lines made a mockery of every single decision she'd made.

She felt dizzy and more than a little sick. Her hands went instinctively to her belly.

A foetus.

A baby.

'Tasha?'

Of all the people she most didn't want to face right now it was Tom. She gasped as she saw him appear at the back gate. Her hand instinctively dropped and she let the small white stick fall through the planks between the steps.

Somehow she forced a smile.

He was wearing his customary jeans and ancient T-shirt. He was smiling at her just the way she loved him to smile.

Tom.

The father of her baby.

She thought she might faint.

'Are you okay?' He knew her well, this man. He opened the gate and came towards her, looking worried, and she made a huge effort and summoned a smile to greet him.

'H-hi. Yes, I'm fine.' And then she thought he wouldn't believe that. She knew she'd lost colour. 'I think I ate something at lunch,' she told him. 'I did a house call on Bert Hathaway and he insisted I try one of his homemade sausages. It's been sitting like a lump of lead in my stomach all afternoon.'

'He makes great sausages.'

'Says the man with a cast-iron stomach. Do you know how much chilli he puts in those things?'

'That's why I know they're safe. No bug could stand the heat. Are you vomiting? Need a nice injection? I'm just the man for the job.'

'I'm sure you are but no, thanks.'

'And I have the all-clear to give as many injections as I want,' he told her, smiling down at her. 'As of today I have my driving licence back. I'm classified normal.'

That was good—wasn't it? She was so confused her head was having trouble operating her tongue. 'Your arm and leg still aren't what they should be,' she managed.

'I'll keep on with the rehab,' he told her. 'But I'm improving every day. Thanks to you.'

'Just because I'm bossy...'

'Sometimes a man needs bossy,' he said, and sat down on the step beside her.

She didn't want him to sit down. She wanted to get up and run.

The sun was almost down. The sky was tinged with the gold of a truly amazing sunset. Grass parrots were settling in the gumtrees around the house, squawking as they fought for the best nesting perch. A cat was purring across her feet. Two more were prowling under the steps.

She was sitting on the back step with the man she loved with all her heart, and all she wanted to do was run.

'Tasha,' he said gently, and her heart did a back flip.

'I… Yes.'

'A letter came to the surgery today,' he told her. 'It was addressed to Dr T. S. Blake. I'm T. R., but I didn't notice. It was in a pile of specialist letters. They all look the same and I didn't even think. I opened it and read it before I realised. I'm sorry.'

And he flipped a letter from his back pocket, tugged it open and handed it over.

It was a formal letter from the IVF clinic.

Dear Dr Blake
We have received your letter advising us that you wish us to cancel your appointment and dispose of the sperm held in your name. To do this, however, we need you to complete the attached legal documents.
    You are required to have the forms witnessed…
    Please return the forms to…

Documents were attached. This was the formal acknowledgement that she wished never to have a child.

That she wished for no more pain.

She held the letter in her hand and watched the letters blur, as the lines on the pregnancy test had blurred moments ago. Her head felt like it might explode. She wanted to shrink into nothing. Disappear.

'I guess Paul used your married name when he deposited the sperm,' Tom said helpfully from the sidelines. 'Though I would have thought they'd use your full name.'

'I'm sorry,' she said, because she couldn't think what else to say.

'You don't need to apologise.' He put a hand over hers. 'Tasha, was this decision because of us? Were you intending to try for another child and cancelled because of what happened between us?'

'It's nothing to do with you.' Except it was. Now it was.

'I can't bear it,' he said at last. 'That I hurt you…'

'You didn't hurt me.'

'I know I wasn't meant to read it,' he said. 'But this letter tells me you'd made the decision to try again for a baby, and now you've cancelled.' He shook his head. 'Tasha, they attached a copy of your letter. You wrote it the day you moved out of my home.'

'I should be grateful,' she whispered. 'I'd forgotten how much love hurts. All you did was remind me. This decision is all about me, not about you.'

'Tasha…'

And then he paused, his attention caught by what was happening at his feet.

Two cats had been snooping under the steps where they'd been sitting. They were agile, curious Burmese, ready to play with anything.

Neither Tasha nor Tom had been paying them attention but they'd been playing with something. Batting it forward.

Now one creamy paw batted their plaything out from the narrow opening under the bottom step. The cats had to go sideways to get out, so for a moment their toy lay untended.

It was a white plastic stick. It showed two red lines facing upwards.

Tasha couldn't move. She sat frozen as Tom reached forward, almost idly, as if it was of no importance at all that he was picking up a pregnancy test stick and reading the results.

The cats yowled their protest that their toy had been taken from them. The parrots kept on squawking overhead. The surf was a faint hush-hush in the background.

All Tasha heard was white noise. The world spun. And then Tom was pushing her head down between her knees, holding her, supporting her while she decided whether to retch or faint—or do nothing.

Nothing was safest. Nothing was what she wanted most in the world.

Tom sat silent and let her have her nothing.

It couldn't last. Of course it couldn't. She sat, head bowed, while Tom ran his fingers through her curls and the silence between them built to a crescendo.

When Tom finally spoke his voice sounded as if it came from a long way away. 'Tasha…' He stopped, cleared his throat and tried again. 'Tasha, are you pregnant?'

'I… Yes.' There was nothing else to say.

He looked at the stick again, then set it aside to pick up the letter and re-read. 'This means… Tasha, did you contact the IVF people to cancel *before* you knew you were pregnant?'

'Yes.' What did he think? That she'd deliberately used his sperm instead? The thought made her want to laugh but there was no way she could laugh. She was so close to hysterics.

Unbidden, her hands went to her belly again. Tom noticed. She knew he'd noticed.

He started stroking her hair again, as one would stroke a wounded wild creature, giving reassurance that help was at hand. Only help wasn't at hand. She was flailing. 'We were careful,' he said, and she heard shock underneath the caring.

She had to make herself talk.

'One of my professors once said the only sure contraceptive is a brick wall,' she managed. 'Tom, I'm sorry.'

Her voice was muffled. She had to straighten. She did but heaven only knew the effort it cost her. To sit up and face the world…

To sit up and face Tom.

'When did you find out?' he asked, still in that strange, neutral voice.

'I've been off colour for a couple of days. This morning…' She bit her lip. 'I woke up and knew. I just knew.'

'So just today.'

'Y-yes.'

'And it's mine.'

That was harder. She had to struggle to make her lips move. 'Yes.' She should say something else, she thought, but she couldn't make herself think what.

Would he be angry?

He didn't sound angry.

Of all the sensations whirling around them right now, anger didn't seem one of them.

There was a long silence. It must have hit him like a sledgehammer, she thought, but the sledgehammer had been at work on her as well and she didn't have a clue where to take this. But finally he spoke.

'Tasha, could you bear to have it?'

And there it was, out in the open.

Could she have Tom's baby?

The thought was so immense it took her breath away. To carry a baby for nine months? To give birth to a little one who looked like Tom? To watch Tom fall in love with his child as she knew instinctively that he would?

Family. The chasm was right before her but instead of running away she seemed to have stepped forward so one foot was in mid-air. Maybe both feet were.

'Tasha, don't look like that.' He turned her face with his lovely strong hands, forcing her to meet his gaze. 'Love, this little one's safe. You know the odds of what happened to Emily are so small that they melt into insignificance. There's nothing to say our baby won't be perfect.'

There it was. *Our baby.* She was trapped in her own terror. Her hands still clutched her belly.

Tom's hand closed over hers and held.

'Tasha,' he said, strongly, forcefully. 'This will be okay. This will be good. We can do this.'

We. There it was again.

'Tasha, you can trust me.'

At least he got it, she thought. At least he understood the chasm of faith that was required—faith that she was unable to give.

But she couldn't answer him. She tried but no words came out.

'Cup of tea,' he said, suddenly cheerful. He schecked out the stick's red lines again, then tucked it into his pocket. 'Yep, I'd call that a definite positive. We should keep this. It's the first entry in our baby's memento book. But meanwhile, tea with lots of sugar. I could handle a beer but just this once I'll forgo it. Two mugs of tea coming up.'

Tasha stayed on the step, gazing at nothing. Tom headed into the kitchen, found the mugs among the kitsch and made two mugs of tea.

And tried to come to terms with what he'd just learned.

Tasha was having a baby.

His baby.

Their baby.

The thought was almost overwhelming.

He'd never imagined this. As long as he could remember, he'd thought of himself as a loner. Relationships couldn't be trusted. He couldn't be trusted. He'd never met a woman who he'd known he could commit to for the rest of his life and he'd assumed he never could.

And then there was Tasha. For the first time he'd felt the beginnings of trust in himself. For the first time he'd thought that here was a woman he wanted to spend the rest of his life with. Betrayal was out of the question because this was Tasha. Hurting Tasha, betraying Tasha's trust, would be like ripping out a part of himself.

He suddenly found himself thinking of that tiny grave high on the headland. Of Emily. Of the way her tiny fingers had curled around his. Of the way her wide eyes had struggled to focus. Of the feel of her tiny body against his. Her newborn smell.

He wanted it. He ached for it.

He wanted a family.

How far had he come since he'd met Tasha?

And how to ease her pain now?

He took the tea outside and she was still staring sightlessly down at Rhonda's pot plants. He stared for them for a while, too. They were pretty boring.

'Seen one geranium, seen 'em all,' he ventured, and Tasha hiccupped on something that might have been a sob. He sat down and pressed her tea into her hands.

'Drink.'

'I don't need—'

'Doctor's orders. Drink.'

She did. Slowly. He drank his, too, and by the time they'd finished the sun had set and it was almost dark.

'I don't know what to do,' she whispered at last.

He took her empty mug and set it down on the veranda and tried to find a way in.

'Do you want a termination?' The words were a slash across the silence of the night and she drew in her breath with a shocked hiss.

But she didn't answer straight away. It's on the table, he thought, and the sensation hurt.

The silence stretched on. Finally her hands went back her belly, the movement a protective gesture as old as time itself.

'No,' she whispered. 'How can I? It's real. A baby…'

'Our baby,' he said again into the night, feeling almost

light-headed with relief. He'd never thought he wanted a child. Why was he suddenly desperate for this one? His hands rested against hers as he searched for the next thing to say. The right thing. 'Tasha, whatever else is between us, this is non-negotiable. You're not doing this as a single parent. I'm with you every step of the way. I know you don't trust me. I know you don't want a relationship between us and I accept that. But you will need support...'

'So here it comes again,' she managed, suddenly sounding dreary. 'You support me during Emily's loss. I support you after your injury. You support me while this one's born... We're taking turns.'

'It doesn't need to be taking turns,' he said softly. 'We can support each other forever.'

'Tom...'

'I know—you can't,' he said. 'So we'll do what we need to do to care for this little one with all the love we can muster.'

'I don't want to stay here.' It was a wail and he gave a rueful smile.

'There's no need for you to stay.'

'But it's your baby.'

'And if I need to, I'll leave Cray Point.'

She turned and stared at him in stupefaction. 'You'd leave...'

'I've hardly thought this through,' he said ruefully. 'But my initial feeling... Tasha, if you need to return to England, then maybe I can, too. Don't worry. I won't turn into some weird stalker. We can still live separate lives but I'll not ask you to parent on your own. I can get work wherever.'

'But you love it here.'

'I love you.'

The words seemed to take all the air from her lungs. She was flailing. 'Tom...'

'I never thought I'd say those words but it's true,' he

continued. 'You don't want it and I accept that, but, Tasha, I will love our baby. I'll be there whenever you need me and whenever he or she...' He frowned. 'Who is this, by the way.'

'I have no idea,' she snapped, torn between tears and laughter. 'The pregnancy test doesn't come with blue for boy, pink for girl. It's currently the size of a tadpole.'

He grinned, that gorgeous smile that had her heart twisting. 'I wasn't talking about our baby's gender. I was talking of names. Hey, my grandma used to call tadpoles pollywiggles. How's that for a name? Yes? Okay, I'll be there whenever Pollywig needs me. Birth? If you want me there, check. Teething? I sing a cool lullaby as long as she's into Pink Floyd. First day at school? I'll probably cry.'

'Tom!' She was practically crying herself. 'You can't put your life on hold...'

'See, that's what I hadn't figured,' he said gravely, and his hands tightened on hers. 'But finally I have it sorted. Life isn't Cray Point. Life is family.'

'Tom, I can't...' It was practically a wail.

'You don't need to do anything,' he told her. 'You definitely don't need to commit to me. All I ask is that you accept you have family. I'm your ex-half-brother-in-law who's now the father of your baby. That seems pretty much family to me.' And before she knew what he was about he leaned forward and kissed her lightly on the lips. It was a feather kiss, a fleeting touch, a gesture of reassurance and warmth. Surely nothing more.

'Are you sure you don't need anything for nausea?' he asked. 'I'm starting to not believe your sausage story.'

'It was a fib,' she confessed.

'So...morning sickness?'

'Nothing I can't handle.'

'Tasha, you will ask for help?'

She took a deep breath. 'I will ask for help.'

'And you'll stay for the next two weeks at least.'

'I will do that.' Because what option did she have?

But suddenly she thought, *The terror has faded.* The overwhelming, paralysing fear when she'd seen those two lines had dissipated.

'Pollywig...' she said tentatively, and he smiled and touched her hair.

'It's a fine name, but we can discuss options if you like.'

'I like Pollywig.'

'So do I.' He rose and smiled down at her. 'And I like Pollywig's mum. But Pollywig's mum needs to head to bed and get her head around the new norm. And me... I'm heading out behind the wheel of my little car to celebrate the fact that I can drive again. And I'm going to be a dad. It's been quite a day.'

'It has. Tom...'

'Mmm?'

'Thank you.'

'Think nothing of it,' he said grandly. 'And don't you dare go to bed and tremble. Together we can cope with one cute Pollywig. Together we can do anything.'

And he leant forward again and his lips brushed her forehead.

And then he was gone and the night was darker for his going.

Who could sleep?

She lay in bed and stared up at the darkness and called herself all kinds of coward.

Tom loved her. She knew it. She could see it in the way he looked at her. She could feel it in the way he touched her. She just...knew it.

It would be so easy to walk into his arms and let the future take over.

Become Mrs Blake again? Pregnant.

Rhonda and Hilda had left strict instructions as to the temperature the cats needed for comfort. The house was constantly overheated, but right now she was cold.

Why was she shaking? It wasn't as if she was frightened of Tom, and surely logic would decree that this pregnancy should be fine. The odds were on her side.

She was pregnant with Tom's baby. She suddenly felt a burst of warmth amid the fear.

This baby would be Tom's. He wanted to be its father.

Pollywig.

'It's a lousy name for a baby,' she said out loud, and she almost found the courage to smile.

Tom had said he'd move from Cray Point to be a father. She couldn't make him do that.

So live here? He'd suggested a medical partnership.

But part of her shut down at the thought. Working with Tom every day... She couldn't.

Why? she asked herself, but the same part refused to answer.

Because she loved Tom? Because she couldn't bear to see him every day?

Because she was a coward?

None of those things, she told herself savagely. It was just that there was an attraction between them that couldn't be denied, and she was being sensible. She wanted no part of it so she needed to leave.

But she couldn't go back to England. It wouldn't be fair to Tom.

Or to her?

For home felt like here.

'It does not.' She said it out loud and one of the cats wandering past her bedroom door leaped in fright and bolted for the company of his mates. 'I don't have a home.'

'You'll need to make one. So think about sensible.'

Sensible was what she needed. She needed to make

plans, get herself under control again, stop the crazy vortex in her head once and for all.

'Summer Bay.' There was a sensible thought. Summer Bay, where Tom had gone to rehab, was a town big enough for a large medical centre with half a dozen doctors. She could get a job, relieving at first, and then as Pollywig grew maybe full-time work.

She had money from Paul's life insurance. She could buy a wee house.

Maybe a puppy…

Tom could visit. The towns were only half an hour apart. It was a sensible distance, where Tom could be as involved as he wanted with Pollywig but their lives could be as separate as they needed to be.

'I wouldn't even have to know who he was dating.' She said that out loud, too. It should have sounded sensible. It should have sounded reassuring but instead it came out a bit…petty?

All of a sudden she felt silly and just a little bit small. To not have the courage to trust…

'I can't help it,' she told the night, and the night just had to listen. 'I'm not built to trust again.'

'You're a coward.'

'Yes, but I'm a pregnant coward and I need to look after me for my baby's sake.'

'That's an excuse and you know it.'

'Okay, I'm afraid,' she said out loud. 'I'm a great blob of yellow custard, quivering at the edges, and there's not a thing I can do about it. So go to sleep.'

She closed her eyes but sleep wouldn't come. The quivering wasn't helping.

CHAPTER TEN

RHONDA RETURNED THE next day. Hilda was arriving later, with their father. 'There's been a hitch in his visa arrangements but he should be here in two weeks,' Rhonda told Tasha, and Tasha thought that was excellent. That'd give her two weeks to finalise things here and find somewhere to live in Summer Bay.

'How's Tom?' Rhonda asked, and Tasha thought of all the things she could say—but didn't.

'His recovery's remarkable,' she said instead. 'He still has left-sided weakness but it's fading almost to unnoticeable. Another month and he should be back to normal.'

'But you're only staying for two more weeks?' Rhonda looked at her sharply. 'And you've moved in here. Conflict? Tom's women?'

'He's not dating at the moment but that's part of it,' she agreed. 'I didn't want to get in the way of his lifestyle.'

'You do know he doesn't enjoy his lifestyle very much,' Rhonda told her. Rhonda's luggage was still in the hall and the cats were tangling themselves round her legs in ecstasy, but she was homing right in on Tom as if she'd been worrying the entire time she'd been away. She probably had.

'There are lots of good women in Cray Point,' Rhonda told her. 'Our Dr Tom is quite a catch. He's always been a looker, and he's lovely. Clever and skilled and kind. But even when he was a teen he dated girls who were older,

more experienced, less likely to be clingy. His mother used
to worry. Why didn't he find himself a nice girl who wanted
to settle down and have babies? We could see it, though.
His mother was a watering pot. She never disguised the fact
that Tom's father broke her heart, and she never let Tom
forget the fact that he looked just like his father.

'"Don't you ever do that to a girl," she'd say over and
over, and she'd say it to everyone. "I do hope he doesn't
turn out like his dad." She was a beautiful ninnyhammer,
our Marjorie, and I reckon it's affected Tom all his life. If
you say something to a child often enough, he'll believe it.
At least no one's saying it to him now but it's probably too
late. How can we get our Dr Tom to commit?'

She already had, Tasha thought bleakly. He had committed.

But she'd done just what his mother had done.

She'd accused him of being like his father. And his
brother.

Worse, she'd believed it. A part of her still did believe it
and she wasn't brave enough to walk away from that belief.

For the next few days things seemed to slow down. Life felt
in slow motion. It was a strange sensation but that was how
she felt. She had slight morning sickness but not much. She
kept waiting for the signs of miscarriage but none came. She
kept feeling the pregnancy was some sort of dream, but a
week later, when she went to see the charge doctor of the
Summer Bay medical group about a job, she confessed that
her work would be part-time. And because Adam Myers'
specialty was obstetrics, she confessed why and ended up
having a full examination.

'Lovely and normal,' Adam told her, and when she told
him what she was most afraid of, he pulled the stats up on
the internet and told her what the chances were of it happening again.

'Somewhere between infinitesimal and none,' he told her. 'We'll scan at twenty weeks. A good paediatric cardiologist should pick up on any problems then, but I'm willing to bet my new employee's monthly wage cheque on a good outcome.' His kindly face creased into a smile of concern. 'It'll be great to have you on board, Tasha. Having a new emergency physician will be amazing. But tell me...' He hesitated. 'Why are you leaving Cray Point? I hear Tom Blake's desperate for a partner.'

'Tom's my ex-brother-in-law,' she said, trying to sound diffident. As if it was of no moment. 'That's why I came here in the first place, to help him while he was ill. But I don't want to work with him.'

Adam nodded and then looked studiously down at Tasha's notes. 'And your baby's father?' he said gently. 'Would he be on the scene?'

And there was no use hiding it. If things went to plan, this man would be delivering her baby, and Tom had made it quite clear he wanted to be there for her.

'Tom's the father.'

She waited for shock. She waited for condemnation but none came. Instead, Adam searched her face with concern. He was a man in his sixties, with the air of a doctor who'd seen it all, and was surprised by nothing. 'I know Tom well,' he said at last. 'I suspect he'll make an excellent father, if he's involved.'

'That's what he wants,' she admitted. 'I'm not sure it's what I want. This pregnancy...wasn't exactly planned.'

He shook his head in mock disgust. 'Really? I have no idea what they teach medical students these days, but I'm thinking I need to write to the people who trained you.' There was another silence while who knew what went through the obstetrician's head, but finally he beamed. 'Well, well,' he said. 'Planned or not, you should make this work. You and Tom... Cray Point and Summer Bay aren't so far apart. Barring complications, you can deliver here in Summer Bay hospital. We're small but we're good. You'll find this a supportive practice and with Tom supporting you as well...'

'I don't need his support.'

'There's no one I'd rather have as my support person,' Adam said gently. 'As a doctor, Tom Blake is one in a million. I have no idea what he'd be like as a partner or a father but I'm guessing good.' And then he shook his head. 'But that's none of my business, so all I'll say is welcome to Summer Bay, Dr Raymond. We'll be very happy to have you on board.'

She still had a week to go at Cray Point. She drove back feeling faintly ill but it wasn't morning sickness this time.

Why was everyone telling her what a great guy Tom was? Why did she feel that everyone was seeing something she couldn't see?

Or was it the other way round? Was it that she was seeing—fearing?—something that wasn't there?

Tom wasn't pressing her. After that one night on the back steps with the cat and the pregnancy stick he seemed to have retired into the background. He let her be.

She still saw him in morning surgery but she'd stopped going to rehab with him. As far as she knew he was back to setting candles and flowers on the veranda.

'You really are a coward.' She said it out loud as she drove back along the coast road but there wasn't anything she could do about it. Her fear was too deeply ingrained.

'I love him,' she said out loud, but admitting it made the knot of fear tug even tighter.

'So I'm a coward,' she told herself. 'I can't take a chance, but to do anything else seemed impossible.'

Tom wouldn't pressure her. He'd be there for her baby and that was lovely. Sort of.

If she only had the courage…

'I don't,' she whispered. 'And there's not a thing I can do about it.'

Three more days.

Hilda and her father were due back on Tuesday. Tom still wasn't operating at a hundred percent but he was coping.

There was a nice little hospital apartment waiting for her at Summer Bay.

She'd done what she'd come for. She needed to move on. With baby.

But she was trying very hard not to think of baby. It was so early. She could still miscarry. Anything could happen.

'You're a wound-up ball of emotion,' Rhonda told her. 'Why not relax, dear? Tom wants to take over. Why not let him? Enjoy your last weekend. You could even go surfing. Tom reckons he'll be back in the surf any day now.'

'All the more reason for me not to relax,' she snapped, and then she recovered and apologised.

What was happening to her? She was turning into a grouch.

Maybe that's what terror did.

She spent Saturday morning thinking about packing but most of the time she sat and stared out the window to the bay beyond. She needed to organise her own car. She needed to organise her new home, to move on, but she seemed trapped in a fog of lethargy.

'It'll be fine,' she told herself. 'I have a great new job. I have a neat apartment and I can choose a lovely new car. I'll…'

And then she paused because she couldn't think past that.

I'll what?

Carry this baby to term? Have a safe delivery? Live happily every after?

Without Tom.

Without courage.

She was feeling so bleak she was close to tears, but tears were stupid. When the phone rang she was so desperate for distraction she almost ran to it, but Rhonda beat her. And as Tasha reached the hall she saw Rhonda's face lose colour.

'It's Tom,' Rhonda said, putting the phone down, and the look on her face scared Tasha to the bone.

'Another bleed?' Please, God, not another bleed.

'Tasha, no, sorry. I've scared you more than Karen's just scared me. No, Tom's okay.'

'Karen?'

'You know Karen, our taxi driver. She's rung to say three lads have been bird-nesting on the cliffs above the bluff. Alex, James and Rowan. Of course, those three again! Of all the idiots… It's loose shale and a sheer drop to the rocks and surf below. Stupid, stupid kids. It was Rowan who almost killed himself last time and came close to killing Tom with him. Rowan only suffered bruises but Tom ended up with a cerebral bleed. Now it's James at the bottom of the cliff, and Tom's saying he's climbing down to help him. With his weak leg and arm. Karen says can we come because someone's got to stop him, but the lad's in trouble and Tom says he's going anyway.'

It should take ten minutes to get from Rhonda's to the bluff but Rhonda covered it in what seemed two, driving like someone in a James Bond movie and swearing all the time.

'Idiot, idiot, idiot,' she kept muttering. 'He thinks he has to save the world. Where would this town be without him, and he risks it all for one stupid kid? Again.'

'Do we know how badly James is hurt?' Tasha asked in a small voice as Rhonda took the next turn on two wheels. Tasha hardly noticed.

'Broken leg. Pete Simmonds has gone down—they

called him first because he's a climber. An abseiler. He went down, risking himself, but he says there's hardly room on the ledge for one. Apparently he's anchored James and come up again to let a medic go down. Karen says there's something urgent needs doing with James's leg that can't wait for the rescue chopper. So Tom's saying he's going down and Pete's just realised how weak Tom's leg is and Karen says you need to talk sense into him.'

Talk sense into a Blake boy? She didn't think so but Rhonda swung the car off the road onto the bluff and skidded to a halt beside the Cray Point fire truck, and Tasha was left with no choice but to try.

Tom was already kitted up. He was wearing a harness. He was kneeling by the cliff edge, sorting gear into a backpack, looking grim. He didn't look up as Tasha approached. He didn't see her until she put her hand on her shoulder and held. Hard.

'What do you think you're doing?' she asked, and she was a bit stunned by how her voice came out. She sounded angry.

But he kept right on packing. 'I need to go down,' he told her. 'James has a compound leg fracture. Pete says it's bent back at an impossible angle and the foot's cold to the touch. He's conscious, ten feet above the surf. The rescue chopper's caught up with an overturned boat and might be an hour. I'm going down now.'

'Have you abseiled this type of cliff before?'

'Pete's told me how.'

'So that's a no?'

'I can do it.'

'With a gammy leg and a gammy arm.'

'There's no choice and you know it.' Still he didn't look up. 'If I don't go down, he loses his leg. He might die.'

He was moving morphine ampules from his bag into

the backpack. She stooped, took the ampoules from him and put them in herself.

'Just pack the light stuff,' she said. 'You can lower saline, oxygen, anything heavy I need when I'm down there. I'll need a thinner loop line attached as well so we can guide stuff down.' She looked up at a man who must be Pete—he was big, burly and carrying a coil of businesslike rope. 'Can we organise that?'

'Sure, Doc,' Pete said with an uneasy glance at Tom. 'I'm so sorry I can't do stuff myself but I never learned any first aid. Blood makes me want to pass out and the last thing the kid needs down there is me unconscious on top of him.' He hesitated. 'So you reckon you're going down instead of Tom?'

'Of course I am.'

Tom sat back on his heels and stared.

'Of course you're not. I can do this.'

'You might be able to,' she said, meeting his gaze square on, 'if you're lucky. But you have no climbing skills and you still have left-sided weakness. Pete, what are the odds on a first-time climber making it?'

'I don't like it,' Pete said. 'It's loose shale. You can't depend on footholds. The kids were damned fools to be here. It'll take skill.'

'I have skill,' she said evenly, and then both men were staring at her.

'You,' Tom said, as if she'd suddenly grown two heads.

'It's called trying to keep up with Paul,' she said. 'He wanted to climb things, and for a while I tried to go with him.' She managed a smile. 'I gave up in the end—Paul was never happy unless the climb was dangerous and it turned out he didn't want me with him anyway—but I learned from good people and I've climbed places more difficult than this. Take off the harness, Tom. This is my call.'

'It's dangerous,' Tom said.

'But you were going down.'

'I'm not pregnant,' he retorted.

And suddenly she grinned. Suddenly it seemed like she was back in her emergency ward in London, arguing responsibility with a macho colleague. Equal rights for women had come a long way in medicine but there were still male doctors with a deep-seated belief in their own superiority.

She'd learned to bypass them with humour, no matter how grim the situation. Now she simply reached out and tugged Tom's harness. She took one shoulder, Pete took the other and the harness was removed from Tom before he could react.

'You're right, I'm pregnant and you're not,' she agreed equitably. 'At least I hope you're not. But I don't exactly have a bulge big enough to get bumped. Next objection, Dr Blake?'

'You can't. Hell, Tasha... I'll go nuts if you go down there.'

'Because?'

'It's dangerous.'

'You've already said that. So you'd rather I sat up here and thought the same about you.'

'Yes!'

She smiled again, then looked at the people clustered around them. 'Okay, let's make this democratic. Rhonda, Pete, Karen, we need to vote. On this side of the argument I give you an experienced emergency medicine specialist with solid abseiling skills. I've done much harder climbs than this. I'm fit and I'm prepared. I'll admit I'm also in the very early stages of pregnancy but I have no side effects and that shouldn't make a difference at all.'

'But that's my baby,' Tom groaned, while the onlookers' collective jaws dropped.

'That makes a difference how?' Tasha asked serenely. 'It

seems Pollywig's about to have an adventure. You taught me with Emily to introduce my baby to life early. So... Pete, Karen, Rhonda, on the other side of the equation we have Tom, a skilled doctor admittedly, but with no experience in this sort of climbing and residual left-sided weakness. We need to vote. Now.'

But there was no voting to be done. Pete was clipping her harness on, and after a moment's loaded silence Tom finished loading the bag. His face was drawn, his mouth grim.

He rose and helped her on with the backpack. 'You dare fall...'

'I don't dare anything,' she told him, taking the backpack and meeting his gaze square on. 'It's the Blake boys who dare. I'm using my skill set. There's a difference.'

'I shouldn't let you.'

'Sense, Tom, instead of bravado. Who's the most sensible candidate for the job?'

He closed his eyes and when he opened them again she knew he agreed. He still looked grim but he also looked resigned.

'I'm with you every inch of the way.'

'I know.'

And then he smiled, a weary smile that said he was hating what was happening but he knew it was inevitable. Then he took her shoulders and tugged her forward and kissed her.

It was a fast kiss, as circumstances dictated it must be, but it packed a punch. It was hard and strong and an affirmation of worry, of fear. Of love?

And there was also something else. When he pulled away she saw an expression that could only be described as pride. 'You're one amazing woman, Tasha Raymond,' he told her.

'I'm a doctor doing her job,' she told her, and only she

knew just how much she wanted to sink back into his arms. But there was work to be done. 'Let's get me down there.'

She'd sounded confident when she'd talked her way into this job. In truth, she was a long way from confident. Climbs could be graded in difficulty and this was high on the scale. The shale and the lack of footholds, the knowledge that her feet could dislodge rock that could fall to the boy below, the steepness of the slope and the roar of the surf...they combined to make a climb where she had to use every one of her skills to keep herself safe.

Pete must have known but he hadn't said, she thought as she manoeuvred herself down the cliff, and she thought Pete would probably prefer it was her risking her neck rather than Tom. Because Tom was the town's doctor and the town loved Tom.

As she loved Tom. His image stayed with her, as did the look on his face as she disappeared over the edge of the cliff. There wasn't a person there who didn't look frightened, but Tom...

He looked haggard and she hated that he looked like that.

Every trace of her concentration was taken with climbing, keeping herself steady, not disturbing the shale, but deep within she was conscious of an almost subconscious undercurrent of thought.

Tom was almost as terrified for her as she'd once been terrified for Emily. But he'd let her go. He'd conceded she had the skills and he'd stepped aside, even if it had almost killed him.

She was suddenly thinking of Rhonda's words.

'It was Rowan nearly killed himself last time and nearly killed Tom with him. Rowan ended up only with bruises but Tom ended up with a cerebral bleed.'

And suddenly she was thinking of the meaning behind Rhonda's words. Maybe she hadn't asked enough questions. She'd assumed Tom had been injured doing his own reckless, Blake boy thing, but maybe he hadn't. Maybe he'd been in the position she was in now, where he was the one with the skills. He'd been able to surf so he'd been the one to rescue Rowan.

Smashing his head might not have been because of reckless behaviour. It might not have been no more reckless than what she was doing now.

She'd categorised him as a Blake boy. A womaniser. A testosterone-driven risk-taker.

Maybe she'd been wrong.

She was two-thirds of the way down now, closer to the boy at the bottom than she was to Tom, but suddenly she felt so close to Tom it was as if he was physically beside her.

It had taken courage to let her go. She knew it had. How much harder to stand aside and let the one you love take the risks...

She was taking a risk now, she acknowledged as she fought to keep herself steady, fought to stop herself spinning and hitting the shale.

How much greater a risk was falling for Tom?

How much greater a risk than falling was loving someone who loved her?

And then she found herself thinking of Iris and Ron and their appalling relationship, and then back to her own dreadful marriage. And suddenly she was swinging on a rope half way down a cliff, thinking she must have had rocks in her head until now.

'Because Tom's been my very best friend for almost two years,' she whispered. 'So how can I possibly compare? I think I must have been a little bit mad.'

He was going quietly crazy.

Pete was doing all the work, feeding out line, keeping

in radio contact to give advice, keeping Tasha as safe as he could, so for the moment there was nothing Tom could do.

Pete's face was grim. He knew the risks. He knew what Tasha was being asked to do.

James's parents were clinging to each other. James's friends were huddled against their parents, turned from defiant teens to children again, wanting comfort.

'We were just trying to reach the easy nests from the top,' Rowan was muttering, and his dad gave him a clout across the shoulders and then hugged him.

That was pretty much how Tom was feeling. Anger and love. Anger that Tasha should be in this position. Anger that she'd even offered to go. Fury and frustration that he'd had to accept that offer.

Pride and love that she was down there, working to save a life.

Tasha. The woman he loved with all his heart.

He'd never thought he could feel like this.

His father and his half-brother had walked out on women they'd sworn to love, betraying them in the worst possible way.

'They didn't really love.' He said it out loud, not caring who heard, and suddenly Rhonda was beside him, putting her hand in his.

'She'll be okay.'

'You don't know that.'

'We all love her,' Rhonda said. 'And she's amazing. You know that, too. All she has to do is climb down a few more feet, straighten one leg and wait for the chopper. What's hard about that?'

But her hand tightened convulsively in his as she spoke and he glanced down at her and saw his fear reflected on her face.

We all love her.

Cray Point had taken her to their hearts. He'd taken her to his heart.

He wanted her.

'Dear God, let her be safe.' He'd wanted her for himself but it didn't matter. He'd barter everything if she could be okay. She could go and live in Summer Bay. She could go back to England if she wanted.

Just let her live.

She made it.

James was huddled in a ball of fear and pain and hardly acknowledged her arrival. Apart from a brief murmur, a touch of reassurance, the first few moments had to be taken with finding herself safe footholds and attaching anchors. There was practically no room. How James had fallen onto what looked like the only outcrop that could hold him was a miracle.

Pete had anchored James as best he could, but he'd also placed a harness on the boy's shoulders and attached a rope. He'd taken the other end back up to the top when he'd left.

That was worst-case scenario, Tasha knew. That was in case the ledge crumbled or James fell. Anchors were only as solid as the cliff face they were attached to.

That was the reason she stayed in her harness now and wouldn't release the tension of the rope from above. It was her link to safety.

To Tom.

James was huddled hard against the cliff, as far from the edge as it was possible to be—which meant there was about eight inches between his back and the fall to the waves below. He stirred as she arrived but he didn't turn to look at her.

She had to balance on the edge of the ledge to examine him, fighting an instinctive urge to cling to the cliff itself.

'James, you know me,' she told him, bending close so

he could hear her over the sound of the surf. 'Doc. Tasha. I saw you when you had a sore throat last month.'

'T-Tom,' James groaned. 'Where's Tom?'

'Up the top of the cliff, where you should be.' She was doing a fast visual assessment. The boy was scratched and bleeding from multiple lacerations. He must have hit shale all the way down. His clothing was ripped and blood-stained. He had a deep cut above his left eye but it was already congealing.

She felt his pulse. It was steady and strong, which was a small reassurance. If he had internal bleeding he'd be in shock by now. She felt his ribs, his abdomen and found nothing obvious. He was conscious, and the kids had said that he'd called out to them as he'd landed, so a head injury was unlikely.

But his leg was twisted at an impossible angle.

She touched the skin at his ankle and winced. Pete was right. His foot was blue and bloodless and cool. This was a compound fracture with compromised blood supply. The tiny amount of blood getting through wasn't enough to keep the foot alive.

He had no massive haematoma or obvious bleed. That meant the vein was probably intact but kinked like a garden hose.

If he wasn't to lose his foot, she had to straighten the leg. Help.

She needed a theatre. She needed an orthopaedic surgeon, an anaesthetist and a full complement of theatre staff.

'Tasha?'

The voice in her headphones was Tom's and it steadied her. She took a deep breath and answered, one doctor to another.

'I'm down. James is conscious but in a lot of pain. I'm about to give him something to ease it. Five milligrams of morphine intravenously?'

'Right,' Tom said, and it helped to hear him agree. She knew she was right, but saying it out loud settled her. It was as if she had a colleague beside her.

She did have a colleague beside her. Tom was with her every inch of the way.

'James, I'm giving you a shot of something that'll dull the pain,' she told him. 'It won't stop it completely but it'll help.' Then she spoke directly into the speaker attached to her headphones. 'Fractured leg with almost nil blood supply to the foot. Tom, work with me. I need anaesthetist advice.'

'Give me a moment.'

'Thank you,' she said, knowing he'd guessed, grateful that she didn't have to say out loud that she was afraid the morphine wouldn't be enough, that reduction in such circumstances might send James into shock, that she needed to talk to a specialist. He'd guessed she was afraid.

She injected morphine. She washed the worst of the grime from James's face. She worried about how long that leg could stay viable.

And then Tom was speaking again.

'The best option's methoxyflurane,' he told her. 'It's a rapid, short-term analgesic using a portable inhaler and it's in a pack at the base of your backpack. Do you know it?'

'I've heard of it,' she said cautiously. 'I haven't used it.'

'It's mostly used by paramedics and people like me who operate outside the confines of a major hospital. We use it when we need to do acute procedures fast without an anaesthetist, or for high-dose pain relief during transfer. Relief begins after six to eight breaths. As long as James is haemodynamically stable…'

'He is.'

'Then we can use it. Can I talk to him?'

'Sure.' She tugged off her earpieces and put one on James. Then she unashamedly stooped and held the other a little way back so she could listen.

'James, this is Tom. How's it going?'

'B-Bloody,' James managed, but Tasha could tell by his face that even this minimal contact with a doctor he trusted was a reassurance.

'Tasha says you've busted your leg. Idiot,' Tom said, but he sounded almost cheerful, businesslike, as if this was little more than a scratch that had to be disinfected. 'She's given you some morphine, which will make you nice and dopey, but the problem is that your leg's a bit bent and the blood's not getting through to the foot.'

'I can't…see.'

'Nor would you want to,' Tom said. 'Bent legs aren't pretty. So Tasha's going to straighten it. She needs to do that before there's long-term damage to your foot, so unless you want to limp for life you'll need to put up with what she does. Sorry, mate, but it's going to hurt. But not for long. Tasha's good, she's fast and we'll get the leg straight and you up the cliff before you know it.'

'I don't want to be here.'

'Yeah, well, you fell down,' Tom said unsympathetically. 'But we're getting the chopper to lift you up. Your mum and dad are up here, ready to give you a good telling-off for bird-nesting in such a dumb place, but they want to give you a hug first. But first your foot. To ease the pain you need to breathe in through the inhaler Tasha gives you. After six to eight breaths the relief will kick in. What Tasha does will hurt but it's just a momentary thing while she sets your leg in position. If you keep breathing through the mask, concentrating on breathing and not the pain, it'll settle. Would you like me to keep talking as she works?'

'Y-yes.'

'Then let's go for it,' Tom said. 'Tasha?'

How did he know she was listening? 'Yes?'

'Go for it, love,' he told her. 'You can do this. I'm with you both.'

* * *

She needed X-rays. She needed her patient under a general anaesthetic. She needed a nice clean hospital, and space to work. And an anaesthetic strong enough to hold the pain at bay so she could manoeuvre the fracture slowly, figuring out the best way to re-establish blood supply.

She had none of those things and Tom could only guess at the stress she was under. Pete had taken photos of the smashed leg on his phone before he'd come back up the cliff. The photos were not great quality but Tom could see splintered bone, a mess, a nightmare to try to straighten in these circumstances.

He wanted to tell Tasha not to beat herself up if she failed. He wanted to tell her he expected her to fail, that what she was doing was a long shot.

He couldn't, though, because she'd put the earphones onto James and his role now was to keep James calm so Tasha could work. As well as that, James's parents were within earshot, hanging on his every word.

He could say nothing at all.

She'd told Tom she could.

She had no choice.

It was incredibly difficult to balance on the tiny amount of ledge space she had. The rope attached to her harness was still taut, carefully played so that as she moved it was pulled out and reined in. She wasn't alone. She had Pete holding her harness.

She also had Tom talking to James while James breathed through the mask. It was almost as if Tom was playing the role of anaesthetist.

She had a whole clifftop of people with her every step of the way.

It takes a village to raise a child. Where had that line

come from? She couldn't remember, but there was a village at the top of the cliff. A village who cared.

She'd worked in emergency wards for almost all of her professional life. She'd been surrounded by a team.

Now she should feel isolated, afraid, but strangely she didn't. Her team—her village—was a little distant but it was still there. And Tom was with her. He was at the top of the cliff. He was talking to James but he was still with her.

He was her rock in all this. Tom.

Despite the circumstances, she forced herself to take her time, to think clearly about the way she'd do this. She knew that she had a tiny window to get the vein unkinked. The anaesthetic couldn't mask such pain completely. After a first attempt James would react, his body would freeze and she'd be lucky if she could get near him for a second try.

But for now he seemed almost relaxed. He was trying out the inhaler, breathing steadily, listening to Tom.

She cut the last of his shredded pants away from his leg and spent a little time familiarising herself with every inch of the fractured limb.

The tibia and fibula were both broken. She could see the breaks. They'd been smashed hard across, splintering.

She could feel a pulse above the break but not below. There was little blood getting through.

She sat and looked for as long as she needed to steady herself, to figure how she should hold the leg, how she should pull.

'Tom says how's it going?' James asked in a fuzzy voice, and she knew the anaesthetic was now as strong as it could be.

'Tell Tom we're set to go,' she told him, and placed her hands firmly—confidently?—where she needed them. 'Tell Tom to stay tuned; your leg's about to be fixed.'

* * *

'Tasha says we're ready to go,' James whispered between breaths, and Tom felt ill. He wanted to be there. He needed to be there.

'It'll hurt,' he warned the boy. 'But only for a moment. Hang on in there, mate, and whatever you do, don't move. Can you do that?'

'Y-yeah.'

'I know you can. We're all with you. Tell Tasha that, too.'

And then he listened as James murmured to Tasha. Then:

'She says she knows,' James whispered. 'She says I gotta lie still and think of playing footy next year. She says if I lie still she'll come and barrack for me.'

'I bet she will,' Tom said unsteadily. 'And I'll come, too. But for now just breathe through the inhaler. Deep breaths…'

And then James screamed.

Seconds felt like hours. She still held James's leg firmly, so he couldn't react by hauling back, twisting, possibly undoing what she'd hoped she'd done.

She could hear the faint sound of Tom's voice speaking to James in the background. He was the one talking James down from the peak of pain.

He had to be. Her hands held James's leg and every trace of her concentration was on the foot below the break. She was holding the leg steady and she was pleading. Please…

And when it came she could hardly believe it. A trace of colour…

I'm imagining it, she told herself, but a moment later she knew she wasn't. She dared to touch his ankle and she felt…a pulse.

'Oh, James,' she said weakly, and then she forced herself to speak more strongly because even though she felt weak at the knees James had to see her as physician in charge. 'Well done, you. Well done, us. Blood's getting through to your foot. You're going to be okay.'

'Y-you hear?' James managed, and she knew he was speaking to Tom.

And then James managed a wan smile.

'Tom says to tell you you're a bloody hero,' he told her. 'He says he knows Mum won't let me swear but that's what you are. But, strewth, Doc, that hurt.'

The chopper arrived twenty minutes later. It was a complex operation, getting James onto a cradle with his leg firmly fixed, securing him, then swinging him up to the top of the cliff.

For a while Tasha was left sitting by herself on the ledge, and almost as soon as the cradle swung outwards she started to shake.

When they finally came for her, they had to treat her as a patient. She was shaking too much to be of any assistance.

'Got you, sweetheart,' the cheerful paramedic said as he harnessed himself to her. They swung off the ledge and hung momentarily over the ocean. 'You're safe.'

She didn't feel safe. She didn't feel safe until she was lowered onto solid ground on the clifftop.

Until she was gathered into Tom's arms and held.

Until she was home.

CHAPTER ELEVEN

Tom went with the chopper to Melbourne. The paramedic
in charge accepted Tom's offer with relief.

'I'll say yes, mate,' he told him. 'You guys have done
brilliantly, getting that blood supply working, and I don't
want it blocking again on my watch. If you're in the back
with him we have more chance of doing something if it
blocks again.'

So Tom gave Tasha a hard, swift hug and followed James
into the chopper.

'Look after her, Rhonda,' he ordered, and Rhonda took
over the Tasha-hugging and nodded.

'She'll be looked after. Every single person in this town
will be offering to make her cups of tea but I'm first.'

'I wouldn't mind a whisky,' Tasha told her, but managed
a smile. 'But tea will be great. I'll stay on duty.'

'I know you will,' Tom said, the warmth in his smile a
caress all by itself, and then he swung himself into the helicopter, the engine roared into full power and he was gone.

She went home with Rhonda, who bullied her into a
bath, then made her eat, then left her to relax.

Tasha knew where she needed to be. She walked slowly
up to the headland, to the cemetery, to a tiny grave. Who
knew how long she sat there? She didn't know. All she
knew was that the tumult that had been in her head, seem-

ingly since the time she'd learned of Paul's betrayal, had somehow settled.

Tonight there were things that needed to be said. She might as well say them first to her daughter.

'Tom's right,' she told her. 'He's not a Blake boy. He's just Tom.' And then she thought about her words and decided they needed changing.

'But he's not *just* Tom,' she said. 'He's my Tom and I love him. And maybe it's time I realised what brave really is.'

Once the chopper had landed at The Melbourne, once a specialist medical team had wheeled into motion and once James's mum and dad were assured James was in the best possible care, Tom was free to leave. There was a bus in the morning. He could get a bed at the hospital and Tasha was in Cray Point tonight to cope with any emergencies. There was no need to hurry back. Regardless, he hired a car. What was the point of finally being permitted to drive again if he didn't? He headed home.

To Tasha?

He needed to stop that train of thought, he told himself as he drove. Tasha was leaving. Living in Summer Bay, he'd see her often, as a friend, as the mother of his child, but for now he needed to back off and let her be.

But he wanted to see her, and he wanted to see her *now*.

What excuse did he have? None, he thought, but as he drove into Cray Point it was all he could do not to turn towards Rhonda's.

He had no reason to take the turn. Tasha would know James was safe. Rhonda had been on the phone demanding frequent updates, and he knew she'd have passed them on to the town.

Tasha would know everything she needed to know.

Except how much she was loved?

She knew that, too, he told himself, but it didn't make any difference. She didn't want him.

What a joke. He'd finally met a woman he wanted to share the rest of his life with, and she had the same mistrust of commitment he'd spent his life with.

He turned the last bend towards home, feeling black.

The lights were on at his place. All the lights.

He pulled to a halt under the veranda and saw the table was set outside. A mass of candles formed a centrepiece to the table. A huge spray of wildflowers trailed under the candlelight.

Tasha was in the doorway.

His breath caught in his throat. She was wearing a sliver of a shimmering, silver dress, a dress that accentuated every luscious curve. Her curls were loose around her shoulders and her face looked almost luminescent.

She was smiling out at him as his car drew to a halt and he'd never seen anyone look more beautiful.

'Hi,' she called, and heaven knew the effort it cost to get his voice to work to call back.

'Hi.' He climbed from the car and glanced at the table, the crystal, the silver cutlery, the best dinner set, his grandmother's finest stuff he never used even for his more elaborate dinners. 'You're expecting company?'

'I'm expecting you.' She waved an airy hand towards the table. 'Rhonda said you were on your way back. Have I forgotten anything?'

He made his way cautiously up the veranda steps, feeling it behoved a man to be cautious. The look of her... He'd only ever seen her in casual and work clothes. This dress... He wanted to put his hands on her waist and hold.

She was stunning.

He was stunned.

'This looks a bit overkill for my usual dinners,' he said cautiously, and she smiled, a smile that lit her whole face.

'It's not a usual dinner,' she told him. 'Your seduction settings are for your trail of assorted women...'

'I do not have a trail...'

'You do have a trail,' she told him, lovingly though, as if she finally understood him, as if she wanted him just the way he was. 'They're very assorted. Rhonda tells me you've had fun and the women you've dined here have had fun as well. So I thought...maybe we could have fun, too.'

'You're offering to be...a part of my trail?'

She shook her head. She still stood in the doorway and he hadn't made it further than the top step. There seemed a vast distance. A distance he wasn't sure he could cross.

'Not a part of your trail,' she said softly, and for the first time she sounded a bit unsure. As if it was taking courage to say what she had to say. 'The end of your trail. And even though my trail hasn't been candles and flowers, I'm hoping it's the end of my trail, too. If you want me.'

The words took his breath away. He should step forward and sweep her into his arms right now, but somehow he forced himself to stay where he was. There were things he needed to sort. There were things he needed to know.

'You don't trust me,' he said at last.

'Past tense. That's my blindness and I'm sorry.' She wasn't moving either. She was leaning against the doorjamb as if she needed its support. 'I've never been very brave, you see.'

'I don't understand.'

She shrugged and tried for a smile that didn't quite come off. 'My parents were adventurers,' she told him. They were both in the army, and they put their hands up for any exciting conflict going. There were dramas all through my childhood—one or the other of them was always getting injured. That was practically the only time I saw them, when they were recuperating. When I grew up I thought

I'd be a doctor. It was a nice, safe profession, filled with good, dependable people.

'Only I must have had some of my parents' drive for adventure because I joined Médicins Sans Frontières and I met Paul. I fell for him. Heaven help me, I even tried to keep up with him. There were so many attempts at brave there, and every one of them was a disaster. After Paul I went back to being safe but then I thought I'd really like a baby. That felt huge. It felt totally unsafe but I did it anyway. My final brave.'

'And then Emily died,' he said softly, and she closed her eyes for a moment.

'Yes,' she whispered. 'And I thought that's the end. But there was a niggle that had me wanting another baby. Aching for another baby. Maybe I could summon enough courage to try one more time. But then…then I fell in love with you and I thought how like Paul you were. And I realised that I couldn't trust myself. The whole idea of a baby, of a future seemed to disintegrate and I thought, I don't have enough courage for anything.'

'Tasha, you're the bravest—'

But she shook her head. 'Wait. Please.' She took a deep breath and forced herself to go on. 'Tom, brave or not, I've finally figured…today I figured… I've had the definition wrong. Somehow in my muddle of a mind I equated brave with stupid. I thought you were like my parents. Like Paul. Like your dad. Taking risks for risks' sake.'

'It's not like that.'

'I know it's not,' she whispered. 'This morning when I thought you were climbing down the cliff, I was as terrified as I'd ever been. There you go, being brave again. Being stupid. And then Rhonda told me about your surfing accident. You went onto the reef deliberately to save Rowan. And on the cliff today… If you'd been Paul, there'd have been no way you'd have let me go down in your stead. So

I went there expecting to be terrified while you did your foolhardy thing. Instead, you accepted facts, you weighed risks and you let me go.'

'And I was terrified instead.'

'I know you were,' she whispered. 'And that's when I realised there's brave and brave. Brave isn't always about putting your life on the line. Brave's also about watching from the sidelines, letting the man you love take the risks he has to take, knowing he'll do the same for you.' She took a deep breath. 'Brave is also saying what's past is past and shouldn't affect the future. Brave might also be about saying I want a family. I want Pollywig to have a dad and I want to love her dad. And... And brave's saying I do love you.'

She stopped and the whole world seemed to hold its breath. Tom didn't speak. He couldn't. He couldn't begin to understand the surge of emotion in his chest. He could hardly begin to hope.

'Tom...' Tasha whispered, and he wanted to go to her but still he couldn't. He held out a hand as if to reach her but his body seemed frozen.

'So I thought I'd leave a proposal for after main course,' she said unsteadily. 'How do they do it in the movies? A ring in the chocolate mousse and then a comedy routine where our hero proposes while our heroine gets her stomach pumped to retrieve her diamond? But I'm not that brave.'

'You're brave enough for anything,' he managed, and finally he got his feet to work, finally he strode forward and took her waist in his hands and drew her to him. 'Love, what are you saying?'

'I'm asking whether this seduction scene has finally worked like it's supposed to,' she whispered, her voice muffled now against his chest. But then she pulled back. He held her at arm's length, gazing down into her gorgeous eyes, and she managed to smile up at him. And all the love in the world was in her eyes.

'I'm saying that finally I get this brave thing,' she whispered. 'And I'm going with it. So, Tom Blake, here's the thing.' She took a deep breath. 'I love you and I want to spend the rest of my life with you. I want to carry your child and I want to share. I want to be brave with you and occasionally I want to be a coward with you. I love you just the way you are, Tom Blake, and I can't wait until after the main course and I don't have a ring anyway so therefore...'

But he wouldn't let her go any further. He put his finger on her lips and shushed her and then he smiled, a smile that felt like it was turning him into a different person. A man who could walk forward from this moment.

'Allow me some pride, my love,' he told her. 'Damn, where's a diamond when you need one?' He glanced around at the ornate table, at his grandmother's silver napkin rings. He seized one and dropped to his knee.

'Tom...' Tasha was half laughing, half crying.

'Shh,' he told her. 'This is important.' And he took both her hands in his and gazed up at her. 'Tasha Raymond, it's my turn to be brave,' he told her. 'So I'm risking everything here, including the messing up of one heirloom napkin ring set. But what the heck. Tasha, will you do me the honour of becoming my wife?'

And what was a woman to say to that?

There was nothing to say. She dropped to her knees as well. He put the crazy, too-big ring on her finger and it almost fitted her fist. He smiled down at it and then he smiled at her.

He drew her into his arms and kissed her.

Tasha had gone to some trouble with the dinner. She'd made a casserole, with expensive steak and wine.

The casserole burned, for taking the casserole from the

oven when the timer went meant risking breaking the moment, and who were Tasha and Tom to take risks?

They weren't risk-takers.

They were very safe indeed.

There was no hospital at Cray Point. There was one at Summer Bay, though. With Adam Myers in charge, it had good obstetric care, so with all the scans showing normal, Tom and Tasha decided that's where their daughter would be born.

One beautiful autumn day Tasha went into natural labour.

For some reason Tasha had woken thinking the weeds had to be dealt with *immediately*. Tom had his way first, though, and they'd had a gentle morning's surf.

Tom had taught Tasha to surf on their honeymoon, but now it was as much as she could do to lie in the shallows and let the sun play on her bump. But that had felt pretty good.

They'd come home. She'd had a nap while Tom had started on the weeds and then she'd joined him. There were no medical imperatives. The soil was damp and still warm, so weeding was easy. Tasha finally confessed her contractions to Tom but she didn't want to stop.

'Let's get this bed done first,' she told him. 'I fancy sweet peas and cornflowers in spring.'

So—reluctantly on Tom's part—they weeded on, and Tasha grew quieter but more and more adamant that she wanted to stay where she was.

Finally she straightened and stretched and winced and gave in to what her body was telling her. 'Maybe it's time to go,' she admitted.

Tom needed no second telling. He'd packed the car the moment Tasha had admitted to her first contraction, and had taken Rambo, their six-month-old cocker spaniel, to

Iris for safekeeping. Keeping on weeding had been a superhuman effort on his part.

'We'll wait until the contractions are ten minutes apart and regular before we head for hospital,' Tasha had reminded him.

How many times had he told his patients that? Yet when it was his own he wanted to break every rule in the book.

But finally she was agreeing. She went inside to wash—and he found her at the sink, bent double with the force of the next contraction.

Tom practically carried her to the car, but as he helped her in, another contraction hit.

'That's less than two minutes,' he said blankly.

'I told you it was time,' Tasha managed when she could catch her breath. She was trying to sound serene but not quite managing it.

He practically ran to the driver's side. As he hit the ignition Tasha moaned with yet another contraction.

'You've got to be kidding!' The contractions seemed to be rolling into one.

'It's okay,' she muttered. 'There's plenty...of time.'

'Tasha...'

'Just drive.'

He turned out of the driveway, up along the headland towards the road to Summer Bay but he knew before he'd gone five hundred yards that they weren't going to make it.

'Um...' Tasha was arching back, moaning. 'Oh, Tom... Oh, whoops... I can feel... Tom, sorry, I might have mistimed... I thought we might...' She moaned through another contraction and then: 'Tom, stop!'

They were high on the headland. The land here sloped gently down to the sea in a vast sweep of lush autumnal green pasture. The view was breathtaking. How many times had they walked up here to lay flowers on Emily's grave, or to sit and talk, or simply be?

It was their favourite place in the world.

'Tom, stop this minute. Stop! *Oh-h-h-h...*'

There was nothing for him to do but pull to a halt.

Their baby was coming.

Help. He had obstetric supplies in the trunk—of course he did—but he didn't want supplies. He wanted a fully equipped hospital, specialist care, someone other than him...

There was no one. The sun was low on the horizon, sending a silver shimmer on the ocean that would soon turn to tangerine. It was late Sunday afternoon and the day trippers had long gone. The road was deserted, and Tasha was unmistakably moving into the second stage of labour.

'I think I need to push,' she said, quite conversationally, and Tom decided to panic. He was feeling as cowardly as he'd ever felt in his life.

'Hey, Tom, we can do this,' Tasha breathed. 'We've been brave before.'

'We take turns, remember?' It was a dumb thing to say but it was all he could think of.

'This time we share.'

He had no choice. He hauled himself together—somehow—grabbed a resus blanket from the trunk and laid it on the lush grass under a stand of gumtrees. He folded his jacket for a pillow.

He rang for the ambulance.

'Sure, Doc.' The paramedic sounded almost as if he'd expected the call. 'We're on our way. Keep us on speaker phone if you're worried. We'll talk you through it if you need us but you know what to do better than us.'

Strangely Tasha looked almost peaceful. The grass was long and soft underneath the blanket. A couple of cows were hanging their heads over the roadside fence, looking on with interest. The surf was a faint hush-hush below them and, now she was settled on her blanket, Tasha was riding each contraction with determination.

In between she seemed almost relaxed.

Tom wasn't.

'We've rehearsed this,' she managed, as the next contraction passed.

'We rehearsed me being up at your end with an obstetrician being at the business end.'

'Tom…'

'Tasha?'

'This is good,' she told him, but then another contraction hit, stronger than those before. Her serenity slipped and he heard the edge of panic. 'Okay. Maybe…maybe this wasn't a good idea,' she whispered. 'I think…I'm losing it.'

What wasn't a good idea? Had she planned this type of birth?

But it was too late to worry about that now. She needed him.

And wasn't that the whole truth? he thought as he gripped her hands while she rode out the next contraction. Tasha needed Tom. Tom needed Tasha.

Family…

And somehow things settled. Somehow the world righted on its axis.

He and Tasha were together and they were about to welcome the next addition to their family. All indications were that this birth was completely normal. What did he have to be brave about?

And finally he moved into medical mode.

'Small breaths,' he told her. 'Let's see if we can take this labour off the boil for a bit. The ambulance should be here soon. Pant.'

Tasha told him where he could put his panting.

'Tasha…'

'Let's…have…our…baby…' she managed. 'Oh…'

And two minutes later a perfect baby girl slithered out into the arms of her waiting father.

Tom sat back on his heels and gazed down in incredulity at the miracle in his arms. A daughter. He and Tasha had a daughter.

'Is she okay?' It was a whisper, a feather breath.

'She's perfect.' And then he caught himself. Skin to skin was almost the first rule of obstetrics. Now their baby was born, he needed to get her onto her mother's breast, and here he was, staring down like an idiot.

At his daughter.

She wasn't crying. She was wide-eyed, as if she was gazing straight at him.

He wanted to weep. Instead, he managed to be a tiny bit professional. He covered his daughter in his sweater and placed her on her Tasha's breast.

And then he forgot for a moment that he was the doctor in charge. This was his wife. This was his daughter. Who could stay professional?

He gathered them both into his arms and he held them as if they were the most precious creatures in the world.

As they were. His wife. His daughter.

'Rosamund?' Tasha whispered. 'After your grandma, right?'

'If that's okay...'

'It's perfect,' Tasha breathed, and her smile was so cat-that-got-the-cream that he pulled back a little.

'Did you plan this?'

'No,' she whispered. 'Or...I might have hidden a couple of contractions. I sort of wanted...'

To deliver her baby here, in peace, away from the clinical efficiency of the hospital, from anywhere that would have brought back memories of past pain. High on the headland where she could see all the way to the Antarctic. Where she could see the tiny township of Cray Point—their home.

Where she could even see the graveyard where Emily had been laid to rest.

He'd never have agreed, but it was too late to protest now, and indeed it was perfect.

They lay on the blanket, Rosamund warmly wrapped, enclosed between her mother and father.

Family.

They lay as the sun slipped further towards the horizon and started losing its warmth.

'We need to move,' Tom told her. 'Love…'

'Maybe we do.' She sighed and she wriggled a bit and found her phone, which was lying by her side. It was still showing a current call. Speaker phone was on.

'Maybe we do,' she said again. 'I think we're ready, guys.' And then she grinned at Tom, a smile that contained cheek as well as joy. 'You think I took a risk?' she said serenely. 'I never would, not with our family. I might be brave, but I'm not stupid.'

And within a minute the ambulance rounded the bend and pulled to a halt. Out of the ambulance came two paramedics, plus Brenda, plus Adam Myers, the Summer Bay obstetrician.

They moved seamlessly into action, a full obstetric team. Leaving Tom gobsmacked.

'You orchestrated this…' he managed.

'I hoped,' Tasha told him, smiling and smiling. Rosamund was sucking contentedly at her breast. Brenda was fussing with warm blankets. Adam was doing something about the placenta but who cared what? 'What's the point of being doctors if we can't have our tribe help us when we need them?' she asked. 'So I talked to Adam and he agreed…'

'I don't usually do home births,' Adam said gruffly. 'But this wasn't exactly a home birth. A birth with an ambulance parked right around the next bend, with all the equipment we could possibly need, with the two of you doctors… We were ready to pull out at a moment's notice if anything went wrong, and if there'd been some other medical emergency needing the ambulance—or even if the weather was bad—we never would have tried it. Tasha agreed to that but we pulled it off.'

Then the gruff obstetrician paused and glanced out over the cliffs to the sea beyond. 'We pulled it off,' he said again, sounding supremely contented. 'Given our time again, my wife and I might even have risked the same thing. Congratulations to you both. And, no, there's no need to thank us,' he said as Tom tried to think of what he could possibly say. 'The planning was fun and isn't that what life's supposed to be? We put up with the grey for the gold, and this is gold. All of us will remember it.'

And then he smiled at them both. 'But the sun's almost down,' he told them. 'There's a chill in the air. It's time to load you all into the ambulance and take you to a nice warm bed. It's time for you to move on to the next part of your lives.

And Tasha looked at Rosamund and smiled and smiled, and Tom looked at his wife and daughter and thought life couldn't be any more perfect than it was right now.

His Tasha. His one true love.

His brave heart, his soul-mate.

'I love you,' he whispered, and he gathered them close. His wife. His daughter. His family. And Tasha lifted her face to be kissed.

'I love you,' she whispered back.

And then they let the world take over as they moved seamlessly into the next stage of their lives.

Together.

* * * * *

THE SURGEON'S
BABY SURPRISE

BY
CHARLOTTE HAWKES

Published in Great Britain 2016
By Mills & Boon, an imprint of HarperCollins*Publishers*
1 London Bridge Street, London, SE1 9GF

© 2016 Charlotte Hawkes

ISBN: 978-0-263-92624-8

Dear Reader,

There are some truly brave and inspirational individuals in this world.

When I first came up with the idea of a heroine in need of a kidney transplant I knew I needed a woman who was strong, determined, and courageous enough to overcome her fears. The more I researched, the more moving stories I read about just such women. Women who, with their partners' support, had risked everything to have a precious baby of their own.

Then I stumbled on a support site for Living Donors—people who had donated one of their kidneys to family, friends, or even complete strangers. It was truly humbling, and so Annie, my heroine's older sister and her very own Living Donor, was born.

I do hope you enjoy reading *The Surgeon's Baby Surprise* as much as I enjoyed writing it. I'd love it if you dropped by my website—charlottehawkes.com—or found me on Twitter @CHawkesUK.

Charlotte

To my wonderful little boys, Monty & Bart.
I love you both '*to a million pieces*'—xxx

Books by Charlotte Hawkes

Mills & Boon Medical Romance

The Army Doc's Secret Wife

Visit the Author Profile page at millsandboon.co.uk.

PROLOGUE

'DIFFICULT CASE, DR PARKER?'

Evie snapped her head off the cool glass of the vending machine at the unmistakeably masculine voice and tried to quash the fluttering of attraction suddenly tumbling in her stomach, despite her inner turmoil.

When was she going to get over this particularly inopportune attraction?

A moment ago, her brain had been swimming with a particularly challenging case. After a day of fighting for her patient and consistently hitting a brick wall, she was feeling drained and unhopeful, but a question from one of Silvertrees' foremost plastic and orthoplastic surgeons, Maximilian Van Berg, and she felt more fired up than ever.

Just as she did every time she was around the man.

Evie hastily dredged up a bright smile. Professional but not too flirty. He liked professional, as demonstrated by his use of her title rather than just using her first name as other colleagues did. And he didn't care much for flirts— any more than Evie cared to be thought of as one.

'Nothing I can't handle, Mr Van Berg.'

None of this *Dr* Van Berg for Max. He was old-school, trained by the Royal College of Surgeons, and he used his right to revert to *Mr* to reflect that.

'That I don't doubt,' Max murmured to her surprise before turning to the vending machine. 'Has this thing been swallowing money again?'

Wait, did he just compliment her—and in a voice that was sexy as hell?

Her nerve-endings tingled at the uncharacteristic gravelly tone. She was used to his clipped all-business tone with colleagues. In fact it was a shame Maximilian Van Berg wasn't a paediatric plastic surgeon—she got the feeling he wouldn't put his own reputation ahead of the best interests of a patient. He had attended the Youth Care Residential Centre where she normally worked a few times, and they'd always seen eye to eye on the cases then. Part of her itched to run this case by him, too, but he would certainly deem that unprofessional of her. She needed to push all thoughts from today out of her head for the night, think about other things and come back to it, refreshed, in the morning.

Instead, Evie allowed herself a covert assessment of the man beside her. He was wearing off-duty gear, which, she concluded grudgingly, only managed to underscore a muscled, athletic physique more suited to some chiselled movie star than the gifted surgeon the man actually was. As a psychiatrist, Evie only came to Silvertrees when she referred a case from her centre for troubled teens, but even she knew that Max was the golden boy of the hospital. And it hadn't surprised her to learn how high a proportion of the hospital staff had apparently attempted to land the man, succumbing to the heady combination of undeniable surgical skills and brooding good looks.

But it seemed that what made him most irresistible was the fact that Max was also intensely private. He was committed to his career, notoriously elusive, and inflexible in his rules about keeping emotions and personal life out of his department; on the rare occasions he was snapped by the media at high-profile events, his dates were always the most stunning media starlets, hanging perfectly on his arm

He strongly disapproved of co-workers dating and had even earned himself the moniker Demon of Discipline. She had never known him to break his own rules, and she could still hear the censure in his tone when he'd heard about her semi-relationship with one of his colleagues.

And yet, during her not infrequent visits to Silvertrees, hadn't she sensed some kind of spark between the two of them whenever they'd met?

Not that she meant to act on it, of course. She knew his rigid reputation only too well, which was one of the reasons she'd enthused about whatever—in reality, lacklustre—relationship she'd been in at the time they'd first met. And it had worked: Max had relaxed in her company, assured that she wasn't flirting with him. Still she'd sometimes felt there was an uncharacteristic softness from him during the rare moments they'd been alone together.

'Dr Parker?' He broke into her musings. 'I asked if the vending machine has been swallowing money again.'

Evie glanced through the glass panel to the item currently lodged, frustratingly precariously, on the half-open metal distribution arm, and sighed.

'The last of my small change...' she nodded, unable to help herself from adding '...and I'm starving.'

Evie tried not to gape as he fished in his pocket for coins for her. Or to notice the way his trousers pulled tantalisingly taut around well-honed thighs as he did so.

'What were you after?' he asked, his eyes not leaving hers.

Evie startled. If it had been anyone else offering to buy her a vending-machine snack she doubted she would have hesitated, but with Max it somehow seemed a more intimate gesture.

'It's just a granola bar, Dr Parker.' He sounded almost amused, as though he could read her thoughts.

She was being ridiculous; she gave an imperceptible

shake of her head. It was foolish to allow her own futile attraction to him to lead her to imagine there was more to the simple act than he actually intended.

'As it happens,' she managed wryly, 'it was the raspberry and white chocolate muffin.'

'A sweet tooth.' He smiled. 'I didn't imagine that.'

A charge of heat fizzed through her. Logically, Evie knew he meant nothing by it but she couldn't shake the idea that he'd imagined anything about her at all. Just a shame it wasn't the same X-rated images she'd been unsuccessfully fighting whenever *she* imagined *him*.

'It's a weakness.' She fought to show a casual smile, but she couldn't help her tongue from darting out to moisten suddenly parched lips.

As Max's eyes flicked straight down to the movement, Evie could have kicked herself for giving too much away. All she could do now was hold her ground and feign innocence, fighting the tingling heat as his eyes tracked up to meet hers. Boy, she hoped he couldn't really read her thoughts.

'Mine's dark chocolate,' he replied eventually, releasing her gaze as he turned flippantly back to the machine.

'Sorry?' She drew in a surreptitious deep breath.

'My weakness. At least seventy per cent cocoa solids, though probably not more than eighty-five.'

As weaknesses went it was hardly significant yet she felt a thrill of pleasure. In all the time she'd known him she'd never once known him to make such small talk. It loaned her an unexpected confidence.

'I didn't think the lauded Max Van Berg had any weaknesses,' she teased daringly.

'I have them.' He met her gaze head-on again. 'I just make it a point not to show them.'

She swallowed abruptly before taking the proffered muffin from him and promptly tearing off a chunk as her empty stomach growled its appreciation. It had been a long, busy day.

'I can't believe you're still here, going through patient files. Shouldn't you be home, sleeping after a long shift? Or is that another weakness in your book?'

It was meant to be a joke but in her nervousness it came out more clipped than she'd intended. Fortunately, he didn't seem to notice as he cast a grim gaze up the corridor.

'No, I was boxing off my open cases before I leave next week.'

'Oh, that's right.' Evie dipped her head; she remembered hearing something about that. 'You're going away to work with Médecins Sans Frontières, aren't you?'

'An eight-month project in the Gaza Strip,' he acknowledged grimly, shadows chasing across his handsome profile as he turned his head away. 'Helping burn victims, performing reconstructive surgery, amputations.'

'From the fighting?' Her heart flip-flopped at the idea of him risking his life in such an environment.

'Sometimes.' Max shrugged. 'But around seventy-five per cent of my patients will be kids under five years old.'

'I don't understand.'

'Electricity is cut off on a daily basis so the people rely on power from domestic-size gas containers for cooking or to heat their homes. But because the canisters are such poor quality, explosions are an everyday occurrence, and children are usually the victims.'

'It sounds like...rewarding work,' she managed weakly, studying his expression of grim determination.

'It is,' he agreed.

And it was essentially Max Van Berg. On the occasions she'd been to Silvertrees, Evie had found he was the surgeon every trauma doctor wanted to hear was on call for any orthoplastic cases with trauma victims from the A&E.

She certainly wasn't surprised that MSF had snapped up a surgeon of Max's calibre.

'I wish every surgeon had your desire to help,' she murmured.

'Problems?'

Why was she hesitating? What did she have to lose?

'It that why you were leaning on the glass, staring so grimly into the machine when I first came into the lounge?' he enquired. 'Because it wasn't for your lost muffin.'

Evie wrinkled her nose. He moved to the coffee machine as she followed on autopilot, refusing to let him intimidate her and trying to ignore the defined muscles that bunched and shifted beneath his black tee shirt.

'I was just thinking about my patient,' she hedged.

'Go on.'

She smiled as his interest was instantly piqued. She could have taken a bet on that. Anything patient-related and it had Max's attention.

'Like I said, nothing I can't handle.'

'I imagine you can,' he repeated. 'We've worked together a couple of times now, Dr Parker. You're focused and you're dedicated to your patients but you don't make rash decisions. I respect your opinion as a psychiatrist, Doctor, and I like that.'

She stared at him in delight until the happiness turned to heat as he pinned her down with an intense gaze of his own.

'I like that a lot,' he repeated, his voice a low rumble. 'In plastics particularly, it's important to me to know who wants my help, and who truly needs it to turn their life around. Sometimes it's easy to tell but other times it isn't so clear-cut.'

Caught in his regard, she felt the atmosphere between them shift slightly. Heat began to rise in her face, travelling down her neck, through her chest until it pooled at the apex between her legs. This was the effect Max always had on her. Sometimes, the way he looked at her almost convinced her he was attracted to her, too.

But that was just fanciful thinking, wasn't it? She'd give anything to know what he was thinking, *right now*.

'Thank you, I—'

'So, how's she doing?'

'Sorry?'

'Your patient with the significant breast asymmetry.'

Another thrill fizzed through Evie. *Had he been watching her?*

She hastily reprimanded herself. It was the cases Max was interested in, not the fact that she was on them. She shouldn't be surprised that he knew the patient. She would bet he kept track of all the cases that came through his department—he was that kind of conscientious surgeon.

'That *is* why you were staring so distractedly into the vending machine, I take it? I also heard you've been reading the Riot Act to one of my colleagues. Are you always this passionate about your patients, Dr Parker?'

Evie blinked, suddenly thrown. His guess might be off, but his assessment of her state of mind was surprisingly on the money.

She had always got deeply involved with her patients, it was true. Her work at the centre had always been more than a job; it had been a calling. But he was right, this case felt personal. She needed to win this battle and help this young girl change her life.

Because this week Evie had received the worst news of her life. Her own body was failing her and soon she might not even be able to help herself, let alone anybody else.

It hadn't been completely out of the blue. Fifteen years ago she'd been diagnosed with polycystic kidney disease, PKD, but she'd never shown any symptoms. However, during her routine check-up this week, to her shock, decreased kidney function had been detected. Her nephrologist had warned her that, whilst she could continue as normal for now, within the next six to twelve months she would begin to feel too exhausted to even continue as a doctor, and within a couple of years she would need a kidney transplant.

If she didn't get a new kidney she would never be able to help another troubled child, never have a child of her own. Worst-case scenario, she might not even have her life.

She hadn't confided it to a soul. She hadn't wanted to. And part of her had an inexplicable urge to spill all her fears to this man right here, right now. If she could trust anyone with this secret, it would be Maximilian Van Berg.

Yet another part of her held back. Better to stay away from her personal problems, concentrate on someone she *could* help: her patient.

Evie drew in a breath and sipped tentatively at the hot drink to steady her nerves.

'Honestly, it's just that my patient really does need this operation, not just for the obvious physical benefit but, as far as I'm concerned, for her mental well-being. She's on the brink of psychological depression, becoming more and more disruptive in school, and becoming so reclusive that her social skills aren't developing.'

'The issue, as I've seen, is that one of her breasts is barely an A-cup and the other is almost a D-cup, so the need for an operation in the future is inevitable?' he stated abruptly.

'Right.' Evie nodded as Max frowned. So he *had* been looking into the case file.

'She can't wear a bra that fits, she can't go swimming with her friends, or go to friends' houses for a sleepover. She can't even change in front of them for a basic PE lesson in school without being taunted. It's making her withdraw socially, and she's now developing stress-induced Irritable Bowel Syndrome.'

'I read the file, Dr Parker,' he responded, removing his drink from the machine and taking a generous gulp.

The man must have an asbestos mouth.

She gave an imperceptible shake of her head to refocus her thoughts.

'However, the paediatric surgeon we spoke to doesn't want to operate due to her young age. He doesn't want to operate when the patient is still growing and developing, and he doesn't know if she could cope mentally with the procedures, including an implant.'

'He has a point.'

'I appreciate that, and you must know how cautious I am about making such recommendations. But I've worked with this girl for almost a year. I don't believe its body dysmorphic disorder, and I know it's a fear of all paediatric plastic surgeons that they could miss such a diagnosis. In this case it clearly isn't an imagined or minor so-called defect in her appearance. It is something which is understandably imposing significant limitations on her life.'

'And what about realising the impact of these procedures? Does your patient understand that her body will never be perfect, that she will have to deal with the scars from the operation?'

'She absolutely does understand that. But, in her own words, the scar is something she could live with. It wouldn't prevent her from wearing a bra, or a swimsuit, or a prom dress. All things she currently can't do.'

He pinned her with a look that was more about the undercurrents running between them than the conversation they were ostensibly having.

'And your assessment is that this procedure isn't just

about rectifying the physical problem but is necessary for developing well-being?'

'I think it's essential to her self-esteem and her social development at this crucial time in her life, Mr Van Berg.'

Her hands shook as she took another steadying sip of her coffee, her eyes still locked with his over the plastic rim.

'Then I'll take a look at the case before I leave.'

'You would do that for her?'

'I told you before, I respect you as one professional to another,' he growled. 'So, how's the boyfriend?'

Evie stiffened. As it happened her latest attempt at a boyfriend had resulted in being unceremoniously dumped when his mother had deemed her *not good enough* for her precious son, after Evie had revealed that she would never be able to give the woman the longed-for grandchild.

She hadn't loved the guy, but, still, it had been painful. It had hurt being told that she wasn't good enough, an echo of the hurt she'd felt when her father had walked out all those years ago.

But surely Max couldn't know about her pathetic love-life? She'd be a laughing stock. Hospital gossip was an unstoppable machine, everyone knew that, but, not working at Silvertrees permanently, she'd always convinced herself that she escaped the worst of it. Still, if people *did* know, then she couldn't afford to lie to Max now.

'Gone.'

She fought to affect nonchalance.

'Good. He didn't deserve you anyway,' Max murmured, his hand reaching slowly up to lower the cup from her lips.

'You didn't know him,' she protested mildly.

'I know if he lost you, he's a loser.'

Evie swallowed hard, unable to tear her eyes away from his.

'I'm going to check on your patient now. All I ask in return is that you join me for a drink in the bar across the way as soon as I can get away from this farewell party I'm supposed to be at right now.'

'What about your business and pleasure rule?' she whispered.

'In a few days, I won't even be in this country, let alone this hospital.' He gave a lopsided grin, so sexy it made her toes curl. 'I think we can bend the rules this once, don't you?'

His head inched closer until his nose skimmed hers. It was like some kind of exquisite torture.

She knew she should be strong, back away. But didn't she know only too well that life was short?

Stretching her neck, she closed the gap between them, a small sound of pleasure escaping her throat as her lips met his.

Max responded without hesitation. One hand slid around the back of her head as the other pulled her firmly to him. The reality of the feel of his solid body even more impressive than the eye had allowed the mind to imagine. His teeth grazed her lips as his tongue danced seductively. He might seem dedicated to his career and refuse to date within the hospital pool, but there was no doubting that Max had dated. He knew exactly what he was doing to her.

It was all Evie could do to raise her hands and grip his shoulders and she hung on for the ride.

'Is that you?'

'Is what me?' she muttered, frustrated that he'd pulled away from her.

'The beeper.' His voice was laced with amusement.

Slowly a familiar sound filtered into her head.

'Oh, that's me,' she gasped as her brain slowly clicked back into gear.

'Yes…' the corners of his lips twitched as she stood dazed and immobile '…Evangeline. You need to go now.'

'I do,' she murmured, muscle memory allowing her legs

to start moving, backwards but in the right direction, even as her brain felt frazzled.

'I'll go and see your patient. When you're done with whatever your message is you can come and find me. I'll be back in my office.'

'I... Okay, I'll...see you later, Mr Van Berg.'

She watched Max turn smoothly and walk towards the double doors at the far end of the corridor, unable to stop him or say anything. It was only when her back slammed into something solid that she realised she'd reached the double doors at her own end.

She wanted to say something, but no words would come.

'Oh, and, Evangeline?' Max twisted his head to call over his shoulder. 'For the rest of tonight shall we agree that it's *Max*, and not *Mr Van Berg*?'

A slow grin spread over her face as he disappeared through the doors.

CHAPTER ONE

EVIE PACED THE hospital corridor.

The wait was excruciating. The squeak of her shoes sounded unusually distracting as she slowly turned on the polished floor. The ever-present smell of disinfectant pervaded her olfactory senses in a way it never had before, so strong that she could almost taste it. Once she'd been a doctor here, now she was a patient like anyone else. She could wait in the visitors' room but there was already a woman in there who seemed to want to talk every time Evie was in there.

And anyway, out here she felt more in control, and closer to her sister-in-law, Annie. Beyond the double doors, Annie was going through yet another set of checks to confirm that she was still suitable to be Evie's living donor for a new kidney. But after almost a year and a bombardment of test after test to confirm compatibility and eligibility, these final cross-matching and blood-pressure checks still had to be run.

She subconsciously touched her lower abdomen, more out of habit than pain since the cramps had already subsided after today's dialysis session. Less than a week and this whole nightmare would hopefully be behind her.

Yet that wasn't even what had her heart performing its real show-stopping drum solo, as it had every single visit she'd made to Silvertrees since that night with Max, almost one year ago to the day. The double doors clanged at the end of the corridor, causing her to whirl around, her heart in her throat, just as it had been every other hospital visit in the last four months since he'd returned from Gaza. But it was always just patients or hospital staff she didn't know or barely recognised. Evie had no reason to think she would ever just *bump into* Max here. The transplant unit was in a dedicated wing set slightly apart from the main hospital. And yet every time she feared—and hoped—that the next person to walk through the doors would be him.

She could have chosen a different hospital, the one closer to where she now called home, but Evie's referral to the state-of-the-art facility at Silvertrees was like gold dust and she'd have been a fool to turn it down for fear of bumping into a man who, for all intents and purposes, had been nothing more than a one—okay, five—night stand.

At least, that was the argument she told herself, and the one she was sticking with. After the two catastrophic attempts she'd made to contact him when he'd still been in Gaza, to tell him about the baby they had created together, she wasn't about to admit out loud that some traitorous part of her secretly dreamed that Fate might intervene. That, in the silence of the night, a tiny, muffled voice challenged her to venture into the main hospital and find him.

Not that she had any idea what she would say to him. How she would even attempt to begin to explain the choices that she'd made. In her heart she knew everything she'd done had been for their baby—a miracle, given the deterioration in Evie's kidney condition at the time of the pregnancy—but it didn't make her feel good about herself.

And still.

She'd hardly been in a state to think clearly when she'd accepted the hush money. In a daze from her premature baby and her kidney failure, rushing between NICU and her dialysis sessions. So when Max's parents—the people who should have their son's best interests at heart—had told her that neither they, nor their son, would want anything to do with the baby, a fiercely protective new-mother instinct of her own had kicked in. She'd worked with enough troubled teens to know how damaging it could be when a child was unloved, unwanted. And she had her own painful experience of being left by her father, too.

Both she and Imogen deserved better than that. They deserved to be cherished, not made to feel like a burden. And so Evie had allowed herself to be persuaded it was in her precious baby's best interests not to tell Max Van Berg he was a father.

But what if she'd been wrong? What if Max *would* have wanted to know about his daughter? Her head whirled with doubts, drowning out the sound of the double doors slamming open once again.

'Evie?'

Goosebumps swept across her skin. She didn't turn around; she couldn't. The voice was painfully familiar and intensely masculine. It evoked a host of memories that Evie had spent a year trying unsuccessfully to bury. A prong of doubt speared her insides. Had she been wrong to believe he didn't care? Because in that perfect moment Max actually sounded happy—albeit a little shocked—to see her.

She swallowed ineffectually, her mouth too parched, and her heart wasn't so much beating in her chest as assaulting her chest wall. Whatever she'd imagined, she wasn't mentally prepared for this but there was nothing else for it.

Steeling herself against the kick from the moment she laid eyes on Max again, Evie lifted her head boldly and completed a slow one-eighty.

She hadn't steeled herself enough.

'Max.' She gritted her teeth, striving to sound calm. In control.

'What are you doing here, Evie?'

There was still no trace of chilliness in his tone. *Was that a good thing, or a bad one?* It suggested he knew nothing about Imogen, so maybe there was still hope. But then again, it also meant he'd been happy with their fling and certainly hadn't been thinking about her these last twelve months so the bombshell of a daughter wouldn't be well received.

So she stayed silent and contented herself with drinking in the man she recalled so very intimately.

Time apart had done little to diminish the sheer physical presence he exuded and she was grateful for the few feet of space between them, acting as something of a safety buffer, both mentally and physically. But space couldn't erase everything. The way Max looked and the authority he exuded. The feel of his skin beneath her hands and her body. The way he smelled—no overpowering aftershave for Max, but instead a faint, intoxicating masculine scent underpinned with a hint of lime basil shower gel she remembered only too well.

'Are you working here again?' he pushed.

'No.'

Silence hung between them.

'Evangeline, why are you here?'

She had to say something. She was standing in the middle of a dedicated transplant unit—she had to explain her visit somehow. So she settled for a half-truth.

'My sister-in-law has some tests before her appointment with Mrs Goodwin,' Evie started carefully, studying his face for any kind of reaction.

'Arabella Goodwin?' He frowned. 'The nephrologist?'

'That's right,' she confirmed slowly.

'Is it serious?'

Evie searched his face; she needed to be careful here. Really be sure of herself before she said anything.

Admittedly, he seemed genuinely interested, but that

meant nothing. This was the side of Max she knew, his sincere concern for his patients and their families. But it didn't mean he wanted a family of his own. It just meant he was dedicated to his career.

Just as his parents had cruelly reminded her.

Just as they'd made her see that, for Max at least, their short-lived fling had been just that. It certainly hadn't been the start of something. He hadn't asked her to wait for him whilst he was away in Gaza. He hadn't even told her that his parents were the renowned surgeons she had read about, attended guest speaker talks to see, studied, throughout her medical studies.

In short, they had shared five nights and four days of intense, unparalleled intimacy, yet told each other so very little about their lives beyond the bedroom.

What if she told him everything now only for him—out of some ill-considered knee-jerk sense of obligation—to involve himself in their lives, only to resent his daughter's existence every time it even threatened to impact on his career?

Wasn't that the nightmare scenario his parents had painted for her? Right before they'd offered her enough money to secure her daughter's financial future in the event that her kidney transplant failed and she wasn't around to look after her precious daughter herself?

But it wasn't just what they'd said, it had been their calm, assured delivery. As if they were acting in her interests as much as in their son's. As if they really believed that her taking the money and staying away was the best solution for everyone. *That* was what had convinced her to take their word for it.

The savage protectiveness Evie felt for her new daughter still caught her unawares sometimes. There was nothing she wouldn't do to protect her beautiful daughter from anything which—or anyone who—could potentially hurt her.

If the Van Bergs had been cruel or vindictive, she probably wouldn't have believed them, wouldn't have taken the money. But she'd been frightened. And vulnerable. Between her bleak prognosis and her premature baby, she hadn't been able to face a battle on a third front. And if his parents were right and Max didn't want to know, how could she face yet more anguish? She couldn't risk it. So now, she needed to buy herself time to think. She'd never expected to see Max again.

But was that completely true? Hadn't she always hoped, deep down, when she was stronger, and if the transplant was successful, that she might be able to track him down again? Hadn't she told herself that, if all went well, she would push past her own fears of rejection and loss to finally tell him about his daughter? For Imogen's sake, because her precious daughter deserved so much more.

But now was not that moment.

'Annie's going through final checks for a kidney transplant. Blood pressure and all that,' Evie trotted out.

She sounded more blasé than she'd have liked, but it was better than having to tell him Annie was actually a kidney donor and that she herself was the recipient. And it was better than breaking down and telling him how frightened she was.

She should have known better than to think she could fool someone as astute as Max. Disbelieving eyes raked over her and she tried to suppress the wave of heat at his intense assessment, all too conscious of the toll her illness and the pregnancy had taken on her over the last year. Dark pits circled her eyes, her frame was unattractively thinner, and her skin flat and pallid—no matter how much she tried to lift it with clever make-up.

She squirmed under his sharp gaze.

'God, Evie, I'm so sorry. I had no idea.' The reserved tone was gone again, replaced by an open candour she thought was more *Max-like*. 'Didn't you say you were close to your brother and his wife? No wonder you look so pale— you must be so worried about her.'

Her stomach flip-flopped. He'd actually remembered some of the few things she'd told him. Was that really something he'd have bothered to take notice of if it had *only* been about the sex? Her mind swirled with conflicting thoughts.

She jumped as she closed the gap between them, his hands closing firmly around her shoulders, drawing her in so that she had no choice but to look him in the eye.

'Evie, if you need anything, you know you can come to me, don't you?'

Residual sexual attraction still fizzled between them.

Chemistry. It's just chemistry, Evie repeated to herself, clinging to the mantra like some kind of virtual life raft. But her grip was slipping and a flare of hope flickered into life deep in her chest. At this stage of her renal failure, a man who could make her feel attractive, wanted, who could make her forget her constantly exhausted body and her regular rounds of dialysis, was a rare male indeed.

Only Max could have snuck under her skin in five minutes flat.

She so desperately wanted to let him kiss her, take her, reassure her that she was still a sexy, desirable woman. It would be welcome relief after the year she'd had.

But this wasn't about her, this was about Imogen, too, and Evie couldn't risk her daughter being drawn into some game as a pawn. Hadn't her own biological father used herself and her brother to hurt their mother? First by walking out on them when Evie had been a baby, with no contact for years, and then by trying to play them off against each other when their mother had finally found happiness with a new man. A kind man who Evie considered to be her true father rather than simply her stepfather. A man who had saved her from going down the kind of route that too many of her troubled teens now found themselves stuck on.

Even now, eighteen months on from the fatal car crash on the winding, twisting Pyrenees' roads on what had been her parents' second honeymoon to celebrate their twenty-fifth wedding anniversary, she still missed them.

It was the kind of close, loving relationship she'd always imagined for herself. The kind of relationship Max had never offered—could never offer—her.

She looked up into his dark eyes and shuddered.

Despite all her self-recriminations, the need to give herself up to Max, to take him up on his offer of support and to give in to her body's welcome burst of energy and unexpected ache for him, was all too thrilling.

'Here, put this on.'

It was only as Max was wrapping his coat around her shoulders that Evie realised he'd thought she'd shivered with the cold. She couldn't help casting a glance up and down the corridor, spotting a couple of nurses at the far end. Too far away to hear their words but watching their exchange with interest.

'Max, please,' she whispered. 'We're being observed.'

He followed her gaze to their curious audience and, muttering a low curse under his breath, turned her around and propelled them down the corridor.

'In here,' he ground out as he bundled her into an unoccupied room off the corridor. And so help her, she let him.

'What's going on, Evie?'

It took everything in Max to push her away from him when all he wanted to do was pull her into his arms and remind himself of her taste, her touch, her scent.

'I don't know what you mean.'

She was lying.

He'd spent the last year unable to get this singularly gentle, funny, sinfully sexy woman out of his head. So much for telling himself, before giving into temptation with her that night, that it would be a one-time fling. He'd always been a firm believer in avoiding dating workplace colleagues, something he'd had no problem adhering to before Evangeline Parker had come along. He wasn't exactly short of willing dates with women who had nothing to do with the hospital, or even the medical profession at all, yet no one had ever got under his skin as Evie had.

She was the first person to ever make him think about anything other than his career as a surgeon. To ever make him wonder if there was more out there for him than just reaching the very pinnacle of his speciality. It had only been that phone call from his parents, on the last evening of his time with Evie, that had unwittingly brought him back to earth.

They were skilled surgeons but cold, selfish parents, and his childhood had been bleak and lonely, a time he rarely cared to look back on. Talking to them that night had reminded him why he would not put any wife, any family, through the only home life he had known. It was a choice. Be a pioneering surgeon, or be a good family man. Never both.

And he could imagine that a family was what Evie would want. What she would deserve.

So he'd thrown himself into his eight-month tour in Gaza, appreciating the challenging working conditions, the difference he was making—and the fact that it was providing a welcome distraction from memories of that one wanton, wild, yet exquisitely feminine woman. However many amazing, lifesaving surgeries he'd performed, he'd always gone back to his tent at night wishing he could share the day's events with Evie. Wishing he were sliding into his emperor-sized bed with her rather than dropping onto his tiny cot, alone.

Yet now she was standing here in front of him, and he wanted her as much as he ever had, telling himself that the only reason he hadn't walked away from her was because she clearly needed someone to talk to. A flimsy excuse, since she clearly wasn't jumping at the chance of opening up to him. Just as they'd revelled in the sex but both been so careful to avoid much personal conversation those five hot-as-hell nights together.

'I think you do know,' he contradicted quietly. 'This is about more than just your sister-in-law and her kidney transplant, isn't it?'

Evie bit her lip, refusing to meet his eye.

'What do you mean?'

She didn't want to talk. But she probably needed to.

'You're concerned for her, frightened for her? That's understandable. But I'm guessing this is more about you feeling as though you need to be the strong one because you're the doctor, and people are looking to you for the answers.'

She chanced a glance at him but didn't answer, so he pushed on.

'It's very different being on the other side of the fence when you're used to being the one making the decisions, but I'm guessing you can't talk to Annie, or your brother, about your fears. So I'm offering for you to talk to me instead.'

'Why would you do that?'

She sounded bewildered. *Was he really that unapproachable?*

'Because I once told you I respect you as one professional to another.'

'I see.'

Was that a flash of disappointment? She shook her head, the moment gone.

'I can't.'

If he simply walked away then he'd feel like a cad. But

if he pushed her then he risked misleading her into thinking that he was open to something more between them.

'Can't, or won't?'

She opened her mouth, closed it, and then opened it again.

'Can't. I want to, Max, more than you know. But I can't.'

There was no reason for his chest to constrict at her words. Yet it did. He gritted his teeth. As long as he could persuade her that there was nothing more between them—that he wasn't remembering how incredible it had been to undress her, lay her on the bed and kiss her until she came undone at his every touch—then she might talk to him. And she definitely needed to talk to somebody.

'Fine, let's discuss the elephant in the room.'

She swallowed hard.

'So, we had a one-night stand—'

'Five nights,' she interrupted, flushing bright red.

He felt a kick of pleasure. *So it mattered to her?*

'Okay, five nights,' he conceded, allowing himself a lopsided grin and watching her carefully. 'Five nights of, frankly, mind-blowing sex.'

She flushed again, crossing her arms over her chest as if to reinforce an invisible barrier between them. But it was too late—he'd seen the way her pupils dilated in pleasure at his words. She might not want to talk to him, but she was certainly still attracted to him.

Her breathing was slightly more rapid, shallower than before, the movement snagging his eye to the satin-soft skin his fingers recalled even now. Her lips parted oh-so-slightly as her tongue flicked out to leave a sheen glistening on her lips. An action that he'd experienced in other ways over those five nights. An age-old response had his body growing taut.

He needed to walk away.

He couldn't.

He closed the gap between them until he could feel her breath on his skin, smell that mandarin shampoo of hers in his nostrils.

'It doesn't have to be over,' he muttered hoarsely. 'Neither of us have the time or inclination for wasting time playing at relationships. But we're both consenting adults, why not enjoy the sex?'

'Just sex?' she whispered again.

He couldn't help it. Before he could stop himself, he reached his hand out and slid his fingers under her chin to tilt her head up. Her eyes finally met his and the sensation was like an electric shock through his body.

'Just sex,' he ground out, as much to remind himself as to convince her.

For a moment he thought she was going to turn him down, but suddenly she raised her hand to catch his and held it against her cheek. Closing her eyes, she rested her chin in his palm as though drawing strength.

'Evie.' His other hand laced through her silky hair to draw her to him; he inhaled her gentle scent, so painfully familiar. The feel of her hands gripping his shoulders then running down his upper arms, the way her breasts brushed against his chest, heating him even through the material that separated them both.

And then his mouth was on hers and Max couldn't be sure which one of them had closed the gap first. He didn't really care. With one hand still threaded through her hair, he trailed the other hand down her cheek, her neck, her chest, feeling her arch her back to push her breast into his palm.

He heard his low growl of anticipation as the hard nipple grazed his palm through the layers of thin cotton, dropping his hand so that he could flick his thumb across it. He dropped down to perch on the corner of the table as she moved over him and his thigh wedged between her legs, which pressed against him so that he could feel the heat at their apex. He dropped his other hand down her back to cup her wonderfully rounded backside, smaller than he recalled. And then she kissed him intensely and it was just the two of them as everything else fell away.

'God, I want you,' he groaned.

'How much?' she whispered.

'You must know the answer to that,' he rasped out, her uncertainty surprising him. The woman he'd known last year hadn't needed validation or reassurance, she'd been sexily confident in her own skin. Still, if she wanted him to show her then he was more than willing to oblige.

But before he could act, Evie had tugged his shirt out, the buttons opening easily beneath those nimble fingers of hers. Dipping her head, she nipped and kissed his body that was leaner and tighter than ever. It ought to be—he'd been hitting his home gym hard ever since his return from Gaza, the only way he could burn off excess energy since he hadn't wanted to sleep with any other woman since Evie.

As she made her way back up to his lips Max pulled her back into him, his hands sliding under the fitted blouse that followed the curves of her pert breasts, revelling in the way her breath caught in her throat.

Suddenly he froze. Her once slender form felt thin. Too thin. He could actually count her ribs. He drew back shaking his head; nothing was as clear or sharp as usual. *Was he missing something?*

'Evie, stop...'

And then Max felt her slump slightly, as though the sudden flame of energy she'd had had just been stamped out without warning.

He was a first-class jerk. Evie was worried about her sister-in-law and he was only interested in rekindling the connection between them.

'I'm sorry, that should never have happened.'

Evie shook her head, and as she pulled away from him he clenched his fists by his sides just so that he didn't pull her back.

'No, it was my fault, Max.' She sounded distraught. 'I shouldn't have come back here.'

For the first time, Max wondered if he'd made a mistake. It wasn't a feeling he was accustomed to. He could read charts, he could read patients, he could read histories. He'd never been bothered to learn to read relationship signals before.

Dammit. Had he got it all wrong?

'Evie, is there something else going on here?'

'Leave it, Max. Please.' She stepped back so abruptly that she almost fell, but it was the pleading in her eyes that stayed his arms from catching her.

Max watched some inner battle war across her features, then, apparently unable to trust herself to say another word, she straightened up and forced her legs to move. He knew it wasn't the moment to stop her. He had some investigating to do before he charged in there.

He forced himself to stay still as she stumbled out of the room, the slamming door reverberating with raw finality.

CHAPTER TWO

IT WAS TIME for answers.

Max pulled up outside the unfamiliar house and turned the purring engine off with satisfaction. His sleek, expensive supercar—one of his very few real indulgences to himself—was incongruous against the older family cars and the backdrop of the suburban street. He checked the address he'd hastily scribbled down on the back of a hospital memo.

It was definitely the right place. But the nondescript, nineteen-fifties semi-detached house on a prepossessing street, almost ninety minutes from Silvertrees, was the last place he would have expected to find Evie—it all seemed so far removed from the contemporary flat that he was aware had come as part of her package working at the Youth Care Residential Centre.

But then, what did he know about the real Evie Parker?

And for that matter, what was he even doing here?

Instinct.

Because decades as a surgeon had taught him to follow his gut. And right now, as far as Evie was concerned, he couldn't shake the feeling that there was something fundamental he was missing. Sliding out of the car, he crossed the street, his long stride easily covering the ranging pathway from the pavement to the porch. He knocked loudly on the timber door, hearing the bustle on the other side almost immediately, before it was hauled open.

'Max.'

'Evangeline.' He gave a curt nod in the face of her utter shock, wishing he didn't immediately notice how beautiful she was.

And how exhausted she looked. He'd seen the dark rings circling her eyes yesterday, along with the slightly sallow skin, so unlike the fresh-faced Evie he'd known a year ago. Just like how thin she'd become, all clear indicators of the toll her illness was taking on her body. He could scarcely believe his surgeon's mind had allowed her to fob it off on being concerned for the health of her sister-in-law. But as soon as she'd gone and his gut had kicked back in, it hadn't taken much digging to discover that it was Evie who was unwell, not Annie. That it was Evie who needed the transplant, not Annie.

He felt a kick of empathy. And something else he didn't care to identify. He shoved it aside; he was here to satisfy himself there really *wasn't* something he was missing, and to be a medical shoulder to cry on. Nothing more than that.

Evie stepped onto the porch, pulling the door to behind her, clearly not about to invite him in.

'What are you even doing here?'

Ironic that he had asked her the same question less than twenty-four hours earlier.

'Why did you tell me Annie was the one who needed the transplant?' He was surprised at how difficult it was to keep his tone even and level with her, when at work his professional voice was second nature.

Evie's face fell. He didn't miss the way her knuckles went white as she gripped the solid-wood door tighter.

'I didn't.' She tilted her chin defiantly.

'You implied it, then. It's semantics, Evie.'

'How did you find out?'

'I was concerned. Things didn't seem to add up.'

To her credit, she straightened her shoulders and met

his glare with a defiant one of her own. *That* was the Evie he knew.

'You've been checking up on me? Reading my file?'

'You left me with little choice.' He shrugged, not about to apologise. 'And don't talk to me about ethics—for the first time in my career I don't care. You should have been the one to tell me, Evie.'

'Well, you should be sorry,' she challenged, although he didn't miss the way her eyes darted nervously about. 'You were the one who always used to be such a stickler about doctor-patient confidentiality.'

'Is this really the conversation you want to have?' Max asked quietly.

She stared at him, blinking hard but unspeaking. *One beat. Another.*

'You're right, I'm sorry,' she capitulated unexpectedly. 'Yesterday…it's been playing in my head and now I'm glad you know. I…just didn't know how to tell you.'

His entire body prickled uneasily.

'Are you going to invite me in?'

She fidgeted, her eyes cast somewhere over his shoulder, unable to meet his eye.

'First tell me exactly what you gleaned from my file?'

Max hesitated. There was something behind that question that was both unexpected and disconcerting. The Evie he'd known was feisty, passionate, strong, so unlike the nervous woman standing in front of him, acting as though she had something to hide, as much as she tried to disguise it.

'As it happens, I didn't read your file. You can relax. I just spoke to Arabella.'

'Sorry?'

'Arabella Goodwin, your nephrologist,' Max clarified patiently. 'I told her you'd approached me about the kidney transplant yesterday whilst your sister-in-law was having her tests done. Which, technically, you had done. Imagine my shock when she assumed I knew that Annie was a living donor and that you were the recipient.'

He'd just about managed to cover up his misstep with his fellow surgeon in time.

'Oh,' Evie managed weakly. 'What else did she say?'

'That your sister-in-law was in for the final repeat tests to ensure nothing had changed before the operation could proceed. I understand you're due for your transplant next week but you'll be taken in for the pre-op stage in a matter of days.'

'And?' she prompted nervously.

He frowned at her increasing agitation.

'Do you mean your PRA results and your plasmapheresis?'

He heard her intake of breath before she offered a stiff nod. His frown deepened. Her tenseness made no sense—surely she had to know that the Panel Reactive Antibody blood tests were undertaken by every potential renal transplant patient in order to establish how easy—or difficult—it would be to find a compatible donor?

What was he missing here?

'Evie, it isn't uncommon,' he tried to reassure her. 'You must know that around twenty-five per cent of patients who need renal transplants go through plasmapheresis to remove dangerous antibodies from their blood and increase their compatibility. You've nothing to worry about.'

'Did she tell you anything else about it?'

She asked the question quietly, but he didn't miss the shallow rise and fall of her chest.

'Evie, is this about your previous transplant not working? Is that why you're so frightened?'

'My previous transplant?'

He bit back his frustration at her resistance to confiding in him.

'You have high antibody levels, Evie, so either you've

had a transfusion, a pregnancy, or a previous transplant. I'm guessing it's the latter, presumably when you were a kid?'

It would certainly explain her ever-increasing agitation, if she was afraid her body would reject another kidney.

'You're guessing a previous transplant,' she repeated, almost to herself before twisting her head up to him again. 'You really didn't read my file.'

'Of course not.' Max blew out a breath. 'Although I admit I *was* tempted. But I didn't want to do that to you, or to a colleague like Arabella. I *do* want to hear it from you, though. Like I said last night, I can imagine you're having to be strong for your family and that leaves no one to be there to support *you*.'

Not least since, over the last twelve months, there must have been a veritable battery of tests for Evie. And for Annie, too. But it was Evie who concerned him, right now.

'Since when do you have the time to leave your surgeries?' she asked sadly. 'Or, for that matter, the inclination?'

It was a valid question. He didn't think he'd have even delayed a surgery for a five-minute coffee with a needy colleague in the past, let alone shuffle his schedule so he could drive a three-hour round trip, not to mention the fact that he was determined not to leave here until Evie had confided all her fears and uncertainties.

He wanted to help her. Needed to help her. There was no point pretending otherwise.

'Since it was you,' he answered honestly, 'I *made* the time.'

He'd sensed she needed the shoulder to cry on from the moment he'd run into her the previous day, but he'd had no idea just how much until she stared at him with wide, suddenly glistening eyes, before almost buckling at the door. He moved forward and swept her up before she hit the ground.

'Let's get you inside.'

He had no idea what Evie wanted from him as he carried her through the hallway. She was staring at him, blinking back the tears, and he felt as though she was evaluating him, as though somehow he'd just passed some kind of test he hadn't even realised he was taking.

He crossed over an original-looking, slightly broken-up parquet floor, past family pictures of people he didn't recognise, and past a coat rack sagging under the weight of coats and waterproof jackets in a rainbow of colours. Pairs of shoes and trainers, women's, men's and clearly a young boy's. An old pram and a box of toys.

There was no doubt it was a family house, practically bursting at the seams. And there was nothing of Evie he really recognised about it.

Finally reaching a quiet living room, just as packed with paraphernalia as the hallway, Max lowered her carefully to the floor.

'This isn't where I'd have pictured you. I take it this is your sister-in-law's home?'

'Yes,' Evie answered slowly. 'And my brother's, obviously. I lost my flat at the centre when I became too tired to work there. Annie invited me to move in with them about nine months ago when I… I needed the help.'

She stopped short of whatever she'd been about to say. He didn't think now was the time to push her.

'That can't have been an easy thing to do.'

'It wasn't,' Evie answered, her voice brittle.

'You sound surprised.'

'I didn't expect you to be so sympathetic. I thought you were all about career, career, career.' She chopped her hand in the air to emphasise her words. 'Drink?'

The sudden change of topic caught him off guard. Did she really think him so heartless?

'Okay.'

She left the room and he heard her bustle about the

kitchen. He'd wanted to ask her what yesterday had been about, the way she'd kissed him, their intimacy. Had he pushed her, or was her desire for him genuine? But then, how could it be when she was as ill as she was?

Now didn't feel like the right moment to challenge her; he needed to bide his time. Standing up, Max searched for a distraction, for the first time allowing himself to look properly at their surroundings. A picture on the back wall caught his interest. A photo of Evie with what had to be her brother and sister-in-law at their wedding. His eyes scanned over the other photos, mainly of Annie's family, older ones of a baby, growing into a young boy maybe nine or ten years old. A couple with Evie in them, in various fashions and hairstyles, and Max smiled. There was no denying that Evie and her brother were siblings, with similar features and colouring, and yet, whilst Evie was undeniably feminine, her brother looked strong and confident. Not as if Evie needed Max to support her at all.

It should please him to think that Evie didn't need more help, yet Max found himself bridling at the idea that she didn't need him. Suddenly a baby photo on the bookshelf snagged his gaze.

Recent. Presumably the baby who used that pram in the hallway. The picture was in a double frame with one as the close-up of the baby that had first caught his attention, the other a photo of Evie with a new baby. A new niece most likely. The baby had to take after her father, but the similarities he'd already observed meant that he could imagine it would be what any baby of Evie herself could look like. Max's chest actually constricted. Evie looked particularly ill and yet the look of unadulterated love on her face was unmistakeable. He'd been right thinking this was exactly the kind of life, of family, that Evie would want for herself. The only reason she hadn't got it yet was because of her illness.

He could never give Evie the family she would want, once she got the transplant she needed. And it was fool-hardy pretending he was here just for support for a woman who was, effectively, nothing more than a one-night stand. He needed to go. Get back to his life at Silvertrees. Refocus on his work. Forget about Evangeline Parker.

Moving quickly away from the photos and back to the armchair to wait for Evie, Max sought a way to best extri-cate himself. He'd have the drink she was preparing, and then make his exit.

'Anyway, I just thought I'd make sure you're okay. It's great that you have a living donor in your sister-in-law,' he offered when she came back through the door at last, a jug of orange juice and two glasses in hand.

'Yes.'

'No waiting on a transplant list. The procedure can be done at the earliest opportunity, before the body goes into kidney failure, and before it puts additional stress on your other organs.'

'Yes.'

He tried to bite his tongue as she poured the first juice, but as her hand hovered over the second glass, he couldn't stay silent.

'Are you supposed to be drinking that? I'd have thought you should be limiting your potassium intake.'

'What are you? The juice police?' she grumbled, but he noted that she set the jug down without pouring a glass for herself. Settling herself on the couch opposite him. Dis-tancing herself once again.

'Evie...' his voice was gravelly with concern, startling even himself '...I'm here. Talk to me.'

So much for extricating himself.

Evie had barely managed to stop herself from sinking back into his arms and confessing everything. He was here.

Here.

And more than that, he'd uttered the words she'd never even dreamed she would hear from him. He had *made* the time to come to her because he knew she needed him.

He just didn't know how much, or why. And she had to be sure—she owed it to Imogen. She couldn't bring Max into her daughter's life until she knew it was absolutely worth it. That Max was worth it.

Not that she had a clue how she would even begin to tell him, anyway.

'How are you feeling?' he asked gently. 'Besides the obvious.'

Tears pricked her eyes again. After years of dealing with troubled young adults, her own father, and even the unkindness of Max's parents, she was used to the darker side of human nature. But sometimes other people demonstrated a depth of human kindness that was truly humbling. Not least the way her sister-in-law had stepped up to offer her a kidney, and then the way Annie and her brother had opened their home to her without question.

And now here was Max—the man with whom she'd shared little more than the most incredible and the only five-night stand of her life—and he had tracked her down here because he was a good person. How far would that goodness extend, though?

'Besides the obvious physical exhaustion?' she asked with a weak smile in a bid to buy herself more time. 'I'm feeling mentally drained.'

It might send him running, but at least then she would know.

Max said nothing. Instead, he stood up and crossed the room to sit next to her on the couch. She couldn't hold back the torrent of words any longer.

'There have just been tests. So many tests that I thought they would never end. Not to mention all the tests which

Annie endured just to help me.' Evie lifted her hands to count off on her fingers. 'EKGs to check her heart rhythm, chest X-rays to rule out lung disease or lung tumours, pap smears and mammograms, CAT scans to check for kidney stones, not to mention a whole gamut of blood tests.'

She cast Max a sheepish glance.

'You'll already know that, I'm sorry. It's just I sometimes can't believe what she's put up with, for me.'

'You're important to her.' Max spoke quietly. 'And to your brother. Besides, you can't tell me you wouldn't have done the same thing for one of them.'

That was true. But it wasn't her doing it for them, was it?

'I just wish they didn't *have* to go through this for me. What if Annie gives me her kidney and her son needs it? She and my brother have a nine-year-old boy.'

'Is there any reason to think he would need it?' he asked calmly.

She knew what Max was getting at. PKD was usually inherited. Her nephew was about as healthy as wild, boisterous, vitality-filled nine-year-old boys got.

'My brother doesn't carry the gene, and my nephew was checked out and found clear. But that's not the point,' she objected. 'He could get hit by a car, develop some other undiagnosed kidney disorder, or anything.'

'Unlikely, given what you've just said,' Max soothed. 'Is that what happened with you? You only discovered you had a kidney disease this last year?'

Old memories crashed into Evie out of the blue, sideswiping her. Memories of her mother and her stepfather, and of her brother. How they'd rallied around her as a teenager when they'd first discovered there was a problem. She couldn't have hoped for a closer-knit family back then and, with Annie as her sister-in-law now, she was still so very fortunate. But she missed her parents. Almost every single day. Her heart ached for the fact that they would never even know about their granddaughter. Imogen would never have the incredible memories of loving grandparents that her nephew had.

'Evie?'

She'd been staring off into the distance. With a start, Evie dragged herself back to the present.

'Sorry. What were we saying?'

'Did you discover your illness this past year?'

'No,' she admitted, her eyes meeting his. 'I was diagnosed with polycystic kidney disease when I was a kid, but I only started entering the first stages of renal failure one year ago.'

That had been the same week she'd allowed herself to break her rules and sleep with Max.

'What happened?'

'I'd been working with a particularly troubled young boy when I got kicked.'

'That must have been some kick,' he growled.

'I guess.'

She wasn't about to tell him it had been so forceful it had propelled her several metres backwards across the office. The kick hadn't caused the problem, it had merely been a catalyst. She tried to lighten the tone.

'But it was right over the site of my weakest kidney. Murphy's law, I guess.'

'I see.' Max nodded grimly. 'No wonder you left your job. I would imagine that would have been a hard decision for you. I know how passionate you were about your work there.'

Evie frowned.

'I haven't left for good, I just took leave when I became too exhausted to work there.'

She wasn't prepared for his reaction.

'Evie, you can't possibly go back to work there.'

'Of course I can.' She bristled at his authoritative tone. 'As soon as I'm well again.'

If all was well again.

'Don't be stupid.' He snorted with derision. 'If this is what can happen to you before the transplant, think of the damage it could cause right over the site of a graft.'

Evie suppressed a shudder and folded her arms defiantly across her chest.

'Who do you think you are, ordering me around?'

'I'm not ordering you around.' He gritted his teeth at her, clearly trying to control his frustration.

They stared at each other in silence. Evie wondered whether, like her, Max was questioning how such an argument had come out of nowhere.

'I'm sorry.' Max held up his hands at last. 'You were telling me how you came to find out about your kidney disorder.'

'Right,' she acknowledged half-heartedly. 'We knew from tests back then that my brother wasn't a match, but my mother had been, so...'

She tailed off, unable to finish the sentence. They'd always assumed her mother would be her donor when the time came. As if losing her mother hadn't been bad enough to start with.

'Your mother is no longer around?' Max surmised, the previous heat now gone from his voice.

'She died just before I moved to Silvertrees. Well, to the centre, you know?'

'I see,' he said again.

'It was a car crash,' she choked out, shaking her head.

Clearly he was taking everything she said on face value, listening to her as a friend, not as a surgeon.

He trusted her. She hadn't realised that before.

If he had his surgeon's hat on he wouldn't have assumed earlier that her high-level HLA sensitisation was a result of a previous transplant. He'd have registered that she was talking about end-stage renal failure now and not a previous transplant failing, which would leave him with only two other realistic possibilities for her high antibody levels in her PRA results. A blood transfusion, or the pregnancy.

But it wouldn't be long before he worked it out. And Evie knew she had to get in there first and tell him about Imogen. His reactions this afternoon had shown more concern for her well-being than she could have imagined. Max wasn't as uninterested in her as she'd been led to believe.

'For what it's worth—' his voice cut through the silence '—I think the death of your mother, so close to your own recent diagnosis, is what's causing you not to think straight.'

'Think straight?'

'About Annie being your donor? I can tell you're having doubts, Evie. You're physically and emotionally worn out and you're getting cold feet because the operation is imminent. You know yourself how patients can get before an operation, any operation. I hope you're not considering refusing Annie's offer.'

She'd thought about it. A thousand times. But on the few occasions where she'd raised it with Annie, her sister-in-law had refused to listen, lovingly laying on the guilt as she reminded Evie that she was all Imogen had, and that she owed it to her daughter to accept the kidney.

'I'm not going to refuse. Annie wouldn't allow it,' Evie hiccuped. 'But it doesn't necessarily make it any easier.'

'It's called *the gift of life* for a reason, Evie.' He stroked her hand gently. 'And I understand your initial concerns. But think of it this way—you're clearly a close family and you owe it to your niece and nephew to be the cool aunt you clearly already are to them.'

Evie froze, his words hurling spikes of ice down her spine.

'My niece?'

'I saw the photographs.'

He jerked his head to the bookshelf. Nausea churned up Evie's stomach. *This was it. She had to do it now.*

She couldn't find the words and the room swayed. She grabbed at the couch; the familiar feel of the piping on the cushion was comforting and she plucked at it absently.

'Evie? Are you okay?' His voice was sharp, his hand slipping into her hair to force her to look at him.

The hallway clock ticked audibly, outside the street was quiet—to anyone else it might even appear peaceful—a gaggle of geese passing noisily outside the window.

'Evie.' He snapped his fingers in front of her face.

Slowly she lifted her eyes to his.

'That's not my niece,' she whispered.

He looked surprised but still didn't understand. A gurgle of semi-hysterical laughter bubbled up inside her.

Max Van Berg, the high-flying surgeon who never missed a thing in a patient, was missing the one thing staring him right in the face.

'Imogen is my daughter.' Her eyes raked over his face, willing him to really hear what she was telling him. 'She's *your* daughter.'

CHAPTER THREE

'YOU HAVE A DAUGHTER?'

He knew the words were there but his brain didn't appear to be processing the message clearly. It might as well have been trying to work in a vat of thick treacle.

'*We* have a daughter,' Evie repeated tentatively.

Slowly, slowly, his brain began to pick up speed.

'I have a daughter,' he repeated, his hand dropping from Evie's hair as he pushed himself away from her. 'I have a three-month-old baby, and you didn't tell me until now?'

Evie crossed her arms over her chest, refusing to meet his eyes.

'Five months old,' she answered shakily.

'Sorry?'

'Imogen is five months old. Not three.'

He turned to pin her with a narrow gaze as she reached for his glass and took a generous gulp as though she was parched. It took a moment for him to register.

'That's enough,' he bit out, taking the juice from her and setting it out of reach before pushing himself up from the couch and moving over to the window, reinforcing the space between them.

'Drinking that won't help you,' he muttered, staring out at the uneventful street scene.

'Thank you,' she whispered so quietly he almost missed it.

He could certainly go for a drink himself. A drink of

the large, stiff variety, not a glass of orange juice. And he rarely drank.

'We slept together a year ago. You're telling me the baby was two months premature?'

'That's not unusual given my...condition.'

He had to strain to hear her.

'The baby was born at thirty-two weeks? Thirty-three?'

'Thirty-two weeks. I went onto dialysis five days a week to carry her for as long as I could, but my body was under pressure, so they made the decision...'

Part of his brain told him that she'd done well to get that far. Her health would have been deteriorating rapidly as the growing foetus put more and more strain on her already stressed organs. It certainly explained why she'd gone from healthy when they were together a year ago, to being taken in for her transplant within the week.

'You never thought to...not to have it? For your health? For the baby's health?'

Even the words tasted bitter in his mouth.

He knew instantly that he'd said the wrong thing. If he'd felt he'd somehow passed some unknown test earlier, he knew he'd clearly fallen short of the mark now. A shuttered expression dropped over Evie's features and her voice turned cold.

'That's all I needed to know.' Her voice was shaking. Whether from anger or distress, he couldn't be sure, but his own emotions were too uprooted to care.

'Please leave, Max.'

How had this turned around so that she *was the one furious with* him?

He swung around incredulously.

'Really, Evangeline? For the last twelve months you have wilfully kept the knowledge of my baby from me, and now you're the one acting hard done by?'

'Because you've just told me you thought I should have...never had her.'

'Don't put words in my mouth,' he bit out. 'I was only concerned about the impact on your health as well as the baby's. You admitted yourself that the stress of carrying a baby was too much for your body and they had to carry out a C-section when it was only seven months old.'

'She.'

He looked at her in confusion.

'Pardon?'

'My baby is a *she*, not an *it*,' Evie choked out at him.

'Fine. *She*.' Had he really said *it*?

He hadn't meant to but he was still processing the news. Dead air compacted the room, making it hard to catch a deep breath. Hard even to think.

'So the baby is all right? She's well?'

The look of pride that lit up her eyes was unmistakeable.

'Yes, she's well.'

'How long was she in NICU?'

'Only thirty days. She weighed three pounds and four ounces when she was born. She needed to weigh around four and a half pounds, and be able to feed, breathe, and stay warm on her own before they would let her come home.'

'Of course,' he managed hollowly.

'She was actually pretty good at maintaining a good body temperature without the help of an incubator,' Evie babbled on. 'But she couldn't breathe and swallow at the same time, so feeding was the big issue.'

'Thirty days.' He blew out a deep breath at last. 'Our baby was in the NICU for thirty days and you never once called me. Never once tried to contact me. In fact, you didn't just need that single month to get in touch with me, Evie, you had seven months before that.'

Evie stared at him mutely.

'Nothing to say for yourself?'

'The snide tone is beneath you,' croaked Evie.

'Call it shock,' he bit back.

A bleak thought suddenly leapt out at him and he rounded on her.

'What do you want? Money?'

'No.'

He might have believed her cry of indignation five minutes earlier. Now, he didn't know what to believe.

'Really?'

'Do you…think I did this deliberately?' she croaked. 'To trap you?'

'Did you?' he demanded.

Her aghast look didn't sway him. He couldn't make sense of it.

'You told me categorically that you couldn't get pregnant.'

'I'd been told that was the case,' she replied weakly.

'Come on, Evie, we're both medical professionals. Just because you have PKD doesn't mean you can't have kids, it doesn't even mean you'd have necessarily developed renal failure. Plenty of women with PKD have one or two successful pregnancies without increasing their risk. In fact, the last figures I read suggested that only fifty per cent of people with PKD will have renal failure by the age of sixty, and about sixty per cent by the age of seventy. There's no reason to suggest you would have even had renal failure if you hadn't been kicked by that kid.'

Max stopped, hoping that was enough. Instead, Evie just stared at him as though she didn't recognise him, making him feel like the bad guy when, surely, it should be her?

'I didn't say I couldn't have children because of my PKD.'

Her voice cracked with emotion but she didn't elaborate. Max barely stifled his frustration.

'Then what? The dialysis?' He scrambled to calculate everything she'd told him. 'You said you went onto dialysis *after* you realised you were pregnant. But even if that hadn't been the case, the chances of a woman of child-bearing age falling pregnant whilst on dialysis are slim but not impossible, one to seven per cent, right? So however you spin it, there's no medical reason to support your assurances to me that it was impossible for you to get pregnant. So, I ask again, did you deliberately set out to trap me?'

Her desperate look disconcerted him more than he cared to admit.

'I would *never* have set out to trap you. Or anyone,' she defended herself. 'When I was diagnosed with PKD, I was also diagnosed with an ovulation disorder. I was told that I would likely need fertility treatment to conceive, which would only be given if my PKD wasn't a factor.'

'I see.' His brain felt as if it were working through treacle to process the information. How could he be sure she wasn't lying to him now? He took in her ashen pallor, her pinched nose, her shaking hands. Was he being churlish?

'I'm sorry. I should never have said all that.'

'No, you...you shouldn't have.'

'It doesn't make sense for you to have set out to trap me, to want money from me, because if you had then you'd have hit me up for it as soon as she was born. So at least you have that in your favour. But right now, it's the only thing you've got in your favour, Evie.'

'It's not that simple.'

'Yes, it *is* that simple. How could you have failed to tell me about the baby? If I hadn't had a plastics consult in that transplant unit yesterday, if I hadn't walked into that corridor at that moment, would you ever have sought me out to tell me about her?'

She didn't respond and the silence settled over them like a heavy shroud, bleak and suffocating. Trees moved in the breeze outside the window, creating a gap to allow the sunlight through. The heat warming up his back was a discordant sensation.

'Well, would you have?'

'I wanted to tell you.' She shook her head at last. 'But things were…are…more complicated than that.'

'Bull,' he snorted. 'I have a daughter. I deserve to have been told about her. *You* should have told me about her.'

'I wanted to…' Evie began uncertainly. 'But you were in Gaza and when I tried to—'

'That's pathetic, Evie,' Max cut her off. 'You could have found a way. You could've got a message to me if you'd wanted to.'

'It isn't that simple, Max. Please believe me.'

'Regardless of your claim that it isn't about money, I intend to meet my financial obligations.'

'I don't want you to do anything out of some sense of obligation,' Evie cried. 'That's why I didn't tell you. Imogen and I don't need resentment in our lives because you never wanted to be drawn into a family.'

'And yet here I am.'

She pushed up off the couch with a sudden burst of energy and made for the living-room door. But it didn't escape him that she was clinging onto it for support as much as holding it open for him.

'Then let me make it clear that you're free to leave. I will never contact you again. Imogen will never need you.'

'It doesn't work that way.'

The harsh bark didn't sound like his own voice. His head was swimming, emotions he couldn't identify crowding his brain—all bar one.

Fear.

He was a highly regarded surgeon on his way to the top of his profession. He controlled crisis situations and managed people through some of the worst times in their life. He relished the feeling of being calm and in control.

None of that was helping him now. He hadn't felt such fear since he'd been a kid. Helpless and vulnerable. All because of his parents. He'd sworn he'd never have a family, never put a child of his through the hell that his parents had laid on him without them even meaning to. And Evie was offering him the chance to walk away from a situation he would never, ever have chosen to put himself into.

But the choice had been taken out of his hands. He was a father. There was a child out there who needed him to *be* that father. He could never turn his back and walk away.

But so help him he had no idea what he *was* supposed to do. The only thing he could do was begin with the practical, the bit he knew.

'I'll start making arrangements straight away.'

'What kind of arrangements?'

'I told you.' He straightened his shoulders. 'Financial arrangements.'

'And I told you that we don't need your money.'

'Look around you, Evie. You're living in your brother's home, which is barely big enough for *his* family, and you've got a baby of your own. *My* baby. You need money. My daughter needs money.'

'The only thing my baby needs right now is love. And I have plenty of that. Clearly, you don't.'

And just like that, Evie hit on his darkest fear.

She was right, he thought, about providing for his daughter materially, but beyond that he *didn't* know how to love anyone. How could he?

He'd been given everything that a child could materially need, but he'd never learned what it was like to *be* loved.

Evie watched her knuckles turn white as she clung on to the door for all she was worth. He'd talked about *obligations* and *arrangements*. All the same things his parents had so calmly and logically presented to her. It seemed they were right after all: they knew their son better than Evie did. Of course they did. And they had been right that he didn't want a child in his life.

And she knew how damaging it would be for him to stay only to resent her and Imogen every day that he was in their lives. Better for him to go now. But Max didn't look as though he had any intention of leaving. Instead he started pacing the floor as he raked his hands through his hair.

'If you and Annie are due at Silvertrees for the transplant within the next few days, what's happening with Imogen?' Max demanded abruptly.

What did that have to do with it?

'My brother will look after Imogen.' She couldn't keep the shake out of her voice. 'Although I'll be at Silvertrees, Annie will undergo her operation at her local hospital. She should be able to be discharged within a matter of days, so it'll be easier for her to be nearer home.'

'Whereas you'll be kept in for longer, and the transplant team at Silvertrees will want to do as many of your follow-ups as possible themselves, before transferring you back to a local unit.'

'Right.'

'So I'm guessing they'll complete the nephrectomy on Annie in the morning, prepare the kidney for transport to Silvertrees and operate on you by the afternoon?' he guessed.

What was his point?

'Yes, I think that's the plan,' she replied stiffly. 'Obviously the Silvertrees team need to monitor me closely but with any luck it will go smoothly, the kidney will start working straight away, I won't need dialysis and I'll be out and back home with Imogen within a week.'

'And your check-ups?' He frowned, unconvinced. 'Even

if you are discharged that quickly, and frankly I think you're being unrealistic, you'll need to go in every couple of days for the first week or so, then at least twice a week for several weeks after that. To ensure your body isn't rejecting the new kidney and to balance your immuno-suppressants.'

'I'll make the journey.' She jutted her chin out mutinously. She wasn't going to stay in hospital, away from her daughter, any longer than she had to.

'You won't be able to drive, so you're going to ask your brother to drive a three-hour round trip every couple of days? Taking a five-month-old baby with you? Unless you're planning on leaving her with Annie, of course, who'll still be recovering herself? Or are you intending that all four of you make the journey?'

He was angry, and he had every right to be, but every cruelly thrown word felt like a physical blow. She knew it was asking a lot of Annie, of her brother, but what choice was there? This conversation was painful, and she didn't see it getting them anywhere other than the mess they had now.

'You've already made your position pretty clear, Max. And that's fine. You didn't ask for this, and I gave you no say in the matter. But I'm releasing you now, from any obligations relating to our baby. You have my word I will never come to you again.'

'I'm not walking away from the baby,' Max snarled at her.

The fire in his eyes could have burned the house down around her.

'I am this baby's father, and I will not allow you to push me out of her life now. I won't allow you to let her grow up thinking her father didn't want her. I *will* be there, whenever she needs me.'

It could have just been grand rhetoric but there was an unshakeable resolve behind the words, which made Evie take stock. And Max looked just as stunned as she felt.

Maybe she needed to remember what a shock this must all be to him, learning about his daughter, and her own kidney transplant, all at once. It had been a big enough shock to her and she'd had the advantage that it had all been staggered over the last year, at least.

And hadn't shock also made her act in a way she'd almost instantly regretted, when she'd taken the money from his parents the day after Imogen's birth?

Yet as a low cry began from the room down the hallway Evie was spared the need to respond to his declaration.

'Imogen,' she cried, scrambling out of the room.

She moved quickly down the narrow hallway to the temporary bedroom she shared with her daughter, but as she became aware of Max following her an image of his luxury designer home came to mind. Spacious and minimalist, it screamed wealth. All the things she didn't have—not if she was going to stick to her promise to herself that the cheque his parents had thrown at her would be kept in a trust for Imogen in the event that Evie's transplant didn't work. But money that Max, as he'd so pointedly reminded her earlier, *could* offer Imogen. In spades.

'Wait back there,' she sputtered.

'You've got no chance.'

With the cry of objection at being left alone becoming more insistent, she didn't have time to argue further. Stuffing down the sense that she couldn't offer their daughter the kind of home to grow up in that Max must have enjoyed, Evie set her teeth and continued down the short hallway and into her room.

She practically had to climb over her single bed to get to Imogen's hand-me-down cot, sniffing the air, which smelled, as always, of lavender baby bubble bath and aloe vera baby lotion. Although, to Max's sensitised nose, she couldn't help fearing it would somehow smell of baby sick or dirty nappies, giving her yet another area in which she fell short in his eyes.

But as soon as the tiny, flushed, screwed-up face saw her and eased into a wide smile Evie forgot their surroundings. She lifted up Imogen, cradling the baby to her chest, and inhaled her unique baby smell.

She would never let anyone take her daughter from her, no matter how much money they had.

By the time she turned around, Max was standing braced against the doorjamb and apparently unsure whether to come in or stay put as he searched for somewhere, anywhere, to place his feet. This time, she wouldn't be intimidated.

'This is where you both sleep?'

She feigned a casual shrug.

'It used to be their downstairs office. They made it a bedroom for Imogen and I because upstairs is only two-bed and I wasn't about to turf either them or my nine-year-old nephew out of their bedrooms.'

'No need to sound so defensive.'

'No need to look so appalled,' she quipped, holding Imogen tighter.

He stepped back, allowing her to shuffle her way through the gap and back to the doorway, but she noticed he didn't offer to take the baby. His daughter. *Was she relieved or hurt?*

'So this is where you expect to return to after your transplant?'

'So?'

'So, given that you aren't supposed to bend and lift anything for around six weeks after your operation, you think you're going to be able to vault that makeshift cot-bed, and stretch down to pick up your five-month-old daughter?'

'I'll have help.' She didn't intend to sound so mutinous,

but dammit if she hadn't handed him his argument on a silver platter.

'Help being your sister-in-law, who's having an operation to give you a kidney and who also shouldn't be bending and lifting?' Max clarified. 'Or help from your brother, who I presume will also be trying to look after his wife and son? And what about his work?'

'We'll figure it out,' Evie snapped back, not wanting him to see how close to the mark he was.

What choice did they have? At least, mercifully, he fell silent as he followed her back up the corridor. However, as she turned to the living room Max continued to the front door. She couldn't conceal her shock.

'You're leaving?'

'Yes.'

'Just like that?' she gasped.

'I have things to do.'

Dumbfounded, all Evie could do was stare. She'd told him he was free to leave; she meant it. But for him to do so when Imogen, his daughter, was right there, for him not to even want to see her or hold her...

It was as if her heart were being torn out. She buried her head against her daughter and rained tiny kisses all over her precious skin. Right then she swore never to let Imogen feel unloved or unwanted.

So much for Max's promise to do the same.

'I'll be back by six o'clock tomorrow night.'

She froze.

'I... What do you mean...?'

'What I said.' He huffed out a breath. 'Make sure you and Imogen are packed. I'll pick you up six o'clock tomorrow.'

'Why?'

'Because you're both coming to live with me.'

For the second time in as many minutes Evie couldn't

make her vocal cords work. All she could do was shake her head in objection.

'Don't test me, Evangeline,' Max warned. 'This is best for you and for Imogen. You and your sister-in-law both need to heal after your operations and you need to be close to Silvertrees for the next three months or until your nephrology team clear you after the transplant. And at least at mine, you won't risk hurting yourself clambering over your bed to get to Imogen's cot.'

'Live with you for three months? Why would you do that?'

And why was a weak part of her so tempted, in spite of everything?

'Because I'm the baby's father, Evangeline.' He stuffed down his exasperation. 'It's *my* responsibility, too. Not some stranger's.'

'Annie's family. Not some stranger. And you're a surgeon who's only interested in focusing on his career. You told me that yourself. You don't have time to look after a baby.'

'Then I'll damn well make time. Just like I did to come down here. I'll take holidays—I'm certainly owed them.'

Evie blinked in shock. This felt so unexpected. Max was always so careful, so measured. She'd thought she'd known him well enough to believe he would be responsible enough to be a distant father to Imogen, but not that he would take full responsibility for them both.

'So, pack whatever clothes and belongings you and Imogen need, a few suitcases at most. I'll be back tomorrow night to pick you up.'

'Max—'

'Six o'clock tomorrow evening, Evie. No arguments, no stalling, just be ready. Both of you.'

CHAPTER FOUR

'WHAT HAPPENED TO your car?' Evie blurted out as she followed Max down the front steps. Imogen was in her arms, their cases in his.

He suppressed a grim response, confining himself to the barest minimum of responses as he loaded the bags into the new car.

'I traded it in last night.'

She didn't even try to disguise her gasp of shock.

'Who willingly swaps out his pride and joy sports car?'

He resisted the urge to tell her that it was a supercar, not merely a sports car. Buying his first one ten years ago had signified the moment he'd decided he'd arrived as a surgeon, and every time he'd driven it to and from the hospital it had been the payoff for everything else he would sacrifice for his career. Yet the truth was he'd never felt so ambivalent towards his car from the moment yesterday when he'd walked out of that suburban house—a father.

The satisfaction he'd got from driving the sleek car on his outbound journey hadn't been with him on his homeward trek. In fact, from the moment he'd walked back out into the street and taken another look at all the family cars on the various driveways, he'd realised his whole life had been turned upside down and inside out.

He was a father. The life he'd grown up envisaging for himself was gone for ever.

And somehow, the thought hadn't chagrined him the way he might have expected.

'It was a matter of practicality.' He offered a deliberately nonchalant shrug. 'It wasn't a car designed for a baby seat. Whereas this is a decent family car.'

'Decent? It's one of the most luxurious, top-of-the-range family cars I've ever seen. And you swapped it out overnight? Just like that?' Evie sniffed but he refused to take the bait.

'Just like that, yes. But don't worry,' he added sarcastically, 'I've still made sure all optional extras are included. Any other questions?'

'Plenty.' She clicked her tongue nervously but he could see she was still disconcerted.

He waited until she had finished settling the baby into the baby seat in the back, waiting until she stood back up, closed the rear door carefully and moved to the front passenger door.

'What's the problem, Evie?' He reined in his frustration.

She paused, frowning as she cast another eye over the vehicle.

'I don't want you resenting me. Us. And you will, if you go sacrificing things like your car. Besides, it's only for a few days.'

The irony wasn't lost on Max. He barked out a humourless laugh.

'You kept the existence of my daughter from me, Evangeline. If I hadn't seen you in that hospital corridor two days ago I still wouldn't know about my daughter. And yet you think it would be the fact that I had to give up my *car* which would make me resent you?'

'You resent me?' She turned to him bleakly.

'You weren't going to tell me about the baby, Evie. What the hell do you expect?'

The raw expression on her face turned to one of annoyance.

'It's Imogen.'

'Pardon?'

'We had this conversation yesterday when you insisted on calling her *it*,' Evie sniped. 'Now I'm reminding you that your daughter's name is Imogen. Not *the baby*.'

Had he really just heard her correctly?

'Are you serious?'

'If you're going to take the moral high ground with me, then, yes, I'm serious. You act like your daughter actually means something to you, yet you can't even call her by her name.'

He bit his tongue before he could say any more, sliding into the driver's seat as he fought against a fresh burst of the darkest rage he'd ever known in his life. It had been bubbling constantly, barely below the surface, since yesterday. But he had to control it. If he came on too heavy and scared Evie off, he might lose his daughter. He might never have intended to have a family, but he was more determined than ever that, now he had a daughter, she would never grow up feeling, well, not unwanted exactly, but certainly inadequate. Unloved.

He allowed his mind to wander for a moment. Back to his past, and back to his own parents. *Didn't they used to call him* the baby *or* the boy? Never Max. And certainly never an endearment. He'd hated it, so why was he now calling his own daughter *the baby*? It was galling, but Evie was right.

His parents had given him a good home, nice room, toys, even time as long as it was for academic work. But they'd never had time to come to a rugby match, a swim meet, a school play. Work had always come first. And he'd always known that it was the most important thing in their lives. They'd told him. Sat him down and explained it to him, told him that he was mature enough to understand them and that when he too was a successful surgeon he'd feel exactly the same way. As if a seven-year-old boy could understand that.

'Look, arguing isn't going to get us anywhere.'

Max had never found it so difficult to keep his voice even and calm. He held his hands up in placation as Evie climbed cautiously into the passenger seat.

'We have to find a way past the anger. For her sake if no one else.'

He dipped his head slightly to indicate the baby gurgling obliviously in the back of the car.

'I agree,' Evie acknowledged, her voice still quivering slightly. 'I'm sorry I sniped at you.'

'Right.'

'And I'm sorry I didn't tell you about Imogen. You have no idea how sorry. If I could go back and change things, I truly would. I wish I'd been able to tell you a long time ago.'

'Then why didn't you?' he asked as non-combatively as he could.

'I tried…' She tailed off, her eyes fixed straight ahead, unable to meet his. 'It's…complicated. And I know that sounds feeble but, believe me, I'm trying to find the words to explain myself.'

'Thank you,' he said simply.

Her spontaneous apology was the acknowledgement he'd been waiting for. To know that she knew what she'd done had been wrong. That he'd had a right to know about his baby from the start.

Yet deep down, as the heat of rage was finally ceasing to sear, he was beginning to try to understand her motivations.

'Was it because of your kidney transplant?'

'Sorry?' He saw her head turn to him in his peripheral vision as the engine roared into life.

'Was your kidney transplant the reason you didn't tell me when you first discovered you were pregnant? Did you think I'd insist you put your health first? That you should have a termination?'

A beat of silence.

'Wouldn't you have?' she challenged unsteadily.

Another beat of silence whilst he thought.

'I would have recommended it. Carrying a baby to term for a healthy woman is stressful enough on her body, but, given your kidney disease, it makes sense medically,' he acknowledged. 'But I would never have insisted. Ultimately, that had to be your decision. And I would have preferred to have supported you through the pregnancy.'

He heard her intake of breath.

'You were in Gaza and out of reach.'

'You could have got hold of me if you'd wanted. You knew who I was working with. You'd have had only to contact their head office and they could have got a message to me.'

'I can't imagine you'd have appreciated that call in the middle of your mission out there.'

Max frowned. *Where did she get this unfavourable image of him from?*

'You don't know me at all, do you? I'd rather have known. Just like you, I'd rather have had the option to make decisions for myself. To cut the tour short and come home if I saw fit to do so.'

'I never thought of that.' The words were so quiet, said more to herself to him, that Max almost missed them.

He still had no idea how the baby...Imogen...was going to fit into his life, but he knew that he needed to buy himself some time whilst he figured it out. Evie certainly thought it was a temporary arrangement, and, whilst he agreed with her on that score, he knew it was going to be a couple of months—rather than a couple of weeks—before she would be recovered enough to think about living on her own again. But by then he should have had time to work out a long-term solution, because she was seriously mistaken if she thought he didn't want some kind of relationship with his daughter from here on out. He just had no idea how they were going to achieve it.

'There are very few things you need to know about me, Evie,' he told her firmly. 'I like things straightforward and honest, but I can't abide people making choices which impact heavily on me, without involving me in the decision-making process. Without even consulting me first.'

He'd had enough of that through his childhood to last him a lifetime. Not that Evie needed to know any of that. The contradiction wasn't lost on him.

'Consulting you...?' she echoed slowly.

'I won't accept it, Evangeline,' he stated grimly, struggling to shut out the ruthless memories. 'Do you understand?'

'But, Max—'

'There are no *ifs* or *buts*, Evie,' he spat out, more at himself.

At his own weakness that even after all this time it should still affect him the way that it did. How had this situation with Evie raked up so much hurt that he'd convinced himself he'd long since buried? Shifting in his seat, Max strived to recover his famed dispassion and composure, but it seemed to have deserted him as he opened his mouth again.

'That's the one thing I absolutely won't tolerate.'

She hadn't thought her heart could beat any faster or harder in her chest, every word like a nail in the coffin of her integrity.

How could she possibly tell him about the cheque and his parents now? Decisions that had been made with the express purpose of keeping Max in the dark? Believing she was doing the best thing she could for her daughter.

Evie pressed her shoulders into the plush leather seat back and drew deep breaths. *In through the nose, out through the mouth. In through the nose, out through the mouth.* One minute went by. Then five. Then ten. The nausea subsided a fraction, nothing more.

If she didn't tell him it would only make it harder to do so later. But—after what he'd just said—what if he turned around and sent her and Imogen back home straight away? She might not have shown Max her gratitude at taking her in, but she was indebted to him for the opportunity to allow Annie and her family some space to recover, as well as allowing herself to stay within easy reach of Silvertrees for the first few weeks after the transplant.

Worse still. What if she told him the truth and he tried to take Imogen away from her? She didn't think that was the kind of man Max was, but how could she be sure? Between her actions in taking the bribe, and her precarious health, could a judge decide that her daughter was better off with Max than with herself? Out of the two of them, *she* was the one who would appear to have acted unscrupulously. How had *that* happened?

She didn't realise they'd lapsed into silence for the last half an hour until his voice, deep and smooth and as self-assured as ever, broke into her thoughts.

'I saw one of your troubled teens the other day.'

'At Silvertrees?' She craned her neck to look at him, grateful for his efforts to find a more neutral topic for them to discuss.

'A young lad, in for a consult,' confirmed Max.

'Do you know who it was?'

'Vince Morrison. The sixteen-year-old with gynaeco-mastia.'

'They're finally allowing him to get surgery? That's great—psychologically he really needs it.'

'No, the parents came in to get more information but they left, deciding it was better to wait until he was older again.'

Evie gave a grunt of frustration.

'That wasn't the outcome you'd been hoping for?' Max asked.

'No.' She rubbed one hand over her eyes. 'Vince's deteriorating behaviour in school and at home brought him to us at the centre a couple of years ago. He's lucky, he has a loving family and kind parents, and they were trying to do their best for him. But, honestly, they were despairing as the gentle child they had known had begun to be replaced by a boy they could barely recognise.'

'I imagine he didn't understand what was happening to his body? Probably getting bullied in school.'

'Yep. The boys had been taunting him with the name Moob Boy, taking photos on their mobiles in the changing rooms and texting them around the school. He started fighting and skipping classes. He'd been a keen swimmer—Schools International—and all that stopped. He wouldn't go on beach holidays with his family, or to rugby camp. He was struggling mentally and physically.'

It felt like it had felt in the early days, before they'd slept together. The easy way they'd always been able to discuss cases.

'The procedure to remove the abnormal breast tissue is fairly straightforward—why would there be a problem?'

'I don't know.' Evie threw her hands up. 'His parents thought it was a phase, that he might grow into his body, and that he should learn to live with it until he was eighteen. I felt the psychological damage might be too great by then, and that it was an unnecessary wait.'

'I would have agreed with you,' Max stated.

The simple admission warmed her insides. She could really use that compliment from him right now.

'So do you know why they went for the consult if they weren't going to go ahead with it?' she asked, feeling less troubled for the first time since they'd left the house.

'By all accounts, their son took the family car in the middle of the night and ended up crashing into a wall. They came to listen to what the paediatric surgeon had to say but didn't like the idea of putting him through the surgery. I couldn't understand why, but now you've explained their attitude beforehand, it makes sense.'

'Who was the paediatric surgeon? Couldn't they have talked the parents round? Explained things?'

'Not enough knowledge of the boy's mental-health history.'

'Why not?' Evie frowned. 'Where were all my notes?'

'It's not your notes they needed. It's the passion, the conviction. *You're* what sells these cases, not a set of emotionless black and white notes.'

'Well, what about my replacement?'

'No one can replace you,' Max said, then coughed as he realised the way it sounded.

She felt the flush tingling from her toes to her legs, into her torso and up. It might not have been what he meant, but it felt good to hear nonetheless.

'Listen, how about I go to the centre and speak to the manager, see if I can't get him to set up a meeting with the Morrisons?' Max offered, his professional tone firmly in place. 'Give them my professional opinion and go from there?'

'That would mean a lot, especially to Vince. But why would you do that for me, Max?'

She knew he'd started the conversation in order to find some common ground between them. Talking about the case was the first real conversation they'd had without awkwardness or disagreement in the last forty-eight hours and it felt like a real step forward. Proof that they *could* work together and agree on a solution that would be in their daughter's best interests.

'I want to do it to show how I appreciate your earlier apology,' Max said unexpectedly. 'And I think it's time I made one of my own.'

'An apology?'

'I feel I guilted you into coming to stay with me. As though you owed it to me for not telling me about the baby. Deep down, I think I can understand some of your reasons even if I don't agree. But I wanted you to know this isn't just about the baby...sorry, Imogen...this is about wanting to help you, too.'

'Really?'

She watched him carefully, surprised as he took his eyes off the road for a moment to meet hers.

'Yes, Evie, really.' He turned back to the road. 'I think you should stay with me because I think it will be better for your recovery to stay close to Silvertrees for as long as possible, in order to be checked over by the transplant team themselves, rather than being handed off to a follow-on team too early.'

'And you do *want* to get to know your daughter, right?' She had to check.

'Of course I do. It's important to me that my daughter knows she is loved and never feels she wasn't wanted. More important than I think you can realise. To that end, I want to make sure I do what's best for her, yes.'

He was choosing his words carefully, but it wasn't necessarily helping her. Was he alluding to his parents? She

couldn't even ask, without revealing her own experience
of them. It left Evie feeling thwarted.

'Which brings me back around to how you and I are
going to proceed from here.'

'You and I?' Her mouth felt suddenly dry again.

'You and I,' he confirmed calmly. 'I'll admit I've been
angry that I didn't know about Imogen before now, and
I've been punishing you for it. I was too wrapped up in
myself to consider that you've got enough to deal with at
the moment with your imminent transplant without additional stress from me.'

Evie squirmed in her seat. This was the perfect opportunity to admit the truth to him.

'You do have every right to be mad...' she began.

'Maybe so, but it won't help you get through this transplant. You know as well as I do that a patient's mental well-
being can influence not only how their body copes during
the operation itself, but how their recovery goes afterwards.
In your case, how your body responds—or rather doesn't—
to a foreign organ.'

'I'll be fine,' she managed shakily, not fooling him for
a moment.

'I understand that you've felt like you have to stay strong
for your family all this time, especially with Annie being
your donor. But you can let go a little now and lean on me.'

Hope flickered tentatively, but she still couldn't relax.

'You must still be angry, Max.'

'Evie, I don't know what happened, or why you...didn't
get in touch. But I'm not going to push you on it any more.
However, when you're ready to talk to me, I'd like that.'

'As easily as that?' She tried not to feel suspicious.

'Why not? We can't dwell on what's happened if we
want to find the best future for our daughter.'

It sounded too good to be true, but Evie wasn't about
to spoil it by arguing. It didn't change the real issues, not

least the money, or the fact that she still hadn't told him about it. But it did go some way to re-establishing a rapport between the two of them so that, when she *did* eventually find the right moment and place to confess, Max wouldn't be so inflexible and impersonal in how he reacted to everything she needed to tell him.

She just needed to buy herself, and Imogen, some time.

'You can't go forwards into the past,' she said softly.

'Say again?'

She startled, not realising she'd said it aloud.

'Oh, nothing. It was just something my mum used to say. You can't go forwards into the past.'

She listened as Max repeated it, mulling the words over as he did so.

'It's a good way to put it.' He smiled. 'So, what do you think, Evie?'

'I think,' she began thoughtfully, 'I'd appreciate that very much.'

'So, friends?'

Evie licked her lips and offered him the first genuine smile since their five nights together.

'Friends.'

CHAPTER FIVE

'THAT'S ANOTHER FAIL,' Max exclaimed to his baby daughter as he lifted her off the changing mat only to watch the downward drop of his third nappy attempt in as many minutes.

This was his first morning in charge of his daughter, having taken Imogen off Evie late last night and telling Evie to get a full night's sleep. The drugs Evie would be on for the transplant made breastfeeding an impossibility, so he'd felt free to take Imogen and give her a feed in the night, subsequently going through more nappies than he cared to count trying to change her. Unsurprisingly, his daughter didn't look overly impressed with his performance so far.

He was a skilled, sought-after surgeon—how the heck could a tiny scrap of absorbent material for a tiny baby defeat him? He wasn't accustomed to failing at things, and he didn't like the feeling one bit.

'Right, nothing else for it.'

He carried Imogen over to the LCD home automation panel on the wall. 'Hmm...' he murmured, flicking through the online tutorials. 'Here we go: *Changing a baby's nappy.*'

To her credit, Imogen didn't cry but simply watched him with big, clear, expressive eyes, which were perfect replicas of her mother's, but it didn't make Max feel any more relaxed around her.

Funny, but he'd dealt with babies week in, week out in

a medical and surgical setting, not least with all the work he'd done with the charity, from cleft lips and palates to club-feet, burns to reconstructive. But he'd never changed a nappy. He'd never wanted to change a nappy. That much hadn't changed. He was beginning to realise that his solution of looking after the baby, *his daughter*, whilst Evie was in hospital might not have been one of his most inspired ideas. He clearly wasn't cut out for it and being in charge of such a tiny life, outside the comfort of the operating theatre, was a weighty responsibility.

'Having trouble?'

He swung around, cradling Imogen against his chest as he did so.

'We're fine.'

'So I see.' She grinned, gesturing first to the tutorial, then to the nappy, which was partly over Imogen's hip and partly over her knee.

'Okay,' he conceded sheepishly. 'So I might have a few things to learn. Anyway, you're meant to be resting.'

He'd insisted on giving her his master suite so that she could get as much rest as possible before her transplant, whilst he moved into the second bedroom, with the annexed dressing room now a nursery.

'I am resting. I forgot how comfortable your bed was—' She stopped abruptly, flushing a deep red.

Max quickly shut down any memories of the last time— the only other time—Evie had been in his home. Those five, intense days.

'Wait, *this* is Imogen's nursery?'

'It is.' He stepped back to let her have a full look around. 'Do you like it?'

'It's very…expensive-looking.'

It should be. He'd paid handsomely to have a designer come in and transform the room in one day, with less than twelve hours' notice. Still, he surveyed the room again, this time through Evie's eyes. It occurred to him that it was very different from the makeshift yet altogether cosier homely set-up she and Imogen had shared at her brother's house.

The interior designer had insisted on an oak sleigh cot, matching oak changing table—fully stocked—and oak wardrobe. A jungle theme ran throughout—Max having just about talked her out of a princess theme—from the bedding to the curtains, and the pastel walls with bright jungle mural to add some interest. On one wall a bookshelf overflowed with soft toys and books.

'I don't know why there are so many books.' He shrugged. 'It isn't as though Imogen will be reading for a while.'

'No, but it'll be nice to sit on that wicker chair over there and read to her at night.' Evie offered him a warm smile, but there was a hint of sadness behind it.

'I hadn't really thought of that,' he admitted with surprise.

'My mum used to have this big chair she called the reading chair, and at night we'd snuggle together and she would read to us for hours and hours. Even as a baby I think she used it to get us into the habit of reading.'

That would be why the idea hadn't occurred to him. He couldn't remember either of his parents reading to him. Ever. They'd always been too busy.

'How about *your* mum?'

'What?' he asked sharply, before checking himself.

'Did your mum read to you, too? Is that why you thought to put the chair and the books in here?'

He peered at her closely but there was nothing in her expression but innocence and interest. Slowly the tense feeling receded.

She hadn't meant anything by it—how could she have? She didn't know the first thing about his parents, and he intended to keep it that way.

'I don't recall,' he lied. 'She probably did. But it was the interior decorator who did this room.'

He didn't want his parents to have anything to do with his daughter. He didn't want them to create the same lack of self-worth in their grandchild as they had in him throughout his childhood. He'd been lucky to have that one teacher who had seen what was going on and taken a young Max under his wing. He wouldn't be a surgeon—a top surgeon, no less—without that one gentle, guiding hand.

'Oh, right, of course.' Evie accepted his explanation without question, and he felt simultaneously relieved and guilty.

'So, what are they like?' she asked.

'Who?'

'Your parents. Are they in the medical profession like you? Is that where you got such skills from? And the way you care so much for your patients?'

'No, it wasn't.' He just about held back the bitterness from his tone.

Of all people, his parents could have been his teachers, his heroes. They had expected him to follow them into a surgical career, and they'd certainly pushed him on the academic side. But they had never shown him a caring or loving side. He sometimes wondered why they had even bothered to have a kid, but the answer was simple: it had been expected. It hadn't been something they'd wanted.

Not that he was about to load his, or his parents', shortcomings onto Evie. She didn't need to know any of this.

In fact, he was beginning to realise that they didn't really know anything about each other at all. Evie was the mother of his baby and yet they might as well have been strangers. Maybe, if they were really serious about being friends for the sake of their daughter then he should actually start talking to her, asking about her life and her family. He had to admit, he was interested.

Max observed in silence as she watched her daughter, her eyes filled with affection. Her innate love for Imogen was beyond doubt. It made him feel…good, just to see it. Almost subconsciously, she skimmed her lower abdomen with her hand and he knew immediately what was going through her mind. He'd seen it time and again with his patients over the years.

'You're going to be fine,' he said quietly. Convincingly.

She shot him an unconvincing smile in return.

'I hope so. Thanks to Annie. Just as long as my body doesn't reject the new kidney.'

'You can't afford to think that way, Evie. You have to stay mentally strong. Be positive.'

'I know.' She bobbed her head but the way her shoulders hunched told a different story. 'But let's be fair, Max, we're effectively trying to disguise a foreign organ from my body. My PRA levels were high enough to warrant plasmapheresis. If my body spots it, it'll really attack it.'

'You know it's more complicated than that,' Max began, then stopped. Even doctors were allowed to get scared; it wouldn't help to simply censor everything Evie said.

He searched for something more constructive to say. To help her. But everything that came to mind didn't encapsulate what he wanted to tell her. He'd dropped pat phrases to patients and their families throughout his career, given them words of comfort whilst being sure not to make promises he couldn't fulfil. Promising to do everything he could for a patient wasn't the same as promising them that everything would be okay, because he *would* do everything he could but the outcome would never be exactly the same because every patient was different.

He had no way of knowing how Evie's body would react to the transplant. He couldn't say what the future held. Yet right now, for the first time in his life, he had to hold himself back from pulling Evie into his arms and promising her that everything was going to be okay.

He'd never wanted to believe it so much in his life.

Max cradled Imogen closer, grateful for occupying his hands and the inadvertent barrier she created between himself and Evie.

'All I can promise you is that you're in good hands. Arabella Goodwin is one of the best nephrologists in her field,' he declared brightly. 'All the tests and pre-op care she has carried out, the method she has selected for the transplant itself, the balance of immuno-suppressants, they're all to maximise your chance of success.'

'I know that.' Evie nodded and bit her lip. 'Logically, as a doctor, I know it. But as a patient, I hate not being the one in control.'

He could relate to that.

'So, forget you're a doctor for ten minutes and pretend you're a patient like any other. Talk it through like any other patient would.'

'How do you mean?'

'You're scared.'

She was going to argue, he could see it. Then she changed her mind.

'I *am* scared, yes. My body's antibodies are so high. The plasmapheresis is just to get me even close to being able to undergo the transplant, but after the operation there's bound to be more.'

'So think of it like both the transplant and the induction drugs are a mortgage deposit, and the maintenance drugs are your monthly mortgage payments. The bigger your initial deposit, the lower your monthly repayments need to be. In other words, the better the transplant takes and your body responds to those initial immuno-suppressants, the less chance your body will reject the kidney in the future, so the less maintenance drugs you're going to need.'

'It doesn't mean that a month, six months, twelve months down the road, my body might not suddenly decide to reject it.' She sucked in a breath.

'No, but we have to start somewhere. There's no way to predict who will suffer a rejection episode, but if you do we adjust the medication to attempt to reverse it. You know that a good percentage of transplant patients go through at least one rejection episode but it's mild enough to counter.'

'I know, and some patients have the same transplanted kidney twenty, forty years down the road, and might have had a handful of rejection episodes they've been able to reverse.'

'Right, and the lower your maintenance drugs are, the more room we have to play with to increase them.'

'Yes.'

Without warning, Evie smiled.

'You know, I actually *do* feel a bit better about it all.'

'Good.'

One little word, which didn't come close to how he was feeling. She looked genuinely less tense and his chest swelled a little to think that, together, they'd talked it out.

It wouldn't be the last time she'd need to run through things, to steady herself, but he'd be here for her every time she needed him. But right now, she needed him to move on.

'Are you hungry? If you fancy it I could make something to eat?'

She hesitated.

'It isn't a problem to make breakfast,' he cajoled.

'Breakfast would be nice.' Evie finally held her hands out. 'Shall I sort out Imogen's nappy?'

Max looked at the falling nappy and grinned wryly.

'I'll learn soon enough.'

The buzz of contact as he handed their daughter to Evie caught him off guard. Quickly he retreated to his temporary bedroom to snatch up a fresh tee shirt from the drawer before heading to the safety of downstairs.

Evie watched him go, her heart beating faster.

He'd lied to her. And she didn't know what it meant.

She'd been right that he had a complicated relationship with his parents. But she didn't know whether to be relieved that he clearly didn't have much time for his parents, or concerned that he clearly didn't intend to talk to her about it. The way the topic had come up so naturally had seemed like a good opportunity to ease her way into admitting the truth.

But if Max wasn't prepared to tell her even the first thing about them, then how could she possibly admit she'd met them, let alone that they had paid her to keep his daughter from Max?

And yet, as awful as it sounded, wasn't it better that he didn't appear to be close to them given their utter indifference to their granddaughter? Having experienced both sides of it herself, a loving home with her mother and stepfather, and a difficult relationship trying not to antagonise her father, she knew she would have been just as well off if her father had never been around at all.

She dropped her head to her daughter's. She'd do anything to protect her baby from anyone who could hurt her, mentally or physically.

Almost in response, Imogen reached up and grabbed Evie's cheeks in her chubby little hands, smacking loud kisses onto her mother's face before burying her head into Evie's neck and nuzzling.

Evie's heart swelled. It was a feeling like no other. It hadn't bypassed her that although Max was clearly comfortable holding a baby from his time as a surgeon, skilled enough to be able to keep them calm and confident enough to examine them, he was detached about it. His daughter might as well have been any baby in his care. There was no bond.

Was it just a question of time? Or would there never be a special father-daughter bond there?

What would happen when she was in hospital? In this particular unit? Between going in for the pre-op and the transplant itself, she would be kept in a sterile environment where Imogen wouldn't be allowed to visit for at least a week. Maybe longer.

Her daughter had spent her life being showered with love, kisses, constant affection. From herself, her brother, Annie, even her nephew. Evie had no doubt that Max would meet Imogen's physical needs. But what about those emotional needs? She would need to see him soften towards Imogen, to look at her as his daughter rather than just a baby on whom he was going to operate, before she would be comfortable about being separated from her daughter for so long.

She was just going to have to teach Max how to show his emotions. The prospect filled her with both trepidation and exhilaration. *How exactly was that going to complicate things between the two of them?*

And teaching him how to change a nappy properly wouldn't be a bad idea, either. She stifled a giggle.

'Come on, precious girl. Let's get you sorted out, and find you a pretty baby suit, then we'll go downstairs and show your daddy how neat and tidy you look.'

Evie sniffed appreciatively as she entered the kitchen where Max was cooking on the stove.

'Barely five minutes and something already smells heavenly.' She grinned.

'Imogen's crying,' Max exclaimed, turning around.

'Yes, thank you, I can hear that.' Evie couldn't help chuckling at his expression of horror.

'But...she's with you.'

'So?'

'So, I wouldn't have thought she'd cry with you. I thought it was just me.'

'I'm not a panacea. Once I got her changed and the nappy contortionist had left, she realised how hungry she was.'

Belatedly she realised that if she wanted to encourage him not just to look after his daughter, but actually interact more with her, then teasing him might not be the best idea. With her transplant looming all too quickly, in a couple of days she'd be in hospital; Max would be all Imogen had. But to her relief he laughed along with her.

'Glad my efforts weren't completely in vain—at least they had entertainment value. I can't believe she was as patient as she was with me.'

'Depends on the day,' Evie responded, realising it would be good to show Max there was no magic wand. 'Some days she might be patient, other days everything might unsettle her. She's a little person, and just like you or I she has good days and off days. If things aren't going well one day, don't assume it's something you've done. There's no fix-all solution.'

Max looked even more horrified.

'If she's fed, burped, slept and has a clean nappy, she'll be happy, though, won't she?'

'Usually. Not every time. All I'm saying is don't assume you've done something wrong. Maybe it's her teeth, or growing pains, or her tummy. Just be ready just to cuddle her, that's all I do and that's what she's used to. What are you doing?'

'Getting a pen to write it down.'

'Max—' Evie was incredulous '—you're one of the foremost surgeons in your field. You said you looked after babies and young children in Gaza. You don't need to overthink it.'

'My field isn't babies. And, despite Gaza, I'm not a paediatric plastic surgeon,' he pointed out, pulling a handful of pens and an old envelope from a drawer and proceeding to test the ink. 'Also, when I do see babies in the hospital, they're usually unwell.'

She didn't mean to, but the smile erupted from her before she could hold it back. She'd never seen him anything but authoritative, completely in control of any situation or crisis, the go-to guy for several of his colleagues.

To see him so flummoxed simply by taking care of a baby, his own daughter, was something she hadn't anticipated. It somehow made him more human.

'Here, why don't you take Imogen while I get something ready for her?'

She stifled a laugh as he physically took a step backwards into the refrigerator when she advanced with the now-bawling Imogen.

'I don't think... I'm in the middle of making breakfast.'

'I can wait. Imogen won't.'

Evie held his daughter out in amusement and reluctantly he took her, delighted when Imogen's cries eased up a little. Despite his uncharacteristic uncertainty about keeping a baby happy, he was clearly more than comfortable actually holding one.

Something to do with the surgeon in him who was able to soothe and examine any patient, just as long as they weren't being asked to change nappies or feed them.

'What should I...?'

'Just cuddle her, and show her what I'm doing. Talk her through it—it might distract her.'

'Look, baby Imogen, your mummy's opening the cupboard,' he began awkwardly.

Evie stuck her head inside and laughed quietly. It was surreal watching the super-surgeon Max Van Berg so wholly out of his depth. She'd never seen it before, and she could bet no one at Silvertrees—or anywhere else, for that matter—had ever seen it, either.

'Look, your breakfast. Oh, you understood that, huh?'

She could hear his surprise as Imogen's cries lessened slightly as she turned her head to look.

'Um… Oh, I can see a breakfast bottle, how about you, Imogen?' He loosened up slightly, gaining confidence as his daughter rewarded his efforts with snuffles now instead of cries.

Evie moved around the space easily; nothing had really changed from the last time she'd been here. Except for the circumstances, of course. Max continued talking, albeit stiltedly, to his daughter until Evie was ready and offered to take Imogen back.

His relief was evident as he hurried towards her, and she stamped down a surge of disappointment that he didn't want to feed his daughter himself. It was something she loved to do. Still, he'd made good progress. And it was only the first morning.

'What are we doing today?' Evie ventured as she settled on the chair to give Imogen her feed.

'I have surgeries this morning,' he answered apologetically.

She glanced at the clock on the wall. It was six-thirty already. He was running late.

'I cancelled all the electives I could, or passed them onto colleagues,' he answered her unspoken questions. 'I'm not on the rota for emergencies so this morning I'm clearing my desk of any immediate cases. I should be finished by the time you go in for your dialysis session this afternoon, but if not just go to the crèche and tell them who you are. They've reserved a place for Imogen until I finish.'

'Silvertrees crèche? How did you get her in there?' Evie exclaimed. 'It's a twelve-month wait list, isn't it? There was a nurse who had just put her kid down when I was working in A&E. She was told she probably wouldn't be able to get him in until he was nine months old, and she was pregnant at the time.'

'Perks of being one of Silvertrees' senior surgeons.' Max winked at her.

Her stomach flip-flopped in response.

'Isn't it just,' she murmured distractedly before a concerning thought settled on her. 'Max, you aren't planning on leaving her there every day when I go in, are you? I mean, she's never been to a crèche before. She's always had myself, or Annie. If I'd thought you weren't going to be looking after her, I would never have agreed to come here.'

'I know that, stop worrying. I told you, I have a few cases to clear off my desk but I've sorted out the rest. I've booked two weeks off and I will be looking after our daughter personally. I will not be palming her off on someone else, because I know that's what you're thinking.'

'Well, good.' She refused to apologise for caring about her daughter.

However, she didn't dare ask how he'd managed to secure two weeks off at such short notice. He'd either pulled in a fair few favours, or promised them, and she was grateful for it.

'Right, well, whilst you're feeding the baby, let me finish your breakfast.'

He passed Imogen back to her, each hand-off getting easier than the last. He was clearly growing in confidence as Imogen's father. But she needed his progress to be quicker. Max was obviously thinking of her recovery—it was one of the reasons he'd brought her here, so that she was closer to the transplant unit at Silvertrees. But she didn't know if he realised just how integral their daughter's welfare was to how stress-free her recovery would be.

Evie was determined to see some kind of bond between

the two of them before she went into hospital. It would make her feel a heck of a lot more confident about being away from her precious baby girl.

CHAPTER SIX

THAT WAS THE last of the paperwork cleared up.

Max glanced at the clock on his wall in satisfaction. He was due to collect Imogen within the next half hour and take her to see Evie. Tonight might be Evie's last opportunity to spend time with her daughter before her transplant.

He had one outstanding patient, a particularly complex, long-standing case, which he intended to return to do himself. He'd already approached his colleague, Gareth Collins, to monitor the pre-op tests and pass on the results, but there were just a couple of last points he wanted to go over. Gareth was on call tonight, so Max knew if he swung by A&E he'd likely catch the guy. Hopefully in between cases.

He moved purposefully through the hospital. It was a novel experience, getting ready for time out that wasn't going to be spent out in some war zone with the charity. How was it that he had never once questioned his ability to handle anything they could throw at him, and yet the prospect of a couple of weeks with his baby daughter filled him with a long-forgotten feeling of inadequacy?

Caught up in a sudden memory of his childhood, wondering at nine years old whether he really was cut out to be a surgeon as his parents expected, he burst through the double doors only to come face to face with a familiar—battered and bloodied as usual—face.

'Hey, Dean, been fighting again?'

He crossed the resus bays to where the young boy lay, his mother worried and teary by his bedside, and his broken nose only the start of his injuries by the looks of his chart.

'Punctured lung?' He cocked his eyebrow at the kid to conceal his deep concern. 'You can't let them get to you, mate.'

Not that the boy was in much condition to respond anyway, but the soft touch didn't work with this particular lad, as Max already knew. This was the fourth time the boy had been in in as many months and the injuries were getting substantially more serious. This time it was a fractured rib with a suspected lung injury.

Max's instinct told him it had been a fight where Dean had been on the ground when he'd been kicked in his ribs. A fight Dean had likely started, from everything Max already knew.

And all because he had prominent ears. *Wing nuts. Jughead. Dumbo.* Dean had heard them all and was desperate for surgery to correct the problem. Apparently that wasn't going to happen. Max stepped away from the curtain just as a man shot around the corner and hurtled into him.

Dean's dad.

Max caught the man before he rounded the curtain, leading him a step away.

'You know I can resolve the problem, don't you?'

'Mr Van Berg.' The man recognised him instantly.

'General anaesthetic and ten days in a bandage and it'll all be done.'

He only had to cut away the skin and tissue behind the ear and stitch the ears into their new positions. The main issue was ensuring the surgeon was competent enough to carry out a procedure that required such visual accuracy. Badly done and the patient would end up with ears that either didn't match, or looked plastered down.

Max wasn't worried. His skill wasn't in question.

'We understand.' The father nodded with a sad smile. 'But we just don't know what to do for the best. To the wife and me, Dean's a handsome little lad with a great personality, and so what if his ears stick out a little? But…'

'But…?' Max encouraged.

'But we've spoken to some experts who've said that it's just name-calling and that life can be a lot harsher than that so Dean needs to learn to ignore kids like that. They've pointed out that he can't go through life fighting everyone who says something unpleasant to him, so if we let him have surgery then he's just never going to learn how to deal with criticism.'

Easier said than done, especially when you were eleven years old. But Max appreciated Dean's parents had only their son's best interests at heart. Better than his own parents.

'And what does your gut tell you?' Max shoved away the shadows that stalked the edges of his memories.

Like the time he'd ended up in hospital for exactly the same thing at about the same age Dean was now, for pretty much the same injury. Max had had his own share of fights, and instigated by himself just like Dean. But unlike Dean, he hadn't had a valid reason for them. He hadn't got any obvious physical or mental impairment, and unlike Dean's concerned parents, who were trying to teach Dean to be strong of mind, Max could only remember his own parents expressing disappointment at such childish and *inappropriate* behaviour, before getting back to their all-important careers. But now wasn't the time to push Dean's parents.

Maybe Evie would be the best person to teach him how to go about helping the kid? He didn't know what it was but something about the boy made Max want to do more to help.

'My gut says that my son's coming home with broken bones,' the father exclaimed, torn. 'That isn't something he should have to learn to deal with at eleven years old. But I just don't know.'

'Well, you know where to find me, Mr Foster.' Max nodded. 'Any time you need me.'

Allowing the father to get back to his son, Max continued down the corridor in search of his colleague, but he couldn't shake the desire to do more for the lad. Before the kid ended up in here, and didn't leave. He'd just have to be careful; he couldn't afford to push these parents into something they weren't ready for.

By the time Max had got a moment with his busy colleague to go through the patient's notes, it had already been getting dark outside. He'd long since missed taking Imogen to see Evie, and had been compelled to call the crèche and arrange for another of his colleagues to take the baby to her mother. He'd been inflexible about being informed exactly *who* was taking his daughter, and when they were doing so, even ensuring it was a colleague he knew well. But none of it made up for the fact that he was doing the very thing he'd been so afraid of—the very reason he'd never wanted a family—he'd let them down, broken his promise to them, and all because his career had got in the way.

It had felt like small consolation that he'd subsequently swept through the hospital actively looking forward to collecting his daughter and hopefully spending a little quality time with her before putting her down in her cot.

And now, he stepped into his voluminous hallway at home, Imogen finally in his arms, as the home automation system was already lighting the house for them.

'So what shall we do, hey?' he asked his unblinking daughter.

As if in response, a pungent smell filled the air.

Wait, was that...?

He didn't need to lift Imogen too close to his nose before he had the confirmation he needed.

'Right, little lady.' He headed quickly for the stairs, grateful to be occupying himself. 'You definitely need a change.'

Whether she resented being taken in the opposite direction from her play mat, or simply the fact that she could sense his tenseness, her wail of objection began even before Max lowered her onto the changing mat. Pulling her legs into her tummy and trying to roll over, she made it clear that she wasn't going to make this an easy change for him.

For a moment, Max stared hopelessly. This afternoon's complex procedure had been challenging and exhilarating, but he hadn't questioned his ability for a second. So how was it that now, faced with a five-month-old baby in a dirty nappy, he was filled with self-doubt?

Ridiculous.

It might be true, but it didn't seem to make it any easier. Imogen clearly didn't trust him, which didn't make him feel any more confident.

What would Evie do?

Tentatively he lowered his head and, finding the bare skin on one flailing arm, he blew a brief raspberry. The effect was immediate as the wailing stopped. He lifted his head to let his eyes meet his daughter's. She was watching him carefully, prepared to give him a chance, but woe betide him if he moved too fast.

With a little more confidence, he blew another raspberry, on her cheek this time.

The giggle of response was heart-lifting. Max felt an unexpected surge of pride at the simple achievement of making his daughter laugh. The tentacles of a bond began to reach out between father and daughter, and as his confidence grew so too did Imogen's trust in him.

Within minutes, he had her relaxed and ready to be

changed, as she happily allowed him to unbutton her Baby-gro and open the sticky tabs holding her nappy on.

He'd known babies' nappies smelled; he'd been around a few. But he'd never been this close to a freshly removed one before. Max wrinkled his nose in disbelief.

'That can't really have all come from you,' he teased dramatically, eliciting more giggles. 'What have they been feeding you, hey?'

He pulled a handful of wipes out of the packet, paused, then doubled it. He could hear Evie's soft chuckle of amusement in his head but he didn't care.

Then he glanced back at the nappy with concern.

'You're not coming down with something, are you?'

His head moved automatically to check her forehead, her tummy. There was no suggestion of a temperature, but still.

He'd heard of doctors—good, competent doctors—who reassured other parents about their babies every day, but who had to get colleagues to check things when they had babies of their own because they couldn't trust their own judgement. They'd always claimed it was different when it came to your own children.

He'd always thought it ridiculous. Now he wasn't so sure.

The idea of Imogen coming down with any kind of infection, especially given her additional vulnerability, actually caused his chest to tighten. The edges of a fear he'd never before experienced.

He thrust the thought away. No, the medical bit was the stuff he *could* trust; that bit he understood. Reaching for the LCD screen from the wall, Max typed in a search. Then he compared the image on the screen in front of him with the nappy. Definitely the expected colour. Imogen was fine.

And since when did he panic over nothing? Since when had he ever panicked?

Even so, it took him several minutes of carefully lifting Imogen's ankles and methodically cleaning all traces until she was perfectly pink and clean, and smelling of baby wipes, until his heart finally started to slow down. Then, dabbing a little cream in place, he deftly secured a fresh nappy in place, before lifting her up to check his handiwork.

'Pretty good.' He nodded his head at Imogen. 'We did a good job there, little lady.'

Imogen gurgled as if in agreement, then, reaching out her chubby fingers, grabbed his hair and pulled him in, giggling in anticipation of another raspberry.

'There's a rugby game on TV tonight,' he told her brightly. 'I haven't had a chance to watch a game in years. What say you grab a bottle and I'll grab a pizza, and we can watch it together?'

Imogen snuggled down into him.

'Okay, then it's agreed.' He dropped a kiss onto her head without thinking. 'I don't think this babysitting lark is going to be too bad after all.'

Although, was it really babysitting if the baby was your own? Max wondered, a half-smile moulding itself to his mouth.

Forget all his preconceptions and fears about not being a good enough father. His daughter was incredible enough to make him *learn* to become a good father. The best father he could be.

And if he was father material then surely that meant he was other kinds of family material, too?

So where might that leave him with Evie?

'How are you feeling?'

Guilty, uncertain, scared. Petrified might be more like it.

'Not bad.' She dredged up a smile.

'Good.'

'Where's Imogen?'

'Outside. One of your junior doctors jumped at the chance to cuddle her whilst I came to see if you were up to one last visit with her this morning. Apparently I'm to tell you that she's even more adorable than you made her out to be.'

'That'll be Richie.' Evie smiled again, more sincere this time. 'He's been great. He has three sisters and a brother.'

'Right.' Max nodded blankly.

'You don't know who he is, do you?'

'Should I?' Max was unconcerned. The hospital was a big place—not everyone knew each other.

'He told me he was on your service for six months a couple of years ago.'

'Come to mention it, he did look familiar,' Max responded thoughtfully, not a trace of shame at his oversight.

It was well known that Max never bothered to find out anything about the people he worked with and she knew for a fact that he'd never really considered colleagues' reasons for getting into the medical profession.

'You know, showing an interest in people's lives outside the hospital isn't always a bad thing,' she told him. 'Sometimes it reveals traits or skills you can't learn in a lecture theatre or an operating room, but which can be just as important in boosting a patient's confidence.'

'It also invites interactions with people which aren't case or hospital related,' he argued. 'And if they don't further a patient's treatment or someone's learning, then they're little more than a waste of time.'

'You sound so—' She stopped abruptly. She couldn't tell him how like his cold, unforgiving parents he sounded in that moment.

'So…what?' demanded Max harshly, as though he knew what she'd been about to say.

Wheels spun in her head.

'So jaded,' she offered, relieved when he seemed to believe her. She cleared her throat. 'Anyway, thanks for bringing Imogen back in this morning. I'll take any opportunity to spend time with her before the operation.'

'Okay, then,' he acceded, leaving her room to fetch Imogen.

Evie blew out a long breath. The transplant team would be coming in soon to start the main pre-op process, getting her into a hospital gown, inserting an IV line into her hand and catheters in her neck to monitor her blood pressure and heart.

Her eyes pricked the moment Max rounded the corner, Imogen in his arms.

'Say hi to Mummy,' he told his daughter softly, lowering her gently into Evie's eager arms.

'Hey, sweetpea,' Evie choked out. It was illogical but being separated from her daughter, who she'd never been apart from for more than a few hours at a time since Imogen's birth, seemed like the worst part of this transplant process, so far.

As Imogen reached out, her chubby fingers locking around Evie's hair and tugging, it was frustrating to realise she didn't even have the strength to keep her daughter at bay. The previous day Imogen had been mercifully sleepy and quiet but this morning she was clearly full of energy. When Max reached out silently to take his daughter back, empathy in his gaze, Evie couldn't hold back the sob.

'Don't worry, a couple of days and it will all be different,' he soothed. 'You'll have a new kidney and you'll be strong enough for your daughter to come back and visit you again. Before you know it, your life will be better than you remember it for a long time.'

She flashed him a grateful smile, watching as he easily shifted his daughter in his arms, soothing her objections at being taken from her mother.

It was like watching a different man from the one she'd left thirty-six hours ago. Two nights alone with his daughter and already he seemed much more at ease, holding her and chatting with her. Even as he talked to Evie, he was simultaneously distracting and entertaining their baby. Not to mention the fact that Imogen was dressed beautifully, and not in a mismatch of clothes as she'd seen throughout her career when some fathers had been left in charge of their children.

'You mastered the nappy, then?' She tried for a weak joke, gratified when Max looked proud of himself.

'I have.' He grinned. 'She doesn't see me coming and shriek her head off any more.'

'You look good together,' managed Evie.

She knew she had to stay positive, stay focused, but she couldn't deny that it was a relief to know that, if anything did go wrong, Imogen would still have at least one biological parent in her life. Even though Evie knew that her brother and Annie would always be there for the little girl.

'You're not getting morbid, are you?' he chastised.

'Of course not.' Biting the inside of her cheek, Evie executed the bare-faced lie with grace. He didn't buy it for a second.

She wasn't prepared when, settling on the bed beside her, Max pulled her into his arms. She stiffened, unsure what to do. Then, like a floodgate giving way, she crumpled against him. The silent sobs wracked her body even as Max held her oblivious daughter on the other side of him, comforting her more than she could have imagined with his free hand.

He dropped a kiss onto the back of her head as she bent forward, holding onto him, her forehead resting on his chest, and she lifted her head to look at him.

'We need to talk, Max.'

'What about?' he asked her.

But now wasn't the time to tell him about his parents. Or about the money.

'Not now. If I get through this.'

'*When* you get through this,' Max corrected throatily. 'We need you, Imogen and me.'

We? The word sounded so good to her ears, even if he was only saying it to be encouraging.

For one perfect moment it was just the three of them in a bubble and nothing existed outside them. Not her transplant, not his parents, and not the fact that she and Max didn't really know the first thing about each other.

If her operation went well, then all that had to change. She and Max had to find the best solution with their daughter's best interests in mind. They needed to get to know each other. Spend time together.

Which meant she needed to tell him about his parents. And the money.

There was no more making excuses.

CHAPTER SEVEN

MAX SWEPT TOWARDS the automatic doors of the transplant unit as he had so many times before as a surgeon. But this time was different.

This whole week going backwards and forwards with Evie, even before the transplant, had been different.

He moved down to Evie's wing, pressing the buzzer for access and sanitising his hands thoroughly even though he'd done it the minute he'd dropped Imogen off at the crèche moments earlier.

'How are you?' he asked softly as he stepped into Evie's room.

'Not bad, believe it or not.'

Her voice was a little scratchy from the intubation during surgery and she was lying on the bed, awake but tired-looking. He was hardly surprised to see she was out of her hospital gown and dressed in soft, loose-fitting clothes. If she'd whipped her packed day case out of the wardrobe he wouldn't have batted an eyelid.

'The nurses warned me that you'd got yourself up and out of bed and made them help you dress the instant the anaesthetic had worn off,' he rebuked, but there was no heat in his voice.

'I've already been through this with them, Max.' Evie grinned. 'They encourage you to be active—walking reduces the swelling and expedites the recovery process.

They say you should try getting up and around and into a good routine as soon as the anaesthetic wears off if you can. Certainly the day after a successful transplant, like this.'

'Which means *gradual* exercise only.' He refused to let her browbeat him the way she clearly was doing with her nurses.

'My creatinine is already down to one point four, my potassium is normal, and there're no issues from the steroids. Even the sickness is gone.' She ticked them off on her fingers as though for his benefit. 'The hardest part is remembering to drink enough water after having my fluid intake restricted for so long. Walking for my health is the least I can do.'

'Whilst still remembering what your body has just been through, and what it's trying to recover from.'

'My transplant went perfectly,' she argued.

'Your transplant went very smoothly,' he was prepared to acknowledge. 'But that still doesn't mean you push it.'

'Fine.' She raised one hand dismissively but it was a half-hearted gesture. She was clearly tired. 'How's Imogen?'

'She's great,' he replied softly. 'But she misses you.'

All other thoughts visibly slid from Evie's head as a pain welled in her eyes, and Max felt for her. Evie obviously missed her daughter more than she'd even feared she would. It would be a while before she would be able to cuddle Imogen again, probably close to discharge. Evie was still too vulnerable to infection after her transplant, and babies like Imogen seemed to have a permanent cold or some such virus, even though Max was determined to keep Imogen as safe as he possibly could.

He determined that, after the visit was over here, he'd bring Imogen to the window outside Evie's room so that they could at least see each other, if only through the glass, as long as it didn't upset the baby. Knowing Imogen, it probably wouldn't; his daughter's resilience and strength of character was beginning to blow him away.

'She's amazing, you know.' The words tripped out of his mouth, taking both of them by surprise.

'I know.' Evie nodded vigorously.

'She's incredible, and tiny, and beautiful. And she's *my* daughter. Our daughter,' he exclaimed incredulously, pride swelling up inside him. 'I'd like to be a part of her life. A proper part.'

Time stood still as she tried to process what Max was saying. Her heart hammered in her chest.

'What do you mean by a "proper part"? How?'

'I mean that I don't want to be an occasional father.'

'So, weekends? Holidays?' There was an edge to her voice that she appeared to be unsuccessfully fighting.

'Evie?'

'I'm sorry, I don't know what's wrong with me. I always hoped you'd have a relationship with your daughter. For Imogen to have her father in her life.'

'But?' he prompted.

'Nothing,' Evie muttered, leaving him with the distinct impression there was something he was missing.

Before she could register, he reached out and took her hand in one of his, his other hand brushing a stray lock of hair from her face. He didn't understand what compelled him but it felt so oddly intimate and his chest constricted painfully.

'But how would it work, Max? Would you expect me to disrupt my life, move to be closer to you? Away from my family? The people who have supported me?'

She was trying to pick a fight with him now, he realised. He was *definitely* missing something.

'Just think about it, Evie. Okay?'

It said a lot for how he'd grown to care for Imogen in

such a short time. Would Evie try to deny a relationship between them? He already knew he could never accept that. His daughter was already a part of his life. Nothing could change that.

Another awkward silence settled over them and they both shifted uncomfortably. The room was stifling. He wanted to get them both out of there, into a less claustrophobic environment, but he didn't want to strong-arm Evie.

He didn't need to worry, she must have felt the same way as she was pushing herself up and slowly swinging her legs over the side of her bed, wincing as the incision site came under pressure. He was at her side in an instant.

'Here, take my hand.'

For a moment she hesitated but then reluctantly stretched out her arm and allowed Max to help her off the bed. There they stood, toe to toe, neither of them daring to move, even daring to breathe. *Could it be that she* did *still want him, after all?*

'How do you really feel?' he asked huskily, fire practically crackling along his veins.

'It feels good to be free of the burden of dialysis, free of feeling as though my body was letting me down, free of feeling like I'm too ill to really be...attractive.'

And Max had certainly made her feel desirable with that kiss only a week ago, in that side room.

The gap between them was tiny and yet it felt like a veritable chasm. He was tempted to reach down and press his lips to hers, the way he had done a week ago, but he had no idea how she would react.

Time ticked by and still neither of them moved.

Finally, almost jerkily, Max stepped away, turning his back on her so that she couldn't read his expression. Not that he knew what it would tell her. When he spoke he heard the tell-tale hoarseness in his voice.

'Shall we go for a coffee?'

'Sure, why not?' She tried for an easy smile but it looked tight and uncomfortable on her lips and she gave up before turning away.

'Lead on, Speedy,' he tried to tease, sounding as awkward as she had.

At least that might make her feel a smidgen better.

Making her way out of the room, her body loosening up and appearing less alien with every step, she set the pace down the hallway and to the patient area. The loaded silence slowly gave way to a more companionable peace, as he'd hoped, as they left the confinement of her room behind them.

The unit had its own coffee-shop area for patients. Larger, well-ventilated and more voluminous than anywhere in the main hospital, and off limits to anyone not in the transplant suite, the coffee shop was somewhere post-op patients could go without being exposed to any number of coughs, colds or other bugs.

Settling into a comfy chair without argument, she let him get the drinks and bring them over. Then he selected a sturdy-looking round tub chair opposite her and folded one ankle over his opposite knee before taking a casual sip of the hot drink.

She dragged her eyes up from his thighs and eyed his coffee enviously before casting a reproachful gaze at the glass of cool, filtered water he had handed her.

'Drink it,' he commanded, not unkindly. 'Your fluid input will be noted on your chart later.'

'Thanks for that.'

But at least it raised a weak smile. Max relaxed. They would get there. Together they would find a harmonious balance and, by the time Evie was cleared for discharge, they would know what they were going to do for their daughter's future.

* * *

'I can't believe she crashed like that.' Evie sighed as he headed back down the stairs, having put Imogen into her cot for the first night home since the transplant.

'I can.' Max chuckled from the hallway. 'The excitement at seeing you home again wiped her out. Snatching a couple of hours with you morning and evening hasn't been the same as finally having her mummy home.'

Evie swelled with pride, and Max marvelled at how far the two of them had come since that first day post-op in the hospital. It was hard to believe that was a week ago already. He had visited religiously, bringing Imogen to the window so that Evie could see her daughter and talk to her through the opening. And then Imogen had been able to come in to visit her, and he'd done everything he could to ensure he didn't take his daughter anywhere she could pick up any bugs to pass on to Evie.

Evie. She looked beautiful, and vivacious, and exhausted. He should pack her off to bed.

Alone.

Whilst he did something to distract himself from the fact that as their friendship had burgeoned over the last week, so too had his reviving feelings for Evie. Which was going to be the last thing she wanted to hear from him.

Hence his need for a distraction. Like watching some mindless film on TV.

Although, given Evie's reaction to him in the hospital corridor when they'd first bumped into each other a couple of weeks ago, it was patent that there were still *some* residual feelings of their former attraction to one other. But was it purely sexual chemistry, or was there something more?

And as much as he wanted Evie, could happily take her to bed right now, he knew he couldn't. It would never be the fun, no-strings fling of last year. They had a daughter together and they still needed to work out the best solution for her future, without complicating things unnecessarily.

And yet, sex was all he could guarantee. He was still the same man he'd been beforehand, still committed to his career, unable to risk splitting his focus. He couldn't give either Evie or Imogen the family life they would get closer to their own family.

So he wanted her, he could admit that. He wanted her in the most primal way. But the difference was that he was evolved, and this was one base need he was going to have to overrule.

'Anyway...' he pushed aside all his concerns, as he had been doing for the last ten days '...a good, peaceful night's sleep—for both of you—and you'll be ready for more time together tomorrow.'

'I *am* pretty beat,' Evie conceded reluctantly.

'So get some sleep.'

'I can't.' She shook her head. 'I mean, I know I won't be able to drop off. My mind is still racing and I'll just lie there staring at the clock if I go now.'

Yeah, he could relate to that.

'I thought I might watch a film or something. You want to join me?' she offered.

'A film?' he echoed sharply.

So much for his idea of distracting himself. They'd watched a few films together during their brief fling. After all, they'd needed some rest and refuelling—as incredible as the sex had been, even they hadn't managed it twenty-four hours a day. That said, their film watching had inevitably ended only one way.

'Why not?' She shrugged nonchalantly, her brain apparently not in the same gutter as his. 'I could just do with a bit of relaxing with some mindless entertainment.'

He resisted the urge to make a wry quip.

'Okay, let's watch a film together.'

'You choose one. I just want to change...'

'Into something more comfortable?' he teased, the cliché slipping out before he could swallow it down. 'That is, more comfortable over the incision site?'

He cringed internally. He'd had no intention of revealing to Evie just how fragile his control over himself was right now. Thankfully, she seemed too preoccupied with her own thoughts to notice.

'Right,' she muttered. 'My wound.'

'Okay. Meet you in there when you're ready.' He retreated into the kitchen for something to eat.

He wasn't even that hungry but he felt the need to occupy his hands if nothing else. His mind trying to put the brakes on the X-rated thoughts going on in the background, Max yanked the cupboards open with unnecessary vigour.

A bag of microwavable popcorn. That would do.

By the time he returned to the lounge Evie was gliding in, dressed in a light grey jersey pyjama-style tracksuit. He tried not to look her up and down, but it was impossible. The clothes emphasised long, slender legs, which had once wrapped so tightly around his hips, a slim waist he had held with his palms and, as the light material clung to the contours of breasts he could picture whenever he closed his eyes, his fingers itched to pull down the zip to reveal more than just that delicious glimpse of cleavage on offer right now.

So much for his desire for self-control.

He tried not to remember the sweet hollow spot at the base of her neck, which was on clear view now as Evie's long hair was pulled up into a sleek ponytail. She unselfconsciously reached for a handful of popcorn, oblivious to the less than pure thoughts running through his head right now.

He seriously needed to pull himself together.

'All set.' He gave a long-forgotten *just friends* smile and gestured to the home control pad in his hands as if that clarified things. Selecting the movie, he commanded the home system to dim the lights just as Evie held out the bowl.

'Popcorn?'

As she moved a familiar gentle perfume, essentially Evie scent, reached his nostrils. In an instant, his jeans grew taut over his groin. Odd, how the olfactory sense was so powerful it could evoke the most vivid of images. Not least right now when he had a flashback to Evie, wild and abandoned in his bed as he grazed his teeth over the sensitive skin just below her ear. And the added low lighting certainly wasn't helping matters.

Grateful for the proffered snack food, he grasped the bowl and rammed it almost painfully down into his lap.

Since when had he turned into a horny, fifteen-year-old adolescent? He had a feeling he wasn't going to remember much of this film, after all.

CHAPTER EIGHT

EVIE WOKE UP and lay for a moment in the darkness, trying to get her bearings.

She was back in Max's home. And after last night, living here with Max felt even more loaded with frustrated longing than before she'd gone in to hospital.

The whole week, ever since that moment when she'd been scared before the transplant and Max had reassured her, she'd felt the old feelings resurfacing with a vengeance. And feeling her whole body change, almost overnight, when Annie's kidney had begun to clear out her body naturally, Evie had realised there was no more dialysis, no more feeling sluggish, no more telling herself how unattractive she was, no more missing out on the fun things because she was lacking in basic energy.

Her whole life was going to improve, something she hadn't dared hope before. Her relationship with Imogen was going to be so much better now she had more strength and energy. And her relationship with Max was blossoming a she felt her former confidence returning.

Yet last night...well, what had happened last night?

She didn't remember a single second of the film; she'd been too busy being hyper-aware of every move Max ha made. She'd been sure she hadn't misread the signals; tha they both felt the attraction, and she'd been equally sur that, given half a chance, they could revisit something of their fling last year.

By contrast, Max had been absorbed in the film, and oblivious of her more X-rated thoughts. Hardly the greatest ego-boost she could have hoped for. She didn't know how she'd got it all so wrong, but the humiliation still stung her cheeks whenever she thought about it.

So right now she really needed a release mechanism. A brisk walk on the treadmill in Max's gym would not only meet the daily exercise goals of her post-op recovery, but it would help to expend some of her pent-up energy.

Maybe.

At least the gym being in the basement meant that she wouldn't wake either Max or Imogen. Although with its high-level windows allowing plenty of natural light, it had never felt like a claustrophobic space to her, plus it was well-ventilated enough to more than satisfy her transplant requirements.

Easing herself carefully out of bed, Evie dressed quickly, only struggling to put her socks and trainers on, and then crept quietly out of the master suite and down to the basement.

The last person she expected to see was Max.

A hot and sweaty Max.

She hovered in the doorway and wondered if he'd seen her or if she could discreetly back away.

'Are you coming in, then?' he asked.

Clearly not the latter, then.

Evie scanned the room. A towel was hung over the treadmill and weights were scattered around his bench; he'd clearly been here a while. He looked pumped, slick, and impressively fit.

Of course he did.

'Um, I was after the treadmill, but you're obviously busy. I can come back later.'

'No need.' Max sprang up with enviable energy and ducked across the room to retrieve his towel. 'I finished on there before. I just have a few reps here and I'll be out of your hair if you prefer.'

'No, no, that's fine.'

It wasn't really. She didn't need Max seeing her pathetic attempt to walk a couple of miles whilst he knocked out reps like some elite athlete.

'I couldn't sleep,' she offered, willing her feet to move. After some objection, they mercifully obeyed.

'Me neither. But our daughter is gently snoring her little head off.'

He jerked his head and a baby monitor blinked at her from the small side table. So it wasn't Imogen keeping him awake, then.

'Has she been asleep all this time?'

'No chance. I think the excitement of seeing you home last night got to her.'

Evie smiled warmly. Their reunion, as brief as it had been and given Imogen understood so little, had been the most uplifting experience she could have imagined.

'Just as we suspected, her tummy woke her in the night and she had a good feed and a little play. So she'll probably sleep longer than usual this morning.'

'Oh, right.'

She wanted her daughter to rest, but she was longing to cuddle the little girl again.

And as for Max—did it make things better or worse that it was just overtiredness keeping him awake? For one brief moment she had allowed herself to think it might be the same sexual frustration that she'd been feeling, that maybe last night hadn't been as easy for him as she'd believed. But she'd only been fooling herself.

Stepping onto the treadmill, Evie started off her mid-speed walk and tried to concentrate on the low-level music

Don't look.

At least she was getting fitter and stronger every day.

Think of anything else but the fact that he doesn't even have a shirt on.

And soon she would be back to normal.

And what else?

Then she could take Imogen back to Annie's.

Nope, it was an exercise in futility.

Her eyes snapped inexorably back to Max. She hungrily drank in the sight of his body rippling and pumping oh-so-deliciously as his muscles worked in exquisite harmony. She had no idea she'd been effectively ogling for a good twenty minutes until he wound up his reps and she glanced at the screen on the treadmill.

'So, how are you going?' he asked, sauntering casually over once he'd cleared his weights away.

She was only grateful she hadn't chosen to wear a heart monitor. It would be bleeping like crazy right about now, and it had nothing to do with how hard she was pushing herself in an attempt to drown out her lamenting libido.

'Not too bad.' She breathed out hard.

Max frowned.

'Are you sure that isn't too fast?'

'Brisk,' she countered. 'That's the key. Once I've got over the first few weeks, I can probably start on a bike, or the cross trainer.'

'Fine, I'll show you how to use that one over there when you're ready. It's not the most user-friendly model I could have chosen.' Max slotted his water bottle into the holder on her machine. 'Here, drink this.'

Evie didn't answer. Did he really expect her to still be here in a few weeks' time? Wouldn't he be expecting her to leave soon?

'Okay, I'm going to leave you to it. Imogen will be waking soon and I wouldn't mind a shower before the nappy changes and feeding begin.' He chuckled.

He was trying, but they were both aware how stilted the conversation was.

'Good idea.'

'Everything okay?'

How was it he could read her so easily?

'I'm just a bit tired, that's all,' she lied, hating the fact that she was using the transplant as an excuse but not wanting him to guess at the real reason for her distraction.

Evie waited, only releasing her breath as he dipped his head in a curt nod, then left the room. She threw herself into her walking for the next twenty minutes, but once the timer ended she still wasn't ready to return upstairs. Everywhere she went in this house had X-rated memories haunting every inch of her brain. Selecting a harder, longer, uphill programme, Evie was determined to clear her mind of everything but getting better.

By the time she finished the second exercise programme and left the home gym to climb the first set of stairs from the basement, she already knew she'd pushed too hard. Every muscle ached. The last thing she needed was to collide with the rock-solid, Max-shaped wall with an undignified *oomph*.

'What the...? Have you been in the gym all this time?' he demanded angrily. 'No, don't answer that, I can see it for myself. You're practically white, Evie.'

'I think I did a bit too much,' she admitted quietly, wondering if she was going to be sick or whether she just *thought* she was going to be.

'You think?'

'I just... *Hey!*' She panicked as he scooped her up into his arms. 'I need a shower—what are you doing?'

'I'm doing exactly what it looks like. I'm carrying you into the kitchen because, frankly, you're never going to make it upstairs by yourself, and I think you could do with something inside your stomach. Your shower can wait, unless you want to risk collapsing?'

'You're right,' Evie answered slowly, trying to ignore the way every nerve ending in her body felt it was on fire beneath Max's touch. 'I think I probably am a bit hungry.'

At least her stomach didn't let her down, giving a thunderous rumble of agreement at the mention of food.

She wasn't quite prepared for the indignity of Max instructing her to peel off her damp tee shirt and handing her his warm fleece jacket. Not even the sight of her in her bra caused a raised eyebrow from him, she thought glumly. A far cry from the fervour with which they had repeatedly devoured each other a year ago.

But within moments she was seated on a chair, a mouthwatering glass of no-longer-forbidden orange juice in front of her, Imogen in her line of sight and playing happily with some soft blocks, whilst Max whisked up two omelettes.

Evie watched in silence considering how, to an outsider, it might have looked like a scene of blissful domesticity. How wrong they would be. She pushed the thought from her head, wondering why she felt so down. But last night had only proved that whatever attraction had once bounced between her and Max, it was now gone. At least, on his part. So she might as well just enjoy the here and now with him as the father of her child, if nothing else.

'D'you know I haven't been able to eat a whole-egg omelette for almost a year?' She forced herself to smile, realising that it wasn't all that difficult as Max set the warm plate down in front of her and slipped into the far seat so that he didn't block her view of their daughter.

'Well, I make a mean omelette if I say so myself. Plus there's a bagel with cream cheese and some smoked salmon if you want it.'

'You remembered.' She was surprised. Not that she

could eat all that now, but it had been her favourite breakfast when working in the hospital, and Max had made it for
her a couple of mornings during their fling. When they'd
dragged themselves out of bed, that was. Or the shower.
Or the swivel office chair.

They ate in companionable silence before Evie reluctantly pushed her chair back, carrying her plate over to
the worktop.

'Thanks,' she told him sincerely. 'I guess I'd better go
and get a shower before the sweat dries on me and I get a
chill. Can't imagine Professor Goodwin would be amused.'

'Not really,' Max agreed. 'Leave that, I'll sort it.'

Pivoting on her heel as best she could, Evie headed upstairs, finally allowing herself the indulgence of breathing in Max's unique scent from his fleece. A bittersweet
sensation, which brought back memories of their time together, as well as a sadness that it would never be like that
between them again. And there wasn't a damn thing she
could do about it.

At least the shower in her bathroom called seductively
to her and, after checking her blood pressure and temperature were within the expected ranges, Evie headed into
the tiled area, the underfloor heating making the floor as
pleasant to walk over as she remembered.

'*Hello*, power shower,' she murmured, looking at the
oversized walk-in shower she had fallen in love with in
those few days before going into hospital.

Turning the chrome-spoked wheel and selecting the wa-
terfall setting, Evie stepped back and flashed a triumphant
smile as the steaming-hot water spilled out. Now all she
had to do was strip off.

Easier said than done.

It took her almost five minutes to divest herself of her exercise outfit. Stretching still pulled at the incision, especially

after having overdone it in the gym, and she didn't want to give the wound any reason to seep and not heal perfectly.

She was in the uncomfortable process of twisting her arms back to try to reach her bra clips when she realised she wasn't going to be able to lift her arms high enough to wash her hair. Not a pleasant prospect given the way she'd sweated in the gym, trying to empty her mind of wanton thoughts of Max. Evie stopped, leaning on the marble countertop as she tried to decide the best course of action.

Leave it. Or ask Max for help.

She chewed on her lip nervously.

What was a realistic solution? She really couldn't afford *not* to wash her hair, but she could hardly bend double over the sink—her body wasn't quite recovered for that yet. Short of getting into the shower with her, how was Max supposed to help her? She froze at the images that conjured. Not least the memories of the shower they'd shared during their nights together. She could almost feel the water coursing over her skin as Max had explored her with his mouth.

Stop right there, she warned herself silently. If the way he'd divested her of her top downstairs was anything to go by, he'd be professional, polite and not in the least bit attracted to her. She'd do well to follow his lead, and if he could be detached then so could she.

Besides, there was nothing else for it.

Slamming off the shower and snatching up a towel, she squared her shoulders and went in search of Max. Grateful to see him coming up the stairs as she reached the landing.

'I need your help,' she announced without preamble. 'Please?'

She didn't dare look over her shoulder to check he was following her as she marched back into the bathroom, grateful for the steam, which offered at least the psychological semblance of privacy.

Professional, polite, detached. Professional, polite, de-

tached... She repeated it like a mantra so by the time she faced Max she was more composed than she'd been before.

'You want my help...for a shower?'

He sounded aghast but she refused to let it get to her.

Professional, polite, detached. She could do it. She would do it.

'To wash my hair,' she explained. 'We can keep underwear on—it'll be like a bikini for the beach.'

Well, no, not really, but she could pretend that was what she was thinking.

'This is ridiculous,' he muttered, shaking his head and walking out of the bathroom without another word. Evie watched the empty doorway and tried to quash the sense of loss.

The minutes ticked by, and still Max didn't return. *Talk about adding insult to injury.* He wasn't attracted to her yet the idea of stepping into the shower had appalled him that much, he wouldn't even entertain helping her. It was a sobering realisation.

Did it matter if ten other men found her attractive in the future? Wouldn't she always remember that the one man who really counted, at least in her head, had been so shamefully turned off by her?

There was nothing else she could do. She would just have to try her best to do it alone. With a shake of her head, she resumed her attempts to unhook her bra.

'You've done your obs?'

Evie swung around, dropping her arms too late and folding them across her chest as he reappeared in the doorway, the baby monitor in his hand.

'*That* was where you went? To check on our daughter?'

'Where else?' he managed, surprised at the relief in her tone. Where had she thought he'd gone? 'You didn't answer me, though. Have you done your obs?'

'I have,' she confirmed awkwardly. 'How's Imogen?'

'She's asleep. Like I said, long night teething and she didn't sleep in as long as I'd expected this morning. She just wanted a bit of a play and some breakfast of her own to fill her little tum and she was ready for a catch-up nap.'

His gaze dropped to her chest as it peeked out from behind her forearms.

'So, do you need some help?'

'No,' she squeaked, coughing to regain her normal voice. 'I'm fine now.'

A beat passed.

'Clearly you're struggling.' Max blew out a breath and walked back into the room. 'Turn around.'

'No, I'm fine. I just…'

'Quit stalling and turn around, Evie.'

He had to stay composed, not give away just how much she still turned him on. He'd managed it downstairs in the kitchen when he'd got her to strip off her wet top, though it had taken some effort. He just had to remember that she wouldn't recover if she wasn't relaxed, which meant not making her feel uncomfortable, as though he might pounce on her any second.

He had to think of her like any other patient. He was never attracted to them no matter how attractive they were.

Except that she wasn't any other patient. She was Evie. And that was what made her stand out from anyone else he'd ever known.

The heavy silence hung between them as Max reached around and unhooked her bra in one simple, efficient movement.

'Hey!' she gulped.

'How did you get it on?' he asked.

'Sorry?'

He cocked an eyebrow at her.

'How did you get the bra on? If you can't get it off?'

'I put it on forwards and turned it around.' She flushed prettily. 'But, like you said, I did a bit too much this morning and my muscles have already started to tighten up.'

'So, do you need help with your briefs, or can you do that?'

'They stay on. And you can hook my bra back on, too. Like a bikini, remember?'

'Evie, I'm supposed to be here to help you. I'm a surgeon, and we're both adults. I'm sure we can see this for what it is and control ourselves.'

Why did that sound like a challenge to himself?

Still, he'd always relished a challenge.

Deftly he slid the item from behind her towel and slung it into the wicker laundry basket without even turning round. The corners of her mouth twitched despite her nerves.

'Fluke,' she teased him unexpectedly.

He stuffed down the flare of attraction.

'Entirely,' he agreed. 'Now, get in the shower.'

They were dancing dangerously close to the flames, he thought as he shed his own clothing, watching her silhouette through the steamed-up glass panel of the shower. He had no idea what he thought he was doing, agreeing to wash her hair like this, but he hadn't been able to stop himself. The fact that his body was already reacting to the shadowy pink silhouette wasn't filling him with hope, but he could hardly change his mind now. Stripping down to his boxers, Max dumped everything in the laundry basket, schooled his thoughts and picked up her shampoo and conditioner before stepping into the shower. An all too familiar, soft, perfect backside drew his gaze and his body tightened further. He was going to have to keep his distance.

Quickly, he stretched his arm around Evie to place the bottles on the marble-tiled alcove, making a conscious effort to avoid contact with her skin. Then, picking the shampoo bottle back up and squeezing out a generous amount for her long hair, he lathered it onto her scalp. As he worked his way through, he watched her place her fingers on the alcove to brace herself and gave a satisfied nod. She wasn't as strong as she liked to make out; her body was still recovering and this shower would have been too much for her alone. With a renewed sense of vindication, Max concentrated on sectioning out her hair and shampooing.

Despite their wildly insatiable desire for each other last year, it was this simple activity that felt the most intimate to Max. Something that people having a basic fling would never do for each other. A quietly affectionate gesture, to wash her hair like this.

He rather liked it.

It was only when the first few strands began to come away that he realised what was happening. It wasn't a lot, but temporary hair loss or breakage was one of the known side effects of some of the medications Evie was taking, until the nephrology team had chance to balance her doses. Max contemplated whether or not to mention it to her now. She would already be aware of the probability, but did she really need the added stress of it actually happening now? And to his mind, it didn't make her any less attractive, or any less of a woman.

He finished shampooing her hair and gently leaned her to one side so that as he rinsed her hair the suds didn't run down on the incision side of her body. Then he started all over again with the conditioner.

Finally, his task complete and his body reined in, Max reached for the tortoiseshell clip he knew she used, twisted her hair up and tied it back. It wasn't exactly neat, but it would do, and it kept her hair from sweeping across her back and dripping any residual hair product near her wound.

His eyes swept over the smooth skin of her back, which his hands remembered so well.

'Here.' His voice was gruffer than he'd intended. 'I'll do your back since you can't reach it.'

She froze momentarily before relinquishing the body puff to him. Swiftly, he soaped her shoulders and back then over her sides, taking care not to linger or to go too close to the wound. Eventually he felt Evie begin to relax. He worked his way downwards using circular movements, covering the backside that was causing his body such difficulties, and bending down to cover the backs of her legs.

There. Done. Give her the body puff back and stand up.

Slowly, almost against his own will, his hands reached up to her waist, his head in line with her hips as he angled her slightly towards him, ignoring her initial resistance, still using the body puff to lather the hip closest to him. He turned her more until his face was inches away from the apex of her thighs.

He could recall the way she tasted, the way she felt. His body tightened in response and he moved the body puff across her abdomen as if to remind himself of what he was supposed to be doing. He inched up, his eyes now level with her incision, her hand hovering over it as if to hide it from him.

'Let me check it?' Half-question, half-command.

She paused, before slowly moving her arm.

Max inspected it. It was healing well.

'Looks good,' he concluded, glancing up at her.

Evie's face was flushed, embarrassed, her eyes closed and her head turned slightly away, as though she didn't dare look at him.

As though she was ashamed of him seeing her scar. As though she was ashamed of the new softness around her abdomen after carrying their daughter, he realised incredulously.

Max ran a hand down over her belly, her flinching confirming his suspicions.

He opened his mouth to tell her not to be embarrassed, that they were a symbol of how strong she was, after all she'd been through this year. But then he realised she wouldn't believe him. Still, he didn't need to say anything; actions spoke louder than words, right?

He dropped his gaze to the full breasts that his hands ached to touch. The perfect brown nipple he longed to take in his mouth. Before he could stop himself, with one hand still on her hip, his other hand trailed up the opposite side of her body to her ribcage, the underside of her breasts. He left it there whilst he placed a kiss on her belly.

She moved one hand to hide the skin but didn't push him away.

'If this is about your scar or your body, I don't want to hear it,' he growled. 'But if you really want me to stop, you say so now and I will.'

The wait almost killed him, but she said nothing as her breathing shallowed and the underside of her breast skimmed his knuckles. It was the signal he needed.

He flicked out the thumb to caress her nipple and, despite the hot shower, Evie's skin goosebumped instantly in response, a low sound escaping her lips. He hardened immediately, straightening up until he could replace his thumb with his tongue, revelling in the way Evie slipped her fingers through his hair without any more hesitation, her other hand on his shoulder. He drew the hard nipple into his mouth, his tongue playing with it, his hands roaming the satiny skin of her body as she gripped his shoulder harder, arching slightly against him.

'Kiss me, Max.'

The instruction was shaky but it was there, and Max slowly straightened up, his mouth claiming hers in one movement. Still, he was only too happy to oblige when she took his hand and returned it to its earlier ministrations of her breast, her own hand reaching for him as she gave a small sound of pleasure when he flexed in her palm.

Her hand closed around him, exactly the way she knew would get him, and he groaned with need, wanting to touch her, taste her, fill her. He stepped back to give his hand room to reach down between her legs, but as he removed his support from her she swayed and stumbled.

What the hell was he doing, pushing her like that?

Evie was still recovering. She might be trying to act as though she were recovering quickly but that didn't mean she was ready for this no matter how she'd reacted. He should have known better than to act on it. He was supposed to be taking care of her, looking out for her. Not giving in to his desire for her.

Drawing away, he reached for the taps and spun them closed. Then, grabbing a bath sheet from the towel rail, he bundled Evie up and lifted her into his arms.

'Max, what are you doing?'

Wordlessly, he carried her through to the bedroom and lowered her gently onto the master bed, before leaving the room. He needed to get to work and start his day. And maybe a couple of nights on call at the hospital would be the best thing for both Evie and himself, too.

CHAPTER NINE

PULLING THE CAR into the garage, Max leaned back in his seat and rubbed his hand over his neck. It had taken three days of gruelling surgeries, just to keep himself busy, sleeping at the hospital, and stop any wayward thoughts of Evie.

He didn't know how to even begin to apologise to her for pushing her the other morning in the shower, his desire for her overwhelming his sense of what was right. He doubted she would be happy to see him this morning. He would have stayed away longer if he could and afforded her more space, but she had a post-op check-up in a couple of hours and he needed to ensure she didn't miss it and was recovering well.

Despite everything, an inner peace had descended on him the moment the garage door had closed neatly behind him and he'd turned the engine off.

Home.

Sliding out of the car, he walked quietly through the connecting door to the hallway, careful not to make too much noise, which could wake Evie or Imogen, when a shadowy shape flickered in his peripheral vision.

'What the…?'

Sidestepping the figure as it suddenly advanced towards him, he snapped the light on and spun around. A white-faced Evie blinked back at him, the loft hatch stick gripped in tight knuckles like a cricket bat. Her shoulders sagged slightly as she realised it was him.

She looked fierce, and frightened, and adorable. He tried to stop his lips from twitching.

'I didn't mean to scare you, sorry.'

'Where the heck have you been?'

The anger in her tone was undeniable and Max's heart sank. If he'd held out any faint hopes that she might have forgiven him his indiscretion with her, then he knew now that wasn't going to happen. He couldn't blame her, but still it cut him to think that she was that furious with him. That he'd betrayed her trust so irrevocably.

So much for the friendship truce he'd promised her a week earlier. He had to tackle it head-on, before she could say anything to make him feel worse than he already did.

'Evie, I'm sorry about the other day. It shouldn't have happened. It was a serious misstep on my part and one which I can assure you will never happen again.'

'A misstep?' She narrowed her eyes at him and his brain whirred.

Was calling it a misstep too flimsy? Dismissing it as less important than it really was?

'A mistake,' he stated flatly, thrusting aside the voice that argued it hadn't felt like a mistake at the time. It had felt natural, and right, as if the two of them fitted together.

What was wrong with him? He felt his face twist into a sneer. Clearly Evie didn't share his rosy version of events or he wouldn't have felt it best to stay away until now.

'A dreadful mistake,' he emphasised. 'For which I am entirely to blame.'

'Oh.'

She sounded less than impressed.

'Anyway, what's all this?' He reached over to prise the long loft-hatch pole from her fingers, hoping in vain to lighten the atmosphere.

'I was frightened you might be a burglar,' she snapped coldly, pursing her lips.

'And you thought you'd come down here and confront them? With a thin stick of wood that would shatter as soon as it made contact with something hard, like a human skull?'

'It was all I could find quickly.' She eyed him defiantly.

'You seriously thought you could cause damage with this thing? You know the house is armed to the nth degree, right?' he rebuked gently. 'If I really *had* been an intruder, you should have stayed upstairs, locked the doors and called the police.'

'And let them come and get us? No chance,' spluttered Evie. 'Although you really need to have a rounders bat or a cricket bat hanging around. That would have been a lot better.'

'You didn't think that it might just be me?' He chanced another attempt at coaxing her out of her fury. 'It *is* my house.'

'Apparently so,' Evie ground out, furiously refusing to be placated. 'Yet you abandoned me here.'

'Abandoned?' he scoffed. 'That's a bit overdramatic, surely?'

'Abandoned,' Evie repeated angrily. 'You beat a hasty retreat to your safe haven of the hospital the minute things got a little...*muddied* here. It didn't exactly fit with you dragging me from the security of my family with the claim that my recovery here would be better than it would have been with them.'

Max folded his arms across his chest, ready to argue with her, before realising she had a valid point. Or, more accurately, another valid point. He *had* wrestled her from her brother's house claiming he would take care of her and Imogen. And he *had* left her alone when he'd come on so strong. But he'd assumed that would be what she wanted.

'I thought you'd prefer some space,' he managed, less certainly now.

'You left me here, with no word as to where you were or how long you'd be there. When you'd return here, *if* you'd return here. I have no one I know around me, and it was just Imogen and I for the last few days. And you think I preferred that?'

She spat the accusation at him as he stood, dumb-founded.

'You knew I was at the hospital, though. And I asked Edina to make sure you were okay.'

'Oh, yes, your cleaning lady. Thanks for your concern,' Evie choked out sarcastically.

Max hesitated. He *had* been concerned. More than he'd cared to admit. But he'd thought Edina was the most neutral party to check Evie's welfare.

'After…what happened, I assumed you'd prefer me not to be around for a while.'

Evie opened her mouth, then blew out hard.

'You assumed wrong,' came her eventual clipped response. 'It's quiet here. And lonely. I'm used to the bustle of family. You should have asked me, checked with me.'

'You're right,' Max acknowledged.

She was hurt, he realised with a jolt.

It was an eye-opener. He'd expected Evie to be furious with him for coming back so soon. But he hadn't considered she might be hurt that he'd left her alone in the first place. *Abandoned* her, as she'd put it.

She didn't even seem to care about what had happened that night before he'd left, apart from her initial dislike of him dismissing it as merely a misstep.

'Do you want a coffee?' he asked gently. 'A tea?'

'Geez, Max,' she grumbled, but the initial heat had dissipated from her voice. 'It's so early it's still practically the middle of the night. I'm going back to bed.'

'Right.' He swallowed abruptly as she stomped back up the stairs and he noticed her attire for the first time. A strappy vest did a poor job of covering generous curves, whilst light pyjama bottoms followed the contours of her bottom.

He dragged his gaze away but the heat was already suffusing his body.

He was in serious trouble. One tiny indication that she might not be as immune to him as he'd first thought and his resolve was crumbling again, faster than a chocolate sunbed on a sunny beach.

This was shaping up to be more of a roller coaster than their fling had been, and all he could hope to do was hold on and see where the ride took him.

'So, that brings us to section six: *Sex after transplantation.*'

A low groan of objection escaped Evie's lips and she shifted uncomfortably in the consultant's office chair.

After her humiliation of the other day, and their cringe-worthy row earlier this morning, the last thing she wanted to do was to discuss the intimate details of her libido whilst sitting a foot away from the man who stirred said libido but who couldn't have been less attracted to her.

'I really don't think we need to go into that now.'

Undaunted by her lack of enthusiasm, however, her nephrologist shot her a smile as she slid a pamphlet across the coffee table separating them.

'Evie.' Arabella Goodwin cocked an eyebrow at her. 'We're all adults here and, whilst I appreciate you and Max kept your relationship impressively discreet whilst you were working between here and the centre, we do nevertheless need to consider the fact that you clearly have a healthy sexual relationship.'

'Oh...no...we don't...that is, there is no...relationship.'

'I do understand you don't want to be part of the rumour

mill, Evie,' the woman cut in, not unkindly, 'but I also understand that you have a daughter together, and therefore we really do need to cover this material as part of your post-operative care. However, please rest assured that nothing said in here will leave my office.'

'No...it's just...' Evie tried again, her cheeks stinging with humiliation as she felt unusually flustered. She wanted to look to Max for support but was concerned that he might not wish to be dragged further into it. Besides, she couldn't bring herself to meet his gaze. As a doctor she might have asked similar kinds of personal questions without thinking twice, but it was very different from discussing her own sex-life with former colleagues. And, again, there was that little issue of doing so in front of Max.

As if reading her mind, Max shifted in his own seat and cleared his throat calmly. She waited for his icy tone to set his colleague straight once and for all.

'Please, Arabella.' His voice was controlled, polite. 'As you say, we kept things discreet when we were colleagues but, yes, we have a daughter together. Do continue.'

With a squeak of embarrassment Evie snatched her hand away from the pamphlet.

She snapped her head around, no longer too ashamed to look him in the face, only to be met with his steely gaze. Clearly he wasn't encouraging—what threatened to be a deeply intimate—conversation for his own entertainment or to make her feel any more humiliated than she already did. But his expression was unreadable. She was going to have to go along with it, for now, but she made a mental note to challenge him just as soon as they were alone again.

Not that *that* was a particularly thrilling prospect at this moment, either.

'Thank you. Let's start by noting that there are many

factors which can influence sexual desire after transplantation, not least a patient's self-confidence.'

With a *whoosh* of breath, Evie resigned herself to the inevitable conversation, which already had her feeling as uncomfortable as she had when, as a teenager, she had been caught with her boyfriend at the time by her bumbling stepfather, who had subsequently attempted to have *The Talk*. She reached subconsciously once more for the pamphlet as Professor Goodwin continued.

'During the pre-operative period, especially when on dialysis, there are obviously more toxins around the body, which might have influenced your physical health. But also going through the process of dialysis could understandably have made you feel less confident in yourself?'

There was an expectant lull and Evie realised with a start that she was expected to offer her personal experience here.

Oh, joy.

She cast a surreptitious glance at Max, but he was steadfastly ignoring her, focused on the nephrologist. She twisted the pamphlet in her hands, buying herself a few more precious moments. With her palms sweating she felt more like an adolescent than a woman, and a doctor to boot.

'It's not exactly the…sexiest thing, being on dialysis, is it?' she mumbled.

'So you experienced a loss of sex drive?'

Her whole face felt as though it were on fire. This was excruciating. How many times had she replayed their wild, sensual explosive five nights together, just to get through the last year?

'Not exactly a loss, no.'

Both Max and the surgeon sat—one waiting stiffly, the other waiting patiently—for her to carry on. Clearly they weren't about to let her off the hook. She saw Professor Goodwin, glancing down at her lap, pucker her eyebrows. Following the surgeon's eyes, Evie finally noticed the shredded pamphlet on her own lap.

Giveaway or what?

'I know this isn't the easiest conversation to have, Evie. But understanding what point you're at both mentally and physically, in terms of your sexual needs, is an important part of the recovery process. Which is why it helps to acknowledge where you were before the transplant and where you hope to be post-transplant, as your recovery progresses.'

Evie jerked her head into something resembling a nod, working her tongue into a response.

'It was a difficult year,' she started, falteringly. 'My renal deterioration was quite rapid, especially being pregnant with Imogen, and I went from feeling completely healthy eighteen months ago, to needing dialysis five times a week during the last few months of carrying Imogen.'

'So which do you believe had the greater impact on your sex drive? The physical drain of the pregnancy and dialysis, or the psychological effect of them?'

'I don't know.' Evie tapped out some unknown tune on the wood as she stalled for time. 'A bit of both, I suppose.'

'And can you remember…? When was the last time you wanted physical intimacy?'

This was the question she'd most wanted to avoid. Especially here, in front of Max. A fresh wave of heat flooded her cheeks, but what choice did she have?

'A few days ago,' she muttered awkwardly.

She felt Max's eyes burning into her neck, and kept her gaze resolutely forward.

'Hmm, you're currently…' Professor Goodwin checked her notes '…eleven days post-op, so that's very positive. And did you actually have physical intimacy?'

Evie shook her head.

'Was that because of a lack of energy? Because the desire waned? Or something else.'

'Something else,' Evie managed.

'Right?' Both a statement and an encouragement to continue.

Evie chose to ignore the latter. She couldn't bring herself to tell anyone, least of all in front of Max, that it was because her attraction wasn't reciprocated.

So she flailed around in her head for an alternative explanation that might sound convincing, but nothing came.

'Evie…?' Arabella urged gently, smiling kindly as Evie could only stare helplessly at her.

Evie opened her mouth but nothing came out.

'Let me get another of these for you.' The surgeon stood up unexpectedly. 'I'll be back in a moment.'

Evie watched her leave gratefully. Clearly Arabella Goodwin was not only a good surgeon but a compassionate individual. This was a perfect excuse to give Evie and Max a moment together, and Evie a chance to compose herself. The woman couldn't have known that Evie could easily have clung onto the woman's immaculately tailored suit and begged her not to leave herself and Max alone in the room.

As the door closed with a soft click Evie stared into her lap, waiting for the inevitable questions.

'You're still…attracted to me?'

He actually sounded surprised, and a little put out, and for a moment Evie forgot her embarrassment. She jerked her head up to stare at him. *The man did look in the mirror, didn't he?*

'Yes,' she answered slowly. 'I can't help that you don't feel the same. My kidney…situation is hardly a turn-on, but you don't have to act as though I'm so completely undesirable as a woman. You were attracted to me, too, once.'

'Is that what you think?'

'That you were attracted to me?' Evie was confused.

'No—' he actually clicked his tongue at her '—that I don't find you desirable.'

She barked out a humourless laugh.

'I think the fact you walked out on me the other day, whilst I was lying practically naked on the bed, is pretty much all the evidence I need.'

'Because I thought I was taking advantage of you,' he exclaimed in a low voice. 'You're only a week post-op. A *major* op, I should add, and you needed my help to even wash your hair in the shower. And there I was, reacting to you. I thought you felt somehow...obligated to me.'

Obligated? Evie's head raced. *No wonder he'd looked so disgusted. But not at her, as she'd assumed. At himself.*

A bubble of happiness wound its way up inside her chest.

'So you don't find me undesirable? Unattractive?'

'I think our curtailed week last year makes it clear just how desirable I find you,' he refuted, his voice thicker than usual.

But any response died on her tongue as the door opened up again and the surgeon walked back in.

So, Max had *wanted her?*

Had he really walked out because he was disgusted at himself, wanting her the way she'd wanted him? Had he really stayed away because he hadn't been sure he could control himself around her and not, as she had surmised, because he had abandoned her?

She chanced another look at Max, who was now also toying with the pamphlet the nephrologist had placed on the table.

A grin played at the corners of her mouth.

She wondered if it was time for a bit of fun. Everything had been so serious lately. Fears weighing so heavily on her, between her own health and Imogen's. And the shock of finding out he had a daughter must have been incredible for Max. But what if they could rediscover some of the fun they'd once shared? The wild side they'd seen in each other during their brief fling.

Yes, the sex had been incredible. But they'd also had fun, laughing and joking in such a way that any outsider would have thought they were in a relationship rather than just indulging in a brief fling before Max disappeared overseas.

Was it possible? Or was it a foolhardy idea? There was only one way to find out.

It was like a switch clicking in Evie's brain as a cheeky thought slid inside.

'I didn't lose interest in sexual intimacy.' She met her nephrologist's eye boldly. She couldn't risk looking to her side. 'I still thought about it, even if I didn't have the opportunity I'd had before my daughter was born. I thought about it a lot, in fact. Especially in the beginning, and then again in the last week before my operation.'

When she'd moved in with Max. Let him work that one out. In her peripheral vision, she could see his head twisting around to look at her, but she didn't dare acknowledge him for fear of laughing.

'That's interesting,' her surgeon noted, oblivious to the significance of the statement. 'And did you feel able to act on it?'

'Not really,' she answered honestly. 'Having an infant isn't exactly conducive. And then there was the dialysis as we talked about before. Although they weren't the only factors.'

'And how do you feel now?'

'Now?' She affected an air of nonchalance. 'I feel very much back to my old self already.'

'So where does that leave us?' Max's deep voice reverberated around the room.

Evie twisted her head around. A wry smile hovered on his lips as his eyes narrowed at her. He'd clearly decided two could play at that game. She felt a kick of pleasure low in her abdomen, rippling down through her core.

'Let me be clearer,' he added robustly. 'Is Evie ready for us to be intimate again? Is that normal?'

'Well, for the most part, I'd say that's entirely up to Evie.' Arabella smiled. 'And I hesitate to use words like *normal*, Max. You know as well as anyone how differently patients can bounce back after any operation.'

Evie could practically feel the anticipation warming her skin. It felt good. She felt alive in a way she hadn't in a very long time.

'But in your case,' the surgeon addressed Evie again, 'where you had a willing donor and therefore didn't have to wait for your transplant or spend too long on dialysis, it's a very positive sign.'

'I see,' Max growled.

'So, Evie, you'll probably find you feel ready for sexual intimacy sooner rather than later. And I really would encourage you, if you do feel well and *want* to resume intimacy, to start exploring it together as a couple.'

'Together,' Evie echoed confidently. 'Got it.'

'However, we do advise you to avoid penetrative intercourse for four to six weeks after your transplant. This is purely to allow the incision site time to heal and not to do with causing any kind of damage to the transplant itself, you understand.'

Oh, no, that had to be a cruel joke, right?

'Don't let that put you off exploring your changing libido as a couple, however. Many people get confused and think that sex only refers to the actual penetrative act of intercourse. However, lovemaking can include multiple things.'

'Such as hugging? Kissing? Touching each other?' Evie asked, beginning to enjoy herself.

'Exactly.'

Evie might have known not to underestimate Max.

'And what about more than that?' His low voice rumbled through her chest, winding a hot path down. Lower and lower. Images of his tongue skilfully caressing her until he brought her to orgasm filled her head, and a shaft of heat shot through her.

'Again, that's entirely up to you. As long as it isn't too vigorous and therefore doesn't put too much strain on the incision whilst it's knitting.' Professor Goodwin leafed through her notes. 'And once the four to six weeks are up, be aware that fertility in a woman, post-transplant, can increase and, whilst oral contraception can be taken, we would recommend using the barrier method.'

Not as sexy but a valid point, Evie conceded.

'Some institutions recommend you don't become pregnant for at least a year after your transplant, even with stable kidney function, whilst others say two years. Here, we prefer to say eighteen months to two years.'

'That won't be a problem,' Max announced confidently, leaving Evie to wonder whether that was because he had every intention of using protection this time. Or no intention of needing anything to start with.

'Okay.' The nephrologist nodded. 'Then let's move on to your serum creatinine levels and how we expect these check-ups to progress during the next few weeks.'

CHAPTER TEN

MAX LEFT EVIE to complete the final tests whilst he checked on the recovery of the patients.

It was a welcome escape. The air had been loaded with expectation since their conversation with Arabella Goodwin. They were both acutely aware that once they left the hospital to go back home, sex would be on both their minds. And, despite everything that had been said, Max was still conscious of not wanting to push Evie into anything she wasn't ready for.

He saw the person lingering outside his office long before the woman saw him. Something about the way she was hovering intrigued him, shifting from one foot to the other, playing with her long hair and toying with her clothing, first pushing the sleeves of her flannel shirt up in the heat of the hospital, then pulling them down again. He crossed the heavy-duty linoleum hallway in a couple of long strides.

'Do you need something?'

She jumped back from the doorway to glance nervously at him. She could be here to see anyone, but instinct told him she was one of Evie's troubled teens.

'I was wondering about Dr Parker? I didn't realise her transplant was last week and she'd already been discharged. They told me to come and see you.'

'Right.' He wasn't prepared to give anything away.

'How…how did the doc's transplant go?' the young woman asked tentatively.

His eyes swept over her. The flannel shirt—incongruously heavy for the day's temperatures—was open over a lightweight top and trousers, but it was as the young woman messed with her sleeves again that Max caught sight of the scars that lay on her forearms. Multiple thin, parallel lines of silvery-white scars from razor blade or knife lacerations.

Hastily the young woman pulled the sleeves down again, her eyes sliding away from his for a moment, before changing her mind, standing a little taller and making herself meet his glare.

The tacit action garnered his respect, but still he was guarded.

'The transplant went very smoothly,' he answered finally. 'Dr Parker responded very well to the procedure.'

The young woman's relief was visible.

'Good. That's good. Great, in fact. Where is she staying? Can we come and see her?'

'She needs her rest,' Max cut in pointedly. Evie hadn't once mentioned expecting a visit from an ex-patient to him.

'I know she's still recovering,' the woman agreed. 'I just wanted to know she was all right. They won't tell me anything, even though Dr Parker said she'd put my name down to visit as soon as she was cleared for visitors.'

'She doesn't need her focus to be split right now. Do you understand?'

The young woman's brow furrowed in confusion. He suppressed a stab of frustration and smoothed his voice out.

'Dr Parker is very committed to her work, I appreciate that, even though she hasn't practised for quite a few months now, but she needs to take the time to recover and look after herself. If she feels she's needed somewhere else then she's going to try to rush the healing process in order to get back to work.'

He was surprised to see the woman offer a soft smile of recognition.

'Yes. I can just see her doing that. Well, can you tell her that I was here because I wanted to know she was okay? We all did.'

'All?' It was Max's turn to frown.

She jerked her head towards the waiting room chairs down the hall where a group of kids, surrounded by a cluster of small bunches of flowers, home-made fruit baskets and cards waited. They were all watching the exchange between Max and the woman intently, without crowding the two of them, which was why he hadn't noticed them before.

'Who are they?'

'Some of the kids from the centre.'

A lot of the kids from the centre by the look of it. And gifts from even more of them, judging by the mini-mountain. Max stared in shock.

'You look surprised, but Dr Parker has helped so many of us turn our lives around. That's a big deal.'

She narrowed her eyes, assessing him, then clearly decided she had nothing to lose.

'You saw my scars.' She lifted her still-covered arms before dropping them back down to her sides. Nevertheless she met his stare head-on, her chin tilting defiantly.

'I used to self-harm for years, ever since I was a kid. I couldn't even admit it to myself, let alone tell my family. Eight years ago I met Dr Parker and I've been cut-free for seven years now, and I'm working on keeping it that way.'

'Understood,' Max acknowledged.

Max considered the strong young woman standing in front of him, surprised at her inner strength and matter-of-fact way of talking to him.

'So you're all here just to see how Evie...Dr Parker is?' He eyed the group with fresh eyes.

'Yes. Dr Parker was there for us, supporting us, when

we needed her. Now we all have good futures and she was hugely responsible for that. So we just felt this was *our* chance to be here for *her*, now.'

Evie clearly meant a lot to them, and he knew the feeling was mutual. Having to resign her post must have been an agonising decision for Evie to have made.

'So, will you give the gifts to Dr Parker, and tell her we were here?'

The woman's voice broke into his musings.

'Of course.' He dragged himself back to the present but his words were sincere.

'Okay.'

'Okay,' he echoed thoughtfully, watching as the group gathered themselves together, offering him a selection of nods, smiles and even a tentative farewell wave or two.

These kids to whom Evie meant so much.

Gathering up as many of the cards and gifts as he could, he began the first of several trips to his office. He'd load them into the car later. At least it might give them a distraction. Something else to talk about other than the inevitable after today.

It was only as he entered with the final armful that he heard Evie's voice behind him, in the corridor.

'Max?' Her hazy tone filled him with emotions he didn't recognise. 'What are all those?'

'Gifts for you. They were dropped off today,' he answered honestly. 'I'll bring them home at some point and you can look at them when you've rested. Today's checkup must have taken it out of you.'

'Yeah, I'm pretty beat,' she agreed sheepishly.

'Then I guess it's a good job I anticipated this and brought you special fuel to keep you going until we get home and eat.'

With a flourish, he produced a muffin from his pocket, unsure whether she would remember.

'White chocolate and raspberry. You remembered?'

He had expected confusion at worst, a laugh of recognition at best, but he hadn't been prepared for the intense look she suddenly shot him. A look that told him she'd already fast-forwarded past their impulsive encounter that very first evening and to the five nights that had followed. And the flush that leapt to her cheeks, the way her eyes rapidly dilated, convinced him that X-rated images were flicking through her head. The same X-rated images that were now flashing through his brain.

His body tightened in primal response.

He coughed, trying to clear his head. The white-chocolate muffin was supposed to have made her chuckle. A thoughtful gesture. Yet now he couldn't seem to shake this electric charge from coursing around his whole being.

'I'll go and get Imogen from the crèche.' He didn't want her wandering through the main hospital exposing herself to any number of germs or viruses. 'Take the car keys. I'll meet you in the car.'

The conversation with the surgeon had brought up the physical side of their relationship again, and it didn't look as though either of them were going to be able to contain it, now it was out there.

The sooner they gave into it, the better.

'Is everything okay, Max?'

Since she'd discovered Max really did still want her the way she wanted him, she'd been unsuccessfully striving to ignore the way the atmosphere felt as though it were *fizzing* around them. Their conversation had been stilted on the drive home, even though they'd both been trying. Perhaps too hard.

Whilst Imogen had been awake they'd had common ground to talk, but now she'd gone to sleep, with just the two of them, it was back to strained politeness. Not what she'd expected after the fun of their exchange in the nephrologist's office. It felt as if they were taking two steps back for every step forward.

'Those gifts you saw me with earlier, they were from a group of your former patients, your so-called troubled teens,' he announced suddenly.

The conversation starter took her by surprise.

'Really?'

'Well, I say teens, but one of them looked more like she was in her twenties. Long dark hair, self-harm scars on her inside forearms?'

'Sally came to hospital?' Evie fought to keep her tone light. 'With which others? Why didn't you tell them to wait?'

'Sally,' he mused. 'I didn't know. I never asked her name. And I certainly wasn't going to suggest they wait for you—you're still too vulnerable for that many visitors. Remember—no confined spaces, no peak-hour transport, no big welcome-home party.'

'I know. How *was* Sally, then?' Evie changed the subject. 'Still doing well?'

'Yes, according to her.' He drew his lips into a thin line. 'But she's no longer one of your patients. Not since you gave up your position and moved away.'

'She's a friend.'

He clicked his tongue.

'You need to learn the difference between a patient and a friend.'

'And you need to learn not to be so dispassionate about either.'

She tensed, preparing for an argument. None came.

'I was thinking something not too dissimilar.'

'You were?' That didn't sound like Max.

'As it happens,' he confirmed tightly, but didn't elaborate. 'So, Sally said she'd been with you for eight years.'

'No, I've known her for eight years but she hasn't been my patient for the last five of them.'

'So she never talks about any problems.'

'I told you, she's a friend. Friends do discuss problems sometimes, you know. But I don't talk to her in exactly the same way I did when it was purely doctor-patient.'

'What kind of problems?'

He sounded genuinely interested, rather than interrogating her. But still, she didn't want to break any confidences.

'I don't feel it's my place to discuss things she's told me in confidence.'

'I thought you said it wasn't a doctor-patient relationship any more.'

'It isn't. Not telling you is a matter of choice, not ethical boundaries.'

'I see. It was only that she seemed very open when I talked to her.'

That was true. Sally was open.

'I suppose you're right. Sally's always felt that by talking about what she's been through it will bring it to more people's attention and lessen the stigma of it—especially considering she's managed to turn her life around, get a good degree and good life experience. But she still can't seem to get a job, because every time anyone sees those scars they discount her without another thought.'

'That really bothers you, doesn't it?' He was suddenly curious.

'Yes, it does. Because she fought hard to understand why it started, what her triggers are, and what alternative outlets worked for her so she didn't harm herself any more. But because the visual scars are always there, she's never allowed to move forward and get on with her life.'

'Okay, so tell me how she started.'

She hesitated again, about to tell him again that it wasn't her place to tell him. But that wasn't what Sally would want.

Evie gave an almost imperceptible shrug.

'She started self-harming just before she hit her teens. Her parents were going through a particularly acrimonious divorce, which included fighting over custody of her older sister—the more accomplished of the two of them. She felt as though she was the one neither of them wanted.'

'So, why cut? Divorce happens to a lot of kids.'

'And self-harm happens more than you'd think, too. A&E records suggest around fourteen per cent of kids aged between eleven and sixteen can self-harm. But the real figures are likely to be significantly higher because many cases go unreported.'

'How? How does it get missed, Evie?'

His cool, unemotional tone suddenly grated on her. She'd fought daily to convince enough individuals and institutions without having to convince Max as well.

'I don't know. Perhaps because not everyone has people interested enough to notice,' Evie cried in exasperation. 'Or because not everyone is as thick-skinned and self-possessed as the great Maximilian Van Berg. Unlike you, the rest of us are human, and what other people say or how they treat us can hurt.'

'What the hell is that supposed to mean?' he growled angrily.

'It means I hate that these kids sometimes feel they have no one on their side. Some might grow out of it before it gets noticed, especially with boys who find other ways than cutting, which they think is more a girl's thing. But just because they punch themselves, or walls, or initiate fights where they know they'll get hurt doesn't make it any less self-harming than cutting is.'

'You're saying if boys fight they're replacing cutting themselves with getting beaten up?' he said scornfully. 'Boys fight, it's a normal part of growing up. It's a way of letting off a bit of steam against another kid who has got under your skin. Better than the social exclusion some girls use against others. Isn't it that kind of ostracising which contributes to some kids self-harming?'

'Yes, but I'm not talking about evenly matched boys taking the occasional argument into the playground, Max, I'm talking about some boys who purposefully get into fights every single day, especially if they choose older or bigger kids who they know will easily beat them up and hurt them.'

'A broken nose, even a broken rib, depending on who they choose to fight?' Max demanded unexpectedly 'If kids call them names because they have a big nose, or ears which stick out?'

'Sometimes it's that,' Evie agreed. 'Other times it's following a traumatic event. But it doesn't even have to be so clear-cut. It might just be a sense of feeling they don't measure up somehow. And they might not fight other kids, they might wait until no one's around and punch walls, or deliberately put themselves into dangerous situations. That's when it goes from boys fighting as a normal part of growing up, to them finding a way of self-harming without actually cutting.'

She expected him to come back at her. Instead he stared at her, unexpectedly silent, his face set into an expression she'd never seen before. It worried her.

'What is it?'

'Nothing, I'm sorry.' He seemed instantly contrite.

'Max?'

'It's nothing.' He was really making an effort to sound nonchalant. Anyone else might have bought it. But not her.

'Max? What's wrong? Talk to me.'

CHAPTER ELEVEN

MAX FROZE. HER WORDS were like an unexpected bombshell. And then it was as if a red-hot rod seared through his gut.

Evie had no idea of the emotional Pandora's box her words had just opened. How could she? He'd never told her. He'd never even realised it himself. He'd seen it in people like Dean, although he hadn't recognised it for what it was. But himself? Never.

And yet, for the first time in his life, he felt as though he was looking at someone he could actually trust.

It wasn't just about the sex.

The thought slammed into him like a lorry jackknifing into his chest. For all the banter and teasing in Arabella's office, he knew Evie was more than just that one fling. And it wasn't just about the daughter who would now connect them for ever. He *wanted* that connection with Evie. He *wanted* her to be in his life. Her and Imogen.

And that meant talking to her, confiding in her, in a way he'd never anticipated confiding in anyone in his life. It meant trusting Evie. But he could do it, because he owed it to her to be as honest with her as she'd now been with him.

'Was that you, Max? Were you that kid?' she asked gently, and he was reminded that he wasn't just trusting Evie, the mother of his child. He was trusting Dr Parker. He didn't know who he was talking to right now, but he didn't suppose it mattered, just as long as he talked.

'I used to come home every night with a bloody nose, a black eye or cracked ribs,' he started hesitantly.

'Why?'

He shrugged, unable to find the words. He'd shut off his past so firmly that he'd almost forgotten about the fighting. Now it was hard to articulate it.

'Did you want the attention from your parents?'

'No,' he snorted. 'And if I had it would have had the opposite effect. They found it hard enough to tell me they were proud of me when I achieved all they expected of me—they could never have dealt with talking about any problems I was having. I think that would have made them retreat into their careers even more.'

'Your parents didn't think you *ever* had problems? Almost every kid has a problem growing up one way or another.'

'Not me,' Max disagreed. 'As far as they were concerned, I was intelligent with a stable background and parents who made sure I went to school, and did my homework to get good grades.'

'What about talking about general growing-up issues?'

'What issues?' he asked flatly, echoing his parents' attitude. 'I was a kid—how could I possibly have issues?'

'So you started fighting?'

'Yeah. I didn't like bullies, so it started there. If I saw another kid getting picked on I'd go after the bully. They got bigger and harder, and I got angrier.'

'How long did it go on for?'

'A while.'

Longer than he cared to admit.

'And what did your parents do?'

'Nothing.' He closed his eyes for a moment. 'One single teacher noticed and took me under his wing. He got me into a mandatory after-school sports programme with swimming, cycling and running.'

'And the fighting stopped?'

'Yeah. All the kids had gone home by the time I got out, so the same opportunities to fight were gone. Besides, I'd always been too busy and too knackered to fight after that.'

'And your parents?'

'It was like it never happened.'

'You're in contact with them?'

There was an odd note in her voice.

'They called when I got back from Gaza.'

'To tell you they were proud of you?' she guessed.

'No,' he answered flatly. 'They called to say they were glad I was safe and to remind me I should write a medical paper on the medical practices out there.'

'Do you...that is...what do you think they'd make of Imogen?'

'Honestly? I don't know.'

They would probably tell him that he'd made a grave mistake, and that he'd never be able to focus on his career the same way with some kid in the background. But he couldn't tell Evie that. He couldn't hurt her that way.

It shocked Max to realise that he might have felt a similar way himself once, before Imogen had burst into his life and enriched it in a way he would never have considered possible.

She shook her head but her silence spoke volumes, her eyes trained on the coffee mug, around which her hands were cupped tightly.

'Just don't be so quick to believe nothing has ever got to me,' he continued, his smile not quite reaching his eyes. 'I'm not as infallible as you seem to think.'

Or indeed as he had thought himself. Shocked by his own revelations, Max changed the conversation to something less charged. Something that he knew Evie would jump to discuss.

'Tell me more about Sally.'

Her questioning glance made him smile.

'I'm interested. Please, humour me.'

'Okay,' she said slowly. 'Like I said, she struggled with issues of feeling unwanted. Like…you, I guess. She somehow managed to get herself into university but she wasn't ready for the demands of the course and she really started to spiral. She started going out clubbing and drinking, every night to excess.'

'Like most students.'

'Not exactly. Then she started on recreational drugs. But when she was with the campus counsellor about to be thrown off her course she had enough guts to tell her what was going on. That's when she came to me.'

'And you helped her to turn it all around?' Max asked.

'Yes, but only because she wanted to do it herself. She just needed the support. There's obviously a lot more to it than that, but ultimately she managed to get back into uni and graduate well. She could get a good job, too, if only health-assessment boards would look beyond the scars of her past to see what she's like now.'

'I could do something with them.'

'Sorry?'

'I could help her with the scars,' he repeated quietly.

'How? There are too many of them over too large an area, and they're deep into the subcutaneous level. How would you eradicate them?'

'I'm not saying I can eradicate them,' Max replied. 'But I could abrade the cicatrised area and then use a split thickness skin graft to over-graft. She'll still have a scar, but it won't look like those lined scars from cutting any more.'

'So people won't stigmatise her?' Evie's voice caught. 'That would be incredible, but she can't afford it.'

'I know that.' He blew out a breath. 'Call it my charitable act.'

'You would do that for her?'

'I'd do that for you,' he responded quietly. And part of him felt the need to do it for himself, as well. It was incredible but after his unexpected confession he wasn't dwelling on the past; in truth he felt lighter than he had ever felt before. Telling his secrets to Evie had been cathartic, not because it was her job but because he felt as though he was sharing a part of himself with Evie that no one else even knew existed. Right at this moment, Max knew he'd never felt as close a connection to another human being as he felt to Evie.

But he knew his confession had startled her, even though she was doing her best to conceal it. So right now he needed them to get back to the fun of earlier that day, and forget everything else but the fact that they'd both realised how much they still wanted each other.

'Oh, and one last thing.' He shot her a wicked smile. 'So there are no further misunderstandings, let me make it perfectly clear. I still want you. Whenever you're ready. You're sexy, exceptionally desirable and, for what it's worth, you're also someone I want to be with.'

And Evie could take from that whatever she wanted.

'Our daughter's out for the count and she looks perfectly angelic.' Evie managed a shaky smile a few hours later as she descended the stairs from checking on the baby. 'You want to see her?'

She was stalling; she couldn't help it. The need for Max, intimately and completely, had been gnawing at her ever since their easy exchange in the nephrologist's office. She'd spent so long feeling bad about herself since her illness, but Max was the one person who made her feel like a whole woman again.

The whole day had been one of revelations. The fact that he hadn't abandoned her the other night but that he'd been uncertain as to how much she wanted him, had always wanted him. His acceptance that her job meant so much to her, and his offer of helping Sally. But, most incredibly, Max's confession about his childhood, which had made her feel simultaneously closer to him, yet all the more disconnected.

She needed to tell him. But the closer she got to him, the more scared she was of him turning against her. So she would first need to convince him that they could be more, so much more, than just co-parents of a beautiful daughter. They could be a proper family.

And even though she wanted to prove to Max that the two of them could be so much more than just incredible sex, right now it still seemed like the best place to start.

So, when he took her hand and drew her up the hallway, Evie silenced the last voice of doubt.

'Tonight I'll take your word for how angelic our daughter is. But right now, Evangeline,' he uttered, his voice gravelly with desire, 'I don't want to wait any longer for you.'

In spite of her fears Evie actually giggled as she raced him up the hall, tumbling to her bedroom together and stopping still by the door.

She could feel Max's breath on her skin. Her heart picked up speed as her own breathing came shallow and fast and when she dared a glance at Max, he was watching the rapid rise and fall of her chest. Then his mouth crashed onto hers with exquisite need.

She responded without hesitation, drinking in his taste, his touch. He dipped his head to kiss a scorching trail from her lips, down her throat and to the sensitive hollow. Arching towards him as he dropped his hand to lazily skim the exposed skin of her chest then cup her breast, his thumb drawing slow whorls over her hard nipple through her top, the fabric proving a frustrating barrier for her. But Max didn't seem to be in any great hurry. He seemed happy teasing her, exploring, nibbling.

She slid her fingers up his thigh, making for his crotch, a thrill coursing through her as she felt him hard beneath the rough material, but his other hand reached down to still any further movements.

'Slow down, Evie.'

His voice was thick with longing and he practically growled, but it only turned her on even more. She pushed his hand off hers and propelled them both towards the bed, pushing him gently down and moving across him so that she was sitting on his lap, her legs wrapped around him, ignoring the stab of pain at her incision site. She was determined not to wince; she didn't want to give Max any reason to insist they take things slowly.

She shifted, wondering if he could feel the heat from her body, when he sucked in a sharp breath, and she gave a wicked gurgle of triumph. *That would be a* yes, *then.*

Evie slid her hands down and tugged at the hem of his tee shirt, pulling it up and only pausing in their kissing for long enough to haul it over his head. She balled the fabric and threw it across the room with a grin.

'Making a point?' he muttered, amused.

'Might be.'

Her hands reacquainted themselves with the muscled chest she'd been dreaming about for the last twelve months. Weaving her fingers into the smattering of dark hair, Evie pushed him back onto the bed, her eyes grazing over him hungrily.

'Like what you see?'

It was a challenge. Almost a dare. Evie smirked at him wickedly, feeling more sexually assured than she ever had before.

'Purely a professional assessment.'

Max quirked one eyebrow.

'Oh, really, *Dr Parker*?'

'Mmm-hmm,' she murmured, tracing an unhurried line along the tense chest muscles, which were, incredibly, even more impressive than she'd recalled. Lowering her head, Evie pressed a kiss into each of them. 'Pectorals.'

'You liked your anatomy classes?' he managed.

'I did.' She dipped her head lower. 'Rectus abdominis. Upper.'

'Yup,' but his voice quivered slightly as she kissed again. Evie moved across.

'Transversus abdominis.'

Another kiss. And this time he didn't offer any kind of quip.

Lower again, Evie ignored the pain shooting across her side. She wanted him more than she was prepared to give in to anything else. Which meant she was ready.

'Evie…?'

'Shh…' she instructed. 'I'm fine, don't ruin it.'

The moment with Max felt too precious, and too fragile to risk breaking. Besides, she needed to prove this to herself. She wasn't just mentally recovered, she was almost physically healed, too.

'Oblique.'

The requisite kiss and she could feel his body straining against her forearm. A sense of power surged through her. He was relinquishing control to her because she was claiming it. It was a heady feeling. She moved back to his middle.

'Which brings us back to rectus abdominis. Lower.' Her voice sounded thick with lust as she dropped a final kiss before straightening up to offer him an innocent stare. 'So, *Mr* Van Berg, where should I go from here?'

Her hands moved to his belt buckle but before she could do anything else Max pulled her to him, hooking his hands around her backside, and stood up with her legs still wrapped around his hips.

'You made your point,' he growled. 'You're healing well. But I can make a point, too.'

Before she could worry that he was going to back away from her like last time, Max set her back on the bed and reached for her zip, waiting a few tantalising moments before he divested her of her top. Her bra didn't last much longer. Then he pressed her gently down until her back sank into the soft mattress, and covered her body with his, taking care not to place any weight on her. Skin to skin now, the muscles Evie had just been kissing grazed her breasts, making her nipples stiffen even more in response.

Obligingly, Max lowered his head and circled them with a hot, wet tongue before taking them into his mouth. She squirmed underneath him, desperate for more, but he locked her down, taking his delicious time.

It was pointless to resist, Evie reluctantly concluded a few moments later as she gave herself up to the butterflies currently performing spinning and twirling Viennese waltzes throughout her entire core. When he seared her skin with his lips it was all she could do to hold still, contenting herself with familiarising her hands with the solid contours of his back and shoulders. And when he raised his head back up to reclaim her mouth she matched him, demanding kiss for demanding kiss. Evie ached to hold him in her hand again, feel him rock solid and so turned on by her that she could barely circle him with her fingers. But he held himself too far away, making *her* the sole focus of the evening's intimacy, and, given the skill with which Max was arousing her, it wasn't exactly a hardship to relinquish the power again. By the time he finally trailed a line with his tongue down her lower abdomen and to the waistband of her jersey trousers, she was powerless to contain her moan of anticipation.

The last of the Steri-strips had come off and the scar was looking less angry and welt-like than it had a few days ago, so Evie forced herself not to cover up the incision as Max paused for a moment to inspect it. Satisfied, he finally slid her jersey trousers down over her hips, cocking an eyebrow at her as he saw she'd replaced her comfy knickers with a scrap of lace that sat well below the scar.

It was on the tip of her tongue to claim that was all she had left, having thrown the rest of her underwear in the wash, but she figured that might be as transparent as the turquoise lace, and instead she ignored the unspoken question, focusing instead on the aching need for him to touch her right where she needed him most.

As if reading her thoughts, Max hooked his finger around the scrap and brushed a knuckle against the aching bud. Evie gasped, instinctively lifting her hips to deepen the contact but he moved his hand away again, in exquisite torment. She laced her fingers through his hair.

'Max.' The raw voice didn't sound like her own. 'I need you inside me.'

He barely paused in his attentions.

'Not tonight.'

It was a wrench but Evie forced herself to pull away from him, lifting her shoulders off the bed so that she could see him.

'You heard the nephrologist—four to six weeks post-op,' he reminded her, moving to lower his head again, but Evie pressed her hand against him, stopping him.

How could he sound so casual about it? This was torturous for her.

'Max…'

'That's a minimum of two weeks, three days and twenty-two and a half hours.'

'You're counting in days and hours?' A gurgle of laughter escaped her. He wasn't as composed about all this as she'd thought. And she was glad about that.

'From the moment we made that damned deal,' Max

ground out. 'And it's taking more willpower than you can possibly imagine not to take you right now. So will you please shut up, and let me concentrate on just...*exploring* you?'

Evie hesitated. This wasn't exactly going as she'd planned in her head.

'Max...' Her objection evaporated from her brain as Max pulled aside the lace material again and flicked his tongue against her swollen skin. Unable to keep herself upright any longer, she fell back onto the pillows as he sucked and licked at the sensitive bud, sending mini fireworks exploding through her belly.

Max slid his finger inside her, his mouth unrelenting in its devilish benevolence as she jiggled in response. She gave a guttural moan moments before the orgasm shattered through her, and Max instinctively slid his hands around to hold her bottom in place, stopping her from writhing away; his tongue and finger coaxing a longer, more intense orgasm than she'd ever known. Evie's body shook with the impact of it as she cried out his name, but he didn't let her go until he was convinced he couldn't tease anything more out of her.

Falling back down, she held her breath in anticipation until Max pulled himself up the bed to haul her into his arms. Evie nestled against his shoulder gratefully, wishing she would never have to leave the security of his embrace. It had been too long. Not just since the last time she'd had sex. But since the last time she'd been with Max. There would never be anyone else for her who would match up to him.

But if there was to be any chance that this could be more than *just sex*, she knew she was going to have to start by telling him about the fact she'd met his parents. And she needed to do it now.

Okay, tomorrow.

Or maybe the day after that.

She needed to be more sure of how Max felt about her. His love for his daughter was clear, but what then?

Lying down, Evie allowed Max to snuggle her in his arms. For all her efforts to take the lead, in the end her confidence hadn't been as high as she'd hoped and she'd been only too happy to let Max take over. So for now she was just going to enjoy this moment. She'd been dreaming of it for long enough.

CHAPTER TWELVE

'So this is Silvertrees Old Town?' Evie breathed. 'It's incredible up here, so peaceful. And I can see for miles.'

Max watched her angle her head to let the rays of sun heat her skin, despite the cool breeze of the high viewing platform, her hands resting on hip-height grey stone wall.

'It *is* stunning,' he agreed quietly.

'Do you get chance to come here that much?'

He dropped his hand to cradle the back of Imogen's head as she nestled against his chest in her baby harness, buying himself a moment to think whether he wanted to answer.

Somehow, it felt like something particularly personal. Ever since they'd first been intimate again, he'd begun to open up more and more to Evie, trusting her in a way he had never trusted anyone before.

'When I can, usually on a run,' he found himself admitting with more ease than he'd anticipated. 'Especially if I want to clear my head before a particularly complex operation. Although I come here less during tourist season—you wouldn't believe how busy it gets then.'

'Really?' She glanced around, taking in the boarded-up stalls. Barely a soul was around at this moment, except for a few artists sketching or painting the spectacular vista. Only the ticket office was open, although a couple of owners were taking advantage of the off-season to repair and repaint their little shops built into the rock face.

Max nodded, feeling himself relax more and more as Evie seemed to fall for the beauty of the place the same way he once had. It was like another small confirmation of how well matched they were.

'It used to be Silvertrees itself before the hospital was built a mile out of town and all the housing sprung up around *that*. Then the hospital took the name Silvertrees and this place became the Old Town, or Outer Silvertrees,' he explained. 'How is it you've never been here?'

With a rueful smile, Evie lifted her shoulders at his light teasing.

'I only ever came here to go to the hospital, either for work or for myself. I didn't even know they had a funicular railway here.'

He arched his eyes in surprise.

'Did you know it was built in the late nineteenth century?'

'Oh, right.' She only hesitated a fraction of a moment before following suit. 'But it's electricity-powered?'

'Good eye.' He nodded, impressed. 'It was rebuilt in the forties specifically for that reason. And the original wooden cars were replaced with lightweight aluminium carriages. But the original line used a simple system of gravity and water. They pumped water into a two-thousand-gallon tank underneath the top car until it outweighed the lower car. Once the top car reached the bottom station they emptied the tank and pumped it back up to a tank at the top station.'

'You know a lot about it,' Evie remarked with a grin.

'I originally wanted to be an engineer when I was growing up,' he answered evenly. No need for Evie to know that she was the only person, outside his parents, who he'd ever told.

Still she glanced at him sharply.

'What happened?'

Max opened his mouth; best to tell her that he'd changed his mind as he'd grown up.

'My parents told me not to be so stupid. That I was going to become a surgeon like them, and that was all there was to it.'

He forced a smile as her eyes slid over him, assessing.

'Oh. Well, for what it's worth, there are thousands and thousands of patients out there who are very glad you were their surgeon.'

'Thanks.' He grinned wryly. 'I appreciate you not trying to psychoanalyse me.'

'At least out loud,' she couldn't resist. 'For the record, though, I can also see you taking that funicular-style technology with you to some foreign country. And manually building one out there for them, if they needed it.'

'Yeah, I guess that's the geeky side of me coming out.'

'I like it,' Evie offered shyly before teasing him. 'It's better than being the *demon of discipline*.'

'Oh, I see. Hitting below the belt, are we?' he quipped as he stepped towards her, careful not to crush Imogen as he drew Evie into his arms.

The kiss was slow and thorough, and full of promise.

Something was changing deep inside him, something fundamental. It felt as though Evie was finally unlocking a part of himself he'd never even known existed, and he liked it.

More than liked it. He welcomed it.

Eventually they pulled apart with reluctance as Imogen made her objections known. Evie dropped a kiss on her daughter's head before lifting her head to meet his gaze. Something indefinable *clicked* inside him, and Max slid protective arms around both of them.

'I think I could live here.'

'Sorry?' He pulled his head back to look at her.

'In Silvertrees,' Evie clarified nervously. 'Back at my

brother's house when you first talked about Imogen and I coming up here, I told you that I wouldn't want to move that far away from him or Annie. But, if it meant you and Imogen having a closer relationship, then I could learn to love living here.'

None of the words that came into his head seemed to adequately express his emotions at Evie's generosity of spirit. Instead, he just pressed a hard kiss to her lips, gratified when she smiled her relieved acceptance.

But that indescribable *something* still hovered on the periphery of his mind. What *was* it? And why was he finding it so difficult to express?

'We'd better get back so you can get ready for your three-week check-up.'

They were starting to extend the time between checkups. It was a good sign, it meant Evie was making good progress.

In companionable silence, they wandered off the viewing platform and slowly rambled alongside the long stretch of stone wall towards the railway, which would take them back down towards the lower section of Old Town.

'Mr Van Berg?'

They both whirled around as a man hurried towards them, a large sheet, clearly just torn from his sketchpad, in his outstretched hand. It was one of the artists from before.

'You saved my sister's hand a couple of years ago when she got it crushed in a car door.' His voice was heavy with gratitude. 'We never knew how to repay you but…well, I hope this goes some way towards it.'

Before Max could reply, the man had thrust the painting at him and was hurrying back off up the wide, cobbled tourist route, only turning briefly to wave his hand in acknowledgement. Turning the sketch around, Max lowered his head.

His heart drummed a tom-tom solo in his chest.

'It's amazing,' Evie whispered, her chin resting against his arm.

And it was. A striking likeness of the three of them, capturing the moment Evie had dropped a kiss on their daughter's head, the two of them encircled protectively in his embrace. But more than that, an intense love radiated from the drawing, the lines, fine here and thicker there, drawing the viewer deeper into the picture.

And the simple caption. *Family.*

Max stopped dead. That one word finally gave him a name to that *something* that had *clicked* inside him earlier, to the feeling playing at the edges of his mind.

Family.

The idea of Evie moving to Silvertrees in order that he should enjoy a better relationship with his daughter was commendable, but it wasn't a good enough reason. He needed Evie to want to move here for herself. To be with him. Because he wanted to be with them *both*. He wanted them to be a family in every sense of the word. For ever.

'What is it?' Evie had pivoted in concern as he stopped so abruptly.

'Wait,' he commanded hoarsely, desperately trying to clear his head of the crazy thoughts now swarming.

How much time had he wasted? How much energy? Focussing on his career and excluding the possibility of anything else, anything more, just because he didn't want to be the kind of parent his own had been to him.

Now he knew he never would be like them. It wasn't who he was. He wasn't emotionally unavailable as they were, and Evie had been the one to show him that.

'Max? Is everything all right?'

She was obviously worried, and yet he still didn't know how to tell her. What would he say? It wasn't as if he even knew that she felt the same way he did. What if he told her he wanted more than they'd ever agreed only to scare her off? He suspected she felt as he did, but, then again, family life with him wasn't something she had ever suggested she wanted.

'What about you?' he rasped.

Her eyebrows knitted together in nervous confusion. 'Me?'

'You talked about living here in order that Imogen and would have a closer relationship. But what about us? Would you and I have a closer relationship, too?'

He heard her breath catch in her throat.

'Is that what you want?'

'It is,' he confirmed without hesitation, but held back from saying anything more.

'Right.' Evie nodded, swallowing hard.

'Is it what you want?' he echoed her question carefully

She nodded again but said nothing more.

He couldn't be sure what that meant, but in that moment he swore to himself that he'd prove to her they could be they *should* be, a proper family. In every sense of the word

Evie quelled the flitting butterflies in her abdomen as she stood in the doorway to Imogen's nursery and watched Max lower their sleeping daughter into the ornate cot. Quietly she backed away down the hall and into the master bedroom, into which she'd pretty much decamped after that first night of sexual intimacy.

But since their venture into Old Town together five days ago, something had changed. It wasn't just about their sexual intimacy, but about their emotional intimacy.

And that was on a whole new level.

Max loved her. She could feel it. She knew it. And from the moment he'd seen that sketch entitled *Family* she'd known Max knew it, too.

She just didn't know whether he was ready to acknowledge it to her, yet. And so she bit her tongue and reined herself in, wanting him to tell her when he was ready. In his own time.

Which, she had to admit, was having its perks.

Every day that Max tried to tell her he loved her but couldn't, he resorted instead to trying to show her how he felt. Ways which were growing more and more intensely passionate as though to compensate for the words that were eluding him. And Evie had never felt so desired, or needed, or wanton.

But as exquisite as it was, tonight she intended to take matters into her own hands. She'd tried a few nights ago, with her sexual assessment of his anatomy, which had been even more fun than she'd hoped. But in the end, when Max had taken charge again, she'd bottled it and let him. But this time, she was going to run things if only to prove to him that she was the same woman he'd known a year ago, not this vulnerable, ill Evie, as he'd begun to think of her. And if he couldn't tell her he loved her after *that*…well, she was just determined that wouldn't be the case.

She heard Max creeping out of the nursery and heading down the hallway and ducked into the shower room, shedding her clothes quickly and efficiently. It was another boost to her self-esteem that she was now able to do this for herself, a far cry from when she'd needed Max to help her to wash her hair.

This shower experience was going to end up very differently from back then, Evie determined. Just as long as Max adequately interpreted the trail of clothes leading from the bedroom door. Her heart lodged somewhere in her throat; it would be just her luck for the door to have closed on her artfully placed heeled shoe and for Max to walk straight downstairs.

With relief Evie saw his shadow entering the room and heading towards the bathroom door, only hesitating slightly as he heard the sound of running water.

'Everything okay, Evie? Do you need any help?'

She was touched by his consideration. Just because they'd been intimate every night he didn't take it as his right to simply walk in. She licked her lips despite the shower water running over her from head to toe.

'No help.' Good job her voice didn't betray her racing heart. 'But company would be nice.'

Through the steamed glass she watched him round the corner, entering the doorway and approaching the shower. Standing as proudly as she could, she indicated the spacious shower area with a confident jerk of her head.

Her skin heated as his eyes swept slowly over her, taking in the head-to-toe view, darkening appreciatively as the pupils dilated, turning them almost black.

She held out the soaped-up body puff.

'Well, are you going to join me, then?'

He didn't need a third invitation.

Within seconds he'd stripped down and stepped around the expanse of glass. Tall, proud and wickedly masculine, his desire for her was unmistakeable and Evie didn't bother to suppress her grin of delight.

He took the proffered body puff but before he could make use of it, he was pulling her against his hard, already gleaming wet body, and bringing his mouth down on hers. Hot and demanding, more so than any nights before.

She slid her hands around to his back, moving them over strong shoulder muscles, down to his athletic waist, and lower to cup his backside and draw herself closer to him, right against the heat between her legs. Carefully, Evie rocked her hips against him before bringing her hand around to stroke him, gripping him more firmly as he flexed against her. She remembered only too well just how Max had liked it when she'd taken the lead a few times during their fling, and tonight she intended to replicate that. Banish the idea of her as weak and vulnerable, once and for all.

Tightening her grip slightly, she moved harder, faster, all the while nibbling at the hollow of his neck and up to his jawline.

His husky groan sent a shiver rippling down her spine. It felt good to wield sexual power over a man like Max, but she had to be careful; she was barely hanging onto her own sense of control by her fingernails.

She rocked against him again, feeling his whole length flexing, solid against her skin. The sigh escaped her lips before she could stop it, only for Max to react to the sound in the most primitive way. Desire flooded straight down to her core. Parting her legs slightly, she nestled him even deeper against herself, not doubting that he could feel how hot and slick she was. How ready for him.

'Stop,' he managed hoarsely, breaking the contact with what was clearly supreme effort. 'We need to slow it down.'

'No,' whispered Evie cheekily, 'we don't.'

His eyes locked with hers, narrowing slightly as he saw her intent.

'Evie, you've no idea how much I want you, but we can't. Not yet. Your incision—'

'Is fine,' she cut him off before he could finish. 'I checked today. They said it's up to me. It has been almost a month.'

Then she saw it. That brief moment of hesitation before he shook his head.

'No, it's been three weeks, five days. I won't let you risk it. Not yet.'

Too late. She grinned inside. She'd seen all she needed to see. Max wanted her as much as she wanted him, and tonight she didn't intend to wait any longer.

'What difference will two more days make? They're satisfied the wound is healed, that I won't cause any damage or stress on the site. As far as they're concerned, now it's all down to when I feel ready. And I feel ready *now*.' She chuckled weakly, hoping to cover up her nerves.

'That's why you asked me to get Imogen whilst you had that last appointment,' he exclaimed. 'You wanted to ask them without me there.'

'I knew you'd argue we should wait for the full six weeks. But it's my body and I know how strong it is. And I can't wait. I don't want to. I need you and I know you feel the same.' She grinned to soften her next words. 'So will you please just shut up and kiss me, Max?'

She barely had time to exhale after her hurried monologue before his mouth crashed down on hers with a ferocious desire, chasing every other thought from her head. He slid one hand around to slip between her legs. Gripping hold of Max's shoulders, Evie just clung on and prepared to let herself be swept away, but then she recalled the split second before he'd kissed her, and the air was sucked from her chest without warning. The way he'd looked at her— no man had ever looked at her with such intense longing before, making her feel more confident than she ever had.

Summoning all her strength, she pushed him away and took the unused body puff from his hands as she turned the water off. It wasn't exactly what she'd planned but in some ways that made it even better to know that neither of them were completely in control.

'Shall we take this through to the bedroom?' she managed hoarsely before giving an apologetic smile. 'There's protection on the nightstand.'

She might be feeling good enough to bring forward the sex part of things, but she knew there was no point in being stupid and risking a pregnancy on her still-healing body. And by the expression now crossing Max's face that had been one of the worries holding him back.

As if to prove her point, he suddenly bent down and

scooped her up into his arms, carrying her out of the shower and through to the bedroom in an echo of that previous encounter. Only this time, Evie was confident it wasn't going to end with him depositing her on the bed and walking out.

She was right. Lowering her down, Max immediately joined her, intent clear in his dark eyes as he began to move down her body trailing whorls on her stomach with his tongue as he moved lower. She fought the urge to simply give herself up to him.

'Uh-uh,' she croaked out, catching his head. 'This time it's my turn. Get on your back.'

Max only paused for a moment before obeying, but when she straddled him and began to move down his body, just as he had with her a moment earlier, he let out a deep groan.

'I don't think I can hold out much longer.' He gritted his teeth. 'You really got me in the shower before, and I've wanted you for too long.'

'I feel the same,' whispered Evie.

She could save that for later; right now she just wanted a release with him. To recapture some of the connection she was sure they'd made a year ago, and to remind them both how it had been before all this transplant business had tarnished things.

Leaning over him to retrieve the condom from the bedside table, she wasn't prepared when Max reached up and cupped her breasts, his mouth moving from one tight nipple to the other. She shifted to offer him better access, her hands fumbling as she distractedly tried to open the foil packet whilst sensations jolted through her body.

'So beautiful, so perfect,' he murmured against her skin.

But this was about her taking control, she reminded herself through the haze. Pressing her hands to his shoulders to keep him down on the bed, Evie sat up, sliding down his legs enough to access his solid length, putting on a slight show as she languidly sheathed him and revelling in his shallow, faster breathing as his eyes were riveted to her every move.

Everything about Max screamed strength, power, masculinity, but having him lie here now, allowing himself to be at her mercy, gave Evie a sense of control, which she desperately needed. She felt capable, reassured and absolutely all-woman again as she met Max's intense gaze and held it, not allowing herself to look away as she covered him, running her hands over his taut, muscular chest as she slid carefully down to take all of him inside her. As if they were designed to fit together perfectly.

Even as he gasped, his hands gripped her hips to hold her from moving and Evie could feel him holding back, worrying about hurting her. She traced a pattern down his lower abdomen, over his Apollo's belt, and placed her hands over his, lifting them enough to stop him restricting her movements.

'My timings,' she reminded him shakily, before rocking over him and feeling his reaction deep inside her.

'Evie. You're so tight, so wet,' he muttered, finally gripping her hips as if he meant it as he thrust up to meet her movements.

She was too primed, too ready to hold out for long and it seemed that Max hadn't been lying when he'd said the same. Within minutes she felt him stiffen as she exploded, climaxing together as wave after wave crashed over her.

There was no doubt any more that she loved Max, completely and utterly. But if he didn't love her back the same way then she would still always be grateful to him for showing her that, kidney transplant or not, she was still all-woman.

Wanton, desirable, and utterly powerful.

CHAPTER THIRTEEN

'KEEP YOUR EYES closed and walk where I guide you,' instructed Max, careful not to let her bump against Imogen, lodged happily in the baby sling on his chest. It was the first family outing they'd had since that incredible night when they'd slept together again.

'What happened to the brisk training walk you promised me?' She giggled nervously.

'We took a detour first. Keep them closed.'

Trusting Max to lead her safely along, Evie kept her eyes closed but her mind whirred. The last thing she'd seen before Max had asked her to close her eyes was that they'd driven through the stunning National Park and through imposing gates and past a gatehouse lodge onto private parkland. A huge hall had stood in the distance but Max had turned onto a smaller single-track road, past a chapel and a hunting lodge.

That was when he'd first asked her to close her eyes.

The temptation to sneak a peek as the car glided silently along had been almost overwhelming and Evie had drawn on every inch of resolve not to give in to the temptation. Even when the car had finally stopped and parked up, and Max had taken an excruciatingly long time getting Imogen out of her car seat and settled in her sling before he finally came around to lead Evie herself out of the passenger side.

She could feel the heat of the afternoon sunshine on her

back, and cobblestones beneath her feet, and was glad of her walking shoes. The air was full of the scent of freshly mown grass, whilst the only sounds were the calls of birds and water, like the rippling of a runnel. And then the clicking of a wooden latch, possibly an outside gate.

Still allowing Max to lead her along, she felt the slight drop in temperature, and just as she was about to assume she'd stepped indoors the heat of the sun hit her again and she realised they'd walked through some kind of archway but were still outside.

She opened her mouth to ask but Max spoke before she could.

'You can open your eyes now.'

Not sure what to expect, Evie obliged. Blinking in the sunshine, it took her a few moments for her eyes to adjust. She gave a gasp of awe.

She was standing in an expansive cobbled quad, at the centre of which an old stone fountain trickled water into a moss-covered stone animal water trough. Large, multi-leaf sets of sliding doors offered tantalising glimpses of the single-storey rooms inside, a couple of which were already open to reveal a large black baby grand piano.

Turning around, Evie looked up at the double height, yellow sandstone building behind her.

'The old coach house for the main hall,' Max offered by way of explanation. 'Shall we look around?'

'Are we allowed?' she found herself whispering. 'It looks like someone's home now.'

'It is.' Max grinned. 'But it's up for sale.'

It took Evie a few moments to process what he was suggesting.

'You're thinking of moving? To a family house? For you and Imogen?'

Not that it could be considered your average family

house. She shook her head in disbelief. *You could house about five families in a place like this.*

'For me and for Imogen. *And* for you,' he corrected, the first hint of nervousness in his voice. 'If that's what you want?'

A family house? For them to be a proper family?

Evie could only gape at him, unable to answer as two warring thoughts crowded out her mind.

It was more than she could have ever dreamed of with Max. But she still hadn't told him about his parents and the money.

There was no avoiding it any longer. No saying she should come clean with him only to let herself bottle out before it came to actually doing so. This time was it.

'What are you doing tonight?' she blurted out quickly.

'Tonight?' He looked taken aback at her sharp tone.

'I mean, are you on call? Do you need to go into the hospital at all?'

'I wasn't planning on it, no.' He frowned. 'Do you need anything?'

She darted out a tongue to moisten her dry lips.

'I want us to talk. More accurately, there's something I need to tell you…something I should have said a while ago.'

His face closed off, and she could see him mentally withdrawing from her.

'I'm sorry, I've obviously misjudged the situation. We should go back.'

'No, Max.' She reached out, taking his arm and not letting him pull away from her. 'This is beautiful. Incredible. I'd love to live here with you, and Imogen. Be a proper family.'

His eyes scanned her face as though assessing her sincerity.

'I love you, Max.' The words escaped her lips before

she realised it. 'I think I've been falling in love with you ever since I met you.'

There was a fatal beat of silence before he opened his mouth and Evie wished she could take back her involuntary declaration. Not because it wasn't true, but because she was afraid it was too soon for Max.

She didn't want to hear him deny her. Before he could speak, she launched herself forwards, her hands protecting Imogen from being crushed as she planted a kiss on Max's lips.

She'd meant it to silence him, but as he held her in place, deepening the kiss, exploring and teasing, Evie found she couldn't pull away.

Only the ringing of his mobile finally made them reluctantly separate. As he glanced at the screen Max's lips tightened into a thin, disapproving line.

It was irrational, but she couldn't help a shudder of apprehension rippling down her spine.

'I have to take this,' he told her. 'Go inside, look around. I'll catch up with you in a moment.'

Against her better judgement, Evie watched him leave as she continued a tour of the stunning house alone.

She knew the moment he walked into the room that something had changed. That something was very wrong.

'Max...?'

'That was my parents.'

She could actually feel her blood pressure dropping, draining from her head, as her heart slowed down. She reached for the back of a chair to steady herself.

'Your parents? I didn't think...that is...you said you didn't have much contact.'

It wasn't what she meant.

'They were calling to ask me if I'd submitted a medical paper yet on my work in Gaza. I decided it was time they knew about you and Imogen—after all, she is their grandchild. So imagine my surprise when it turns out they already knew all about you both.'

'I wanted to tell you myself—' Evie stumbled but Max interrupted.

'Did my parents *pay* you to keep Imogen a secret from me?'

Quiet fury radiated out of every fibre of him.

She should have told him everything from the very start, instead of bottling out every time she came close.

'Whatever you think, it isn't like that.'

It sounded clichéd and hollow, but it was the best she had.

The flat, emotionless resonance of his words had cut into her. Whatever she said, it wasn't going to make a difference. An overwhelming sadness consumed her. A sense of grief for what might have been, and the pain of losing yet another person she loved—except this time, it was all her own fault.

'Did you cash their cheque?'

He didn't even realise he'd been holding his breath, fervently urging her to deny it, until she offered a short, jerky nod.

Dammit, he was such a fool.

His whole life he'd looked down on people who believed in love, in others actually loving each other, caring for each other, wanting the best for each other. When he was a child, his parents had mentally knocked any such foolishly romantic notions out of him.

A few minutes ago Evie had promised him that she loved him. Yet lying to him was how she defined love? His response had been on his lips when she'd landed that kiss on his mouth and effectively silenced him. Thank goodness he hadn't told her he loved her in return.

He'd learned to trust himself and his career. Nothing more, nothing less.

And then Evie had come along and shattered all the fortifications he'd built around himself, like a sledgehammer to a landmine.

He had trusted in her. Believed in her. He'd even begun to rewrite his future, a family life with Evie and the beautiful daughter they'd somehow managed to create in that wild week together.

Never once had he thought he could be hurt—no, *wounded*—as deeply as he felt in this moment.

'Please, Max, you have to understand…'

She tailed off on a hopeless cry. He wanted to walk away. He wanted to shut down whatever apology or explanation she was about to offer, but he couldn't. So help him, his feet refused to move.

'All this time, I thought you kept Imogen from me because you felt you would be better off without me. I never once thought it was because you felt you were better off with my parents' money.'

She winced as though the accusation actually hurt her physically, but Max didn't care. He felt too raw, too angry.

'It wasn't like that.'

'Then how was it, Evangeline?' He managed to keep his voice level. He didn't know how.

She started to speak then stopped, shaking her head. The taste of acrid disappointment filled his mouth.

'So it *was* like that,' he bit out in disgust. Though whether more with her, or with himself, he couldn't be sure.

His legs finally began to work again and he turned for the door.

'*No.* No, it wasn't,' she exclaimed. 'Wait, Max, please. I'll… I'll explain everything.'

'I don't want to hear it.'

'Then for Imogen's sake. Please.'

He whirled around, enraged.

'Don't ever, *ever* use our daughter like that again.'

'I'm sorry. You're right.' She stared at him, wild-eyed and teary. 'I don't know why I said that. But I *can* explain. Please.'

He should keep moving. Leave. Every fibre screamed at him to do so.

'You have five minutes,' he ground out.

She nodded, still staring at him in silence.

'Four minutes, forty-five seconds.'

'I wrote you a letter when I first found out I was pregnant,' she blurted out.

'I didn't get it.'

'No. Your parents turned up at Annie's house instead.'

Max glowered, trying to work out whether she was lying or not.

'How would they have known?'

'I didn't know how to contact you out there, and I didn't want a letter like that sitting on your doormat for months, so I went to HR and got your emergency contact details.'

'And my parents' address,' he realized, raking his hand through his hair. 'Why didn't you just send it to the charity to forward on to me?'

Evie looked aghast.

'I never thought of that.'

And so she'd trusted that his parents would pass the letter on. But they never had.

The truth hit him again and a fresh wave of nausea bubbled in his gut.

'What did your letter say?'

'It…explained how I first found out I was going into first stages of renal failure when I came to Silvertrees. The week we first slept together. Then, a month or so later, I found out I was pregnant.'

'So they read your letter to me, and visited you at your brother's house?' he reminded her flatly.

'Yes,' Evie answered after a moment. 'They accused me of deliberately setting out to trap you.'

Just as he had. The irony wasn't lost on him. His parents were undoubtedly the people he least wanted to emulate and yet here he was, more like them than he had ever realised. It didn't make him feel any better about himself.

But neither did it change the fact that Evie had betrayed him. Lied to him.

'And what did they say?' he asked grimly, not wanting to ask but needing to know their response.

'They told me that losing the baby would be for the best.' Evie gulped, clearly struggling to contain her emotions. 'They told me that if the baby did survive, given that we knew my PKD had developed into kidney failure by that point, the chances of him or her being completely healthy were slim. They also said that you were a successful surgeon with a promising career and they weren't going to let me ruin it.'

A firewall of fury swept through Max. No one should ever treat anyone in that way, least of all someone as kind and giving as Evie. He knew his parents were callous, but even he wouldn't have believed they could stoop so low.

And any promising career only reflected well on them, Max knew. Their consideration had nothing to do with him, only with themselves.

As Evie hiccupped beside him, he realised she was still fighting to compose herself.

'They told me you weren't interested in a family—which I already knew—but that you would feel obligated to *do the right thing*.'

That brought Max up short. Obligation had definitely been his motivation in the very beginning, but that had quickly, subtly—so subtly he hadn't even noticed it at first—changed. Now he missed both Evie and Imogen when they weren't around, and actively looked forward to going home to them.

Or at least, he had done, until that phone call had turned everything on its head.

Now he felt used, unwanted, a means to an end.

Just as his parents had made him feel as a kid.

'I once told you the one thing I couldn't accept was people making decisions which impacted on me, without even consulting me about it,' he snarled.

'I know. But they told me you would end up resenting me for curtailing your career and ruining your future. More importantly that you would end up resenting Imogen for it.' Evie gave a helpless shrug. 'I could never put my daughter in that position.'

'So you took the money,' he surmised curtly.

'No. Not then. I told them I didn't need their money. I'd stay away if it was for the best, but I wouldn't be bribed to do so. I even ripped the cheque up in front of them.'

Max frowned. He hadn't been told this.

'They said you took the money. *You* even just told me you cashed the cheque.'

She took another deep breath, her hair bouncing around her face as she nodded again.

'When Imogen was born, once I knew she was stable and going to make it, I realised I had to tell you. I wanted to tell you I'd understand if you didn't want to be a part of her life, but I felt you had a right to make that choice.'

'So what changed?'

'Your parents came to me first.'

'My parents did?' He could scarcely believe what she was telling him.

'They'd obviously been monitoring my progress because Imogen was delivered in the afternoon and they got there that night, after visiting hours.'

Max grimaced. He'd always known his parents were

emotionally lacking, acting logically and practically, if that seemed somewhat cold to those around them. He could imagine they would have kept an eye on Evie once they'd known about the baby. Not because they were the grandparents—that would have been an emotional connection, which simply wouldn't have occurred to them—but because they would have seen it as their duty. An unwanted obligation.

'I was still groggy, and in shock. I wasn't thinking straight. But then I think a part of me hoped they'd come around, that they'd actually come to see their beautiful granddaughter.'

'It wouldn't have made a difference.' He gritted his teeth.

'No, it didn't,' Evie acknowledged sadly. 'They told me a family was the last thing you needed. And the last thing the baby and I would ultimately want. That we'd end up making each other feel trapped and miserable and that taking the money for my baby would be best for all of us, in the long term. They sounded so convincing.'

'Because that's truly what they would have believed.' Max knitted his brows together, not sure how to explain it to someone who had grown up in such a loving, close-knit family unit.

'They were so…calculated.' She stopped abruptly. 'Sorry.'

'I told you, they don't consult anyone else, they would have simply decided what *they* felt was in everyone's best interests and then acted accordingly,' he said flatly. 'They will never be able to understand the indescribable pleasure I get from my daughter. Before I met Imogen, even *I* thought being a surgeon would always be the most important thing in my life but I was owed the right to make my own choices. *You* owed me that much.'

'And you blame me for denying you that choice?'

'Yes,' he hissed. 'You kept my daughter from me. You

kept your kidney condition from me. You listened to me telling you about my childhood and the way I instigated fights just so that I had a label for the pain I was feeling growing up. And still you never said a word.'

'Because I was frightened, Max.'

'That's it? Fear is your excuse for every decision you made?'

'Yes, because I *was* frightened for my own future health and I was frightened for Imogen's. I was frightened, I was desperate and I was exhausted. The dialysis had taken it out of me and I was staring mortality in the face whilst a tiny, helpless baby was relying on me to get her through her own life. I took the money because I knew it would provide for her if anything happened to me.'

She took a faltering step towards him, her hands outstretched before checking herself. 'I never touched a penny of it, though. You have to believe that, Max. I set up a proper trust for Imogen. It's all her money. It always would have been.'

'I believe you,' he bit out, the closest he could get to re-assuring her.

The fact was, it didn't even matter any more.

The white-hot anger that had initially coursed through him was already beginning to recede. It wasn't about the cheque any more. It wasn't about the money at all. Part of him even felt for Evie, how his parents' reaction must have looked to her. But he still couldn't forgive her for the fact that she'd lied to him.

She'd made every decision unilaterally, impacting on him without him even knowing about it, let alone having any say. And then she'd listened to him tell her about his childhood, about his parents, about his difficult relationship with them, and yet she'd never uttered a word. She'd known about them, met them for herself, and yet whilst he'd been confiding the secrets he'd never told another living soul she'd still kept such a huge secret from him.

That was why he couldn't forgive her.

Max stood, his back to Evie, unable to move a muscle. Even his jaw was locked, preventing him from answering.

For years he'd told himself he would never allow anyone to get close enough to hurt him. The way his parents had.

Never letting himself get close to anyone had been the only way Max had known to protect himself, and to protect others. He'd become used to being alone, felt safe and protected with a buffer between himself and any other person. He'd had no reason to doubt that he'd be as cold a spouse and parent as his own parents had been.

And then Evangeline Parker had come along to sneak under his skin, bringing with her the most precious gift he had never imagined, in Imogen. He'd let her in, trusted her, been prepared to change his life for her. And now he felt more alone than he had in his life.

'You have to understand why I took the money, Max.' Evie's quietly distraught voice dragged him back to the present.

Even the tears shining in rivers down her cheeks didn't touch him now. He couldn't afford to let them.

'Believe it or not, I *do* understand why,' Max grated out. The anger was receding now, leaving him with a dull ache.

And a void.

'Then we can work through this?' she breathed hopefully.

He shook his head.

'I'm here for Imogen. I'll always be here for her—she's my daughter. But as for you and I, there is no longer any *we.*'

'You just said you understood.' She choked back a sob, and he could see her struggle to stay in control, refusing to break down in front of him.

Part of him could even admire her for it. A lesser woman might have cried and yelled and begged.

'I understand you were frightened for your future. You had no idea if the transplant would be successful and you wanted to secure our daughter's future in the event that you weren't able to pull through.'

'And I didn't know you well enough. When your parents told me you wouldn't want to know about a child, I had no reason to distrust them.'

'I understand that, too. We had a week-long fling. Neither of us had any idea that Imogen would be the result of it.'

Evie bobbed her head, her hair bouncing wildly in her confusion.

'So you understand why I did it, even if I didn't go about it the right way?'

'Yes. But what I don't understand—what I can't forgive—is that you continued to keep it from me.'

'I was scared. I'm sorry,' Evie cried. 'I *wanted* to tell you. I tried so many times. But it never seemed like the right time.'

'It would never have been the *right* time, Evie. But the closest *right* time would have been when I found out I had a daughter you'd been keeping from me. Or when I asked you and Imogen to move in with me here. Or when I told you everything my parents put me through as a kid.'

'Stop. Please.' Evie held up her hand, a distraught expression clouding her features. 'You're right and I'm so, so sorry I never said anything then.'

'What I can't accept is that you probably never would have told me.'

'I would have. Somehow.' She shook her head in despair. 'I was intending to tonight. Remember?'

Yes, he remembered. But that didn't mean anything.

He'd been ready to marry Evie. To make them a proper family, once and for all. Now it was all lost.

He turned for the door.

'I'm going into the hospital after all. I'll drop you off at the house and I'll leave straight from there.'

'Please, Max. Can't we just talk about this?'

'I don't want to waste my time. Or yours. And I don't want to risk saying something that either of us will regret.'

'When will you be back?'

'In a few days.' That should give him enough time to think.

'Fine,' she said dully. 'Then we'll be gone by the time you get back.'

Max sucked in a breath and turned around.

'Gone?'

'If you can't forgive me, then it's the best thing, isn't it?'

The last scars of his childhood, which had taken so long to heal but had finally knitted over, were ripped open by Evie's words. He would never heal the same way again. He wanted to tell her *no*, that he wasn't ready for that. But she was right, it was the only way, and he had to find a way to move past this in order to have a future with his daughter.

'The best thing. We will need to discuss custody of Imogen, too,' he bit out. 'Shared custody. I won't be just a weekend father to her, Evie.'

'Fine.' There was a desolation in that single syllable that cracked his heart. 'Then I won't be there by the time you get home.'

Max gave a curt nod, unable to speak.

Home? That house would never feel like a home to him again.

CHAPTER FOURTEEN

'IT'S HEALING NICELY.' Max inspected Sally's new graft. It was good work, maybe some of his best yet. The scars would always be there, but they were no longer the marks of her self-harming years. People wouldn't look at her and judge her, condemn her.

'What's happened between you and the doc—why is she back staying with Annie, not you?' Sally cut across him. 'I saw her before she left and she looked worse than she ever did, even with her kidney and the baby, and that's saying something.'

'It's private.' Max glared at the young woman. The last thing he wanted to do was rake over the crippling pain he'd been fighting against ever since Evie and Imogen had left.

'Which means you're trying to pretend everything's okay.'

Nothing was okay. But this wasn't a conversation he wanted to have, even if he was getting the impression Sally didn't care what *he* wanted. His heart plummeted into his new black trainers. Everything was new since Evie and Imogen had gone. Too many memories.

Sally pressed on regardless. 'I think you ought to cut Evie some slack.'

'She told you that, did she? Shouldn't surprise me.'

'No.' The woman clicked her tongue disapprovingly. 'Of

course she didn't. She won't tell anyone a thing. But I know, whatever it is, she's blaming herself entirely.'

Despite everything a shaft of pain lanced through him. Evie had already been through more than most people would ever have to endure. He couldn't do anything about the failed situation between the two of them, she had hurt him more than he'd ever thought possible, but that didn't mean he wished any more grief on Evie.

'Well, then, there's no more to say.' Max tried to shut the conversation down but Sally wasn't so easily deterred.

'There is more to say. I'm guessing that, whatever it is, it's something to do with that baby of yours. And the doc loves that little girl with all her heart. Whatever she did, she'll have done with her child's best interests at heart.'

'Sally—' Max began warningly. He might have known someone who'd been through all this young woman had wasn't about to be intimidated.

'I can see that you're a posh boy, from a good family. I bet you've got parents who would have done anything for you. So isn't it a good thing that Evie's willing to fight for her daughter so that she gets the same chance in life to end up like her doctor mum or surgeon dad? And not someone who didn't have anyone wanting or fighting for them and ends up like me?'

'You had Evie fighting for you. And look at what you've managed to achieve for yourself,' Max answered before his brain could kick into gear.

He didn't need to see the smug look on Sally's face to know he'd just stepped right into her cleverly laid trap.

'See, deep down you really *do* know that the doc's one of the good guys. And when I didn't give you the chance to second-guess yourself, your instinct made you stand up for her.'

Max opened his mouth, wanting to tell Sally it was none of her business. Ironic that she should be so perceptive in how he felt about Evie, yet so wrong about his childhood being so different from her own. But he stopped.

She was right about one thing. It was better that Imogen had someone like Evie, who showered her with love and affection every single day, and was willing to risk everything to protect her. Two things. He *had* instinctively thought well of Evie.

When it came down to a straight choice between him and her daughter, Evie had protected Imogen. Her baby would always come first. Just as he now knew he would put Imogen first if it came down to a choice between his career, and his daughter.

But that didn't stop it from being painful thinking about the way Evie had hurt him.

Although, thanks to Sally's interference, he was starting to wonder if he was looking at it all wrong.

'Thank you, Sally. Most enlightening,' he managed dryly, before stepping around her to open his consulting-room door. 'Now, if you don't have any more questions about your own post-op progress, I'll see you at your next appointment.'

'Fine.' Sally clicked her tongue again. 'Just think about it, okay? I think you and the doc made a great couple. And I don't like to see her so miserable.'

'Goodbye, Sally,' Max said firmly, ushering her out and closing the door behind her with relief. But the thoughts still crowded into his head, as if Sally had jimmied the floodgates open and now he couldn't secure them back again.

When it was time to scrub in for his next surgery, he'd never felt so relieved. He desperately needed something else on which to focus all his energy.

He was a first-class jackass.

It was Max's first thought as he walked out of the OR to scrub out several hours later. The operation had gone better than he could have planned, yet the only thing on his mind was getting out of here, climbing into his car and going to win Evie back.

Sally was right, even though she didn't know it.

He'd been prepared to forgive his parents for the way they had approached Evie because they assumed he was like them—that his career would be more important to him than his daughter ever could.

They couldn't have been more wrong, and yet he was prepared to forgive them.

Yet Evie, who had tried to protect her own daughter in exactly the same way, was bearing the brunt of his anger. Because he loved her, and so she had an ability to hurt him far more than anyone else ever would.

He was punishing her for being the kind of mother, the kind of partner, he most wanted her to be. The kind who was passionate about those she cared for, and wasn't afraid to show it.

Now he had to show her that he could be the same way. Because Evie—and indeed Imogen—were integral to his happiness, and it was time to bring them home. If they'd let him.

Grabbing the quickest shower of his life, Max dressed and headed to his office.

His phone rang as he slung his bag over his shoulder and headed for his car, but he ignored it. It didn't matter who it was, he couldn't afford to be distracted. All that mattered was getting to Evie, as fast and as safely as he possibly could.

It was only when he was outside Annie's house, plunged into pitch-blackness, when he retrieved his phone to call Evie and find out just where she was, that he saw the missed call was from Annie.

With uncharacteristically shaky hands, he punched the redial button and waited for the call to pick up.

As he listened to the calm but concise voice on the other end, he felt his whole world fall apart.

'I only saw Evie a few days ago, how can she be showing signs of B-cell rejection?'

Evie heard his voice, thick with emotion, through Annie's speakerphone.

'How can she be showing signs of B-cell rejection?'

Evie shifted in the hospital chair, trying not to let herself react to the tone of his voice. His evident concern was heartening but it was only natural given how much he had grown to care for his daughter and therefore, by extension, Evie as Imogen's mother. Such concern didn't mean he forgave her, or that he loved her.

'Overnight she started coming down with flu-like symptoms, aching around the kidney site, and she had increased urine output.'

Evie heard Annie try to deliver the information in as clipped a tone as she could over the phone, trying to control her emotions in order to stay businesslike. It was so un-Annie-like that Evie couldn't help a weak smile of affection at the effort her sister-in-law was trying to go to, just to keep Max informed without asking the question she was clearly dying to ask.

Are you going to come down and see her?

A part of Evie longed to ask the same question herself, but she knew what Max's answer would be and she didn't think she could take another rejection.

'Do they know for sure it's rejection?' he demanded sharply over the speakerphone.

'They performed some tests and the creatinine test showed rejection was likely so they've performed a core biopsy.'

'Is she on bed rest in the outpatients whilst they wait for the results?'

'Yes.'

'And if it's confirmed, what's the procedure?'

'What?'

'Annie,' Max snapped, his voice cracking over the line, 'if they determine that it *is* rejection, what will they opt for? Additional plasmapheresis and IVIG sessions?'

'I'm not sure.' Annie glanced desperately at her.

Evie clenched her hands around the covers, trying to calm the lurch of her heart that Max should sound so frantic and *un-surgeon-like*. Almost like any other relative of a patient, concerned for their loved one.

She shook her head. *Now she was just being foolish.*

'No,' Annie said as Evie realised her sister-in-law had mistaken her headshake for rebuttal.

'Sorry, sorry,' Evie cried. 'Yes, they'll probably look at additional plasmapheresis and IVIG as a first port of call.'

'Evie?' Max's voice reverberated around the room. 'Can you hear me? Just hold on, I'm going to end this call so I can phone your Transfer team down there and get some more information. Okay?'

Evie couldn't meet Annie's gaze as she tried not to let her emotions show, but she was sure the whole hospital could hear her heart hammering a military drum tattoo inside her chest.

Was that professional concern? Concern for the mother of his daughter? Or, could it be possible, genuine concern for the woman he'd realised he loved? And this time, when she tried to reprimand herself that she was being unrealistic, the spark of hope refused to be stamped out.

'All right,' Annie was saying. 'Shall I...? Do you want me to call you with updates?'

'Sorry?'

So she'd got it all wrong.

His surprise at why he should need to be kept informed was a kick in the teeth. Evie tried but she couldn't stop the tears of regret from welling in her eyes. Even Annie's tone changed as she turned her back to speak quickly and quietly into the phone.

'To let you know how Evie is doing? She told me not to bother you, after your conversation the other day. But then we agreed it was better to tell you so that you could decide whether you wanted to come down for your daughter or whether you were happy for my husband and me to look after Imogen.'

'Ah, right.' He sounded genuinely sorry he'd misunderstood, at least. 'Actually, Annie, I think it's probably better for Imogen to stay in a constant environment with your family rather than be pulled from pillar to post coming back up to me whilst Evie is down there.'

A fresh wave of nausea rolled over Evie. It was enough that he couldn't forgive her, but she didn't want to be the cause of a rift in his new relationship with his daughter.

'Fine,' she heard Annie respond flatly, but her irritation with Max was audible. 'Then the baby will stay with us. We'd love to have her longer. Just thought you might, too.'

'Okay. Tell Evie it's going to be fine.'

Evie stared across the room in shock. Max never said that. He never promised anyone everything would be fine. *Never.*

'And tell her I'll be with her in…'

The line crackled as he faded out but it sounded as if he'd said *half an hour.* That couldn't be right.

'What?' Annie's shock was nothing compared to the way Evie's heart leaped. 'I can't hear you clearly.'

Still, that couldn't be right—it was a much longer drive than that.

'Sorry, heading into a tunnel so I'll probably get cut off any minute. I said I should be there in half an hour.'

'How?' Annie voiced Evie's thoughts, but the line cracked again and went dead.

Evie stared at her sister-in-law in disbelief before a heavy tear trickled down one cheek. Hope, confusion, anticipation, expectation—it was all in that one salty droplet.

'Did he mean the Meadowall Tunnel between my house and here?' Annie asked slowly.

Leaning her head back on the pillows, Evie just shook her head and hoped.

'Feeling pretty bad?' The gruff voice woke Evie from her fitful slumber and she snapped her head up in disbelief. She hardly dared to open her eyes too quickly in case she found he wasn't really there.

Nope. He was reassuringly solid.

She drank in the sight, but slowly the dark-circled eyes, unshaven stubble, and slightly haunted expression registered. It gave her something to cling to.

'I'm about as good as you look,' she murmured shakily.

'That bad, huh?' His eyes were loaded with regret.

'Pretty much. I can't believe I fell asleep. When did Annie go?'

'You're exhausted. Annie said you dozed off as soon as our phone call ended and she stayed with you until I got here.'

'Half an hour?'

'Twenty-four minutes.'

'You really were already down here?' A few more restraints of caution gave way.

'Outside Annie's house,' he confirmed quietly.

He stepped towards her and she offered no resistance as he snaked his arms around her shoulders and drew her in. Instead, Evie closed her eyes and allowed his familiar citrusy, musky, masculine scent fill her senses. Max dropped a kiss on her head.

Still they didn't speak.

Beyond her, the rest of the hospital fell away. Just like the first time, it was just her and him, and nothing else.

'Why are you here, Max?' she mumbled against the rock wall of his chest.

'To bring you home.' His words were muffled, spoken into her hair. She had a feeling he was breathing her in just as she'd done with him. Her heart cracked.

'What's changed?'

He paused a bit before saying the word she didn't want to hear.

'Nothing. Everything.'

'Max…' She drew her head back but didn't pull away. 'I *am* sorry.'

He shushed her.

'No, it's my turn now. I should have accepted your apology that afternoon, but I was being pig-headed. I know you were scared to tell me, and that you couldn't have been sure what my reaction would have been. Just because I know what my parents are like doesn't mean you did.'

'What about betraying your trust? You said you couldn't forgive me.'

'I was being an idiot. I'm sorry. I was thinking of my own feelings where you were more concerned about our daughter. That won't happen from here on.'

'From here on?' Evie whispered, needing to hear Max say the words. 'Does that mean you want Imogen and me to come back with you?'

'No.'

She tipped her head back, confused.

'You said before that you wanted to bring Imogen and I home.'

'Yes, but not my old place—why should you two have to move? I'll move down here and we'll get a new place. A home of our own.'

'You're leaving Silvertrees?'

She should be more circumspect but she couldn't stop a tiny balloon of elation floating up inside her, lifting some of the darkest fears about this recent rejection episode.

'You said to me a month ago that this is where you love to be.' Max nodded. 'Your family is here, you and Imogen have ties here. I don't have ties up there. It's just a job. I can find a job anywhere. So we find a house you love near your brother and Annie, and we start a new life together as a proper family.'

'But you still intend that I should give up my career?'

'Actually, no. Sally told me about a centre she visits down here, with a whole new set of kids just desperate for someone like you to believe in them, fight for them. I spoke to one of the board members on the drive down. We need a proper meeting to hammer out the details but they've been hoping to approach you for quite a while. They also know of me by reputation and would be more than happy to welcome me as their new go-to paediatric plastic surgeon.'

'Working together?' She couldn't seem to process what he was telling her.

'Side by side, whenever you needed me.'

It all sounded too good to be true. And yet it was true. Max was here, and he was offering all she'd ever wanted. And more.

'You would do that for me? For Imogen?'

'I would. And for me. I realised that I don't give half as much back as you do, and it's time I started.'

'You've got it all figured out, haven't you?' Evie marvelled.

'Pretty much. There's just one thing left.'

She didn't realise what he was doing until she felt the cool metal sliding over her finger. The ring was stunning, a classic grain-cut solitaire diamond ring set in a platinum band with alternate diamonds and rubies set into each shoulder.

'I never make promises I can't keep. So believe me when I promise I'll love you until the day I die. Marry me, Evie?'

Looking up into his face, she realised how real it was. No more secrets, No more lies. Just the promise of love and support and a future with the man she loved.

A long, long future. She was determined of that.

'Yes,' she whispered with a throaty chuckle, unable to resist teasing him. 'And I promise to love you until the day *you* die, too.'

'Minx.' He grinned against her lips as he slid his hands into her hair to draw her into an intense, toe-curling kiss.

EPILOGUE

'NICE MEDAL. SNAP!' Max teased as Evie ran towards him, brandishing her newest necklace and with her space blanket billowing out behind her like a cape.

'His and hers?' She arched her eyebrows in amusement.

'Quite.' He laughed. 'You looked fantastic coming over that finishing line, by the way.'

'Thanks, I was just glad the whole thing was over. I don't think I could have raced another metre. But this finishers' medal makes it all worthwhile, even if I am somewhere around five hundredth according to the race officials.'

'Yeah, well, never mind the four hundred and ninety-nine. How many of them are former transplant recipients?' Max snorted dismissively. He was immensely proud of his wife and, judging by the beam on her face, she felt just as proud of herself. 'Besides, I heard that over one thousand competitors started this year, so you've beaten over half of them.'

'True,' chuckled Evie. 'So, I got Annie's right kidney round a half-mile swim, a seventeen-mile bike ride and a five-mile run in one hour and fifty-nine minutes. How's her left kidney doing?'

'This is your first triathlon, ever, and still you're so damn competitive.' He dropped a kiss on her nose.

'Mmm-hmm. It's also my transplant's five-year anniversary, with no rejection episodes since that initial blip.'

She snuggled against his chest before pulling her head back excitedly. 'I'm feeling incredible. So, about Annie's other kidney?'

'I actually don't know, sorry,' he relented. 'I haven't seen your brother since the last changeover points where he was waiting for Annie, but I think he said she was about fifteen minutes behind you at that point, and you know you're a faster runner than she is.'

'She'll probably be coming in between two hours twenty and two hours thirty, then.' Evie glanced at her watch. 'Shall we head back to the finish line?'

'Good idea. I said we'd meet everyone there so look out for Imogen—she's probably still commandeering your brother's shoulders for the best view in the house.'

'She would. She's the cheekiest five-and-a-half-year-old I've ever known.' Evie clicked her tongue but Max wasn't fooled; her love for their two children radiated through everything she did. 'What about Toby?'

'He's doing what he always does in the middle of the afternoon...'

'Sleeping,' she chimed in, laughing. 'I bet my brother's pushed him the whole way around in that off-road racer pram you bought.'

'You can count on it.'

They jostled their way good-humouredly against the finishers coming towards them, finally making it back to the finish line to look out for their family.

It felt good to Max.

The last five years had been the best of his life since he'd left Silvertrees to move to within fifteen minutes of Evie's family. Unexpectedly, he'd not only gained a family in Evie and Imogen, but he'd also gained the family he'd never had in Annie's family, too.

The ink had barely been dry on his resignation when the job offers had flooded in, and he had happily accepted a generous promotion package to the top local hospital, which had included a relocation incentive to the house of their dreams. But, more importantly, they had accepted his proviso that he must also have time to work with some of the troubled teens from the new centre where Evie had returned to part-time work along with having time with her family.

The fact that they were doing this race today for Sally seemed so perfectly fitting. Free of the recognisable silvery lines, Sally had easily found her dream job, which had previously eluded her, and it had also given her the confidence to start charity work in her spare time for the residential centre where she'd first met Evie.

Max wrapped his arms around his wife feeling, as he did every day, contented and relaxed.

'Do you know, between you, Annie and I, we've raised money well into five figures?' he murmured into her ear, revelling in the look of proud shock as she twisted her head to look up at him.

'Seriously? That's incredible. Does Sally know? She'll be over the moon.'

'Sally's the one who told me.' Max nibbled Evie's ear, causing her to inadvertently wiggle against him.

'What about you, anyway? How did you do?'

'I didn't do too badly.'

She pulled out of his arms and spun around.

'You didn't win, did you?'

'Who do you think I am? Superman? No, I didn't win.' She poked him playfully in the ribs.

'What was your time, then?'

He grinned until she shrieked with anticipation.

'Oh, come on, Max, you have to tell me.'

'One hour, twenty-seven minutes.'

'Wow…' She soberly bestowed a kiss on his lips. 'That *has* to be a high position?'

'Within the top ten.'

'That seriously deserves a prize.' She adopted a serious expression. 'I feel I should reward you.'

'Oh, really?' He pulled her to him, the crowd surging unconcerned around them.

'Yes, really. Tonight,' she clarified, snaking her arms around him. 'When we're alone.'

'I think I love the idea but I have a feeling that you might be too tired for anything tonight.' He smiled, lowering his mouth to drop a soft kiss on her lips, surprised when she deepened it to something full of promise.

'It's funny,' she whispered, 'but suddenly I find I have untapped resources of energy these days. Must have been the white chocolate and raspberry muffin you gave me this morning before the race, but I feel there's nothing I can't handle.'

'That,' he murmured gently, kissing his wife again, 'I don't doubt.'

* * * * *

*If you enjoyed this story, check out
the great debut from Charlotte Hawkes*

THE ARMY DOC'S SECRET WIFE

Available now!

MILLS & BOON®

MEDICAL ROMANCE™

THE ULTIMATE IN ROMANTIC MEDICAL DRAMA

MILLS & BOON®

EXCLUSIVE EXTRACT

Kate Ashton's night with Sam Ryder leads
to an unexpected consequence—but can he
convince this nurse that their love is meant-to-be?

Read on for a sneak preview of
THEIR MEANT-TO-BE BABY
by Caroline Anderson

'You didn't tell me you were a nurse,' Sam said.

'You didn't tell me you were a doctor.'

'At least I didn't lie.'

Kate felt colour tease her cheeks. 'Only by omission. That's no better.'

'There are degrees. And I didn't deny that I know you.'

'I didn't think our...'

'Fling? Liaison? One-night stand? Random—'

'Our private life was anyone else's business. And anyway, you don't know me. Only in the biblical sense.'

Something flickered in those flat, ice-blue eyes, something wild and untamed and a little scary. And then Sam looked away.

'Apparently so.'

She sucked in a breath and straightened her shoulders. At some point she'd have to tell him she was pregnant, but not here, not now, not like this, and if they were going to have this baby, at some point they would need to get to know each other. But, again, not now. Now

Kate had a job to do, and she was going to have to put her feelings on the back burner and resist the urge to run away.

Don't Miss
THEIR MEANT-TO-BE BABY
By Caroline Anderson

Available February 2017
www.millsandboon.co.uk